WELCOME TO THE DUNGEON

It is a fortress where fantastic twists of time and space hold travelers from a dozen worlds captive.

It is a prison in which cyborgs, swordsmen, eight-legged aliens, and beautiful women struggle side by side against their unknown captors.

It is a trap within whose confines the known laws of nature and of science are suspended and the impossible is commonplace.

It is an island in a dark and distant galaxy, a territory from which there is no return until an adventurer from Earth arrives, seeking his brother.

From the heart of darkness to the edge of the unknown, this is the quest of Clive Folliot, explorer and hero!

Ask your bookseller for the Bantam Spectra Books you have missed:

PHILIP JOSÉ FARMER'S

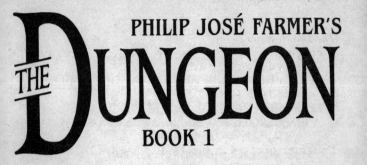

THE DUNGEON

BOOK 1

THE
BLACK
TOWER

•

Richard A. Lupoff

A BYRON PREISS BOOK

BANTAM BOOKS
TORONTO • NEW YORK • LONDON • SYDNEY • AUCKLAND

PHILIP JOSÉ FARMER'S THE DUNGEON, BOOK 1: THE BLACK TOWER

A Bantam Spectra Book / August 1988

Special thanks to Lou Aronica, Amy Stout, Shawna McCarthy, David M. Harris and Gwendolyn Smith.

Cover art and interior sketches by Robert Gould.
Cover design and logo by Alex Jay/Studio J.

The DUNGEON is a trademark of Byron Preiss Visual Publications, Inc.

ISBN 0-553-27346-9

Published simultaneously in the United States and Canada

PRINTED IN THE UNITED STATES OF AMERICA

O   0 9 8 7 6 5 4 3 2 1

▪ FOREWORD ▪

"... listen: there's a hell
   of a good universe next door; let's go."
   So wrote the poet e. e. cummings in his "Pity This
Busy Monster Manunkind."

   He may not have been thinking of science-fiction
and fantasy writers when he conceived these lines.
But he certainly should have been. The writers in
these genres most often set their stories in universes
we do not know and never would—if these writers
did not take us there. On the other hand, cummings
may have been thinking that s-f (science-fiction) writers usually take us to other universes that are worse
than ours—if that is, indeed, possible. In fact, they
are more often than not universes that make ours
look like a rest home. (But rest homes are often not
such good places.)

   The s-f writers play Virgil guiding his Dante (the
readers) through various hells. That is, the universe
next door is an Inferno. That's all right. We all want
to go to heaven, but we do not want to read about it
unless we're looking for a cure for insomnia. Nothing much happens in heaven, and most people there
are bores. Hell is interesting and exciting. Things
move fast and furious there, and the inhabitants
don't know from one minute to the next if they'll be
alive.

   If that description of hell sounds like Earth, so be
it. But our dangers are familiar, whereas those next-
door are anything but ho-hum. We've never encoun-

tered them before, and we don't know just how to react because the environment is strange. And we run across, or into, entities, things, and situations outside our experience. In short, we are in the unmundane among busy monsters most unkind.

I am one of the writers who has, in many of my stories, put my heroes or heroines in the unmundane. And in such messes that even I did not know how they were going to get out of them when I hurled them into them. But I always figured out a way.

I also have used, in some of my works, characters and environments derived from the pulps. And I should add: derived from the spirit of the pulps, exotic adventure.

I have written many stories not connected with the above, but those that are have gotten much attention. Partly, perhaps, because they have become melded into one body. That is, they turn out to be living in one universe and are, indeed, related by blood. At the same time, pulp-originated though they are, they interact with, and are related genetically, to many characters of the classics. Thus, this universe next-door is a new one: pulp-and-classic. Farmerian.

This, plus my love of alien adventures, is why Byron Preiss asked me to edit and oversee the *Dungeon* series. This series is an emulation of the spirit, not the content, of the Farmerian universe next-door, the pulp-and-classic.

First, though, it's best to describe how and why I created this universe.

By the age of seven, 1925, I had read and was in love with the works of Mark Twain, Jonathan Swift's *Gulliver's Travels*, R. L. Stevenson's *Treasure Island*, Dickens's *A Christmas Carol*, the Oz books, London's *Before Adam*, H.G. Wells's and Jules Verne's works, Doyle's Holmes canon and *The Lost World*, and Burroughs's Tarzan and Mars series. I loved Homer's *The Odyssey* and the Norse, Greek, and American-native mythologies.

I was a bookworm yet was very athletic.

In 1929, when I came across the first issues of Hugo Gernsback's *Science Wonder* and *Air Wonder* with their wonderful Paul illustrations, life became even more golden. I plunged into the sapphire seas of the unmundane. I was an amphibian who alternated between the land of reality and the ocean of fantasy. But I much preferred the ocean. I still do, much to my detriment, because the land of reality is where we live most of the time.

Then I found the world of the pulps, the *Argosy* magazine, which came out weekly and carried many s-f and adventure stories. Later, I read all the many s-f magazines, and, in 1931, was captivated by the first *The Shadow* magazine. Money was scarce, though, during the Depression. When the first *Doc Savage* magazine came out in 1933, I had to choose whether to buy *Shadow* or *Savage*, and old Doc won out.

I also read Roy Rockwell's Bomba the Jungle Boy series and the s-f Great Marvel series. Though these were books, they certainly had the pulpish qualities. The stories were fast and gripped you until the end. The characters ranged from flat to caricature to a sometimes excellent portrayal. The writing was a spectrum of near-atrocious to competent to very good. The ideas were often stimulating and sometimes original, often banal, often secondary and derived but with new twists and facets.

In short, just like so-called "mainstream" literature, except that mainstream has no new or unusual concepts. If it does, it is not mainstream.

Of course, in those days I had no literary discrimination. They all read great to me, and many gave me some of the keenest pleasure I've ever had. I was in a Golden Age in my childhood and early youth. There were plenty of bad times, but, as I look back, the intimations of immortality, that blue-tinged, gold-shot thrilling and trembling-on-the-edge-of-revelation, that almost mystical feeling, came as much, perhaps more, from the pulps as from the classics I was reading.

Oh, yes, I forgot that *The Arabian Nights* and The Bible were early influences. There were so many that it's easy to forget some of them.

Later, I dived into the other works of Dickens and the non-Holmesian stories of Doyle, all of Jack London, and then Balzac, Rabelais, Goethe, Mann, Dostoyevsky, Joyce, Fielding, and the poets. When I was twenty, I found the biographies of Sir Richard Francis Burton and the books he had written. All read long before I began to sell my fiction to magazines.

The unconscious is the true democracy. All things, all people, are equal. Thus, in my mind, Odysseus towered no higher than Tarzan, King Arthur was no greater than Doc Savage, and Cthulhu and Conan loomed as large on my mind's horizon as Jehovah and Samson.

The pulps and the classics became fused in my mind. Lord Greystoke lived next door to Achilles and Natty Bumppo. Leopold Bloom met Lamont Cranston and Rudolf Rassendyll at cocktail parties. Milton's Lucifer had his horns polished at Patricia Savage's beauty salon, and She-Who-Must-Be-Obeyed was pen pals with Scheherazade and Jane Eyre. Bellow Bill Williams (a series character in *Argosy*) bellied up to the same bar as Mr. Pickwick, the great god Thor, Falstaff, Old Man Coyote, and Operator #5. D'Artagnan, Thibaut Corday, Brigadier Gerard, and Lt. Darnot argued about military strategy over fine wines and snails. Joshua, Fu Manchu, Professor Moriarty, Captain Nemo, Pete the Brazen, and Doctor Nikola told tall tales around a campfire. Paul Bunyan, Christian the Pilgrim, Hawk Carse, Don Quixote, and the Cowardly Lion argued about the metaphysical aspects of the Mad Tea Party.

You get the idea.

My conscious knows better, now, than to give these equal billing in the literary theater. But the Mother of Minds, the real She-Who-Must-Be-Obeyed, my unconscious, knows no better.

I would be remiss if I did not tell how great an influence the early movies and the illustrations for the books of my childhood had on me. Before I could read, I saw (and still remember) Douglas Fairbanks in *Robin Hood* (1922). Fairbanks's *The Black Pirate* (1926) and, in 1925, Wallace Beery in *The Lost World* and Lon Chaney in *The Phantom of the Opera* thrilled and scared me. There were many more I have not forgotten and which still seethe in my unconscious.

The powerful illustrations by Doré in *Pilgrim's Progress, Paradise Lost, The Rime of the Ancient Mariner,* and *Inferno* and Wyeth's and Pyle's illustrations powerfully affected me. Paul's works for the Hugo Gernsback magazines sparkle in my mind like the massive jewels in the walls of ancient Opar.

These were, you might say, the visual equivalent of the classics and the pulps.

All: books, magazines, movies, and illustrations resonated on the same frequency. They no longer do so, but none of the magic is gone.

I have gone into such detail about the origin of the universe hight Farmerian because I want the reader to understand it. And it's a necessary *prelude* (from the Latin, meaning *before the play* and also, in a sense, *foreplay*).

It is necessary because this strange brew of the unreal and the real, the classics and the pulps, is what caused Byron Preiss, the producer of this projected series, to launch it. The *Dungeon* works are based, in part, on the spirit that dwells in certain works of mine.

These works are also, in part, my tributes to other writers and, in part, derive from my childhood desire to continue the worlds of some of my favorite writers when they ceased writing them.

The works of mine noted below are, in my peculiar way (is there any other?), extensions and amplifications of the beloved fiction of my Golden Age:

The Opar series, based on the Tarzan and Allan Quatermain canons. (The wretched movies based on Haggard's character have no relation to Haggard's great novels.)

The Lord Grandrith-Doc Caliban series, based on Tarzan and Doc Savage. (But they give the darker side of these heroes.)

The Riverworld series, a fusion of my fascination with Burton, Twain and Dante and their philosophies and inspired ultimately by The Bible.

The World of Tiers series, inspired, in part, by the apocalyptic worlds of William Blake, the English poet; in part, by the American native culture-hero, Old Man Coyote; in part, by the exploits of d'Artagnan, Dumas's fictional character and also by the real d'Artagnan, of Rostand's stageplay hero, Cyrano de Bergerac and the real de Bergerac. (The latter also appears in the Riverworld series.) In part, by the wild tales of Thibaut Corday, Theodore Roscoe's French Legionnaire. In part, by Doyle's Brigadier Étienne Gerard, whom Doyle derived from the very real Napoleonic soldier, Baron de Marbot. (Marbot is also in the Riverworld series.)

The Adventure of the Three Madmen, in which Holmes and Watson encounter G-8, The Shadow, and Mowgli the Wolf-Boy, much to their consternation, and end in a lost country in Africa, the inhabitants of which are descended from the Zu-Vendi, Haggard's lost people in *Allan Quatermain*.

The Greatheart Silver series, one story of which is about a final showdown between the aged heroes and the decrepit villains of the pulps.

There are similar works of mine too numerous to mention. Enough said about them. But these have given rise to the novels of *Dungeon*, and these, as I said, emulate the spirit of the above. Universes begetting universes, not parallel to mine but asymptotic.

Richard Lupoff was wisely chosen to do the lead-off novel, *The Black Tower*. He is a man after my own heart, not with a knife, but in temperament. He's an authority on the works of Edgar Rice Burroughs and deeply read on the well-known and the obscure science-fiction and fantasy of the late 19th century and the early 20th century. He has written a number of parodies and pastiches of these. He is also the author of a series of parodies on science-fiction writers. I was one of his subjects, feebly disguised as Albert Payson Agricola, a hack s-f writer justifiably murdered. For those too young to know, Albert Payson Terhune was a very successful writer of dog stories featuring collies, one of which was named Lassie. Agricola is Latin for Farmer.

Lupoff's interest in the "old stuff" is not just a dilettante's. He's taken the early classics and not-so-classics of the pulps and popular books and reworked them. He has given them new life and new colors and new shapes in a thoroughly Lupoffian manner. However, despite often poking fun at these early s-f stories, often shot with ridiculous science, two-dimensional characters, and racism, he reveals a basic love for them. Though one part of him disbelieves them and is repulsed, to a certain extent, by their reactionary premises, another part really does believe in them and has great affection for them.

This is well. A writer who neither believes in nor loves the worlds he's writing about carries no conviction.

Like me, he is well acquainted with the 19th century. He knows that it is the mother of the 20th and that the Earth then still had its terrae incognitae. Africa was still the Dark Continent in a geographical and psychical sense.

And, like me, he used and uses real people among the fictional. *The Black Tower* starts on the Earth of 1878. Early on, we are introduced to some historical persons. A little later, we meet Sidi Bombay, a one-time gun-bearer for Sir Richard Francis Burton. And there is the fictional Quartermaster Sergeant Smythe.

His genius at disguises reminds us of The Spider, The Shadow, Doc Savage, and Sherlock Holmes. It also reminds me of Burton himself, a master of disguise.

In the spirit of my worlds, Lupoff writes a story in which things are seldom what they seem. The familiar and the cozy become sinister. The hero, as in so many of my works, is justifiably paranoid. Somewhere, somehow, somebody or some thing is pulling strings, and, willynilly, the puppets are dancing. But these puppets can think and can fight back.

Above all, Mystery reigns. It is not just the miasmic and misinterpreted atmosphere of detective stories and Gothics, though it is this, too. It's the mystery of the universe itself. Or, as in this case, also the mystery of another world.

One of Lupoff's additions to the universe, Neville Folliot's diary, with its update additions by an invisible hand, reminds me of Glinda the Good's great book. Events as they occur appear daily on the blank pages of her massive and magical volume. I doubt that Lupoff got the idea from the Oz books; it's no doubt his own concept. But it resonates from Oz, nevertheless.

Just as the spirit of both the pulps and the classics, a hybrid found only in our genre, resonates in his novels.

Both human and alien characters in *The Black Tower* are in the Farmerian spirit. I especially like Finnbogg, the bulldogoid, and Chang Guafe, the tortured and monstrous semishapeshifter. And there is the time nexus, where entities from everywhere and everytime are collected, a favorite situation of mine. Collected by whom? For what purpose?

Ah, sweet and sour mystery!

When the series is done, we will see the universe as an organic whole. It will be explained in logical and believable terms.

But, as e. e. cummings wrote:

"—when skies are hanged and oceans drowned the single secret will still be man."

—Philip José Farmer

· ONE ·
THE
ENGLISH
WORLD

· CHAPTER 1 ·
Piccadilly Circus

The curtain rang down on a jolly scene. The brothers James John Cox and John James Box celebrated their reunion. The audience, which had spent the evening in gales of laughter, now burst into storms of cheers and applause.

In their orchestra seats, Major Clive Folliot felt Miss Leighton's fingers close on his arm. Clive had been distracted by his thoughts during the performance, and he knew that Miss Leighton understood his feelings about his absent brother Neville—at least, she did so as well as anyone other than himself could understand those tempestuous feelings.

Is there anyone, other than a twin, who can understand the feelings of one twin for another?

"The play was jolly but it struck very close to home, did it not?" Annabella Leighton asked Clive Folliot. "It must have pained you, Clive."

Clive Folliot did not answer at once. It was necessary for him to compose himself. One did not give way to emotions in public, especially if one was an officer in Her Majesty's military service.

Clive was wearing the scarlet tunic and dark trousers of the Imperial Horse Guards. He brushed his reddish brown mustache with a hand that shook slightly. He turned toward Annabella and managed a grin. "Close to home, yes. But it was a fine entertainment nonetheless. I hope I did not ruin the performance for you, Miss Leighton."

As he spoke, he drank in her beauty with his eyes.

Annabella Leighton was a beautiful young woman—
little more than a girl—some thirteen years younger
than Clive Folliot's thirty-and-three. Her hair was a
glossy jet black. For attendance at the theater it was
done up in coils that glistened so that they seemed to
pick up the cornflower blue of her darting, merry
eyes.

Her shoulders were white and sweetly powdered,
her bosom full and graceful and daringly revealed
by her gown, when she permitted her shawl to slip
from her shoulders. Her waist was slim, even tiny,
albeit perhaps the least bit less so than it had
been when she and Major Folliot had first become
acquainted.

She smiled up at Major Folliot. "Oh, no," she said.
"You could never ruin the performance for me. In
your company, Clive, it could not have been other
than enjoyable."

The theater was clearing around them as English
gentlemen in evening dress or military uniforms and
ladies in wide-skirted dresses slowly filed from their
seats. A few Americans were scattered through the
crowd, identifiable by their loud voices and swagger-
ing way. They were coming back to England in growing numbers now. They had been, ever since the war
between their states had ended—an event, Clive realized with a start, now three years past.

All in all, Clive mused, this audience was a cosmo-
politan crowd. He wondered if all of them had even
understood the dialogue and the songs!

"Miss Leighton," Folliot said, "I do hope you will
not take it amiss if I ask you to accompany me
backstage."

She did not reply at once.

"I don't think it will ruin your reputation," he
added. "But of course, if you prefer not to mingle
with players, we will leave the building at once."

"No, Major. You did mention that one of the players
was your friend. I should be happy to be introduced
to him—if that is what you have in mind."

"Indeed."

The rooms behind the stage were a mad flurry of unfamiliar colors, odors, and sounds. Annabella Leighton felt as if she had fallen down the same rabbit hole that had claimed little Alice in Mr. Carroll's peculiar little book, and she would not have been surprised to encounter a mad hatter or a hookah-smoking caterpillar at any turn.

Major Folliot's friend had played Mr. Box, the printer. For this, he rated a private dressing room, upon the door of which Folliot rapped briskly.

A tenor voice called, "Come ahead, then," and Major Folliot pushed open the door, gesturing to Miss Leighton to precede him.

"Clive!" the erstwhile printer cried. "Close it behind you! I'm almost ready." The actor's back was to the door, a dressing table and mirror offering him the opportunity to observe his callers. When he caught sight of Miss Leighton he spun about and leaped to his feet.

"Don't tell me!" he exclaimed. "This is the breathtaking Miss Leighton, of whom Clive has spoken so often."

Annabella extended her hand.

"George du Maurier," the actor introduced himself. "I am honored, Miss Leighton. Clive never ceases to sing your praises, and now I see the reason for his devotion."

"A splendid production, du Maurier," Folliot said. "I wish I could reconcile with Neville, as did the brothers in your amusement."

"He'll turn up, Clive. Others have been out of communication far longer than Neville has, and emerged unharmed from some jungle or desert."

Du Maurier gave a hint of a bow. "Let's find a more suitable venue for our conversation than this pesthole, shall we?"

Annabella said, "I agree that there could be more agreeable surroundings in which to hold our chat."

Du Maurier clapped a beaver hat on his curly hair,

lifted a light coat from a peg near his mirror, reached past Folliot and Miss Leighton to open the door, and doused the gas. The room remained faintly illuminated, light penetrating through the open doorway from the cluttered backstage area.

Outside they hailed a cab. Du Maurier peered up at the driver and gave the address of his club. To Folliot and Miss Leighton he said, "Artists and writers shall surround us. I trust you approve."

The traffic was light at this late hour, and shortly the cab drew up before an entryway guarded by a uniformed footman.

Once inside, du Maurier said, "We're very bohemian here, Miss Leighton. Ladies are permitted in the bar. There are those who frown upon us, but then, we are as we are." He shrugged.

"Yes." Annabella smiled. "Artists and writers. What can one expect?"

Du Maurier laughed and led them toward the main salon. A servant took Miss Leighton's outer wrap and the two men's headgear—du Maurier's tall beaver and Folliot's military cap. A waiter approached and du Maurier ordered brandy for all.

They were seated in comfortable chairs before a huge fireplace, warming themselves happily.

Turning toward Folliot, du Maurier said, "There is, then, no further word of your brother?"

"None," Clive murmured. "Fourteen months now, and not a word."

"It must be very hard for you to accept," Annabella said.

"Yes," du Maurier agreed. "And to believe, as well."

"I don't know what you mean, Mr. du Maurier. Hard to believe—what?" she frowned.

"He's going to start in," Major Folliot warned her. "I should have warned you, Miss Leighton. George is a brilliant cartoonist—the best that *Punch* can boast—in addition to his talents as comic actor and musician. But he is given to some very strange ideas."

"Strange, are they?" The conversation paused as

the waiter arrived and served the brandies. Then du Maurier resumed. "You scoff, Folliot, you scoff. But 'there are more things in heaven and earth . . .'"

"I know, I know. I should like to believe, or at least to hope, but when there has been nothing for so long, I find it almost impossible."

"But of course, my friend. You have struck to the heart of the matter. To hold that the possible is possible takes no wit or courage. It's a mere tautology at that!"

He waved his hands as he warmed to his subject.

Annabella Leighton watched the two men, du Maurier in casual mufti, Folliot in his scarlet tunic and brass accouterments. The dancing light of the fire set the artist in soft and subtle shades of earth tones, greens and browns and grays. At the same time the flames seemed to dance on the metal buttons and fittings of the major's bright uniform.

"To assert that the impossible is possible," du Maurier continued, "that is what requires imagination. Imagination," he grinned, tapping a long finger against his temple, "imagination, yes, and intellectual courage. And strength."

"I would not have thought, Mr. du Maurier, that you were given to mystical leanings," Annabella said.

"Mystical leanings?" Du Maurier smiled at the phrase, considered for a moment. Then he asked, "But why not, Miss Leighton?"

"We live in an age of science and of rationality, do we not?" The flames were warming her from the outside, the brandy from within. She smiled at the cartoonist.

"All the more reason to consider those things which remain—thus far—beyond the veil of the known. We are learning of new wonders each year. Nature yields her secrets grudgingly, but yield them she does. Chemistry, electricity, geography—life itself! What great beasts once trod these islands, uncounted ages ago, of which we are only beginning to learn!"

"But, du Maurier," Clive put in. "You speak of

things that are produced in laboratories, or found beneath the surface of the earth. Wonders, yes—but wonders that can be perceived with the eye, weighed upon the scale of the investigator, placed in the museum for all to visit and behold."

"And you think I am spinning fairy webs when I tell you that I believe in the works of Dr. Braid and his achievement of trances and new mental states. But I hold that the mind contains powers and abilities we have not yet begun to plumb. I believe that there is life we have never encountered. There may be inhabitants of the other planets and there may even be planets circling the fixed and distant stars, with whose people communication and commerce will someday be possible."

Folliot was about to reply, but Annabella Leighton spoke first. "This is all very wonderful, Mr. du Maurier, as subject matter for philosophical speculation. But what has it to do with Major Folliot's missing brother? Surely you do not mean to suggest that someone had placed Neville in a trance, from which he may transmit mesmeric emanations to Clive. Or do you believe that he has been translated to the planet Mars, where he is at this moment learning the secrets of the people of that world?"

"I do not know where Sir Neville is," du Maurier said.

Clive rose from his chair and stood facing du Maurier, his back to the flames. "You make too much of the mystery," he asserted, "and too little, at the same time."

"Ho!" du Maurier exploded. "Who is speaking in paradoxes now, Folliot?"

"What I mean is this. My brother is lost, truly lost. With all your talk of hypnotism and mesmerism and trances and inhabitants of distant worlds, you merely cloud the issue. Neville went to Africa, not to Jupiter. We know that he explored much of the Ruwenzori Range, and that he then penetrated at least as far as Gondokoro."

He placed his brandy snifter on the mantelpiece and clasped his hands behind his back. He paced the thick Persian carpet.

"What happened to him after he left Gondokoro? That is what we need to determine. Not whether there are winged persons on Mars."

"But vou see," du Maurier responded, "if Dr. Braid's developments on the foundations of Mesmer's work have validity—"

"If?" Folliot cut him off. "If? You who spout the whole line of supernatural foolishness from Paracelsus to Mesmer to Braid, say, If?"

Du Maurier refused to rise to the bait, refused to be distracted from his chain of reasoning.

"If," he repeated, "Anton Mesmer and James Braid are correct, and if we can continue their researches, it might be possible to establish a contact, a direct mental contact, from the mind of one brother to that of another."

"Unfortunately for your notion," Folliot replied, "Dr. Braid has gone to his reward."

"Just so," du Maurier conceded. "But others may carry on."

Miss Leighton said, "I do not wish to cast a pall on your speculations." She looked from Major Clive Folliot to George du Maurier, than back to Folliot. "But you both assume that Sir Neville is still alive. How can you be certain of this?"

Clive Folliot and George du Maurier exchanged glances.

Folliot spoke. "I do not know that my brother is alive. In part, I need to find this out, for if he survives he remains in line to become the next Baron Tewkesbury, and to inherit the lands and buildings and moneys appertaining to the title. If my brother is dead—heaven forfend!—then the inheritance will pass to me upon the eventual death of our father."

Du Maurier pushed himself from his chair and crossed to stand beside Clive Folliot. He put his arm around Clive's scarlet-covered shoulders. "If I had not known you for most of my life, and if I did not know you for the true innocent that you are, I should accuse you of dissembling. 'Heaven forfend,' indeed!"

He dropped his arm again, sipped his brandy. "We'll need another round of these, will we not?" He signaled to a servant, then returned to his subject. "What did that arrogant bully of a twin ever do for you, that you should want to find him and bring him home? Other than thrash you in the boxing ring a hundred times? You're game, Clive, but that isn't enough, in this life!"

The servant returned and refilled the brandy snifters of the three.

"Go out there after him, and fail in your quest," du Maurier went on, "and you're more than likely to pay with your life. Succeed, and what have you achieved? You bring the bully back! Leave him, I say. If he returns of his own accord, well enough—or ill! If he never returns, then when the time comes you will inherit in his stead."

"No," Clive Folliot said. "Neville has his faults, I'll concede."

"Hah! And Napoleon had his ambitions!"

"But he is still my brother," Folliot continued. "And I see my duty very clearly. I must find Neville. Save him if he lives, or at least learn his fate, if he is dead. I cannot leave the mystery unsolved. Even a cynic like you, du Maurier, will concede that I must learn his fate. Else the line will become clouded and I will never truly become Baron Tewkesbury."

Du Maurier snorted. "A mystic in one breath, a cynic in the next—is that what I am?"

"Yes. And the best cartoonist in London," Clive Folliot said. "And my good friend, devil take you."

The two men clasped hands.

"Come along, then, Folliot. Miss Leighton, if you please."

The great clock standing between a portrait of the late Prince Albert and one of Her Majesty sounded the hour.

"A cold supper will be served now," du Maurier said. "I trust you both have at least a modest appetite. Performing always makes me ravenous, and I am prepared to attack something larger than I am if I must, to fill my plate!"

Laughing, they made their way through a cold buffet of poached salmon, langouste, asparagus, potted veal with truffles, and pudding. As he stood, china and cutlery in hand, Clive felt the hand of another descend heavily upon his shoulder. He turned to see a man of below average height, his clothing well cut but stained and carelessly worn, staring at him. The man's hair was wiry and gray; he wore a straggly beard marked with stains of ink.

The newcomer spoke in a low voice, jerking his head toward a far corner of the salon.

Clive excused himself from Annabella and du Maurier and followed the bearded man in the direction indicated.

"I wouldn't expect to see you out tonight," the gray-haired man said to Clive.

"What I do tonight is my business, Carstairs," Clive hissed. "Let me get back to my party."

"Soon enough, fellow. Since we've crossed paths we might as well finish our little business for the moment."

"I don't know what's to finish."

"Your itinerary is set, your passage is booked, your gear has been packed and delivered to the *Empress Philippa*," Carstairs said in his low tones.

"That's no more than was agreed to."

"And you will furnish complete reports to us."

"Of course."

"And only to us. *The London Illustrated Recorder and Dispatch* is not financing your expedition out of sheer benevolence, Folliot. I hope you understand that. One word to a rival paper, and everything is off. No further funds, no sponsorship, no publication for you, nothing."

"Don't think that you are furnishing all my funds, Carstairs. Father is providing cash as well."

Carstairs snorted. "Good old Dad, eh, Clive? Loves his little boy so well he's sending you out to be a hero and rescue your big brother! Well, here's your farewell present from *The Recorder and Dispatch*." He drew a thick envelope from an inside pocket and passed it to Clive.

Clive glanced over his shoulder. Annabella and du Maurier had filled their plates and were chatting while they waited for him to return. He opened a brass button on his tunic, slipped the envelope inside, and nodded curtly to Carstairs.

When he returned to his companions du Maurier said, "I didn't know you were pals with Maurice Carstairs."

"I wouldn't call him a pal," Clive said grimly.

"Nonetheless." Du Maurier peered at Carstairs, who was slinking from the salon, pretending not to have seen the cartoonist. "Take care, Folliot. That *Recorder* gang has an unsavory reputation on the street. Newspapering's a competitive game, and there are a lot of smart players in it, but even so, that gang is about the slipperiest in the business."

"I know what I'm doing, du Maurier! I thought you were hungry, anyway. Perhaps that's what's making you so testy tonight."

"I—testy?" Du Maurier's eyes popped with surprise. "Well, never mind, never mind. I'll see what I can do for us."

Du Maurier secured the use of a private dining room, and they seated themselves around a table covered with spotless linen and polished silver.

A steward brought a tall bottle of Moet & Chandon, and glasses were filled with the sparkling champagne.

The conversation returned to the burlesque *Cox and Box* and to George du Maurier's comic and musical performance. The spirits of the celebrants rose with those of the champagne and the world outside their little group was forgotten.

From the outer salon the standing clock sounded again.

Major Folliot said, "You'll excuse us, du Maurier. I know that Miss Leighton must rise early tomorrow to attend to her academic duties."

Du Maurier stood. "Permit me to accompany you, then."

"No, no. There is no need of that. If the commissionaire will fetch a cab for us, I shall see Miss Leighton to her door."

Du Maurier accompanied them to the main entryway of the club. He stood with them while a cab was summoned. The night had turned colder, and the London fog had thickened into a mist that clung to every visible object, reflecting the few dim lights and giving the street a grim and ghostly atmosphere.

▪ CHAPTER 2 ▪
Plantagenet Court

Major Clive Folliot sat on the dark blue velvet plush stool, his scarlet tunic open, his elbows on his knees. His fingers were laced and his chin rested on his hands.

He was watching Miss Annabella Leighton bathe.

Her hair was piled upon the top of her head and held in place by pins so as to keep it out of the warm water. She smiled at Major Folliot as she soaped herself. His admiration was obvious, and his frank expression of it was equally gratifying to her.

She rubbed a cake of Pear's soap into lather, balanced a shimmering bubble on the palm of her hand, and playfully blew it toward Folliot.

The bubble wafted the few feet from Annabella to Clive and broke against the side of his face. He looked startled.

Annabella laughed. "What's the matter, Clive?"

He shook his head. "Nothing, my dear. Nothing. I was merely—distracted."

She raised herself in the tub, the better to scrub. Her breasts, pale as milk and soft as new snow, were exposed, their generous nipples in dramatic contrast with the color of the rest of her skin.

"Would you help me to dry myself, Clive?" She climbed from the tub and stood on a small carpet while he wrapped a huge Turkish towel around her. She turned so her back was to him, his scarlet-covered arms around her. She took his hands and placed them on her bosoms. "I feel so wonderful after a bath, Clive. So freshened, before retiring."

She turned within the circle of his arms, looking into his face. She gave him a small kiss on the edge of his jawbone. "Come to bed now, my darling. I really do have to rise early in the morning, and go to discharge my duties."

"You shouldn't be teaching the daughters of the rich, Annabella." Clive's voice was angry. "You're as fine as any of them—finer! And yet they treat you as little better than a servant."

"Hush. Come beside me." She had climbed into her large bed. She had a long nightgown with her, but she held the garment in her hands; she had not donned it.

The room was illuminated by a single oil lamp, and a window gave onto the little street, Plantagenet Court, where Annabella had her room. The landlady had questioned her about her entertaining a gentleman in her quarters, but when the landlady learned that the gentleman in question was the younger son of Lord Folliot, Baron Tewkesbury, she soon ceased to ask questions.

Clive continued to stare into the oil lamp's flickering flame.

"It's cold," Annabella teased. "I'll have to slip into my nightgown if you don't come and warm me up, Clive."

He still failed to respond.

She leaned forward, the thick quilt sliding unheeded to her still-slim waist. She took his face in her hands and turned him so they confronted each other.

"Clive, you have been preoccupied all evening. At the play, and at Mr. du Maurier's club. And now—you've never been so uninterested in my companionship. Has some higher-born lady stolen your affections from me? Or was it that unsavory-looking man with the gray beard?" She frowned, then added, "Or has it to do with your brother Neville?"

He looked into her eyes and she could see tears visible in his own.

"Clive, tell me please! What is wrong? I shouldn't have teased you, but—Clive, what is it, darling?"

He drew a breath. "It is Neville—in a way."

She saw the stricken look on his face and drew his head down to rest on her bosom. He put his arms around her and held her, held himself to her.

"Do you want to tell me, Clive?"

He shook his head.

"Then come into bed, and I'll help you forget whatever it is. We can speak of it later. Come now."

She helped him out of the scarlet tunic, ran her fingers beneath his shirt, all the while kissing his face, his cheeks and lips and his closed eyes.

He heaved a sigh and climbed beneath the quilts with her, and did forget his distracting worries for a time. And then he fell asleep.

In the middle of the night he suffered a terrible nightmare and awoke trembling and clutching at Annabella.

"Now you must tell me," she said. "Please, dear, before the morning comes and you must sneak out the back way and I leave by the front. Tell me now what it is."

"Yes. Yes, you're right."

She stirred.

"Don't light the oil," he said, drawing her back. "I can speak better in the darkness, where I cannot see your face, Annabella."

"Tell me, then. You said it was about Neville."

"Yes. And about Maurice Carstairs. The man with the gray beard. And it's about Brigadier Leicester. You know whom I mean, Annabella?"

"Of course. You've mentioned your commanding officer many times. What has he to do with Neville?"

"He has to approve leave before I can set out in search of Neville."

He could not see her face in the darkness, but he could hear the intake of her breath and feel the tension that coursed through her body.

"We've discussed this so many times, Clive. And again tonight, even with Mr. du Maurier. Why must you search for Neville? He'll come back or he'll not, as heaven decrees. Why should you be lost as well? Neville is a cruel bully, Clive. He never let you forget that he was the elder, even though it was only by a few minutes."

"We were born on different days, Annabella."

"Yes, how many times have I heard the story! Neville was born just before the stroke of midnight on January twenty-sixth, 1835. And you were born just after."

"Yes. Making my birthday January twenty-seventh."

"But, Clive! What difference does the passage of a few minutes make? You and Neville are fraternal twins! You had the same father, the same mother!"

"Yes, and that mother died after giving birth to me, and Father has blamed me for it, for thirty-three years! For thirty-three years Neville has been the light of Father's eye, and I have been the bête noir. And now that Father is growing old, and succession is on his mind, Neville's absence in Africa assumes greater dimensions each day."

"Let him stay lost! Then you will become the Baron Tewkesbury. Everyone knows it. Du Maurier knows it. All of London knows it."

Clive groaned. "But Father has agreed partially to finance an expedition in search of Neville. And *The Recorder and Dispatch*—"

"A rag!" Annabella interrupted.

"Even so, they have agreed to pay for the rest of the expedition. Carstairs is their man. He delivered an envelope of bank notes to me at du Maurier's club—it's his, too. With the money I have now, I can go after Neville. But you want him to stay lost, Annabella, don't you?"

"I do! I admit it! You've said you want to marry me, Clive! Oh, why did I ever take you to my bed! You think me a common strumpet! You treat me like a whore—creeping up the stairs to my chamber, sneaking out the back. I'm a kept little whore of the young officer! I should have known! Every nobleman's son in a scarlet tunic has his little plaything tucked away somewhere, and I am yours."

She sobbed.

"I thought you were different from the others. I thought *I* was different from the others. But you're just another whoremaster and I'm your little doxie! How could I not have known!"

"Brigadier Leicester has approved my leave," Clive said softly.

"And off you go to Equatoria to search for your dear brother."

"Yes."

There was a lengthy silence.

Then, "I will marry you," Clive said.

"You've told me that many times."

"I have no money. I cannot divert the funds of the expedition."

"I don't want money. I want a husband, Clive. And a name."

"You weren't so demanding when first we met!"

"I had less reason to be demanding."

"When I get back I shall write a book. They all do, you know. Did you hear du Maurier say it at the club? It's the truth. They all write books, and they all make fortunes. And then we shall marry, whether Neville becomes Lord Tewkesbury or I do. Don't you see? It's our path to freedom! We shall be out from under Father's thumb, if he's still alive, or Neville's if he is not. We shall be independent of them, and we shall make a life of our own. You shall give up your teaching, and I shall resign from the army, and we shall live together, happily."

"Yes, happily ever after, Clive," she said, her intonation heavy with bitterness and scorn.

"But we shall!"

"Don't you know a fairy tale when you hear one? Even when it is your own voice that is telling it?"

He slid from the bed and crossed the room. Even in the nearly complete darkness of Annabella's bed-chamber, Clive knew his way. His bare feet felt the rough nap of the carpet between the bed and table.

Through the tall window, a distant dawn was attempting to send its first feelers of pale gray. The mist of midnight had turned into an icy rain, and Clive knew that in a few hours the city would be clogged with sliding wagons and fallen horses. Many of the latter would break their legs and would be destroyed on the spot, their steaming carcasses hauled away by others of their breed.

Behind him, Clive could hear Annabella's breathing. She did not speak as she waited for him to respond to her jibe.

He found a box of friction matches. He lifted the chimney, long grown cold, from the oil lamp and felt the wick with two fingertips to make certain that it was still damp. Then he wiped his fingers dry and struck the match. When the lamp was burning evenly he held it waist high and turned back toward the bed.

Annabella giggled.

"I did not know I had said or done anything funny," Clive sniffed.

Annabella put her hand over her mouth. "You've never seen yourself stark naked save for a nightcap, holding a lamp like some modern Diogenes searching for an honest man." Before he could respond she grew serious again. "I suppose it's too much to ask that my nineteenth-century Diogenes make me an honest woman!"

Clive felt himself flush. "I have told you, dear Annabella, that I will marry you as soon as I can afford to do so! There is no way that I can support a wife on the pittance the government pays me. I should marry you this very hour—we should rouse some parson and become united before the cock crows!—if only I could afford it."

There was a lengthy silence.

Finally, Annabella said, "Put the lamp back on the

table. Leave it burning, Clive. So your Brigadier Leicester has approved your leave, has he?"

Clive placed the lamp as directed. He said, "He has."

"And when are you leaving on your African expedition?"

Clive did not want to answer. He stood on the carpet, sweating with embarrassment and shame, simultaneously trembling with the chill of the icy room.

Annabella, comfortable in her bed, outwaited him.

Finally, he said, "In the morning. Tomorrow—that is, this day."

"All right," Annabella said angrily. "You'll be gone in the morning, but you're going to have a night that you shall never forget, Clive Folliot!"

She threw back the comforter and quilt to reveal her nakedness. She held her arms toward him. "Leave the lamp burning, Clive! Take off that ridiculous nightcap and get back into this bed!"

He stood on the wooden pier, looking up at the gray ship that loomed above him. The *Empress Philippa* was one of the hybrid craft that were coming to dominate the sea lanes. She carried both sail and steam power, the former being regarded as more reliable and economical; the latter, as providing greater speed. Power was already up in her boiler; her sails were furled and clouds of dark smoke rose from her stacks.

Gray ship, gray Thames, gray London sky! Clive looked down at his less-than-fresh appearance. Before acquainting himself with the captain of *Empress Philippa* he would have to find his cabin.

▪ CHAPTER 3 ▪
Aboard the *Empress Philippa*

Luncheon was an informal affair, but at dinner Clive did make the acquaintance of Captain Wingate.

The captain was a retired Royal Navy officer, a veteran who had fought in the Burmese war fifteen years earlier. The captain took an interest in Clive and invited him to his quarters for an evening's chat.

Planted in a comfortable chair in his own quarters, Wingate admitted that he missed serving the Crown and envied Clive his opportunity.

"But they don't want an old sea dog like me in the fleet, any more than they want old soldiers around. We're an embarrassment to the youngsters who want to rise."

The captain leaned back in his chair. "Tell me, Major, why has an officer of Her Majesty's army left his unit and booked passage to Zanzibar? That is, if my question doesn't sail too near a reef, if you take my meaning."

"I believe I do, Captain. And there is nothing secret about my mission. Doubtless you have heard of my brother, Sir Neville Folliot."

"To be sure, Major! All the explorers have come in for their share of fame. Now that peace has laid her gentle hand on Brittania's brow, we must seek elsewhere for our heroes than the battlefield. And the exploration of exotic realms seems to have filled the bill—as well as giving our officers something to do other than ride to parade."

He turned away from Clive, opened a heavy-lidded

humidor that stood upon his table, and extracted a cigar. "Would you care for one, Major?"

Clive accepted, and they lit their smokes.

"I will confess, Major, that I did not at first connect you with the explorer. If you'll forgive my saying so, the name Neville Folliot is almost a household word these recent years, while that of Clive Folliot, well . . ." He exhaled a plume of fragrant smoke and waved it away.

"There's nothing to forgive," Clive said. "You speak nothing but the truth when you say that Neville is famous. And that I am for all practical purposes unknown."

He gazed out a porthole. Through the glass he could see a cloudy sky and a dark sea. Beyond, he knew, lay the coast of France. Soon *Empress Philippa* would pass the imaginary extension of the border between France and Spain. Clive's journey was just beginning.

"So after you debark at Zanzibar you'll head for the mainland and try to pick up Neville's trail, is that it?"

"Precisely."

"I don't recall your shipping much gear, Major Folliot. Aboard the *Empress,* that is. And you seem to be traveling alone. Surely you don't intend to carry out this expedition single-handed!"

Clive shook his head. "I have read the reports of as many of the explorers as I could lay my hands on. And I've spoken with several of them. Mr. John Hanning Speke and Mr. James Augustus Grant were particularly helpful."

"A shame about Mr. Speke, don't you agree?" The captain leaned toward Clive.

"A pity—killed in a hunting accident the very day he was to debate Sir Richard Burton."

Captain Wingate lowered his cigar, crossed his arms on the table before him, and said, "There is something strange about the headwaters of the Nile, Major. You are aware that Burton and Speke both claimed to have found the source of that river."

"Indeed! That was to be the subject of their star-crossed debate!"

"Aye! And Neville Folliot was seeking to make the same discovery, and he has disappeared."

Clive Folliot leaped to his feet. "Surely you see no connection between the incidents!"

The captain laughed. It was a slow laugh, coming from deep in his throat, a deliberate *huh-huh-huh* sound. "I'm just an old sea dog, Major Folliot. I served my queen and country as long as I was permitted, and now I serve the shipping line running this crossbred three-master from London to Zanzibar, from Zanzibar to Ceylon, from Ceylon to Singapore. And so on, and so on, wherever my employers order. Soon Monsieur de Lesseps will finish digging his canal at Suez, and I expect my new masters will discard me again as my old ones did before."

He squeezed his eyes shut and dabbed at their corners with a huge, patterned bandanna. "The cigar smoke, Major Folliot. These are the finest Havanas, but their smoke still makes the eyes tear. You agree with me, surely."

Clive realized that the interview was ended. He returned to his cabin to ponder.

Breakfasts were served to passengers in their cabins aboard the *Empress*, and luncheons were informal affairs, but dinner aboard ship was an elaborate ceremony and the hours afterward were busy ones.

Clive was assigned to a table with three companions. Two of them were a missionary couple on their way to convert the heathen Africans. The Reverend Amos Ransome was a doughy-faced, bespectacled divine who commenced each meal by fixing his thick lenses before his weak eyes, bowing his head over a volume of prayers, and murmuring an inaudible grace. His conversation seemed limited to the works of the late John Wesley, from whose death the missionary had yet to recover.

"I'm sorry," Clive found himself apologizing, "but I seem to have lost track of my church history. Did Mr. Wesley not die some years ago?"

"In the year 1791," the young reverend supplied.

"Can you not put aside your grief?" Clive asked. He found it difficult to keep a straight face. "You don't look much over twenty, Reverend Ransome."

"From such a loss, the world will not soon recover," the reverend replied. "But we will carry the good word to every corner of the earth. When all mankind has come to the Way—then will there be rejoicing throughout the nations."

"Quite," Clive commented.

The reverend's companion spoke seldom and kept her eyes lowered to her plate throughout each evening's meal. She wore voluminous dark costumes. Despite their cut, Clive could not but notice a voluptuous form. Still waters, he thought.

At first introduction Clive had assumed that Lorena Ransome was the reverend's wife, but Amos explained that she was his sister. "As good a helpmeet as any wife could be," Amos explained, "but without the danger of domestic complications to distract us from our holy task." He managed a feeble grin.

The final member of their table was a florid-faced, stockily built man traveling alone. He introduced himself as Mr. Philo Goode, from Philadelphia, Pennsylvania.

Hoping for relief from the reverend's alternating sermons and his lugubrious silences—there seemed no hope of getting his sister to speak during their dinners—Clive turned to the American in desperation.

He wore a glittering stickpin in his cravat and bright-jeweled rings on the fingers of both hands. He spoke grandly of his business interests in the New World. They extended from Maine to South Carolina along the Atlantic Ocean, and included cattle farms in Missouri and a major interest in a diamond mine in Ohio.

The Reverend Ransome exclaimed at each new revelation by the American. Even Miss Lorena Ransome roused herself from her customary silence to comment that Mr. Goode must be very rich.

Empress Philippa had reached a position to the south of the Ivory Coast. Conversation turned to the development of Africa's as-yet-unplumbed riches. Philo Goode boasted that he himself had economic interests in Africa as well as America. They were the reason for his present journey, he said. To check up on his investments in the companies that were even now beginning to exploit the potential of the Dark Continent.

Miss Ransome looked shyly at Goode. "You must be one of the richest men in the New World," she said.

Swallowing the last of his beverage, Goode burst into laughter. "Rich! By gum, everybody's rich in America! I'm a piker compared to some! Why, within the next few years I expect to own a raiiroad and an iron foundry. We're making money so fast in America we can't keep track of it."

"I trust you are in the custom of sharing your good fortune with those who do the Lord's good work," Ransome intoned.

"Am I a tither, do you mean?" Goode asked.

"Some do more than tithe, my friend."

"I don't know why I should give my hard-earned dollars to support some hymn-singing, Bible-thumping parasites," Goode said. He slapped himself proudly on the chest. "I worked for every nickel I've got, and I expect others to do the same."

"Parasites! God's loyal servants, sir!" Ransome was on his feet, his normally pasty face red with anger.

"Parasites, I said. They don't raise food, they don't dig ore, they don't weave cloth. They just eat and preach! Well, I don't need any preaching, least of all from some snivel-nosed four-eyed weakling, and I'll eat my own dinner, thank you very much!"

Goode, ruddy-faced to begin with, was livid. As he spoke he pounded his fists on the white linen.

Lorena Ransome had sat, ashen-faced, during the dialogue. Now she pulled a tiny handkerchief from her sleeve and sniffled delicately into it. She grasped Clive by the cuff of his jacket and turned appealingly to him.

"Can't you stop them? Oh, please, Major Folliot. My brother is not a strong man. I fear they are coming to blows, and he will be no match for Mr. Goode."

Clive managed to interrupt the others. "Our meal is ended anyway," he said. "Perhaps we might retire to more salubrious surroundings."

"I haven't finished my say yet," Goode insisted. "I don't know why that damned purser Fennely put me to table with a pair of pallid petunias like these two. And you're not that much better, you lobster-backed fop! My granddaddy whipped your old King George and sent your soldiers packing, and I'm ready to give you the same lesson if you can't remember what it was!"

"Please, sir!" Clive rose to his feet. "Miss Ransome is present. If you wish to settle your differences with me, there is a proper way. A vulgar brawl at the dinner table is not that way."

The Ransomes were still in their seats. Miss Ransome was staring, alarmed, from Goode to Folliot. The Reverend Ransome had folded his hands and lowered his eyes. Now he murmured a soft *amen* and looked up at Folliot and Goode. "I have prayed for guidance," Ransome said.

"Oh yeah?" Goode jeered. "You must have sent your message by telegraph. What kind of answer did you get? Or haven't they answered you yet?"

"Come," the Reverend Ransome said, "let us retire to the ship's lounge, where we may continue our discussion in calmer circumstances."

Clive expected Goode either to punch Ransome then and there, or to stamp out of the dining salon in disgust and rage. Instead, the American said, "All right, preacher. We'll do that."

They found a private corner in the ship's lounge and seated themselves. A steward approached and offered them beverages. 'We do not take strong spirits," Ransome explained for himself and Lorena. "But a cooling fruit juice would be welcomed."

Goode ordered a brandy and Folliot agreed to join him. When the steward started to turn away, Goode said, "Just bring the bottle and a couple of glasses, sonny. We don't want to bother you with running back and forth all the time." He laughed at his own words.

There were half-a-dozen tables in the lounge. Most of the ship's passengers were male, but a few ladies were accompanied by their husbands. An upright piano stood in one corner of the room. Card games were in progress at several tables, as travelers whiled away the *Empress*'s slow progress southward.

Clive's attention was captured by a most remarkable sight in the far corner. A man had seated himself at the piano, and from the back he appeared to be a Chinese gentleman.

A mere matter of days had passed, and yet the world of the *Empress Philippa* seemed as isolated from England as must George du Maurier's fabled planet Mars. Stranger yet, the mandarin, clad in his Oriental gown, was rendering with perfection a difficult composition by the late German composer Felix Mendelssohn!

Clive shook his head in wonderment.

The steward returned bearing a tray with a glass of nectar for each of the Ransomes and with two empty glasses and a bottle of golden-colored liquid for Mr. Goode and himself.

When the steward left, Goode lifted his glass. "I apologize, Reverend. I'm a hot-tempered man and I react when people tread on my toes. I guess you mean well, if nothing more."

"Half an apology is better than none, I suppose," Ransome said.

"And as for you, Major," Goode snapped a nod at Clive, "we threw out your King George but look what we have now—that fool Andy Johnson! We may yet have to do the same thing to him, hey? Drink up, drink up!"

Clive emptied his glass and Goode refilled it.

"Tell you what, Reverend," Goode went on. "About that tithing business. Never believed in it and don't believe in it now. Let 'em get out and earn their own way, says I. I've never given anything to any damned preacher, but in the spirit of friendship, I'll make you an offer."

Ransome looked mildly at the American. "An offer, Mr. Goode?"

"Let's have a little game of poker. Look at all the fun they're having." He indicated the nearby tables where card games were in progress.

Ransome grew paler than ever.

"Just a friendly little game," Goode repeated. He slapped himself on the chest as he had earlier, but this time he kept his hand pressed against his jacket so that Clive could see the rectangular outline of a deck of playing cards.

"I could never—I am a Christian, Mr. Goode. A Methodist. Gambling is most unchristian."

"Can't do it, hey?" Goode lowered his glass from his lips, added a bit to it from the bottle, filled Clive's glass, and returned his attention to Ransome.

"I'll tell you what, Rev. If I win, anything I win I'll donate to your mission, how's that? And if you win, you can do the same. So it isn't gambling, see? It's just my way of tithing. Got to salvage a little American pride, eh?"

Ransome looked at his sister. He bent his head, spoke a few words to her, then straightened. He reached into his pocket and withdrew his prayer book and his glasses, fixed the glasses on his nose, and studied the book.

After a few minutes he closed the book and slipped it back into his pocket.

He cleared his throat. "Playing cards is still a frivolous and unseemly activity. But the greater sin would be gambling, and as you say, this is merely a device whereby you may contribute to the good works of our mission. So I have decided that it is permissable—although hardly behavior in which I would care to indulge more than this once, Mr. Goode."

Goode turned to Clive. "What about you, Folliot? You in the game? I'll even forgive your damned redcoats for burning Washington back in fourteen."

"Ah—I could hardly keep my winnings, Mr. Goode."

"Philo," Goode said. "Call me Philo, and I'll call you Clive, all right?"

"You may call me Amos, then," the Reverend Ransome added.

"And you may call me Lorena," his sister said. She leaned toward Clive as she said it, and as the bodice of her dress touched his arm he could detect the warmth and pleasant softness of her bosom.

"Why don't you throw in with us, then?" Goode said. "All winnings to the reverend's mission. What could be better than that, Clive?"

Folliot agreed.

Goode reached inside his garment and extracted a package of playing cards. He said, "Plain American poker all right?"

Ransome said, "I fear that my sister and I are not acquainted with the rules of the game. Of any card game."

Goode shot a look at Folliot. "Let's play a couple of dummy hands, to teach Amos the game, okay, Clive? Amos and Miss Ransome, of course."

Clive agreed and Goode dealt an open hand. Clive won with a pair of jacks. The deal moved to Clive and he dealt an open hand and won again with a feeble ace high.

Next it was Lorena Ransome's turn to deal, and under Goode's guidance she distributed the cards correctly, and won the hand as well, with a heart flush. When Clive explained to her that her hand beat both her brother's two pairs and Philo Goode's three tens, she squealed delightedly and hugged his arm.

Clive blushed, and, seeing him do so, Lorena did also.

Soon they started playing in earnest. The ship's purser provided chips, and the steward replenished Amos's and Lorena's glasses and replaced Clive and Philo's bottle.

Amos Ransome was the only one of the four who hadn't won a hand during the dummy play, and for the first half hour of serious play he managed to continue his miserable performance.

Philo Goode lost a few pounds; Amos Ransome, far more; Clive Folliot and Lorena Ransome won in roughly equal amounts.

Every time Lorena won a pot she would squeal and hug a nearby arm—at first alternating between her brother and Clive, then turning to Clive more and more often.

The steward returned again, with fruit juice for the Ransomes and brandy for Folliot and Goode. The luck of the table swung from Clive and Lorena to Philo and Amos. Then Lorena did a little better. Then Philo, Amos, and Clive bid up a huge pot.

Clive held a full house with three acres.

Philo was sweating. He opened his collar, lifted his brandy glass, and set it down again. The betting was furious. Lorena had dropped out early but the three men refused to quit.

Several of the other games had ended, and passengers had moved from their tables and assembled near this one. Even the silken-robed mandarin had ceased his performance of Mendelssohn and joined the crowd of Europeans surrounding the table.

Finally Goode threw his cards face down on the cloth.

Clive had gone deeply into the funds provided by Maurice Carstairs. He looked into the envelope. He'd been drinking brandy and become intoxicated both by it and by the proximity of Lorena Ransome. She had abandoned her practice of squealing and hugging his arm every time she won a pot, but there was now a pressure of her leg against his own, beneath the table, that he found both distracting and exciting.

He laid his last fifty-pound note on the table.

Amos Ransome, his ecclesiastical garb soaked with perspiration, said, "I'll call you, Clive. Is that the right term?"

Suddenly Clive realized that he had gambled away most of his treasury. The friendly game, all for the good of the mission, had turned into his ruin. If he lost this hand, he would be unable to finance his search for Neville. He would never write his dispatches for Carstairs's rag, would never write his book, would never make his fortune—would never marry Annabella.

He laid down his full house.

The Reverend Amos Ransome laid down a straight flush. He reached for the chips and the pile of cash that spelled the doom of Clive Folliot's mission.

A long hand ending in a jade fingernail protector emerged from the sleeve of a silken robe. The carved jade touched the back of Ransome's hand. It appeared to be the gentlest of contacts but Ransome froze into immobility.

"Major Clive Folliot," the mandarin intoned in perfect and unaccented English. "You have been taken in by a trio of brilliant cheats. I suggest that you retrieve all of your money and retire to your cabin. These three will remain where they are while a steward summons Purser Fennely. He will deal with them or turn the matter over to Captain Wingate, as he deems proper."

Lorena Ransome screamed.

Philo Goode shoved back his chair and leaped to his feet. "How dare you, you yellow heathen!" He fumbled at his waistband and drew a hogleg revolver. He pointed it at the mandarin.

The Oriental raised his fingernail protector from the back of Amos Ransome's hand and tapped gently on the barrel of Goode's revolver. The revolver landed on the table with a crash.

Goode stared, dumbfounded. His eyes bulged, and he strained, but he appeared unable to retrieve the weapon.

The mandarin lifted the revolver and emptied the bullets from its cylinder. He dropped them, one after another, into the the brandy bottle. As each bullet landed in the liquor it made a distinct sound, as if a small, heavy stone had been dropped into a half-frozen pond, where the resulting ripples remained as evidence of the event.

Beads of perspiration dripped from Philo Goode's ruddy face. He shouted at the crowd surrounding the table, "You're white men. Are you going to let this yellow devil accuse the reverend of cheating? Stop him!"

The Chinese reached for Amos Ransome's thick-lensed spectacles. He removed them from the preacher's nose and extended them toward Clive, bowing.

Clive looked curiously at the glasses. He held them in front of his eyes and looked at the cards lying on the table. Each was clearly marked with its suit and denomination. No wonder the Reverend Ransome had won so much money! His earlier poor play had been a ruse to lure Clive into betting more heavily. Philo Goode's job had been to set up the game with his studied insults of the preacher. Goode had provided the marked cards. And Lorena Ransome had added to Clive's distraction.

Clive passed the preacher's glasses around to half-a-dozen spectators. Each of them looked through them at the cards and muttered before passing them on to another. Finally they came back to the mandarin.

If it hadn't been for the Chinese, Clive would have been cleaned out and left with hardly a pound to his name, while the preacher—come to think of it, he was almost certainly a phony preacher at that—divided the loot with his female confederate and his other fellow American.

At this point the purser, Mr. Fennely, arrived, summoned by a steward.

Clive explained briefly what had happened. Fennely said, "Reverend, Miss Ransome, and Mr. Goode. You are confined to your quarters. You will go there directly from the salon, and wait for a summons from Captain Wingate. You will consider yourselves under captain's arrest."

He asked Clive if he wished to prefer charges against the three.

Clive said, "What will happen to them?"

"If you prefer charges, Major Folliot, they will be arraigned for attempted criminal fraud, tried by a ship's tribunal, and, if convicted, bound over to the authorities at the first British port."

"And if I don't?" Clive asked.

"Captain Wingate will probably keep them under confinement in their cabins until we reach our first port of call, then put them ashore and wash his hands of them."

Clive considered. The Ransomes and Philo Goode all watched him. Finally he said, "I will not prefer charges."

The purser nodded. "Word will pass throughout the maritime fleet, you may rest assured of that, Major Folliot." Shoving Amos Goode's revolver into his own waistband, he ushered the three cheats from the salon.

Clive looked around for the mandarin, but he had disappeared.

▪ CHAPTER 4 ▪
The Celestial Guest

Folliot slumped in the sole chair with which his cabin was furnished. He held his head in his hands, trying to calm his racing thoughts.

At a gentle scratching at the door he called, "Come in."

Bowing, the mandarin entered. He closed the door carefully behind him, bowed again, and removed his headdress.

Clive stared up in amazement.

"Quartermaster Sergeant Horace Hamilton Smythe reporting, *sah!*"

The Chinese braced to attention and snapped a quivering right-hand salute. But he was no longer a Chinese. He still wore the elaborately embroidered, brightly colored silk robes of the Oriental, but his facial features had altered subtly.

The shape of his eyes seemed to have changed, and the tips of his long, silken, ebony mustache had been curled and waxed.

The color of his skin had not changed, but what had seemed, in the ship's salon, an Oriental yellow could now be seen instead as the healthy tan of an Englishman who has spent years beneath the tropical sun.

Clive sat flabbergasted, staring up at the sergeant.

"I'll beg you not to give me away while we're aboard the *Empress*," Sergeant Smythe said.

"But—but—" Clive stammered.

"With your permission, sah." Smythe indicated the

foot of Clive's bunk. With Folliot occupying the cabin's sole chair, his visitor made a seat for himself on the end of the bunk.

"You were on detached duty from the Horse Guards. Brigadier Leicester—"

"Yes, sah," Smythe assented. "Technically, I am still in the Guards. Although I imagine they've got themselves a new regimental quartermaster sergeant by now."

"Yes, they have." Clive nodded. "And a sorry job he is. We miss you, Smythe. Where did you go? The brigadier was mightily close-lipped about the whole thing, as well as about when you might return to duty."

"With the major's permission, sah, I'm not at liberty to say. But the major might observe my accouterment and draw certain conclusions, if I might so suggest, sah."

Clive said, "I'd like to do something to show my appreciation, Smythe. At least offer you a bit of refreshment. But I'm afraid that I'm traveling light, as they say."

"Quite all right, sah. An enlisted bloke doesn't expect an officer to entertain 'im like no visiting lord, does he?"

Clive nodded. "But you're no ordinary enlisted soldier, Sergeant Smythe. You've been with me from my first days in the regiment. Ah, what a bewildered youngster I was back then. A junior lieutenant may be considered an officer by the Crown, but in matters real he's about as competent as a newborn kitten."

"Yes, sah."

"Smythe, why didn't you just give up on me back then? I know I'm not a great military man, never have been and probably never will be. But back then in fifty-seven, I must have appeared totally hopeless. I was frightened to death, did you know that, Sergeant?"

"Speaking frankly, sah, and off the record?"

"Of course, Sergeant."

"If the truth be known, Major, I could see you was shaking like a leaf. That's normal in new lieutenants. Every experienced soldier knows what a green lieutenant is like. But, Major Folliot, a smart soldier learns real quick like, to tell two things about any officer he has to deal with."

Clive watched Smythe's gestures.

"You learn to tell whether an officer's got it here." He tapped himself on the forehead with his thumb. "And you learn to tell if he's got it here." And with the same thumb he tapped himself over the heart.

"If an officer's got it in those two places, Major, why, a good smart soldier can shape 'im up. Stiffen 'is spine for 'im a bit, sharpen up his skills at square-bashin', teach 'im a little bit o' this and a little bit o' that, and first thing you know you've got yourself a pretty good little officer. But if he ain't got it here and here, then there's nothing a soldier can do with 'im, except try and stay out of 'is way, and not depend on 'im in no battle."

"And you saw me through ten years, Smythe, and I never understood what was happening." Clive sagged.

"Don't feel bad, sah. I had many a good time with the Guards. And you done right by me, as well. Many an officer as holds back on his batman 'cause he don't want to have to train a new one. You never 'eld me back a day!"

Clive uttered a rueful chuckle. "You ought to see the chap I've got now, Smythe. Not a bad soldier, but he'll never hold a candle to good old Private Smythe." He shook his head. "No, I never could have held back on you, Smythe. I was as proud as I could be when you made corporal, then sergeant. You're a legend in the regiment now, you know. They talk about Quartermaster Sergeant Smythe as of some departed titan. Which brings me back to you, Sergeant."

"Sah? I don't quite take your meaning, I'm afraid."

"Clearly you intend to remain reticent about your travels since you left the Guards."

"I've no choice, sah."

"I quite understand. But as much as you feel you can tell me—and where you learned to play Mendelssohn."

Smythe laughed. "Now that, sah, I can tell the major. There was a young lady, sah, a most talented musical performer and instructor, who claimed to have known the late composer in Germany. Well, sah, she was a lovely young lass but somewhat inexperienced in some of life's more delicate matters. She offered to teach me something of music if I would teach her something of other things. By the end of our exchange, I was very pleased with what I had learned from the young lady. And I have reason to believe that she was equally pleased with what she had learned from yours truly, sah."

Folliot stared at the sergeant. "I believe you are actually blushing, Sergeant Smythe."

"Am I, sah?"

The sergeant passed his hand before his eyes.

For an instant, it seemed to Clive Folliot that Sergeant Smythe's features wavered and grew indistinct, only to be replaced by those of the mandarin.

The Chinese rose to his feet. As Sergeant Smythe he had been a diminutive individual, easily four or five inches shorter than Clive's own five feet ten inches. As the mandarin he towered, or seemed to tower, so that he had to stoop slightly to avoid smashing his Oriental headdress against the cabin's timbers.

"This humble one is honored to have assisted the admirable major in a few slight moments of difficulty. This humble one begs that the admirable major exercise discretion until the splendid ship *Empress Philippa* reaches lovely island of Zanzibar."

"But—Sergeant Smythe?"

The mandarin opened the door of Clive's cabin. Beyond the cabin a sultry night of warm air and brilliant stars blazed spectacularly. "In Zanzibar, Ma-

jor Folliot may encounter Sergeant Smythe once again.
For now, humble Chinese individual must seek rest
in own cabin."

He bowed, backed through the doorway, drew the
door shut behind him.

Clive levered himself upright and pulled the door
open again, but the mandarin had disappeared into
the tropical night.

He was summoned to Captain Wingate's quarters
for a discussion of the event. The captain assured
him that the trio of gamblers would indeed be put
off the *Empress* at the first opportunity. This, it turned
out, was the Portuguese port city of Luanda, an ugly,
steaming city where the *Empress Philippa* dropped off
some crates of machinery and picked up a fresh
supply of stores, as well as a few passengers.

Clive confirmed his wish not to press charges against
the trio. He could not help asking Captain Wingate
what he knew of the mysterious Oriental who had
first detected the gamblers' scheme.

Captain Wingate drew up. "I can tell you nothing,
sir, about that gentleman. You are an officer in Her
Majesty's service. You will understand. I can say nothing more on the subject."

There were a few more performances in the salon.
Clive spent most of his evenings there, sometimes in
his uniform, at others in mufti. The mandarin would
appear, render a selection by Berlioz or Chopin,
Donizetti or Liszt, Mozart or Haydn—but most often
Mendelssohn.

But he did not speak. He traveled alone.

One evening, when the mandarin left the salon,
Clive managed to follow him to his cabin. Clive remained in the shadowed companionway, feeling con-
spicuous in his scarlet jacket and brass buttons, for
most of an hour. Then he knocked at the door.

After a moment, it swung open.

Clive had expected the man to revert to his true
identity as Sergeant Horace Hamilton Smythe, but

instead he was greeted by the mandarin in his full regalia and headdress. Behind the Chinese, Folliot could see that one wall of the cabin had been converted into a Buddhist shrine. Before a statue of the Enlightened One, on a cloth-covered altar, joss sticks smoldered in a bowl.

The mandarin bowed to Clive. "Her Majesty's officer honors this humble one. May the humble one be of service to the major?"

Confused, Clive stammered, "Smythe? Aren't you Sergeant Smythe?"

The Oriental bowed. "The officer is mistaken, I regret to say."

Clive stumbled to his own cabin and began work on a dispatch to Carstairs at *The London Illustrated Recorder and Dispatch*. He was not only supposed to chronicle his adventures in pursuit of his lost brother, but to provide sketches for the rag's staff artists to turn into publishable cuts.

"We *are* an illustrated newspaper." He could hear Maurice Carstairs's snide intonations. "We have to give the public their money's worth. And those who cannot decipher words may still enjoy the illustrations."

· CHAPTER 5 ·
Her Majesty's Resident Consul

Empress Philippa's crew had furled her sails and Captain Wingate ordered the engineer to raise a head of steam as the island of Zanzibar hove into view. It was late in the day, and the sun hung like a huge orange ember low above the Indian Ocean. Even this late in the day, the heat was oppressive and the air lay like a heavy weight on the world.

Clive Folliot had been invited to stand on the bridge as the ship made port, and he now watched with keen interest as the colors of the city blossomed before his eyes.

"They are strange people, Major," Wingate told him. "They are great sailors; they do things with their dhows that I should hardly dare attempt with a full-rigged frigate. But they don't have the European's machines, and they crave them with all their heart."

Clive raised his eyes to the cloud of black smoke that poured from the *Empress*'s stacks. "That's why we are steaming into port rather than moving under sail, I take it."

"That is exactly the reason, Major. I shouldn't say that they're so superstitious as to think there's anything supernatural about our steam engines. Although I imagine that the first time they saw a ship moving without sails, with black smoke belching from her stacks, they must have jumped from the ground."

He turned to give the helmsman a command, then returned to what he was saying.

"No, they're not altogether ignorant and superstitious. Some of 'em have been to the great centers of learning, to Berlin and Vienna and Paris and Rome. Some have even been to England. Many of them know a good deal more than we give them credit for. It's their attitudes that are so different from ours, that you have to watch out for."

"I'm not sure I take your meaning, Captain. Although I can tell you that I served in Madagascar at one time. Thus, I believe I can claim a small degree of understanding of the peoples of the region."

"You've mentioned that, Major Folliot. And I think it will serve you in good stead. But don't judge Zanzibar by the Malagasy peoples, and don't judge the black Africans by either. They're all different civilizations, as different in some cases as the Chinese and French, if you understand what I'm telling you."

Clive gave a noncommittal answer.

Captain Wingate shook his head. "Major Folliot, did you ever hear the expression, 'What you don't know can't hurt you'?"

"I have, sir. In fact it is a misquotation from the works of Mr. Sidney Smith."

"Well, it may be a quotation or it may be a miss. I want to tell you, Major Folliot, that in either case, it isn't true. What you don't know can hurt you very badly indeed. It can kill you. Yes, sir!"

The captain issued another command to the helmsman.

A dhow had moved from the harbor under sail, and it now beat its way past *Empress Philippa*. Clive could see the swarthy faces of Arab sailors as the dhow moved gracefully across the greenish water.

"There's only one thing more dangerous than what you don't know," Captain Wingate resumed. "And that is, what you do know that's wrong. That, Major Folliot, is the only thing I've ever heard of that has killed more men than what they didn't know at all. What they knew that just wasn't so."

Clive reached into his waistcoat pocket and withdrew his gold watch. He was dressed in mufti this day, as he had been for most of the voyage out from England.

"Impatient, Major Folliot?"

"Zanzibar is but a way station for me, sir. I must send my dispatch to my publisher, make what arrangements are needful, and then travel on to the mainland."

"I understand, Major. The call of a family obligation. You're a fortunate man to have a family at that."

Clive didn't answer.

"You see that marker?" Captain Wingate pointed.

Clive nodded.

"We've no tide tables for this part of the world. There's much work to be done before the seas are all as safe as the River Thames and the English Channel. That marker tells us the depth of the water just now. The tide is out. We'll drop anchor here and wait for morning. I expect we'll be seeing the sultan's harbormaster shortly, though."

The captain laughed. "Look at that, Major Folliot! Speak of the devil and here he comes."

Wingate pointed once more. A small felucca was beating across the harbor. In the stillness of late afternoon the craft had hard going. Clive could see that the little boat carried two persons, a single sailor and a passenger garbed in grand fashion.

The felucca finally hove to beside the *Empress*. A rope ladder was lowered from the *Empress*'s deck and the little boat was made fast while its two occupants climbed to the deck.

"I hope you won't mind spending one more night in your cabin, Major Folliot." Captain Wingate escorted Clive from the bridge. "We can't dock until morning anyway, because of the tides. I could have sent you ashore in a pinnace, but I expect the harbormaster will want to speak with us first. These Arabs are a suspicious lot. He might take it very ill if you tried to sneak ashore too quickly."

"Sneak ashore? I would do no such thing!"

"Of course not, Major. But you see, the sultan's man doesn't know you, does he?"

Clive peered over the railing to the deck where the two newcomers were greeted by the *Empress*'s deck officer.

Captain Wingate led the way down wooden stairs to the deck.

The harbormaster, garbed in elaborate robes and a red fez, stood engaged in conversation with the officer. The sailor had been separated from his master. Clive saw that a second Arab had come from somewhere and had drawn the sailor aside. They were garbed in similar striped robes and filthy, loose turbans. They were conversing in Arabic, gesticulating toward the harbormaster, the deck officer, Captain Wingate, and Clive.

Clive looked at his pocket watch, then returned to his writing. If he hurried he could complete his dispatch to the *Recorder* and still arrive at the dinner table in time to have his evening meal.

He completed his task, folded the dispatch, and sealed it. He would drop it off with Her Majesty's resident consul in Zanzibar, and it would be forwarded to Carstairs in London with the next outgoing diplomatic pouch. For a moment, Clive contemplated leaving it with *Empress Philippa*'s purser instead, but Captain Wingate had said that the ship was continuing eastward, and the dispatch would be too long delayed if it was carried on the *Empress*.

How much later it was that Clive made his way to his bunk, and how many hours he managed of uneasy slumber, he did not know. All he knew was that he was being roused, much against his will.

"We're gettin' offer this ship, Major," Sergeant Smythe said in a low voice.

"Of course we are. In the morning." Clive was quickly regaining his composure.

"Not in the morning, no, sah," Sergeant Smythe

whispered. "Right now, now, sah. Believe me, you want to get off this ship right now. The old harbormaster—and he ain't the harbormaster, believe me, sah, he's someone else—he's still in conference wiv Captain Wingate and Purser Fennely. The local politics, sah. Her Majesty's consul—Sir John Kirk—he's got his hands in some things you don't want to know about. The sultan of Turkey, the khedive of Egypt, the Frenchies—it's an awful mess, sah. You don't want to stay on this ship!"

He peered into Clive's eyes, nodded in satisfaction. "Now is our chance to get off this ship, and to get off quick and in one piece. Come on!"

He led the stumbling Clive Folliot to his cabin and helped Clive inside. The Arab sailor lay on Sergeant Smythe's bunk, stripped of his garments, bound and gagged.

"Out of your mufti and into this robe, sah," Smythe urged. "And please, Major, be quick about it and be quiet!"

Puzzled by Sergeant Smythe's astonishing message, Clive obeyed.

The Arab's eyes blazed, and he struggled to free his hands and feet. He did not succeed.

As Clive pulled the Arab's robe over his own head he was nearly overwhelmed by the odors trapped in the crudely woven cotton. There was a taint of grease, perhaps the residue of some lamb that the Arab had eaten. There was a musky perfume. There was the acrid scent of stale perspiration. There were other odors whose origin Clive could only guess—and he preferred not to.

"Here, this goes beneath the robe." Sergeant Smythe handed Clive a leather harness with an empty scabbard attached. "Around your leg, like a lady's garter, sah." Smythe nodded to indicate the appropriate place for the contrivance.

Once Clive had strapped it to his leg, Smythe handed him a dagger and indicated that it belonged in the scabbard. In the meantime, Sergeant Smythe had transformed himself into a filthy Arab.

Smythe pulled the hood of Clive's robe up over the officer's head. He shoved him out the doorway of the cabin and followed him into the companionway. "Come on, sah, we've got ter go!"

"But my chest," Clive demurred. "My uniforms and my clothing. My writing supplies. My money. All are in my cabin. Surely we can have them transferred to the shore."

"No, we can't, sah! I'm sorry, but you don't realize yer life's at stake! Bofe of our lives! We've got ter go *now*!"

He hurried Clive through *Empress Philippa*'s companionways. When they reached the deck, Smythe gestured Clive to remain hidden. He peered out, waited for a clear moment, then scurried across the deck. His Arab robe floating about him so that he looked like nothing more than a pale shadow scuttering across the wooden surface.

At *Philippa*'s rail he halted and crouched in a shadow. The storm clouds that had gathered earlier were being torn and strewn around the sky by a cold wind. Raindrops spattered down, alternating with gusts of windborne moisture. Through a hole in the clouds, a tropic moon sent down its rays.

Clive saw Sergeant Smythe gesture to him, and he scuttled across the deck, joining the sergeant at *Philippa*'s rail. "We're lucky they didn't leave a man to guard the felucca," Smythe whispered. "But we might run out of luck at any moment."

As if to punctuate Smythe's words, angry voices rose from above the two Englishmen. Clive glanced up and saw a light on *Philippa*'s bridge. Two figures were silhouetted by oil lanterns. One was the ship's purser, Mr. Fennely. The other was the Arab harbormaster. They were shouting and pointing down at the deck—pointing at the very spot where Clive Folliot and Horace Hamilton Smythe crouched in the shadows. Captain Wingate was nowhere to be seen.

"Now, sah, move!" Smythe urged.

The two men scrambled up and over the rail. Clive reached the rope ladder attached to *Philippa*'s hull first, and began climbing down toward the harbormaster's unmanned felucca. Sergeant Smythe followed without delay. As soon as the two men tumbled into the little boat, Sergeant Smythe cast off her lines and grabbed a pair of oars.

"Get that sail raised, Major," he shouted at Clive.

A few minutes and they were well away from *Empress Philippa*. Lanterns shone from the ship's deck, and voices shouted angrily in English and Arabic and pidgin.

There was a flash from the *Empress*'s deck, then another. Bullets whined overhead or splashed harmlessly near the felucca. One went through the little boat's sail, making a distinctive popping sound as it pierced the linen cloth.

But the sail had caught the swirling wind that swept across the harbor, and Clive, calling on skills learned long ago on the lakes of Scotland, guided the boat skillfully toward the shore and safety.

They made their way among a crazy pattern of dhows, feluccas, and cargo barges anchored in the harbor. Each gust of wind changed the pattern of cloud and sky, darkness and light. Clive was soaked with rainwater and salt spray, chilled to the bone by the cold wind.

"We're lucky it ain't no full-fledged monsoon," Sergeant Smythe said, as if he had read Folliot's mind. "Well, here's a place we can tie up."

They made fast the felucca, dropped the sail, and scrambled onto a crude dock. Almost all the residents of the city had been driven indoors, as much by the foul weather as by the hour. The two made their way through the streets, Sergeant Smythe leading Major Folliot almost as a blind man would lead a sighted one through pitch darkness.

Clive's nostrils were assaulted by all the odors of

the city, but he saw nothing of its sights. In the darkness of the storm there was nothing to be seen.

Smythe drew up at last at an iron gate. It was secured by a heavy lock, but Smythe worked some trickery upon it, and shortly the gate creaked open. Clive and his companion entered.

They found their way to a tall wooden doorway. Smythe lifted a huge iron knocker and dropped it. It landed on the thick wood with a deep boom. After a lengthy wait, the door creaked open.

A sleepy Arab youth in a long cotton gown answered the door. He held a lantern high in one hand.

Sergeant Smythe chattered something at him in the boy's own language and the youth stepped aside, admitting the two newcomers.

In the vestibule, Smythe jabbered again at the Arab youth. The youth disappeared.

"I say—" Clive began.

He was interrupted by the arrival of a thin-faced, blond-haired, mustachioed individual in dressing gown and slippers. He, too, was carrying a light with him, but his was a candle mounted on a heavy silver stick, its flame shielded by a glass chimney like that of an oil lamp.

"Who the devil are you?" the thin-faced man demanded. "Some dirty *fellah* comin' round here to bother me in the middle of the night? I'll have you whipped and thrown out if you've no explanation!"

"I am Major Clive Folliot, son of Baron Tewkesbury, sir! And my companion—" He looked around for Sergeant Smythe, but Smythe and the youth who had admitted them had both disappeared.

"Major Folliot? Tewkesbury?" the other echoed. He peered into Clive's face. "Well, you're the second Major Folliot I've encountered. T'other one claimed to be the son of Baron Tewkesbury, as well."

"That must have been my brother, sir! He passed through here more than a year ago."

"So he did, so he did." He lowered the candle. "So

you're another Englishman, are you? Then what are you doing in that silly get-up? You coming from a party?"

"No, sir!"

"Well, you've come to the right place, anyway, young fellow! This is Her Majesty's consulate, and I am Sir John Kirk, Her Majesty's resident consul. Let's get you a bath and a set of decent clothes, and then I want to know what the devil is going on with you! You're a far way from Tewkesbury, young laddie! A far, far way from Tewkesbury!"

· CHAPTER 6 ·
The Coral Palace

The cry of the muezzin, familiar throughout the Middle East but eerily alien to the ear of the Englishman, came to Clive Folliot in his sleep. He was back in Madagascar, running through a nightmarish landscape of city streets and razor-sharp mountains, wavewashed beaches and steaming jungles.

Something was after him, something whose breath was hot and moist and smelled of death, whose fangs snapped and whose claws clashed with every frantic step.

Clive wanted to look back, to see what it was that pursued, but he knew that a single glance would spell disaster.

He ran faster and faster, stumbled into a native bazaar, crashed into a rug merchant's display. He thrashed desperately, struggling to fight free before he was overtaken. But his every effort only enmeshed him more helplessly in the heavy cloth.

He rolled over, his eyes open, prepared to see the face of death looming above him.

Instead, he saw the face of the Arab youth who had admitted him and Sergeant Smythe to the consulate last night.

The youth had a smooth complexion and huge, liquid eyes of a dark shade that approached purple. He was wearing a clean cotton robe that swept the floor. His bare toes protruded from beneath its hem.

"Is sir all right?" he asked. His voice was soft and

his quaintly imperfect English was pleasant to the ear.

"I'm all right. All right," Clive stammered.

"Shall sir take a cup of tea before rising? After rising, Honorable Sir John has invite sir to breakfast. Honorable Sir John has said, tell sir of breakfast is kippers and scones with marmalade. Shall sir take tea before rising?"

Clive thanked the youth, accepting the consul's offer. Shortly, having shaved with borrowed instruments and clothed himself in a set of lightweight khakis of a vaguely military cut, Clive permitted himself to be led into the consul's presence.

Kirk was seated at a dining table in a sunny chamber that might have been transported from some middle-class merchant's country house. When Clive entered the room, the consul set down his cup, stood, and offered his hand.

"Good to see you cleaned up and dressed like an Englishman, Folliot! I daresay you were a sorry sight last night. Raining like cats and dogs, and there's this thunderous booming at the door, and there you are looking like a drowned rat! Well, you look a lot more human today, I shall say."

"Have you seen—" Clive started to ask.

"I say, sit yourself down, Folliot. Relax. You're not in London now. No need for the frantic pace. Things move more leisurely here in the tropics. You'd best get a knack for it or you'll never survive. Have some breakfast."

He rang a bell and a servant appeared.

"Take Major Folliot's order, Mahmoud. Bring the gentleman something to eat before he perishes."

Clive ordered breakfast and the servant disappeared.

"Lazy as the day is long, these natives," Kirk said. "Have to keep after 'em constantly or they do nothing but sleep all day and steal you blind at night."

"Mahmoud, you said his name was?"

"Mahmoud, Ali, Abdul, it doesn't matter, my dear

Folliot. A native is a native. I say, haven't you been out from the Isles before?"

"Just once, Sir John. To Madagascar."

Kirk shuddered. "Horrid place. Zanzibar is bad enough, but there are worse places to go. Now, Major, what's this all about?"

Clive got out his question this time. "I arrived in company with another Englishman. A Sergeant Horace Hamilton Smythe."

"Sorry," Kirk said.

"What do you mean, sir, *sorry*? We were together. It was Sergeant Smythe who made that—what did you call it?—thunderous booming. It was he who opened the lock in your outer fence. Where is he now, is what I wish to know."

Kirk speared a noisette of lamb from his plate, dabbed it into a hillock of mint jelly, and popped it into his mouth. He chased it down with a draft of tea. "Sorry, Folliot. Never heard of the chap. Did wonder, though, how you got the gate open. We generally lock it up at night to keep the beggars off the grounds. Consulate's attractive prey for them, you know."

He captured a small potato and sent it after the noisette. "Have to get after the staff over that. Can't have Abdul leaving the outer gate unlocked at night, half the city is made up of his cousins, they'll swarm like locusts if you let 'em."

Clive persisted. "About Sergeant Smythe, Sir John."

"Can't help. Can't help. Listen here, a poor chap like myself gets to feeling cut off, way out here. Have to show the flag, of course. Keep the natives in line, protect Her Majesty's interests and so forth. Every kind of wog in the book has his nose stuck into East Africa these days. Appalling, Folliot, just appalling. Not that I'm complaining, you understand. Duty, duty, duty."

He buttered a scone and ate half of it in a bite.

"But"—and he pointed his butter knife at Clive—"you've got to bring me up-to-date on the doings of the realm. What's happening in Parliament? What plays have opened in London? What's the gossip from Buckingham Palace? Prince Albert's been dead for long enough, you know. What's a young and lusty queen like Her Majesty to do, eh? Can't shut herself up in a nunnery for the rest of the natural span, if you know what I mean. Well, let's have it, Folliot, let's have it!"

Miserably, Clive slogged through an interminable meal, filling in his host on what was new in England.

At the end of the meal Kirk led Clive to his study. This was the consular office, complete with desk, official seal, and portrait of the queen.

"Sir John," Clive said, "I do not understand your insistence that you know nothing of Sergeant Smythe. But since you refuse to budge on the subject, I will not persist. Instead, I will ask you to assist me in my mission."

"And what is that, Folliot? An Englishman does not travel to this tropical sink without good reason."

"I am seeking my brother, Neville."

Kirk steepled his fingers beneath his chin. Clive estimated the consul's age at five-and-thirty years, a mere two years greater than his own, yet Sir John had the look and the air of one steeped in decades of cynicism and debauchery. Perhaps it was the result of life in Her Majesty's diplomatic service. Resident consulship in a place like Zanzibar would doubtlessly alter a man.

"Neville Folliot was a good chap. Came through here last year, full of idealism."

"I am attempting to follow his trail, Sir John."

"Going to find the source of the Nile, old Neville said. Burton, Speke, Livingstone, Baker—he was going to outshine them all, outdo them all. Going to be the most famous of the explorers. Hah!"

Sir John Kirk's laugh was unpleasant.

"I told him to go back to England," the consul resumed. "Africa will devour you, I told him. Go back to those cool glades and those civil streets. Don't try to conquer Africa, Africa will conquer you."

He nodded to emphasize his certainty.

"He went anyway. I helped him to outfit his expedition. Took him down to the palace, introduced him to Seyyid. It all just whetted his appetite for Africa. I've seen it before, Folliot. Africa is like morphia, Folliot. Once you've seen it, you crave more. And each time you take more you only increase the craving. I'm as close as I can be, right here in Zanzibar. I'll never set foot on the mainland again, or I'm lost. Neville is lost, and if you go to Equatoria, you too shall be lost. Don't go, Folliot, I warn you!"

"I am sorry, Sir John. My mind is made up. I cannot abandon the search for my brother, until I either bring him out of Africa safely, or at least learn his fate."

Clive rose to his feet. He swept his hand across his chest in a gesture of finality. "I have spoken!" he announced.

Kirk laughed. "Spare me the melodrama, old chap." He heaved a heavy sigh. "All right. I can't stop you and I shan't try. If you're determined to destroy yourself, I shall see to it that you do so with the proper equipment and under approved diplomatic seal."

He called for a servant. While the native stood by, Kirk scribbled a note on a piece of his official stationery. He sent the native off to deliver the missive.

"What was that about?" Clive asked, as soon as the servant had withdrawn.

"That," the consul announced, "was a request to His Magnificence the Sultan Seyyid Majid ben Said, to be carried by hand to the royal palace, to be presented to the sultan quick-time. It should arrive in about an hour, and His Magnificence will clap his illustrious hands and grant the boon requested by Her Majesty's resident consul and the distinguished visitor Major Clive Folliot shall be presented at court this very day."

John Kirk grinned. "So, old chap, we'd better see about getting you spruced up a bit. They're not too demanding in the way of court garb hereabouts. Fortunately. So let's get a move on."

"Aren't you going to wait for the sultan's response?"

Kirk grinned. "Don't be a goose, Folliot. These fellows know who's boss. If the Arabs or the blacks started to kick up their heels, we'd slap 'em down fast. Their headmen are smart enough to have that figured out, and they know that if they don't keep their chaps in line, we'd just dump 'em and get somebody else to take charge who'll do better."

He got to his feet, brushed a crumb from his pale mustache, and tossed his napkin to the floor. "Come along, then, Folliot. We'll see a couple of sights on our way to the palace." He took Clive's elbow and steered him from the room.

As they passed from the breakfast room the consul called back, "Abdullah! Ali! All of you boys, get in there and clean up. This house is turning into a pigsty!"

There was a rush of bare feet as the servants converged on the room and began to clear.

The horses lifted their heads at the approach of Kirk and Folliot. A servant boy held the bridle of each beast. There was a magnificent chestnut with a blaze of white on his forehead for the consul, a pleasant-natured dapple gray for his guest.

John Kirk took the reins of his chestnut and vaulted into the saddle. The consul was garbed in a light-weight suit of white linen. As concession to the day he wore a pith helmet. His gloves, riding crop, and boots were of matching cordovan.

Clive Folliot, still in borrowed raiment, paused to make the acquaintance of his gray, patting the horse's nose and speaking to it for a few minutes before climbing into the saddle.

The consulate gates had swung open for the day, and the horses moved out at an easy walk.

"You'll get along all right with old Seyyid," Kirk told Clive.

"You mean he likes the British?"

"Don't be a fool, Folliot. I mean he's got his own fish to fry, and he's quite willing to do what he can to keep us happy. He wants us on his side if he can have us, or at the very least he wants us to blink now and then at some of the things that go on in his little part of the world. And so long as that suits Her Majesty's interests, we're quite willing to do it."

Clive shook his head. The storm of the previous night had cleared away, and the streets of Zanzibar, briefly converted to mud, were already well on their way back to their normal condition of hard-packed dirt and dust.

They were approaching the bazaar, and a medley of odors assaulted Clive's nostrils. The streets were narrow and crowded with white-robed Arabs, black Africans, and merchants from India and Indonesia. Clive didn't see any identifiable Europeans.

Beggars were everywhere. At first they crowded around the two Englishmen on their horses, but Kirk swatted a few outstretched hands with his riding crop and they fell away. Most of the traffic proceeded on foot, but there were a few donkey-drawn wagons, and an occasional spavined excuse for horseflesh.

And camels!

Clive had seen camels in Madagascar, but that had been years ago. He'd forgotten how large the beasts were, towering over the chestnut and the gray that he and Sir John Kirk rode.

The city itself was built on hilly terrain, and their path wound up for a while, then back down. The odd, rolling pace of the camels surrounding the Englishmen's horses made Folliot feel as if he were back on board *Empress Philippa*. Proud Arabs rode some of the huge beasts, their robes hanging around them, cloths wound about their heads, their ornate, long-barreled rifles lying across their laps.

And the smell of the beasts—there was no other like it! Clive found himself longing for the clean sea air he had breathed from the deck of the *Empress*. Which made him remember—

"Sir John!"

The consul faced around.

"I must recover my gear from the *Empress Philippa*. There was some mix-up last night involving the harbormaster, but Captain Wingate will surely send my belongings ashore."

"He will, will he?" Kirk laughed.

The odor of horses and camels was now mixed with the spicy odors of outdoor cooking. Food vendors lined the narrow street, holding up samples of their wares to tempt the travelers. Metalworkers, potters, leathercrafters filled every opening.

And yet another odor began to be mixed with the rest. It was a human odor, like and yet unlike the musky smell of the long-robed Arabs they moved among. It was an unpleasant, unhealthy odor.

Clive wrinkled his nose.

"Well, what about my chest? At least I can go down to the harbor and try to hire a felucca to sail out to *Empress Philippa* and get it for me."

The roadway had risen once more, and John Kirk reined in.

Clive Folliot brought his gray to a halt beside Kirk's chestnut.

"You see that?" The consul raised one white-clad arm, held his riding crop in a cordovan-gloved hand. He pointed toward the harbor. There was no sign of *Empress Philippa*, but Kirk swung his arm around to the right, pointing in a northerly direction.

A cloud of black smoke was barely visible over the ocean. Kirk asked, "Did your Captain Wingate tell you what his next destination was, Folliot?"

Clive stammered, trying to remember.

"Don't bother your head, old chap. He's gone, anyway. Halfway to Pemba, I should say. Probably swing over easterly from there, head on to India."

"Yes," Clive managed to get out, "I think he did say something about India." He could feel his cheeks and ears reddening. He felt the complete fool.

"Don't worry, old chap. We'll reoutfit you. You can pick up anything you need right here in Zanzibar, but actually, the more things you can pick up on the mainland, the easier a time you'll have of it, don't you see. Lot of bother, loading everything onto a dhow and having to ferry it over. Lot of bother, believe me!"

"I should think that a complete expedition could be prepared in Zanzibar. Roll onto the mainland and simply keep going."

Kirk shook his head. "Why make more work for yourself, my dear fellow? Gather all your equipage here, load it all, transfer it to the mainland, then unload it and reassemble everything and begin your real task. Wasteful, wasteful."

"But can I get what I need on the mainland?"

"You'd be surprised, Folliot. Several towns where you can resupply. It's become something of a local industry, don't you see, outfitting European explorers. Lot of Indian merchants, Arab traders, even some whites who've gone halfway native. Probably your best bet's Bagomoyo. Beastly miserable place, but convenient. You can get everything there, and I guarantee you'll be happy to move on once you're ready."

For the first time since leaving Her Britannic Majesty's consulate, a cultivated area of grass had become visible. The street broadened and the beggars and merchants became fewer. Armed guardians wearing fezzes and vaguely military-appearing garments were in evidence.

A tall fence of wrought iron loomed beside the road, surrounding a parklike area of trimmed lawn and obviously well-tended palm trees. In the center of the park a structure of white coral rose gracefully.

The two riders drew nearer, and Clive could see the geometrical figures that dominated the architecture. Peaked alcoves, bartizaned roofs, pillars, and breezeways were magnificently constructed and meticulously tended.

"The old Sultan Seyyid Said restored this palace," Kirk told Clive. "It was pretty run-down in the days before his reign. Or so the old-timers tell one. My predecessor, Atkins Hamerton, was here in Seyyid Said's time. A fine fellow, the old sultan was. Or so one hears. Hamerton was on the verge of putting in for a return to England, you know, when the old sultan reached the end of his reign."

He shook his head.

An Arab guard came running from the gate of the palace. He looked at the two men and their horses, seized the reins of the chestnut and the gray, and led them toward the palace.

In the moment that he stared up at Clive Folliot, the eyes of the English rider and of the Arab guard locked. They held for the flicker of an eyelash, and then the guard turned his head away.

But that moment was long enough for Clive Folliot to recognize the Arab guard, who may indeed have been a guard, but was by no means an Arab.

▪ TWO ▪
THE
SOURCES OF
THE NILE

▪ CHAPTER 7 ▪
The Dhow *Azazel*

Hot tropical sun beat upon choppy tropical seas as the lateen-sailed dhow beat slowly out from Zanzibar's sweltering harbor.

Clive Folliot squinted against the glare. Despite the shadowing brim of his pith helmet and the relative comfort of his khaki outfit, he was already drenched in perspiration. He patted himself nervously, making sure that he still possessed the royal patent furnished him by the sultan of Zanzibar.

The patent called upon all who beheld it, within the sway of the Sultan Seyyid Majid ben Said, Anointed of Heaven, Most Favored of the All-Merciful, and so forth, and so forth, to give to the bearer, the Englishman Major Clive Folliot, a subject of Queen Victoria and favored friend and servant of the aforenamed sultan, et cetera, all courtesies and assistance in his mission, thereby earning the favor and gratitude of the Most Favored of the All-Compassionate, and so on.

Once Clive passed beyond the narrow coastal strip that recognized—sometimes—the sway of the sultan of Zanzibar, the royal patent might carry no legal force, but John Kirk had suggested that other monarchs who reigned over the kingdoms of Equatoria would, possibly, render him a certain courtesy.

A brilliant light flared in the sky ahead of the dhow and off her port side—to the craft's southwest. The light grew in size and intensity, its color shifting through a range from magenta to dazzling orange to turquoise; then, slowly, it faded.

Clive heard the gasps and exclamations of superstitious Arab sailors as the display continued.

A second light flared and faded.

Then a ring of shimmering lights grew and began slowly to revolve.

It was like a fireworks display over the Thames, but never had Clive beheld so magnificent a show of lights, especially in broad daylight.

The Arabs were exclaiming. The few words of their language that Clive had picked up lately were sufficient to tell him what they thought they beheld.

This must be a display of angels, one sailor asserted. Some great soul had cast aside his bodily raiment and was being welcomed into paradise by a ring of angels and houris.

No, a second sailor argued. The lights were the flaming gates of hell, and demons in the service of Shaitan were preparing to descend upon the earth and make war upon the armies of the faithful. Surely this was the result of their having sailed aboard a dhow with so impious a name as *Azazel*—an angel indeed, but one who had rebelled against the will of heaven and been cast out to become the despised and accursed Eblis!

The dhow's lateen sail had fallen slack during the strange display. Now the sky began to darken and the sound of a distant howling began softly to be heard.

Clive watched as sailors fell to their knees, raising their hands in supplication to their deity, crying out in terrified prayer. He felt a similar impulse himself, resisting it in order to maintain his dignity among these half-civilized Semites. Even so, the aerial display had been amazing and mystifying. What could the lights have represented? And if a phenomenon of nature, they were unlike any Clive had ever before known. And if a phenomenon of human origin— but no, that was too farfetched even to contemplate.

The dhow's sails began to flap fitfully. The ship's captain, a muscular Arab in filthy robes and straggling beard, strode among his men, screaming at them to return to their stations, but to no avail.

The air felt heavy, wet, and suddenly, shockingly, frigid.

Clive drew his lapels around his chin. He clutched them with one hand, the dhow's rough wooden railing with the other, and gazed in awe toward the north.

A titanic black cloud was advancing across the Strait of Zanzibar. Beneath it a swirling mass of blackness extended down toward the water, while from the surface of the strait a column of green extended upward to meet the blackness. Bolts of lightning danced between the cloud and the sea. Some of them shot up and down the sides of the monstrous waterspout. Others discharged inside the column, illuminating it for fractions of a second so that the entire funnel cloud and waterspout were turned into a dazzle of black and green.

The preternatural stillness that had prevailed, a stillness in which every guttural prayer and curse, every creak of the ancient dhow's rotting timbers, could be heard, came to an end. With a single screaming gust of wet brine the waterspout was upon *Azazel.*

Clive Folliot found himself lifted bodily from the deck of the ship. His grip on the railing was broken as if he were an infant from whom a toy had been seized by a bully.

It was a moment of strange objectivity. As if detached from his body, Clive could observe the things that befell him and those around him, but he was utterly helpless to resist the forces that imposed themselves upon him and his world.

Everything revolved. The sky became the sea; the sea, the sky. In his state of objectivity Clive rejected this explanation. Instead, he deduced, he had been turned upside down by the monstrous wind that had seized him and all around him.

He saw sailors floating through the air like graceful terns.

He saw *Azazel* rise from the surface of the Strait of Zanzibar and revolve with dignified grace through the air.

He wondered at the others on board. He recognized the captain's form twisting slowly in the air, his beard whipped sideways by the whirlwind, his face a mirror of astonishment.

He recognized other sailors whom he had seen on *Azazel*'s deck.

For a moment he thought he recognized the face of Horace Hamilton Smythe, but the quartermaster sergeant turned mandarin turned sultan's guard was gone before Clive Folliot could be certain.

He saw the blackish water of the strait rising toward him, and in his mind converted the picture to one of himself plummeting from the sky toward the brine.

Even as he plunged into the water he could hear the cacophonic mixture of Arab wails, crashing timbers, howling wind, pounding waves—and another sound, a strange, distant sound that he was unable to identify, but which he knew in some inexplicable way held the key to his fate.

He might have regained consciousness briefly while still submerged in the heaving waters of the strait, but if so it was only for a moment, and then he lost himself in the darkness again.

When he recovered he was lying on a rock-strewn, sandy beach. The sun was rising over a stand of palm trees while the last stars faded from a fast-brightening sky. He pulled himself to his feet, survived a short bout of dizziness without going down again, and staggered to the nearest boulder. He leaned against it and tried to get his bearings.

The Strait of Zanzibar showed no evidence of the fierce storm that had passed—or of the dhow *Azazel*. Clive felt for his pocket watch and discovered that his clothing had been half torn away by the violence that had destroyed the sailing ship.

His watch was still in the pocket where he had

placed it, but it had been smashed by some impact as well as drenched in brine. With an oath he threw it into the water.

Jetsam from the wrecked dhow littered the beach. Clive surveyed what he could see of it, tramping up and down the sand, his khaki rags and waterlogged boots picking up additional layers of sand every time he knelt to examine some piece of furnishing.

There was nothing useful. Smashed timbers, shredded bits of sail canvas, broken fittings. No utensil, no ship's tool, no blade or firearm. He was a latter-day Robinson Crusoe, and he tried in vain to remember whether the original had found weapons and tools on his desert island or had had to make do with only the raw materials of nature.

Perhaps Clive Folliot would find a Friday to assist him!

He continued along the beach. He thought he recognized the form of a supine human. He sprinted clumsily along the sand, his boots heavy and chafing on his feet.

It was a man—a sailor from *Azazel*!

Clive knelt beside the man and peered into the unmoving face. The horror in the man's eyes struck to Folliot's core. He tried to raise the man from the sand, and realized that the sailor's neck was broken. He laid him back once again and with trembling fingers managed to close his eyes.

Other grisly evidence of the storm's murderous effects littered the beach, but Clive could not bring himself to examine any of the bodies more than was needed to ascertain that it no longer lived.

Am I the only one spared? he pondered. *Did the storm kill every last occupant of* Azazel?

Perhaps Robinson Crusoe was not the model for his situation after all. Perhaps he was more of a modern Jonah.

He made his way to the edge of the jungle that marked the end of the beach. To his astonishment he discovered that he had found his pith helmet somewhere in his wandering, and held it in one hand.

Abstractedly, he placed it on his head.

He tried to calculate the number of bodies he had seen scattered on the beach. Surely there were far fewer cadavers than there had been sailors aboard *Azazel*. The others might have landed farther along the coast or even have been swept out to sea, but it was possible, also, that he was not the sole survivor of the storm.

Could others have survived in the water and been picked up by later, passing craft? Or been washed onto the shore and made their way inland before Clive regained his senses?

He cocked an ear. Somewhere he heard the sound of running water. He turned slowly until he located it, then began slowly walking along the edge of the jungle, heading toward the sound.

He had no appetite for food, but he had swallowed salt water during his ordeal, and then had lain overnight on the beach. Now, as the sun rose toward its tropical zenith, its rays baked him dry and he found himself suffering from a thirst such as he had never before experienced.

He stumbled along the beach for what seemed many hours, yet each time he stopped and estimated the time of day from the position of the sun, he found that only minutes had passed. He staggered back to the water's edge and dipped his hand into the gentle surf. It was amazing to think that this softly curling water had only the night before been a raging maelstrom.

He lifted a handful of the water, held it before his face. He thought that he could smell it, imagined that he could taste its cool freshness on his swelling tongue and splitting lips.

With a moan he let the brine trickle between his fingers.

All too well he knew the price that he would have paid for the moment of false relief that a single sip of brine would have brought!

He broke into a staggering, shambling run. The sound of flowing water was close! He stumbled back to the shade of the jungle's edge, forcing himself to move ahead, step by step.

Before him the clear water of the Wami River cut through the sandy beach and joined the brine of the Strait of Zanzibar.

Clive threw himself onto his belly and slaked his thirst in the Wami. First a tentative taste of the water, to assure himself that it was clean and free of the taint of salt. Then a cautious swallow, and then as much as he felt his parched stomach would tolerate.

He made his way a few hundred yards upstream, walking through tall trees that came almost to the edge of the river. He reached for the leather tube in which he carried his dispatch paper and pens and the few rough maps he had been able to obtain of the area.

Of course—the case was gone.

He tried to find the royal patent from Seyyid Majid ben Said. Not only was the patent lost, the very garment in which Clive had placed it was lost as well.

It was time to get hold of himself. He sat beside the river and strove as calmly as he could to recall the map to his mind's eye. A mystic power like those fancied by du Maurier would have come in handy, but Folliot had only the limited power of human recollection to rely on.

He was headed for Bagomoyo, and he knew that the town lay some miles down the coast from the Wami. And he knew that the Wami flowed in an easterly direction, into the strait. From where he sat on the riverbank, the water flowing from his right to his left, the Strait of Zanzibar marking the mouth of the river, he knew that he would have to cross its waters before trekking to Bagomoyo.

The only alternative was to head north for . . . He tried to remember. If he headed north he would eventually reach the Pangani River. There was a settlement at the mouth of the Pangani, but Folliot had no desire to add the extra distance to his trek. He had no container in which to carry fresh water, and he had come perilously close to yielding to temptation and drinking the brine not long ago.

The Wami looked neither too deep nor too rapid to cross.

Folliot searched up and down the riverbank until he found a limb that had fallen from a tree—he thanked heaven that the common palms were not the only growth in this jungle! He removed his boots, tied the laces together, and attached them to the tree limb. He stripped his trousers and added them.

Clad only in shorts and a ragged strip of shirt, his pith helmet still perched comically on his head, he began to swim across the river. One arm slung over the tree limb, he used it both as a support for himself and as a transport for his boots and trousers.

A few other logs seemed to be floating on the slow-moving Wami. Clive found the clean water invigorating, the sand washing off his body. He was almost to shore when one of the floating logs opened a pair of yellow, catlike eyes and stared at him.

With a flip of its muscular tail the crocodile lunged at Clive, pink-lined mouth opened wide, triangular teeth glistening.

Clive dodged, but it was the arrival of a second amphibian, larger and hungrier than the first, that saved his life.

The second crocodile closed its jaws upon the neck of the first, knocking it sideways and provoking a roar of rage and pain that sent Clive paddling even more frantically for the shore.

The two hungry beasts—the first of them easily twelve feet in length and the second closer to fifteen—thrashed and snapped and roared in the Wami's waters. Clive scrambled onto the riverbank, tugging his tree limb and its precious cargo with him. He stared in horror at the animals that now fought mindlessly, to every evidence having utterly forgotten the presence of a human and his value as a potential dinner.

Clive retrieved his boots and trousers from the limb and pulled them on. The tree limb was too heavy for him to carry, but he managed to break a length from its end, and he took this with him to use as a walking stick and potential weapon, should he find himself in need of one.

The sounds of the battling crocodiles faded as Clive made his way from the river. By nightfall he was exhausted. His thirst had returned, and this time it was accompanied by the stirrings of hunger.

There was no readily visible food, and Folliot was in no state to begin a hunt. He found a tree that he was capable of climbing, crawled to a position he could tolerate, and managed a few hours of fitful slumber.

Stiff in every joint, sore in every muscle, a foul taste in his mouth and a grumbling in his belly, Clive Folliot crept from the tree in which he had spent the night.

He took his bearings and resumed his trek toward Bagomoyo. He considered once more searching for food, but decided that he could make the village by noon, and that he would do better to seek nourishment there than he would here in the jungle.

He was not an experienced traveler in the African jungle, and while he realized that his ignorance was his greatest handicap, he realized also that his awareness of that ignorance was his greatest asset. He would be on the alert, he would be wary of his surroundings, and that watchful caution would keep him alive.

He kept near the edge of the jungle, thereby avoiding the direct sunlight and parching air of the beach without having to deal with the perils of the interior. He watched the branches of the trees above him, ever aware that a great snake or other predator might be waiting to drop on him.

He had hoped to find a trail through the jungle,

one made by black natives or Arab traders—even one made by the wild peccaries supposed to inhabit the region—but he could locate none. Still, the undergrowth was only moderately dense and he was able to progress through it without the assistance of a machete.

It came at him like a swinging pendulum in a tale of terror by the American Mr. Poe, but it was far more terrifying than a razor-edged blade, for it was animated and malicious.

It had rows of eyes that glittered like rubies in the subdued light of the jungle.

It had fangs that dripped venom.

In some obscure part of Clive Folliot's mind he was aware that it must be suspended from a long cable of sticky silk. But Clive had not the time to analyze his thoughts. He could only act by reflex, and it was his reflexes that saved him, though just barely.

He managed to raise his walking stick, the remnant of the tree limb that he had used in crossing the Wami River, before the huge spider reached him.

As it was, the arachnid collided with the stick. Folliot swung the stick almost like a cricket bat. It struck the spider glancingly, not directly enough or with sufficient force to send it aside. But instead of colliding head-on with Folliot, the beast brushed against his cheek.

Folliot felt his pith helmet knocked from his head. A streak of fire raced along the side of his face, from the tip of his nose to the tip of his ear. He whirled in his tracks and saw that the spider had reached the apogee of its course and was swinging back at him.

The spider's swing was precisely like that of Mr. Poe's pendulum!

Clive raised his walking stick and swung again at the spider. It was a gigantic beast—a monster the size of an overfed house cat; its silken line must be as thick as a hawser!

Before the moment of impact the monster managed to disconnect itself from its silken line. Its course, previously a graceful arc, straightened.

Folliot missed the spider with his stick, but the beast's scrabbling legs gained a tenuous purchase on the wood, and it scrambled along the piece of tree limb, onto Folliot's arm, then onto his shoulder.

Clive was knocked to the ground. He could see the monster's rows of ruby-red eyes glaring maliciously into his own. The spider was squatting on Clive's half-naked chest. Its fangs ran with glistening venom.

Something whizzed above Clive Folliot's head and the spider was gone from his chest. Gone in an instant. Folliot struggled to his feet. His head ached and his vision was cloudy. His mind told him dimly that the venom he had received in the spider's first attack was taking its toll.

He leaned against the bole of a tree and looked for the spider. It lay on its back, a six-foot spear impaling its body. There was still life in the creature, and it struggled frantically to regain its feet. Clive watched fascinated as the spider kicked and scrabbled on the jungle floor. At last it succeeded in righting itself.

The native spear still embedded in its flesh, the spider dragged its body forward. Its eyes were fixed on Clive.

Folliot backed away from the spider. Some part of his mind, remote and objective, remembered that he had long ago been told that spiders do not attack enemies larger than themselves. He was larger by far than this spider, huge though it was. Could some professor of natural history not inform the beast that its conduct was abnormal, and persuade it to cease and desist?

With each step Clive felt himself growing weaker, dizzier.

With each step the monstrous spider seemed to grow stronger.

■ CHAPTER 8 ■
Bagomoyo

Something in Clive told him that if he remained in the jungle he would die. He would surely die. He would collapse, and the spider would reach him and inflict upon him a second and fatal dose of its venom.

The two of them, mammal and arachnid, would lie together on the jungle floor, prey for whatever carrion eater first arrived.

Whose spear was it that impaled the spider? Clive had no way of knowing, but whoever had hurled the shaft with such magnificent aim and force showed no inclination to reveal himself or offer further assistance.

Folliot was on his own.

He managed to stagger the few score yards that it took him to clear the undergrowth and find himself on the sandy shore once again. He put some distance between himself and the jungle.

He could hear the scratching of the spider's eight clawlike limbs against jungle growth, the scrape of the spear, and added to those another sound, a weird chirruping ululation such as he had never heard before.

Had the spider a voice?

Was this its hunting cry?

Folliot shuddered.

Brine foamed around his ankles.

He turned back to see the jungle, and at its edge two rows of angry eyes blazed ruby-red at him.

The spider advanced from the shade of the last row of trees onto the sand.

Folliot backed away. He reached for his walking stick and realized with a wave of black despair that he no longer had it—he had dropped it in the jungle and it lay there still, far from his hand, useless to him.

The spider uttered its weird chirruping sound, its fangs raised like twin sabers.

Folliot staggered back a step, another. His boot slipped on something flat and smooth, covered with a shallow layer of sand. He felt his balance sliding away. He toppled backward, landing with a thud at the edge of the surf.

The spider sounded its chirruping again. Folliot saw the arachnid dragging itself painfully forward, the spear extending before it, gore coating its fire-hardened tip. Some dim recess of Folliot's mind pitied the spider the agonies it must be suffering, and admired the courage and determination that drove it to drag itself after its prey even though it must surely be near death itself.

The spider reached Folliot's leg. A drop of venom fell from one fang and splattered against the Englishman's bare flesh where his khaki trouser had been torn away.

It was as if fire played upon Clive's naked nerve endings. Galvanized by the searing pain caused by the venom, his hand reached instinctively for the buried object, whatever it was, over which Clive had fallen.

With a rush of energy he leaped to his feet, the object in hand held before his wondering eyes. It was a scimitar! It's metal blade was shining and free of rust. It must have been carried by a sailor aboard *Azazel*.

What irony of fate had brought the sailor to the shore, then swept his cadaver back to sea while leaving behind his weapon?

Clive stood over the spider. The sun cast his shadow

blackly over its gory, spear-impaled form. Like the angel of death Folliot swung the scimitar, splitting the spider in half.

The killing had been an act of mercy, not of cruelty.

Folliot took the spear by its haft. He walked to the water's edge and carefully wiped the spider's gore and venom from both the spear and scimitar. He did the same for the wound on his face and the burned patch on his leg.

He rubbed the scimitar gently with soft sand until it was completely dry, then wiped it clean and stuck it through the stout belt that held up his tattered trousers.

Spear in hand, he strode back to the edge of the jungle and resumed his march to Bagomoyo.

His head was beginning to swim once more but he kept his wits about him until he reached the edge of the jungle clearing that meant he had got safely to Bagomoyo after all.

At that point he lost his awareness of his whereabouts and of himself. Vague images of the earth and the sky, of great eyes and dark visages and words spoken in an unfamiliar tongue, took the place of sensible recollections.

Then even those faded into darkness and for a time he knew nothing.

There were only flickering lights and dancing shadows and the low sound of distant chanting and drumming and a strange sensation as if a cool breeze was playing intermittently over hot, sweat-coated skin.

Clive Folliot blinked and tried to make out his surroundings. A black face loomed over him, a black face that was attached to a naked form.

He squeezed his eyes shut for a moment, then opened them again to see if the strange vision had disappeared. It had not. The woman squatted patiently beside him, slowly waving a palm-leaf fan. That was the source of the breeze he had felt.

He raised a hand to his face. His skin was fevered

but a poultice of leaves covered the wound that the spider's venomous fang had gouged.

He tried to sit up but the woman placed her hand on his shoulder and pressed him back. His eyes kept straying from her serious face to her magnificent torso. Her breasts were uncovered and hung gracefully before him, swaying with every movement she made. Her waist was slender and her hips generous.

She wore a necklace of wooden hoops painted in reds and yellows and browns. Her hair was daubed with something, possibly mud, that had dried into a high peak.

"Who are you?" Folliot demanded. "Is this Bagomoyo?"

The woman smiled happily. "Bagomoyo," she repeated. Than a string of syllables meaningless to Folliot.

"Don't you speak English?" he demanded.

Her reply was incomprehensible.

"How about French? German? Arabic?" If she spoke Arabic he was hardly better off than if she did not, but perhaps there would be an Arab in the vicinity who spoke one of the civilized European tongues. Many of them did so in Zanzibar.

She shook her head helplessly.

"Aren't there any white men around?" he tried. "Have you ever seen a white man before? A doctor? A trader? A missionary?"

She recognized the last word, or seemed to. Clive was having trouble concentrating on their attempts at dialogue, with her nudity displayed as it was. But she was nodding her head now and smiling happily.

"White father," she said.

"Yes! Is there a white father in Bagomoyo?"

"Bagomoyo! White father, Bagomoyo!" She jabbered at him in her own language, but the words *white father* and *Bagomoyo* kept recurring.

"Fetch him, then," Folliot urged her. "Get me the white father. Bring the white father to me, please."

How much of his speech the black woman understood, Clive could not even guess. But obviously she caught the drift of his words, for she laid aside her palm-leaf fan and left the hut.

Clive lay staring at the roof of woven sticks and thatch, watching shadows dance and listening to chanting and the rhythmic thudding of drums. He felt for his watch, then remembered that he had thrown it away on the beach. He wondered what time it was, how long he had lain unconscious in the hut, and how long he would lie now waiting for the arrival of the white father.

He heard a bustling outside the hut and opened his eyes. The face he saw illuminated by the oil lamp that cast those dancing shadows was round and cheerful and pink, and the fringe of hair surrounding it might once have been red but was now almost entirely gray.

The faded eyes might once have been a vivid blue, but now they peered through thick, wire-rimmed spectacles and they were pale and as gray as the fringe of hair.

"It's true, then," the newcomer said. "T'nembi spoke the truth!"

Clive tried to sit up, and a pair of old hands, work-roughened and strong, helped him to do so. His head swayed, spots danced before his eyes, and a million demons played tympani inside his skull.

The newcomer pressed him back onto the crude pallet where he lay. "A bit too fast, young fellow. You're not ready to leap about yet, that's a sure fact."

"You speak English," Clive stammered.

"There are those who think I do so poorly," the other replied. "But English it is that I speak. Not that I get a chance to use my mother tongue very often hereabouts."

The man leaned over Clive, and Folliot thought he detected a hint of alcohol in the other's breath. The man shook his head. "Perhaps you'll be so kind as to tell us who you are, my fine young hero. You come stumblin' into camp—or so T'nembi tells me—wavin' a scimitar like some wild Turk, shakin' a spear like a native, and ravin' about a spider as big as a house."

He leaned closer, to examine the bandaged wound on Clive's face. The whiff of spirits on his breath was stronger. He peeled some of the leaves away from the wound, nodded gravely, then pressed them back against Clive's skin.

"I can almost believe it about that spider. Dear T'nembi, she's a good girl. Tryin' to learn English, but she's only got a few words as yet. I didn't think she knew *spider*, but from the looks of your face, young hero, I guess she does."

He sat back on his haunches.

Clive pushed himself upright, leaning on one elbow. Again the other reached to help. This time Clive was able to sit facing his visitor without growing faint. He said, "Am I in Bagomoyo?"

"That you truly are." The other nodded.

"And—and who are you?" Clive asked.

"Father O'Hara. My mother called me Timothy F. X. after her dear lost brother and her favorite saint. And the good Lord called me into the service of these poor benighted heathens." He made a gesture that might have included the interior of the hut or the whole of Africa, for all that Clive could tell.

Behind the priest Clive could see the open entryway to the thatch hut. Dawn had broken, the blazing tropical sun rising over the Strait of Zanzibar and vaulting into the sparkling sky above Bagomoyo.

"Do you think you can handle some nourishment, young fellow?" the priest asked.

Clive grunted an affirmative.

Father O'Hara shot a stream of syllables over his shoulder. The black woman T'nembi rose and left the hut. Clive had not even seen her crouching against the wall.

She was back almost before she departed, carrying a bowl of hot mush and a clay jug that she set down beside Father O'Hara.

The priest lifted the jug and downed a long swig. "The native beer," he said. "I do miss the good Irish whiskey, but this beer is better than any I've tasted in the world."

He spoke again to T'nembi, who knelt beside Clive's pallet and fed him mush. It had a bland, woody taste, but as soon as he'd swallowed his first mouthful Clive felt himself starting to regain his strength.

The woman was feeding Clive with her fingers. Apparently dining implements were unknown in Bagomoyo. T'nembi was still nude; to Father O'Hara the sight of the woman seemed as natural and unremarkable as that of a tree, but Clive became uncomfortably aware that T'nembi was not only unclothed but was one of the most exciting females he had ever chanced to behold.

"Well, you know who I am now, my lad," Father O'Hara was saying, "but I've not the remotest idea of who you may be. Nor of how you came to be wandering this dangerous countryside with nary a companion and hardly a stitch of clothing."

Clive looked down at himself and realized just how tattered his costume was.

"I am—I am Major Folliot," he managed.

The priest peered into his face. "That I find hard to believe, young fellow."

Clive started to shake his head, then thought better of it. "But I am. I am Clive Folliot, major of Her Majesty's Fifth Imperial Horse Guards Regiment."

"Oho!" The priest nodded. He took another long swig from his jug, wiped his mouth on the sleeve of his loose-fitting robe. "That I can believe. I thought you were claiming to be Major Neville Folliot, and Neville I've met, and I can tell you that you are surely not he. Although," and the priest paused to study Clive's face, "I'll admit there's a mighty strong resemblance between the two of you."

"You know Neville?" Clive grasped the priest's sleeve in a trembling hand, almost causing him to spill his jug.

"Careful, careful, young man. All will be made clear to you. Just ask your questions and you'll have the answers. Ask and ye shall receive, our Lord tells us."

"Neville Folliot is my brother," Clive told him. "I'm seeking him now. I was aboard a dhow sailing from Zanzibar when—" He stopped, the full horror of the past hours returning to him.

"You were caught in the waterspout, were you?" the priest furnished.

Clive bowed his head. "I believe—that I am the sole survivor of *Azazel*. That was how I came into possession of the scimitar." He gazed around the hut once more and for the first time discovered his weapon—both his weapons—carefully placed against the wall, along with his pith helmet and boots.

"These storms are wicked," Father O'Hara said. "Heaven knows how many souls the Lord has called home as a result of them." He gazed piously toward the thatched roof of the hut. "But—are you certain that no others survived?"

Clive said he couldn't be sure, that he had seen no others once he found himself lying on the beach.

"Then there could be others," O'Hara persisted. "There could be others." He gazed into the distance for a moment, swigged at his jug, then spoke again. "You walked all the way from the site of the wreck, did you? All the way here?"

"Not exactly," Clive demurred.

The priest looked questioningly at him, and Clive told the story of his encounter with the crocodiles in the Wami River, and the attack of the giant arachnid in the jungle.

When Clive finished speaking, the priest nodded. "The spider attacked you, you say?"

Clive said it had.

"Well, that is odd," the priest said. "And thus you came into possession of a fine Arab scimitar and a good spear as well."

Clive nodded. He accepted another bit of mush

from T'nembi. His eyes lingered on her lush body until she looked away.

"But you never told me," the priest was saying, "who it was flung that spear and saved you from the spider's attack. You owe someone your life."

"I don't know who it was," Clive answered. "He just—I don't know, that's all."

"Well, what's to be learned will in due course be learned. But another oddity of your tale, young Folliot—now I don't question your honesty, understand—but you've been through an ordeal, and at such times one may grow confused, even jumble reality with illusion—but you spoke of those fireworks before the storm broke."

"Those lights were no illusion, Father! I saw them! They were dancing in the sky. They were beautiful, beautiful yet awesome, even frightening. And then the storm broke. There was a connection, Father O'Hara, there had to be."

"There was no connection, Major!" O'Hara's voice had a new edge, on his face an expression that Clive had not seen before. "There was no connection because there were no lights, do you understand me? There are no such lights in the sky."

The priest raised his jug and held it tilted to his mouth for a very long time. Clive could see his hand trembling as it held the jug, and when he lowered it at last, his eyes looked first left, then right, then down, but not at Clive's.

Not at Clive's.

Clive slept and ate and regained his strength.

T'nembi came and fed him, and Father O'Hara came and talked with him, but never about the lights.

The priest had indeed met Neville. Clive's brother had passed through Bagomoyo on his own ill-fated expedition, and O'Hara had got to know him before he moved along.

O'Hara admitted that he had helped Neville to hire bearers from among the local populace. Some of them had returned from their expedition with Neville Folliot. Some had not. The wives and children of the men who had failed to return had been adopted by other families, as was the habit of the Africans. The survivors of the lost wept and mourned, as did survivors of the lost the world around, but there were no forlorn widows or orphans in this country.

Clive asked to speak with those who had returned, and O'Hara volunteered to act as interpreter. But the interrogations yielded only sketchy information. Neville had headed inland, then turned in a northerly direction, toward Lake Victoria and the Sudan. That much was no surprise to Clive.

Neville's party had reached a dreadful region known as the Sudd, apparently avoiding an encounter with the fratricidal Mutesa. The Sudd was an area marked by treacherous swamps, dangerous wildlife, and uncertain geography. Some of Neville's bearers had refused to enter the Sudd and had turned back to Bagomoyo. Those were the men Clive now questioned. Others, Neville had bribed or browbeaten into continuing with him—and they had disappeared with him as well.

Once the questioning was over, Clive sat in conference with Father O'Hara. The women of the village had stitched together an outfit for Clive, a strange-looking set of breeches and a shirt of colorful cloth that he wore with his boots and pith helmet. He examined himself in a small, precious mirror owned by Father O'Hara and found himself a ludicrous sight. At least he was able to shave, with a razor loaned him by the priest, and O'Hara had hacked off the Englishman's hair, which had begun to grow long and shaggy.

O'Hara asked Clive if he wished assistance in returning to England via Zanzibar.

"By no means!" Clive snapped.

"But surely you do not intend—"

"Surely I do!" Clive cut him off.

"But, Folliot. You have no party. You have no equipment. And you have no funds with which to hire bearers or to buy equipment. You can't possibly hope to trek hundreds of miles alone, armed only with a blade and a spear. How will you survive?"

"I don't know," Clive muttered. He dropped his chin into his hands. He was strong and healthy again, and in one part of his mind was as determined as ever to find his brother.

But a more practical part of him had to admit that the priest was right. He couldn't possibly carry out his expedition alone, he had no helpers, and he had no money.

There was a stir at the far side of the village.

Clive and the priest looked up, then rose to their feet and stood side by side staring at the apparition that advanced across the packed dirt toward them.

Clive cast a sidelong glance at Father O'Hara. Clearly the priest was dumbfounded by what he saw.

But Clive recognized in a flash the silken-clad mandarin who had played Mendelssohn so beautifully aboard the *Empress Philippa*.

The mandarin was garbed in a dark red and green costume embroidered with gold. He was mounted on the back of a camel, the camel in turn decorated with fine cloth and polished metal. Villagers ran in excited circles around the beast and its exotic rider. Their chief, a man whom Folliot had met through the agency of Father O'Hara, had come out of his hut and stood now staring up at the mandarin.

Father O'Hara and Major Folliot crossed the dirt-packed area that served in Bagomoyo as a village green and stood beside the chief.

Clive started to speak, but the mandarin shot him a look that spoke volumes. If this was Sergeant Smythe—and Clive knew that it had to be Smythe—the man did not wish to be identified, nor his former relationship with Folliot revealed.

Father O'Hara—remarkable man!—began to address the mandarin. His words came slowly and his face creased with concentration and the recollection of long-unused knowledge, but he was speaking Chinese!

The mandarin smiled at the priest and responded in the same language. He too spoke slowly, but he did so with the same confidence and precision with which he had performed at the piano.

Father O'Hara translated for the mandarin and for both Clive Folliot and the chief of the village, speaking Chinese, ki-Swahili, and English in turn. A villager took the mandarin's camel to be watered, while the Celestial climbed from its back and moved with the others into the chief's hut.

While this building was of the same crude architecture as the rest of Bagomoyo, it was by far the largest and most comfortably furnished house in the village. The chief offered seats to O'Hara and to Folliot as well as to the Chinese.

As the latter descended from his camel he had carefully removed a carved chest or strongbox the size of a large volume. This he now placed on the packed earth before Clive Folliot. He spoke for a time to Father O'Hara.

As the Chinese spoke, Clive watched both his face and that of the priest. When the mandarin was finished, O'Hara turned toward Clive, wonder and puzzlement on his features.

"The Chinese gentleman says that he came across this object"—he indicated the strongbox—"on the beach near the mouth of the Wami River. He states that he believes it to be your property, Major Folliot."

Clive looked into the eyes of the mandarin. Had he not known better he would have been utterly deceived into thinking the man an authentic Oriental who spoke not a word of English. To O'Hara, Clive said, "Please tell the gentleman that I believe he has indeed recovered an object of mine which I had thought to lie at the bottom of the Strait of Zanzibar, in the hulk of the dhow *Azazel*. Please tell the gentleman that I am most grateful for the return of my box."

When O'Hara had translated, the mandarin smiled ingratiatingly, inclined his head, and murmured a few words in Chinese. He reached forward and opened the box, revealing a scattering of gold and gems and neatly arranged stacks of bank notes. The notes, issued by the Bank of London, ranged in value from single pounds to thousands.

· CHAPTER 9 ·
Lord Baker

"And how well does the major know the local terrain, sah?" Smythe asked Clive Folliot. The erstwhile mandarin had retransformed himself, and now sported the khaki garb of a European explorer on the African continent. There were no military markings on his clothing, but at this moment it would have been hard to take Horace Hamilton Smythe for anything other than a soldier.

"I know it moderately well, Smythe." Clive was uncertain as to how to address this chameleonic individual, but since Smythe had lapsed into military forms of address, Folliot found himself doing the same.

"Before leaving England I read all the published works I could lay hand upon," Folliot continued. "I also attended lectures given by Sir Richard Burton, and I had the pleasure on one occasion of meeting the lamented Mr. John Hanning Speke."

Smythe grunted. From somewhere in the pockets of his bush outfit he produced a pipe and tobacco pouch, and proceeded methodically to load and fire his pipe.

Folliot waited impatiently while Smythe went through the slow procedure. Folliot knew that the other man could act with speed and decision when the case was urgent, but at his leisure he could spin out the most trivial act until he had tried the patience of saints.

Finally Smythe returned to the topic. "I was hoping," and he paused to puff on his short-stemmed briar, "that the major," and he drew again on the pipe, "I refer to Major Folliot," and he took the pipe from his mouth and nodded in agreement with himself, "Major Neville Folliot, that is, sah—"

"Yes," Clive cut him off, "yes, my brother Neville. What about him, Smythe?"

"Well, sah," Smythe studied his pipe, "I was wondering, I might even say hoping, that Major Neville Folliot had written some letters to his brother, that is, to you, sah."

"Letters from Africa, Smythe?"

"Precisely, sah. I knew the major would understand, sah." Smythe beamed. He put down his pipe, quaffed a quantity of native beer, and picked up his pipe again.

"Neville wrote home to our mutual parent, Smythe. He did not write to me. We were not—are not—on so close or cordial a basis as that."

"Oh." Smythe nodded. "I see." He hummed tunelessly, then looked into Clive's face. "If I may make so bold, sah—did the major—you—chance to read the major's—your brother's—letters to the baron—your father?"

"Thank you, I know who my father is, Smythe. And my brother, for that matter. Baron Tewkesbury was in the habit of reading aloud to me such portions of Neville's letters as were not of a wholly personal nature. They included considerable information regarding the geography of the region, thank you."

"And does the major know the route that his brother followed, sah? Did the major's letters provide that information? The other major's letter, that is, sah."

"Quite so, Smythe. Neville headed northwest from Bagomoyo, skirted the southern shore of Victoria Nyanza, and headed northward. He stopped and refitted at Bukoba, then moved parallel to the Ruwenzori Range—"

"The Mountains of the Moon, sah!"

"Quite. And disappeared somewhere to the north of the village of Gondokoro. At least, that was the place from which he dispatched his final missive to Baron Tewkesbury."

"Perhaps the major will share his familiarity with the region with me. It should make it easier for me to serve the major," Smythe said.

"Quite so, Smythe, quite so." Folliot unlaced his boots and lay back on his field cot. He closed his eyes, wondering at the talents and versatility of Horace Hamilton Smythe, and at the man's density at other times.

By the time they approached Bukoba, the party was not in nearly the fine condition it had been upon leaving Bagomoyo.

A daily routine had been established, with bearers assigned specific duties. There were the beaters and hunters, the animal drivers and equipment carriers, the cooks, and the scouts. Some of the Africans had wanted to bring their women along as cooks and companions, but Clive had vetoed this. His military career had taught him that women on such an expedition meant nothing but trouble.

The men had grumbled at that, and Sergeant Smythe had told them that some of the better prospects for the party had refused to join up when they learned that they could not bring their wives with them. But Clive had been adamant.

The scouts moved ahead of the main party, and others served as flankers. There were no known groups in the region, but after the disappearance of Neville, Clive wished to take no unnecessary risks.

Three days out of Bagomoyo, a pair of men had deserted, returning to their homes and families. "Can't be helped, sah," was Sergeant Smythe's comment. "The men miss their women and children. Those two wanted to bring 'em along to start with. I know those two. Good men, aye, but they miss their mates and kiddies. I'm a lifelong bachelor myself, but if I were a married man, I can't say as how I'd blame 'em. Well, sah, it can't be helped."

Clive was more worried about further desertions than he was about the two men who had already left. He asked Smythe if he expected more men to decamp.

"Can't say as how one can predict that, sah. Treat 'em well, and let 'em know that there's a generous pay packet awaiting 'em at the end of the trail, and they'll likely stay. But if too many men gets eaten up by beasts or comes down with fevers or if the food runs out—well, sah, 'tain't as if they'd taken Her Majesty's shilling, sah. They're employees, if you takes my meaning, sah. Employees. They can quit, you see, sah. 'Tain't as if they'd sworn a soldier's oath, you see."

They lost more men in Bukoba. Word came through the rumor mill of the party, to Sergeant Smythe, and from him to Clive Folliot, of what had happened. Tribal loyalties were strong in East Africa, and word of any important event could spread by jungle telegraph from village to village. The men involved were bachelors with relatives in Bukoba, and when they heard of available brides with temptingly low prices, they opted to make their acquisitions while the opportunity was presented, and not risk losing the brides to other suitors.

Before Smythe or Folliot even knew about it, the eager bridegrooms and their blushing fiancées were gone, en route back to Bagomoyo.

They tried to hire replacements in Bukoba, but the men of that village refused to serve with men from Bagomoyo, and vice versa. It was one thing to purchase a bride in another village. But it was a far more serious matter to travel on safari with men you hadn't known all your life.

Four days out of Bukoba, a hunting lioness brought down a pack mule, and the drivers attempted to kill the big cat. The result was one death among the courageous drivers, and two men slashed by the big cat's powerful talons.

The lioness tore a haunch from the dead beast of burden and loped away with it. Only Clive and Horace Hamilton Smythe carried firearms on the expedition, and neither had been near enough the point of attack to bring down the lioness. It was all over in the batting of an eye, or so it seemed.

Once the lioness was out of sight and order had been restored, Clive drew Horace Hamilton Smythe aside. "We've discussed this before, Smythe. Is this going to cost us more desertions?"

Smythe shook his head. "Don't know, sah. These are good solid men. About as reliable as you'll find on the continent. But they've had a good fright now."

They buried the dead man, and the two who had been slashed turned back to Bagomoyo. It was fortunate that they were both able to walk, and to carry enough supplies and weapons for their own needs.

"Will they get back safely?" Folliot asked Smythe.

"There's no way to know that, sah. Man could walk ten thousand miles unscathed on this continent, then die of a scorpion's sting sitting in his easy chair at home." He paused, rubbed his chin reflectively, then went on. "Couple things we might do, though, sah, to help ourselves. Always a risk, there is, but a smart gambler can help his odds, if the major takes my meaning."

Clive asked him what he had in mind, and Smythe outlined his plan. Increase the number of scouts, set them farther from the main party. Set up a double screen, so that predators that slipped through the first row might be detected by the second. Arrange a system of signals between the main party and the two rows of scouts.

· CHAPTER 10 ·
Into the Sudd

Clive slept not a wink. His mind was in a turmoil of thoughts, images, recollections, regrets, resentments.

Neville had ruined his boyhood. Though twins, the brothers had, technically, been born on different days. And Neville, as heir presumptive to the Barony of Tewkesbury, had received first preference in all things, from the day of his birth forward.

Long before dawn Clive gave up any attempt at sleep. He crawled from beneath the light covering that had kept him warm. He could hear Horace Hamilton Smythe's breathing from the other folding cot in his tent.

He slipped from the tent fully clothed and walked through the encampment. The remnants of a few cooking fires still glowed redly, sending thin fibers of smoke coiling upward into the cool air. At the center of the encampment a watchfire danced and guardsmen kept vigil.

Clive walked to the *boma*. He pulled aside a tangle of vines and twigs and thorns. There was little serious concern at this place; predators were few and were more likely to regard man as a dangerous interloper, to be avoided for safety's sake, than as fair prey.

He stepped onto the plain and closed the gap he had made in the *boma*. He walked quietly beneath equatorial stars. The constellations were strange in this latitude; some of them he had learned, others he had not. Clive seated himself on the ground. He pulled up his knees and rested his elbows on them, gazing into the blackness.

A soft breeze blew from the west, bringing with it still cooler air from the Ruwenzori Mountains. The sounds of small creatures came to Clive from every direction. He felt a sense of peace such as he had known seldom in his life, a communion with whatever god had made this wondrous, spacious continent.

Not only Tewkesbury but London, all of England, seemed not merely thousands of miles away but millions. For all that they mattered now, Clive might have been sitting on a grassy plain on the surface of Mars. If he were indeed on another world, perhaps he could send his thoughts whirling across the millions of miles of interplanetary vacuum to the waiting brain of George du Maurier. Or perhaps, the thought struck him, to that of Annabella Leighton.

What was Annabella doing now? What was the hour in London? Surely it was the next day, and Annabella was up and bustling about her appointed duties, instructing her charges. Unless it was the Sabbath! With a start Clive realized that he had lost track of the day and date.

When had he last sent a dispatch to Maurice Carstairs? He could—

A talonlike hand dug long, bony fingers into his shoulder, breaking the distracted reverie into which he had fallen. He whirled and looked into a face made all the more terrifying by its grin.

The sky was growing lighter to the east. The glittering stars had disappeared against a field of brightening colors, and there was sufficient illumination to reveal a physiognomy as black as the blackest Folliot had seen in Equatoria. The eyes gleamed at him with a feverish intensity. The grin was huge, and revealed a pattern of snaggled teeth that would have sent any London dentist into perforations of rage.

The face was surmounted by a makeshift turban of loosely wrapped white linen. The man wore a thin sheet draped toga-fashion from his shoulder, and leaned on a crooked staff taller than he was.

"Englishman," a rasping voice emerged from the snaggle of teeth, "Englishman, why are you not resting? You have hard times to face."

Clive leaped to his feet, escaping the grasp of the man's talons. "Who the devil are you? What do you want?" He brushed at his shoulder, trying to give the appearance of wiping away the man's dirty touch but in actuality attempting to restore the circulation that the other's iron grasp had cut off.

"I, sir? I am the Englishman's servant, his friend, his helper and guide. I am called Sidi Bombay."

Clive peered into the man's deep eyes. He burst out laughing. "Smythe! Sergeant Smythe! You are indeed a master of disguise, although I cannot fathom your reasons for such conduct."

Sidi Bombay shook his head. "I am not the Sergeant Smythe. I am knowing the most excellent sergeant. He it was who approached me, who asked me to be your aide. A most admirable man is he, yes, Englishman. But I am not he, no, Englishman."

Clive took the man's chin in one hand, rubbed the other vigorously on his cheek. Then he peered at his fingers, then at Sidi Bombay's face. "It isn't greasepaint," he stammered. "It's your real color!"

"So it is, Englishman. My real color, indeed. As it has been my whole life through, yes."

"And you say that Sergeant Smythe hired you?"

The black man nodded.

"But—why?"

Sidi Bombay grinned again. "He and I are acquaintances of old, Englishman. Yes. You are going to the Sudd, this I know. You cannot walk through the Sudd, know you not that?"

Folliot declined to give a direct answer. "What's your job, then? What did Smythe hire you to do? And why the deuce didn't he ask me about it first?"

"I came to your tent and spoke with your sergeant. He told me you were walking about. He said that if he had known I was hereabouts he would have asked you first, yes, but he did not know."

"But—why?"

"I can find boatmen to carry you through the Sudd. I can guide you myself. Otherwise, Englishman, you will die in the Sudd. You will never emerge from the Bahr-el-Zeraf. You will never see Fashoda. No, Englishman, never."

Clive thought of his continuing journey, of the chance of finding Neville and returning safely to England. Even under the most favorable of conditions, the odds he faced were long.

He made his decision.

"Come along then, Sidi Bombay." He started to turn back toward the encampment, but stopped to stare at a single patch of sky that seemed to have remained in night's darkness while dawn filled the rest of the firmament with light and glorious colors. The dark patch was to the north, the direction in which he planned to march.

A few stars remained visible, and even as Clive stared they rearranged themselves into a spiral and began to whirl, to whirl like a hypnotist's disk, faster and faster, tighter and tighter.

And then, suddenly, they were gone, and the patch of darkness was gone. The brilliant tropical dawn had broken fully.

Folliot grasped Sidi Bombay by the shoulders. "Did you see that, man? Did you see that—in the sky?"

He released one of the black man's bony shoulders and pointed.

"I see only the morning, Englishman, yes."

"But—you didn't see the patch of darkness? The spiral of stars?"

Sidi Bombay shook his head. "We must hasten back to camp, Englishman. Sergeant Smythe and the bearers await us. We must be on our way. A long journey awaits."

The *boma* was dismantled, the last embers of the

watchfire stamped into gray ash, tents struck and packed onto the backs of patient animals.

The Ruwenzori Range fell away to the west and the land dipped almost imperceptibly with each passing mile as the party moved toward the Sudd.

The Sudd was where Neville had been when he sent his last letter home to England. He had described the swamp as a fetid region filled with wildlife that ranged from the pestiferous to the deadly. Thus far Clive had traced his brother's path without great difficulty. He had no idea of how much farther he had to go, or of whether he would find Neville alive or dead or not at all.

But the greatest mystery to this point was the strange serial display that he had seen twice, in its differing forms. Prior to the waterspout the stars had turned to exploding fireworks. On the plain outside the encampment they had held a patch of the heavens in darkness when all the rest was light, and had gone into their hypnotic whirl before fading from visibility.

What had happened?

It was almost as if a piece of the firmament had been ripped away, permitting Clive to peer into another realm, another sky. It was as if, for those brief periods, he had stood upon the surface not of the Earth or of any of the sun's familiar worlds, but upon the surfaces of two alien planets circling two alien suns. Suns where the cosmos behaved in a manner unguessed at and undreamed of by the wildest of the imaginers of Earth.

He had tried to discuss the phenomenon with Father O'Hara. But the old priest, otherwise so affable and outgoing, had frozen entirely and refused to admit any knowledge of the subject.

And Sidi Bombay—the man had proved as invaluable an aide as he had promised, and Clive had thanked Horace Hamilton Smythe for engaging him. But the black man, too, had acted oddly when Clive Folliot asked about the remarkable aerial display, and had pretended an ignorance that could not have been authentic.

As they approached the Sudd, the hard African soil began to grow softer and more moist, and to support vegetation far more lush than it had at higher and drier elevations.

At night, after assuring that the camp was secured and the animals watered and fed, the three leaders of the expedition assembled for dinner. Clive Folliot, Horace Hamilton Smythe, and Sidi Bombay sat with their light service set before them on a folding table. Hot meat, rough bread, and native beer were their standard fare. It was not unlike a military encampment, with the three of them comprising an officers' mess—although Clive wondered how his commanding officer, Brigadier Leicester, would have reacted to the sight of a major of Her Majesty's Horse Guards dining with a noncommissioned officer and a civilian associate in black skin and ragged turban!

They had managed a crude map, and at the end of the repast, the tattered page illuminated by a flickering oil lantern, they studied it together.

They had passed between two bodies of water, Lake Kyoga to their east and the far larger Luta Nzige to the west. Gondokoro lay directly ahead, and it was from this point that Neville Folliot had headed northward into the Sudd, never again to be seen.

With the little information they had, the three planned the path of their party to Gondokoro and beyond. Gone was Clive's interest in continuing the search for the fabled source of the Nile. Not that he had ever felt a great desire to trace the historic waterway. He was becoming ever more obsessed with the need to unravel his brother's fate. Other aspects of his journey might be of interest to Maurice Carstairs and Carstairs's readers, but Clive was turning from an explorer into a manhunter!

Days later they passed through Gondokoro. The native bearers had led Clive to expect a thriving village, even a small city, but instead they found only the pitiful remnants of a town depleted by slavers and left, days earlier, in flames.

Cold judgment told Clive that he must keep his men with him, but he could not abandon the few, pitiful survivors of the attack to fend for themselves. More of the bearers left the party to assist the aged, the feeble, and helpless to make their way from Gondokoro back to Bagomoyo.

Folliot's depleted band reached the edge of the Sudd itself the better part of a week after leaving the ruins of Gondokoro.

Sidi Bombay had slipped away from camp before dawn the previous day, and Folliot, distressed, had sought information about the deserter from Horace Hamilton Smythe.

"He's your man, Sergeant!" Clive was furious. Sore feet, insect stings, and sunburned skin did nothing to help Folliot's temper. "He's your man, and now he'd done a runout on us! What's it all about, I want to know!"

Smythe smiled ingratiatingly. "I wouldn't worry none about old Sidi Bombay, Major! He hasn't deserted, no sah! He's off on an errand, is old Sidi."

Clive felt himself reddening. The sun was up and its rays cast a red-gold glow onto everything they struck, but Folliot's redness was not that of dawn. "An errand? What kind of errand? You hired the man without my permission, now you allow him to leave camp on some mysterious errand, also without my permission? Where's the man got to, and what is he doing?"

"I don't know, sah. And I beg to express a disagreement with the major, but I didn't give Sidi Bombay permission to leave the camp. He's his own man, is Sidi. Has been as long as I've known him, which is a very long time I must admit. Sidi don't ask permission. He don't need no by-your-leave, sah. He comes an' goes as he pleases."

"A free spirit, eh? I'm surprised he hasn't been

stood against a wall and shot by now, or maybe strung up to a good tall tree."

"No, sah. Nobody's better try that with Mr. Bombay, sah. Sidi's got too many friends. He's done too many good turns for too many important people, all the way from the Congo to the Mekong. Sidi's a legend and nobody dares cross him, sah. Nobody."

Clive snorted. "Well, get hold of M'Gambi, and get the camp struck and the party moving. And when we reach the water there"—he pointed ahead, toward the great swamp that lay ahead, covered this early in the day by a blue-gray miasma—"we'll need to see about some sort of pontoon or raft arrangement."

Horace Hamilton Smythe grinned behind his hand and did not quite render a military salute—Folliot had opposed that idea—before facing smartly about and pacing away to perform his duties.

Birds screamed overhead and unseen reptiles slithered through the tall grass at water's edge.

Clive examined his boots and found them coated with mud almost to the knees. Even as he stood on a bit of what appeared to be solid ground, surrounded by tussocks of tough, sawblade grass, he realized that he was sinking slowly into muck. He pulled his feet clear and replanted them. The earth seemed dry and solid enough, but within seconds Clive realized that he was sinking in once again.

The morning mist had burned off the Sudd, and for a few hours the party had moved in bright daylight. But by midafternoon a new bank of odoriferous moisture had risen from the earth and mud and water that made up this part of the Sudd. Tall reeds poked from the assortment of moist grasses. There were little splashes, hisses, and less frequent screeches and roars.

The Sudd was alive, and Clive Folliot was beginning to fear that it was malevolent. He looked around and realized with a chilling start that he was alone.

"Sergeant Smythe!"

"Right here, sah!" The man appeared like an apparition from a bank of drifting fog.

"Sergeant Smythe, I'm afraid that we've committed a miscalculation of serious degree. Here we are. I doubt that the horses or mules can go any farther in this stuff."

He pulled one boot out of the muck and kicked a gob of semiliquid matter off it before setting it down and repeating the operation with the other boot.

"I've even certain doubts about the men. Have you sounded out M'Gambi on the question? Will our bearers stay loyal, or will they turn away from us now? I've heard a good deal of grumbling since leaving Gondokoro. They're afraid of slavers, and now they're afraid of the Sudd as well, it would seem.

"Can't blame them," Smythe replied. He imitated Clive's procedure in clearing his boots and resetting them onto drier land. "Ever wonder where you'd wind up if you just kept sinking into this stuff, Major? Almost quicksand, it is. If you just let yourself sink, maybe put on one of those new diving suits that German bloke invented, and sink and sink into the stuff . . . where d'you think you'd wind up, sah?"

Before Clive could respond, a shadowy figure became visible through the mist. It was tall and gaunt and shrouded in white, and seemed to glide rather than to walk.

Clive grasped Smythe's khaki-clad shoulder and pointed. "Look at that!" he exclaimed. "It—can it be—is it a ghost?"

The form glided nearer. The mist parted. The black and cheerful visage of Sidi Bombay, surmounted as ever by his ragged turban and clad in his shroudlike white robe, assumed full clarity. He stood like Charon in the stern of a narrow barge. The barge drew only a few inches of water, and Sidi Bombay poled through the shallow swamp, using his long staff as if he were moving peacefully on the surface of the Thames.

As silently as a ghost, Sidi Bombay raised one thin arm, pointed a bony finger at Clive Folliot, and gestured him to enter the barge.

Simultaneously, Horace Hamilton Smythe removed Clive's hand from his shoulder, took Clive by the elbow, and half-guided, half-propelled him forward.

As he moved toward the barge, Clive noticed for the first time a small discoloration on the back of Smythe's hand. It was a pattern of dots, as if Smythe had been tattooed like a sailor. The dots were arranged in a roughly circular pattern that reminded Clive of the weirdly circling stars he had seen in the morning sky. As Clive stared in amazement, the stars shifted, swirled, spun, until they were a blur against the sunburned brown of Smythe's flesh.

Dizzy, Clive stepped into the barge. He sank to his heels. The sound of water lapping against the barge's rough-hewn wooden hull, and the suck and slap of Sidi Bombay's knobkerry as he poled the barge stern-first away from the shore, were all that Clive could hear.

They were surrounded by fog and mist. The distant cry of unidentified creatures of the swamp penetrated to Clive's ears. He felt rather than saw Sidi Bombay swing the barge about and begin to pole it deeper into the mysterious Sudd.

▪ THREE ▪
WHAT
WORLD
IS THIS?

▪ CHAPTER 11 ▪
The Ruby Heart

The bearers who had carried Clive's supplies all the
way from Bagomoyo were left behind. There was no
need to worry about them, and if the truth be known
Clive Folliot had little thought to give to them.

What had happened? What secret did Horace Hamilton Smythe and Sidi Bombay share? For how long
had the abduction of Clive Folliot—and no other
term could fairly be applied to the event—been
planned?

Surely there had to be a connection between the
mysterious symbol tattooed on Smythe's hand and
the stellar formation that Clive had observed, but
what in heaven's name could it be?

Clive demanded an explanation of Smythe.

The reply was a shake of the head.

Folliot persisted.

"I'm sorry, sah," Smythe apologized. "It's as much
a mystery to me as it is to the major. Surely there was
no way those bearers could have followed us, though.
P'raps old Sidi Bombay knows what he's doin', sah.
In fact, I'm sure he does. Sidi's never let me down
before, sah, and I'm sure he won't let us down this
time."

Clive's brow was clammy. The Sudd was hot but
the mist was strangely chilled, and droplets precipi-
tated on his skin. He removed his pith helmet, wiped
his face with a bandanna, then slipped the cloth back
into a pocket of his khaki trousers.

Smythe wore clothing similar to Clive's, but for

headgear instead of a pith helmet he wore a leather-visored military cap, sans insignia. A belt of cloth webbing cinched Smythe's bush jacket, and a holster hung from his hip.

Clive dipped one hand into the water alongside the hull of the barge.

"I wouldn't do that, sah."

Clive looked into Horace Hamilton Smythe's eyes. "Why not, Sergeant?"

"Not safe, sah. Please, sah!"

A rush. A splash. Clive jerked his hand out of the water in time to avoid serious damage, but a row of razor-sharp teeth scraped across his knuckles, leaving a pattern of zigzag lines. Blood seeped from the scratches. Clive pulled the bandanna from his pocket and wrapped it around his hand.

"I'm sorry, sah."

"What—what was it?" Clive stared in the direction the thing had moved, but it was long gone, even its wake hidden in the slowly drifting mist. He had caught a single glimpse of something colored a metallic blue, its body smooth, its movements sinuous and graceful, that moved away with astonishing speed.

"Please, sah. Don't put your hand in the water again, sah. The major was very, very lucky." Smythe raised his eyes to gaze into the mist. Then he lowered them to look at Clive. "Good many dangerous critters in the water hereabouts, Major. Not so many flying ones. Wouldn't hurt to keep an eye out nevertheless, but there ain't so many flying ones as there are swimmers."

Clive looked about himself. "You've been in the Sudd before, Smythe?"

"No, sah. I've heard about it, is all. A dangerous place. That's all, sah."

The mist was thick and chilly and damp. The water was black and nearly opaque, and as to what creatures lurked in its blackness Clive was reluctant to speculate. There was no single source of light, no sun or moon to suggest the time of day or night.

The mist itself glowed with a luminescence, and particles of it glimmered like dust motes dancing in a beam of sunlight.

Now and again a creature would splash in the black water.

Less frequently the flapping of great leathery wings would be heard overhead, and Clive would peer upward to see a shadowy form, vague and dark and menacing, circle and dip and then rise again and disappear into the shimmering mist.

Only once did such a shadow come close to the barge, and Clive saw Sidi Bombay freeze into petrified immobility at its approach. The creature had a long head marked by dark, glittering eyes and a bony jaw that opened to reveal rows of teeth that caught the light of the luminous mist and threw it back as a gas lamp through a London fog. The wings were wide and featherless, of a dark brown color. The formation of bones was clear through the creature's skin, and claws marked the forward peaks of the bone structure.

As the creature swooped past the barge it uttered a strange cry, a cry unlike any that Clive had ever heard before and one that caused a cold chill to creep along his spine and a shudder to pass through his limbs.

Now objects began to appear through the mist, rising from the surface of the water. Tall tree trunks rose, and from them gaunt branches stretched like accusing fingers. Moss hung from the limbs like the sleeves of monks' robes, and astonishing orchids bloomed in the moss; while huge spiders—the cousins, perhaps, of the monster that Clive had slain on the beach near the River Wami—scuttled up and down strands of moss, their eyes glowing malevolently through the pale mist.

Jagged rocks rose, and the huge spiders scampered across their faces, glaring after the barge, their fangs working, their legs swaying and bending as if to an invisible and intangible current of air.

A scream echoed from somewhere afar.

Another sound, closer in distance and yet more alien in spirit, was heard. It might almost have been a chuckle, and Clive breathed a silent prayer that if it was indeed a chuckle, it was that of a hyena and nothing worse.

At first the rocks rising from the water were gray and jagged, like mounds of granite, and the water through which the barge moved was still and motionless. Then the rocks changed. They were taller, more massive, more varied in color. There was a suggestion of form and plan to them. Clive wondered if they could be remnants of some ancient civilization, the monuments of a race that had disappeared from the Earth before Pharaoh raised the very pyramids of Egypt!

The water through which they moved began to swirl and foam.

The pitch and volume of animal sounds increased— screeches, roars, screams ... the splashing of fins unseen through the black water, the flapping of wings hidden by thickly swirling mist, the scrape of claws or mandibles.

If the carven rocks were survivors of a nation that had lived and died uncounted centuries before, the creatures of the swamp might be the survivors of ancient species that had disappeared from all the rest of the Earth millions of years ago!

They passed a crystal-like rock as large as a brougham, as clear as a carven blue diamond. Within the crystal a light the color of a blood ruby pulsed, as if a giant heart were beating. A creature crouched upon the rock, something like a spined lizard with huge, facetted, insectile eyes. Its limbs were abnormally long for such a beast, as long, in proportion to its size, as those of a plains baboon.

The creature launched itself with a frightful cry.

Horace Hamilton Smythe and Sidi Bombay reacted simultaneously.

Sidi Bombay shifted his position, attempting to

fend off the thing's attack with his staff. In the same moment Horace Hamilton Smythe drew a large revolver from his holster. He fired a single shot at the attacking creature.

The report of the firearm echoed through the Sudd, returning again and again to the men in the barge. The creature splashed into the water and swam away at astonishing speed, stroking with its apelike arms and screaming its rage.

In the moment of the creature's attack, Sidi Bombay had been distracted from guiding the barge. The craft had turned toward the crystallike rock. Just before the prow struck, Clive shouted a warning. He realized that it was too late to avoid a crash, and in the same instant realized that there would be no crash. The rock revolved, revealing an opening.

The barge penetrated the pulsing light, the beating heart of the crystal.

Thud! The heart pulsed, the barge entered its crimson glow. Clive felt himself bathed in the color. No, he was more than bathed in it. He was penetrated, suffused, absorbed in the ruby pulsation.

And then the barge emerged into another realm.

A strange state of calm came over Clive. He felt isolated from everything that had happened, isolated even from himself. He felt as an automaton might feel, could such a mechanism have consciousness, aware of his own thoughts and actions and words and yet divorced from them.

He laid his hand on Sergeant Smythe's wrist. "Let me see that," Clive commanded. Smythe held out the revolver for Clive's inspection.

It was long-barreled, plated with nickel—if not with silver. The barrel was covered with ornate engravings, and the hilt was decorated with polished black stone. Black obsidian or midnight-blue onyx, Clive could not tell.

"That is hardly royal issue, Sergeant. Where did you get it?"

Smythe seemed actually to blush. "I spent some

time in America, sah. Played at cowboy for a while. It's—well, sah—you might say, a sort of souvenir, sah."

Clive released the man's wrist.

As Smythe returned the revolver to its holster, he turned it for a moment, revealing the other side of the grip. In the blue-black stone Clive saw the glimmer of a pattern of points of light. They might have been specks of white stone, inlaid against the black, or they might have been glittering chips of diamond.

They were set in the pattern of the swirling stars.

Before Clive could say anything further to Smythe, the barge surged ahead. The water was glowing here like a rapidly moving creek.

Sidi Bombay drew his staff from the water and laid it in the barge, dropping to a kneeling posture in the bow of the craft. The wooden craft surged even faster, and the darkness grew deeper. Peculiar odors assailed Clive Folliot's nostrils, and the air whipping past his face seemed filled with peculiar shapes, writhing, gibbering, taunting him, performing unspeakable acts with organs of unimaginable purpose.

There was a flash of darkness, of absolute black that stood against their surroundings as a flash of lightning will stand against even a bright daytime sky, and a clap of thunder that left Folliot's ears ringing.

He thought that the astonishing flash of darkness had blinded him, but in a while vague images appeared, indicating that his eyes were adjusting to the darkness that now surrounded him.

The barge had come to total stillness, and the air that had so oppressed Clive in the swamp was suddenly sparse, icy, crystalline. White shapes swirled like swimming creatures, their forms barely visible in the dimness.

Where were they?

Surely they were no longer in the Sudd. Perhaps they were no longer in Africa—or even on Earth! An errant thought flittered across Clive's mind: *How George du Maurier would love this, could he be in my place! And how I should love to be safely back in London, in his!*

"Sergeant Smythe? Sidi Bombay?" Clive heard his own voice, realized that he was whispering.

"Not yet, O Englishman." To Clive's surprise it was not Horace Hamilton Smythe but the black Sidi Bombay who spoke. "A little longer, O Englishman, a little time only. Wait until you can see."

Perfect silence descended on the barge. There were no sounds now of animals calling, of fish or reptiles swimming, of the flapping wings of aerial creatures. There were no sounds of flowing water. Clive could hear the rush of his blood and the pounding of his pulse. He could hear the deep, steady breathing of the stolid Horace Hamilton Smythe and the shallower inhalations and exhalations of the cadaverous Sidi Bombay.

Clive blinked uncertainly. In the distance, not high above eye level, a fuzzy patch of light no larger than a penny appeared. The light was pale, a faint white that pulsated slowly. It seemed to revolve, and to resolve itself into still smaller points of whiteness. The points arranged themselves into a spiral.

The slowly revolving spiral rose from eye level to a point overhead like the sun rising from horizon to zenith, but the lights separated also, increasing in brightness as they did so until they spanned the sky from horizon to horizon, slowly swirling so that a hypnotic trance threatened to overtake anyone who watched them too long.

Their brightness increased until Clive could see himself and his companions clearly, and could make out their wooden craft and its immediate surroundings.

Within a word the three men rose and climbed from the barge. It had become beached on a shore of jet-black sand that led away to a landscape of the same composition. It was like finding themselves reduced to the size of ladybirds and placed on a carefully sculpted model of a world, a world carved all of a single piece of perfect black obsidian and lighted by a swirling spiral of tiny, brilliant diamonds.

They walked from the barge, from the shore.

There was no sound.

Clive peered back to the way they had come, searching for a sign of the passage through which they traveled.

There was no such sign. The crystalline rock with its pulsating ruby heart was gone. For all that Clive could determine, there was no passageway. There had to be, his mind told him. But it was gone. If it existed at all, it was beyond his senses, beyond his reach. Whatever place he was now in, he would have to deal with.

Sidi Bombay and Horace Hamilton Smythe were waiting for him. Smythe stood at a proper parade rest, feet slightly spread, his hands clasped behind his back, the butt of his pistol showing in the holster on his hip. Sidi Bombay, tall and gaunt, his black skin almost invisible against the black backdrop, stood with an arm outstretched. Clive was reminded, oddly, of a portrait of the Christ calling men to come to his side.

They began a trek across the black landscape. To eyes increasingly accustomed to the weird landscape, the illumination provided by the swirl of stars was sufficient for practical use. But a mood of depression slowly overcame Clive Folliot.

Everything was blackness. The sky, except for the slowly revolving points of light, was the sky of midnight. The earth beneath his feet was a dead black. There was vegetation—grass underfoot, taller brush, and then tall trees not far away—all of them, dead black. Still farther off, hills rose black against a black horizon, their shape distinguishable only by some subtle suggestion of texture, or perhaps a deeply buried sense of distance and mass, against the remote blackness of space.

No animal sound was heard—in fact, the only sounds were those of the three men walking abreast. And no animal life was seen; no rodent or ruminant scampered for safety, no predator stalked the three—or at least, no predator that gave evidence of its presence. No flying creature flapped its wings, be they feathered or fleshy.

Sidi Bombay floated like a ghost, his gauzy robe and tattered turban visible against the darkness.

Horace Hamilton Smythe maintained a soldierly bearing, almost marching across the landscape. His face was more visible than Sidi Bombay's; his khaki outfit, too, was visible. Now and again, as the swing of hips and the lay of the uneven landscape might dictate, the butt of his revolver could be seen protruding from its leather holster. The midnight-blue stone was black in this place, and the glittering diamonds that mirrored the swirling spiral in the sky seemed to move in cadence with the stars.

The landscape tended upward.

They had moved away from the edge of the black water where their barge had beached, and Clive Folliot's leg muscles were beginning to cry out for a respite. The other two men, Clive assumed, would suffer similarly from fatigue.

"Time for a rest—and a conference," Folliot suggested. He had more reasons than these for calling a halt. Aside from the need for a respite and an exchange of information, he felt a need to reassert his leadership of the party. Sidi Bombay and Horace Hamilton Smythe were both ostensibly in his employ and consequently subject to his command.

But increasingly, Clive had felt control slipping away. Smythe maintained his courteous and subordinate air, but there was an edge of independence beneath it. And Sidi Bombay—Sidi Bombay had appeared with the barge and conducted the party to this place. Who was this man? What master did he serve? What did he intend?

Clive found himself wondering what purpose the

expedition now pursued. It's own bare survival, per-haps! The pursuit of the disappeared Neville Folliot seemed a remote goal, now—and yet it remained a goal that Clive could not permit himself to abandon.

The three men seated themselves on the earth. Clive looked closely at the local plant life, the grass and minor shrubs. These seemed normal except for their dead black coloration. The air was cool and clear, with only a slight and unidentifiable but al-together pleasant tang.

"I wonder," Clive mused aloud, "could we start a campfire here? Were we to gather some dry wood and strike flame—would it burn?"

"It might indeed, Englishman." Sidi Bombay's voice was reedy and unfamiliar in this unfamiliar world. "But we dare not stay in one place too long. We have a distance to go. There would be no gain in tarrying."

"Go—go where?"

"Ahead, Englishman." Sidi Bombay nodded, his white turban dipping and rising in the blackness.

"Surely we are not still moving to the north? Toward the Sudan?"

"To the north, Englishman?" In the ghostly light of swirling stars, Sidi Bombay's irregularly spaced teeth reflected the light of distant stars like white rectangles set in a mask of blackness. "One might suppose, Englishman, that in a sense we are still moving toward the north." Again the white turban dipped and rose in mocking assent.

"But where are we? We have surely left the Sudd. As strange a place as that is, it is still Earthly. There are crocodiles there and hippos, trees and cattails and nesting birds. The sun rises and sets there, the sky is blue and the earth is brown and the plants are green. And there is life, life all around one. But here—here—"

He gestured to indicate their surroundings. "All blackness. All—death." He had not meant to be melo-dramatic, but involuntarily he uttered the last word in a whisper that held some portion of a sob. He looked at his companions pleadingly. For all that he was a field-grade officer and Smythe only a quarter-master sergeant—and Sidi Bombay a mere civilian guide—Folliot felt helpless and dependent upon the others.

"Buck up, sah," Smythe encouraged. "Everything will sort itself out in time."

"You know that, Sergeant?"

"I hope it, sah. If I may say as much, I pray it."

"But you don't know it?"

"P'raps we'd best be on our way again, sah." He reached into a pocket of his khaki trousers and pulled out a massive stem-wound turnip watch. For some reason the incongruity of the action made Clive Folliot laugh. He was reminded of the white rabbit in the Mr. Dodgson's fantasy.

Smythe caught the laughter and joined in.

Even Sidi Bombay permitted himself a dry chuckle.

But Folliot realized that he had scored a partial victory. He had reasserted himself as a figure to be reckoned with. He said, "Very well. As none of us is suffering from excessive fatigue—or hunger or thirst—let us continue."

Their path led steadily upward, upward into the blackness. The air grew perceptibly thinner and cooler, but the swirling, spiraling stars that provided their illumination continued on their majestic courses. Other than that, there was no indication of the passage of time.

They might have marched for hours or for centuries, but in fact, Folliot mused, they marched through some timeless realm where neither hours nor centuries had meaning. Clive wondered what hour Horace Hamilton Smythe's pocket watch would indicate—but then he realized that it would not matter in the least. Should the watch indicate that it was six o'clock or twelve o'clock, it would make no difference.

He uttered a solitary chuckle. He found himself humming familiar tunes beneath his breath. One of them, he realized, was an air that his friend du Maurier had sung in the burlesque *Cox and Box*. He smiled ruefully. *Oh, du Maurier, if you could only see me now. If your mystical mental communion were actually linking our minds at this moment . . .*

Renewed thoughts of du Maurier brought his mind back to thoughts of London, and of Annabella Leighton. Her lips, her face, seemed to float in the air before him. The eerie blackness of this weird world set off the redness of her lips, the whiteness of her flesh. He saw her partially disrobed, her curves illuminated by the warm hearth of her London flat. How she teased him at times, as she slowly removed her garments, posing in camisole and garters, smiling at him and—

"Englishman!"

Folliot drew up short, Sidi Bombay's bony hand clutching his shoulder through the khaki bush jacket. Clive was standing on the brink of a precipice. The black landscape had risen to a bluff. Inches beyond his boot tips the terrain fell away, dropping what must be thousands of feet in an almost vertical cliff.

"One more step, Englishman, and you would learn the answer to all the mysteries of being!"

Stretching for miles from the base of the cliff was a black landscape. Brilliant starlight glimmered even to this height from the surface of a river that flowed from the base of the cliff across a stark plain.

And far out on the midnight plain, lights glittering enticingly, a magnificent city thrust black towers gracefully, high into the cold black night.

Clive Folliot stood side by side with the gaunt, white-robed guide, drawing breath after slow breath, letting the awesome sight sink slowly into his consciousness.

Then, "Major Folliot, sah! Sidi Bombay!"

Sidi Bombay dropped his hand from Clive's shoulder and they turned toward Horace Hamilton Smythe.

"Come and see what's been left here," the sergeant urged.

▪ CHAPTER 12 ▪
The Silent City

Clive sprinted to the side of Sergeant Smythe.

"Have a look, sah!"

Smythe had fallen to one knee before a round-topped, oblong object. It was as black as the rest of this world, carved of smooth black stone. It was as long as a man is tall, as wide as a man is wide, and deep enough to hold . . .

"It is a coffin, yes, that it surely is." The dry voice of Sidi Bombay sounded from behind Clive Folliot's shoulder.

"But whose—what—?" Clive stammered in bafflement.

"Don't see how it could've got up here, sah?" Sergeant Smythe inquired, his voice husky.

Sidi Bombay held out his arms and intoned, "The coffin of the Prophet rose through the air and was taken into Paradise. Surely the coffin of some lesser one could be lifted to this mountain peak."

Smythe grunted. "Huh! That's as it may be, Sidi Bombay. I don't banter theology with the likes of you."

A ghastly smile split Sidi Bombay's scrawny features. "The English sergeant has learned when not to challenge, I see, yes."

"But whose remains can it contain?" Clive returned to the subject.

"There is but one way to learn that, O Englishman." Sidi Bombay moved closer to the coffin. He searched for a way to open it, but his manner was more that of a man seeking for something he knows is present, than that of a man merely exploring. There were no visible hinges, but an inlaid panel showed a different texture of blackness.

Clive Folliot, watching over Sidi Bombay's shoulder, caught a glimpse of the now familiar star-spiral pattern. He watched long, bony fingers play over the glittering points in a sequence of moves too rapid to hope to duplicate.

As if on perfectly machined gears and hinges oiled to utter silence, the whole propelled by a tightly wound spring, the lid of the coffin arced away from the three men. Within the casket, lying against glistening black satin padding, lay a cadaver.

The face was utterly like that of Clive Folliot: only the different style of facial hair marking the one man from the other. The skin was pale in death, the clothing was the uniform of a major of the Royal Somerset Grenadier Guards. The corpse's hands were folded across the chest of its brilliant uniform tunic, clutching a small leather-bound volume.

"Neville!" Clive Folliot cried.

Sergeant Smythe placed a strong hand on Folliot's shoulder. "Steady, sah! Steady on!"

"But—it is my brother! My twin! My—" Clive Folliot fell to his knees beside the coffin, his forearms resting on the obsidian edge, staring thunderstruck into the face of the cadaver, the face that so astonishingly resembled his own.

"He never made it through the Sudd. Somehow he passed through that same—passage, channel, gateway—that crystal and ruby portal. He came here, also."

"Yes, Englishman. So must he, for behold, here he is, indeed." Sidi Bombay had moved closer to Clive. As he nodded his head, his ragged white turban fell and rose solemnly.

Clive raised his face to address Sidi Bombay and Horace Hamilton Smythe. "That gives me no answer as to how he died, or why he is here. But it proves that he was not alone here, for he is laid out in this casket and the whole has been placed here for some purpose—and by some persons."

He paused, then went on. "With due respect to your religion, Sidi Bombay, I do not believe that Allah carried Neville up here in his coffin. Someone living and material did that. Probably," and he extended his arm over the open coffin, pointing at the cluster of graceful towers that rose from the black plain beneath the mountain wall, "someone from that city."

Sergeant Smythe pushed himself upright and stood at the edge of the bluff. "Maybe your Allah can fly us down there, Sidi Bombay. If not, it's a long walk round the edge of this mountain, till we find some way down. We can't go back the way we came, I don't think."

"Allah could carry us in the palm of His hand, O Sergeant. To the All-Merciful the task would be as naught. But we are our own masters here, and it is ours to make what we will of our plight."

A cold sweat had broken out on Clive's forehead. "There may be a clue . . ." he whispered. With trembling hands he reached for his dead brother's fingers, to unclasp them from the journal. The fingers were icy and stiff, and Clive had to pry them away from the book.

As soon as it was free he pulled it from Neville's dead hands and rose to his feet, holding the book before him. When he attempted to open it he found that a small lock, like those used by giggling schoolgirls to protect their diaries, held it closed.

Clive turned the book over, searching for a clue as to how to open it. As a last resort he or his companions could smash the lock. He studied the book in the weird light of the swirling stars. It was bound in jet-black leather and bore no title on its cover or spine. The only marking was a miniature representation of the starry spiral Clive knew so well.

A sound like the whisper of hands on cloth made

Clive look up. Sidi Bombay and Horace Hamilton Smythe had stepped away from the casket, and the cadaver of Major Neville Folliot seemed almost to struggle, moving restlessly within its casket.

But Clive realized that this was not at all the case. Neville Folliot—if this was truly Neville—was crumbling away. The flesh that lay pallid and drab against the casket's padding was disintegrating into death's final dissolution. The uniform Neville wore—the splendid parade dress of his Guards unit, with its brass trim and frogging of woven gold—was shredding and turning to tatters and threads.

The very skeleton of the man, the rounded skull with its now-vacant sockets where only seconds before eyeballs had stared blankly at the black sky, cracked and fell away, revealing cold vacancy where once a living brain had contemplated the theorems of Aristotle and the verses of Homer.

An errant breeze swept across the mountain peak, lifting the dust of Major Neville Folliot from the satin of his casket and the wool of his uniform and scattering it across the emptiness beneath the bluff.

Clive felt himself shudder but brought himself back under control. "I have found my brother. I have now accomplished the first part of my charge. But to know that Neville Folliot is dead is insufficient. I must find out how he died. Why he died, and at whose hand. This journal will tell us much, but I must also see what lies in the black city yonder before I consider returning to England."

He gazed out over the black plain. "How can we get down there?"

"Coffin looks awfully tall, sah." Sergeant Smythe was kneeling beside the casket. He reached in, lifted a corner of the shimmering satin padding. The edges of a false bottom showed clearly in the light of the swirling stars.

"Lend a hand, Sidi Bombay. You heard the major."

To Clive's astonishment, Sidi Bombay complied with the sergeant's command. The two men pried the false bottom from the coffin and stood back to observe its contents. "Look at that, sah! Just what the doctor ordered, I'd say!"

Smythe pointed into the coffin. Carefully arranged in the volume beneath the false bottom lay a complete set of climbing equipment—grapnels, ropes, pitons, picks.

"This'll be a test of our skill and our courage, I'd say," Smythe asserted.

"And of our faith," added Sidi Bombay.

Clive stared at the white-clad man. At one moment Sidi Bombay seemed to know all that was to be known, seemed to have appointed himself the controlling influence of their party. At another, he appeared a mere traveler, a faithful retainer. Clive said, "Very well. There's nothing to be gained by delay. Let us set to our task!"

Clive had taken the point position in their descent. He felt it his duty as the commander and leader of the party.

Sidi Bombay had taken the center position of the three, linked with both Folliot and Smythe by a safety line. His tall, almost scrawny frame weighed little, and despite his sometimes startling toughness, Clive feared for the survival of that dry, ancient body.

Horace Hamilton Smythe, physically the strongest of the three, anchored the party, the safety line knotted around his waist. Should Sidi Bombay fall, Smythe's strong muscles and firm grip might save him. Should Clive Folliot fall, in all likelihood Smythe would find himself bearing the weight of three.

The descent itself had been physically draining but, other than that, less difficult than Clive had anticipated. As a youth he had climbed the tall hills and gentle old mountains of his native land. He had mountaineered for sport in the Swiss and Italian Alps. He knew that the demands of a descent were those of concentration, caution, and thought more than they were of brute strength or great skill.

He planned each step, each grip, each placement of finger or toe before he made it. Whenever possible he planned not one move ahead but two, three, four—like a chess player plotting an attack.

When he saw the fissure he welcomed it for the hand- and footholds it offered, for the opportunity to brace and rest that it might provide. It was only when he braced himself in the opening and peered into the slit in the mountainside, which opened like the iris of a titanic cat's eye, that he saw movement.

The organ that shot out at Clive could have been anything long and flexible and deadly. The arm of a huge orangutan. The tentacle of a giant squid. The tongue of a monstrous batrachian.

Like everything else they had found in and of this dark world, it was a dead black. It uncoiled, swept past Clive's face with a deadly whir, and drew back into the fissure. Clive barely caught sight of the serrated edges of the tentacle, and as it withdrew they buzzed audibly against something. From the swirling stars in the midnight sky faint rays of light penetrated the opening in the mountain and were reflected from the glittering eyes of the creature.

With a chill, Clive realized that it was his safety line that the serrations had buzzed against. Intentionally or otherwise, the thing had cut that line. Clive was now unprotected by the line and disconnected from the two climbers above him on the mountain. If he lost his grip there would be no help from Sidi Bombay or Horace Hamilton Smythe.

He braced himself, leaned as far away from the mountainside as he could, and peered upward. He could see Sidi Bombay some twenty yards higher on the escarpment, making his way slowly downward. Another fifteen or twenty yards up, Clive saw Horace Hamilton Smythe.

With all his breath, Clive shouted up to his companions, pleading with them to drop their weapons to him. He had to repeat himself, but at last they heard.

Sidi Bombay released his staff and it tumbled toward Clive. Folliot caught it with both hands, pressing desperately against the walls of the fissure, bracing with spread knees.

He held the staff in one hand, bracing with his elbow, peering upward at Horace Hamilton Smythe. The sergeant was a speck of blackness silhouetted against the blackness of the night. He called down to Clive and let go of his pistol.

It tumbled downward. To Clive it seemed that time was frozen. The revolver fell with infinite slowness, turning end over end, its pattern of diamond stars appearing and disappearing with each revolution, larger and brighter with each revolution, until the revolver was only a yard or so above Clive's head.

There was a sound from deep within the fissure, a slither mixed with a scraping as if great legs covered with stiff, bristly hairs were moving against rock walls.

Clive dared not take his eyes from the falling pistol, not for a fraction of a second. If the thing was moving toward him he would have to trust to providence that it would not arrive before the pistol reached his hand.

The diamonds whirled past his vision once more, gleaming with the brightness of a constellation of suns. Then, with an impact as audible as it was tangible, the revolver thudded into Clive's hand.

He swung his arm, his palm and fingers closing around the revolver's grip at the same time as his forefinger moved through the trigger guard. He pointed the revolver into the fissure and sighted along its silvered barrel.

For the fleeting instants, the fractioned seconds it took to perform these acts, Clive had neither thought nor will. He was a passenger in his own body, an observer inside his own skull. Someone or something else seemed to take him over. Some instinctive or reflexive knowledge guided every muscle in his frame.

He experienced his forefinger squeezing the revolver's trigger, without thinking or willing himself to do so. The fissure was illuminated by the flash that emerged from the revolver's muzzle.

The light appeared and disappeared more rapidly than the blink of an eye. In that tiny fraction of a second Clive saw something that would stay with him for the rest of his life, whether that span should be measured in moments or decades.

A face.

A monstrous, terrible face.

Not a human face, but one that held in it something of the human, something warped, anguished, pain-filled and even more hate-filled, that might once have been human. And something of the insectile, for the eyes were huge and faceted and gave back the flash of the revolver in a thousand fractured fragments. And something else, too, something obscene and hateful and infinitely filthy.

It had been the face's tongue, Clive decided, that had whirred past him and buzzed against his safety line and severed him from the white-robed Sidi Bombay above him.

And then, as that fleeting flash of light faded, the bullet fired from Horace Hamilton Smythe's American revolver struck that face, struck it dead center, and smashed it like an overripe tomato hurled at a poor entertainer in a cheap music hall in the worst section of Whitechapel.

The report of the revolver echoed in the fissure, echoed in Clive's ringing ears. And coupled with the thunder of that explosion was the sickening liquid sound of the face. Smashed. Smashed.

It exploded, and chunks of flesh and pieces of gore and freshets of its vile blood and even more disgusting fluids, hot and stinking like the deepest pits of hell, washed over Clive.

He braced Sidi Bombay's staff against the walls of the fissure, stuck Horace Hamilton Smythe's revolver into his waistband, and clung, clung desperately, to the inside of the fissure.

Gobs of protoplasm hissed past his ears and fell

away toward the black plain beneath him. Where hot fluids struck his body he felt an immediate and disgusting abnormal warmth. He blinked and looked down at himself. He was drenched with gore, but even as he examined his clothing and the exposed parts of his body in dismay, the stuff hissed and steamed and bubbled away, dissipating into the cold, dark, dry air of the mountain.

Hot bile rose in Clive's throat but he fought it back and fought to calm and steady himself before turning his face upward to the others. He called to them, and at his instructions Sidi Bombay climbed down until the upper end of the severed safety line hung within Clive Folliot's reach.

Carefully, Clive reconnected himself to the safety line, knotting the severed ends tightly.

He continued his descent.

The march from the base of the mountain to the black city was uneventful.

Nothing lived on the black plain, no living creature swam in the black river. At least, none that revealed themselves to Clive or Smythe or Sidi Bombay.

By the time they arrived at the black city they realized that it was even taller, even more overwhelming, than it had appeared from the bluff where Neville's coffin had been found.

Within the city the light of the swirling stars penetrated but little. Instead, points of brilliance danced in the air like dust motes in a sunbeam. Each point gave out a minuscule bundle of light, dancing and dipping, intangible and uncapturable. By the uncounted millions the light-motes swarmed, providing an illumination comparable to a gloom-laden twilight.

The buildings varied in size and shape, but all were constructed with a combination of grace and massiveness that spoke of the nature of their designers. All were black, the only variation in their material being that of texture: some were glossy and shimmered in reflected starlight and mote-light; others were dull as matte.

It was not difficult to find the center of the city, for here a vaulting monolith curved skyward, its slim black peak disappearing into the blackness of the heavens. The tower was a monolith in more than appearance: it was obviously a single piece of stone. This was true of each and every structure in the city, and Clive Folliot came to suspect that the entire city was in truth a monolith, a single titanic sculpture, or possibly a casting of some black basaltic material that was formed and hardened in one unit

What if the entire black world was a monolith?

He shook his head and strode first into the curving tower.

Through a tall archway he proceeded to a grand black hall. There he observed what appeared to be an altar, and upon it a casket, a miniature of the one in which his brother Neville had lain. Beside the altar stood a gong as tall as a man, and beside it a mallet.

Without difficulty, Clive opened the casket. Within it lay an object ordinary in shape but nevertheless startling in appearance. It was a key, a small and ordinary key no more than an inch in length.

But it was made of bronze. It was not black.

Unhesitatingly he lifted the key from its casket, fitted it into the lock of his brother's journal, and twisted.

He turned to the final entry in the journal. *If you have come this far,* he read, *you must have found the altar in the Tower of Q'oorna. The Tower of Q'oorna marks the center of the City of Q'oorna. This world is the Dungeon of Q'oorna. Strike the gong, Clive. For now, that is all you must do, but whatever qualms you may have must not stay your hand. MY BROTHER CLIVE, I ADJURE YOU, STRIKE THE GONG!*

There was no question in Clive Folliot's mind that the journal had been written by his brother. He had known that hand all his life; it was similar to his own but was not identical.

Perhaps he should turn back to the beginning of Neville's journal and read the earlier entries before complying with this one, but he had not the patience. Not now.

He resented the position in which he found himself. All his life he had been subordinated to his brother and dominated by his stronger will. The very expedition that had carried him from England to Zanzibar, from Zanzibar to Equatoria, and now to this strange world called the Dungeon of Q'oorna— all this had had Neville Folliot at its center, as its driving motivator. Clive had felt no real desire to travel to Africa. He was a quiet man at heart; he fancied himself an intellectual, and it had been his ambition to devise a means of leaving Her Majesty's service and returning to a quiet and contemplative life in England.

Instead he had traveled thousands of miles, endured hardship and peril, and found his brother —dead.

But even that had not released Clive from his elder twin's domination. From beyond the grave itself Neville had reached back and commanded Clive's actions. From beyond the grave itself!

Clive laid the journal on the altar, nodded solemnly first to Quartermaster Sergeant Horace Hamilton Smythe and then to the gaunt, turbaned Sidi Bombay. In a few strides he reached the gong. He raised the mallet and swung it once.

The sound of the gong was soft but almost unbearably sweet, an infinite harmony of under- and overtones that filled his mind with points of sound that danced and swirled like the light-motes in the city and the spiraling stars in the sky.

Even before the sound had faded into silence, Clive heard the pounding of feet and the shouts from the City of Q'oorna.

▪ CHAPTER 13 ▪
The Khalif of Q'oorna

Clive Folliot whirled. The hall was filled with soldiers. They were Arabs and Nubians and mamelukes. They were armed with spears and with scimitars and with long-barreled, ornately engraved rifles, with bows and arrows, with crude wooden clubs and even stone-headed war axes.

They came howling forward, brandishing their weapons and uttering threatening sounds and gesturing fiercely, but none actually attacked the three outsiders.

Clive had returned Sidi Bombay's staff and Horace Hamilton Smythe's American Navy Colt when they safely reached the foot of the black cliff, after Clive's nearly fatal encounter with the face in the fissure. Clive himself was armed—if that is the right word—with the mallet he had used to sound the gong. He held it in one hand, his brother's journal in the other.

Now Smythe crouched defensively, his American revolver held before him.

"Don't shoot, Smythe," Folliot commanded. "Hold steady, men. We don't know what they want. Perhaps we can parley with them." He wished that he had something more deadly than a mallet in hand— his military saber, or even the scimitar he'd found on the beach and used against the giant spider. But those weapons were long gone, the saber sunk with the wreckage of *Azazel* and the scimitar left behind in Bagomoyo.

There was a shout from the rear of the motley army, and with an inarticulate roar the oddly mixed soldiery attacked.

A Nubian's spear whizzed past Clive's cheek. He saw Sidi Bombay parry a flashing scimitar with his staff. Sidi Bombay wielded the heavy stick as if he were Little John battling Robin Hood with his quarterstaff.

A warrior, stark naked save for daubings of mud and strings of beads, swung a club at Clive. Clive parried with his mallet, and as the warrior lurched past him he clipped the man neatly behind one ear. The man slipped behind Folliot, and Clive had no time to look after him.

From the corner of one eye Clive saw an orange flash. There was a report that echoed like magnified thunder in the cavernous room. He whirled and saw a dagger-bearing dacoit fall to the black marble floor. He had launched himself at Horace Hamilton Smythe, and Smythe had dispatched him with a single shot from his Navy Colt.

Sidi Bombay, tall and gaunt and cadaverous, was surrounded by attackers. Calmly, he swung his staff, turning to face opponent after opponent, keeping clear a circle six to eight feet in diameter, with himself its revolving fulcrum.

Attacker after attacker went down. Blades flashed, firearms boomed, heavy sticks were hefted, and Sidi Bombay, his expression one of serene detachment, seemed always to swing his staff to the right point at the right instant. Where a scimitar flashed downward, it clashed once against the staff and reversed its arc, whirling away through the air above the attackers. Where a rifle was hefted, Sidi Bombay's staff became a blur of brown wood against the black architecture, the rifle would clatter to the floor, and an Arab would stagger away clutching cracked knuckles.

Almost unconsciously the three companions had formed themselves into a triangular formation, back to back to back. Smythe aimed his Colt, fired, aimed, fired. Every shot brought down an attacker. The man did not miss once.

Clive swung his mallet steadily. He was in a strangely detached state of mind. He could see himself, think through each peril and counter. He issued commands to his body, to his arms and hands, to his feet, telling them to shift, to turn, to parry and thrust now like a master of foils, to poke like a bayonetier, and in extremism to swing his mallet like a berserk Viking, slamming it against his enemies, now pounding aside a thrusting dagger, now crushing a foeman's skull like an eggshell.

How many attackers were beaten to the marble floor, there was no way of counting. How high the bodies piled, how redly the blood ran over smooth black marble, there was no way of knowing. A rage compounded equally of fire and of ice flowed over Clive, flowed through his veins. A goddess of battle sung in his ears.

But the outcome was inevitable. The odds against Clive and his friends were overwhelming, little short of infinite.

When Sergeant Smythe's revolver was empty, there was no possible chance to reload. A razor-edged kris was plunging at his tunic and he dodged aside and clubbed the empty revolver against the turbaned Malayan who wielded the kris. The man sank to his knees and Smythe seized the weapon from his hand, instantaneously reversing it to hold the next attacker at bay.

Clive heard a dreadful sound, a combination of a thump and a crack, and to his other side saw Sidi Bombay holding two objects upward. For the first time in the battle, the expression of serenity on Sidi Bombay's face had disappeared, transformed into one of dismay. The gaunt Sidi Bombay's staff had broken in two, doubtless snapped by one too many impacts against an attacker's ax, club, rifle barrel, or skull.

Clive's own weapon, the black mallet, was suddenly seized by a breechclouted mameluke. The man tugged at the mallet, and Clive, setting his heels against the marble floor, yanked back. The mameluke flew toward Clive. The last thing Clive saw was the top of the man's head rushing toward his own face, too rapidly to avoid.

There followed a period of darkness and silence punctuated with flashing lights and roaring winds.

Clive opened his eyes and looked up into the worried face of Sidi Bombay.

"The Englishman lives yet. I thought you had been gathered to the bosom of the Creator, O Clive Folliot. Yes."

Sidi Bombay was crouching over him. The thin, dark face was streaked with blood, as was Sidi Bombay's tattered white robe. The gaunt man helped Clive to achieve a sitting posture. Clive gathered his breath and his strength, then climbed to his feet.

He found himself back in the room of the black altar. The stone altar had been converted to a throne, on which sat the fattest man Clive had ever beheld. He was huge, both tall and broad as well as fat. He must have been close to seven feet in height—or would have been, had he stood. As he sat, his weight must have approached eight hundred pounds.

Tiny, glittering eyes peered out of the folds of flesh that he might have called a face. He was dressed in luxuriant satins and wore a magnificent turban upon his head. A great purple ruby gleamed from the front of his turban, and his costume was decorated with diamonds and emeralds and sapphires. Little of his flesh was exposed, but that which was— most notably his hands—was as distended with fat as his porcine physiognomy.

He wore a ring on each of his fingers, no two alike, and he played with them, one by one by one, seldom looking up from the intricately worked metals and the precious jewels.

Clive found himself standing between Sidi Bom-

bay and Horace Hamilton Smythe. Smythe was as
battered as Sidi Bombay. A quick look told Clive that
Smythe's nose had been smashed, a long gash had
been sliced along his cheek, and one of his eyes was
closed and discolored.

The huge man facing them began to speak, and in
a fleeting instant, even as he did so, Clive took note,
somewhere deep in his mind, that the gash on Sergeant Smythe's face had been crudely sutured closed.
If the procedure had been painful, it might yet save
Smythe from death by bleeding or infection.

Who had done the work? Sidi Bombay? Or one of
their captors?

The fat man was speaking to them. His words
flowed in a rapid, uninterrupted jabber. Clive could
not understand his drift. A few of the words sounded
vaguely familiar, like a slumgullion of Chinese and
Spanish, ki-Swahili and Hindi. There were occasional
familiar words, scraps of French and German, Latin
and Greek, something that sounded like Hebrew,
and even a syllable or two of English.

Once, Clive thought that he even heard his own
surname spoken.

But he did not understand the message.

Only now did he begin to pick out the other figures who ringed the room, illuminated by this time
with flickering torches mounted in brackets against
the walls.

A man whose costume reminded Clive of a vizier
at the court of the sultan of Zanzibar stood near the
throne.

The ruler finished his peroration. The vizier turned
to face Clive and his companions. The vizier's arms
were folded across his chest. He appeared to await
an answer.

Without warning, Sidi Bombay fell on his face
before the ruler. The ruler spoke a few more incomprehensible words and Sidi Bombay rose as far as his
knees. He began to jabber, not at the ruler but at the
vizier, in Hindi.

"What's the fellow saying?" Clive whispered to Horace Hamilton Smythe.

Smythe whispered back, "I can only follow a bit of it, sah. But Sidi Bombay is pleading for our lives."

Before Clive could respond he was yanked forward and thrust face downward before the throne. The vizier had not performed the indignity upon him. A pair of savage Dayaks had advanced silently on bare feet and caught him from behind.

Clive tried to struggle but he felt something cold and sharp against his neck and caught the glint of polished steel from a corner of his eye. With an almost silent moan, he lay still. He was spread-eagled on the polished marble. He was unharmed, save for the aches and bruises he had sustained in the battle. His head ached monstrously but that was to be expected, and he was fairly sure that he had broken no bones. But he realized that he was in imminent peril of his life. That fact was coupled with the affront to his dignity: a member of the English aristocracy and an officer of Her Majesty's military service, forced prostrate and helpless before some savage ruler!

Clive managed to get a view out of the corner of his eye. Sidi Bombay, still on his knees, conversed with the vizier. The vizier passed Sidi Bombay's statements to the ruler. Only the vizier, apparently, was permitted to address the giant who sprawled on the throne.

Sergeant Smythe was no longer visible. Clive hoped that Smythe was still there, still behind him, merely out of the range of his vision—that nothing drastic had been done to him. A pair of naked brown feet also impinged on Clive's view, one ankle decorated with a strand of small bones and teeth.

Clive recoiled at the sight, only to see that very foot raised and to feel it planted firmly on the back of his skull. One more move, it seemed to say, and cold steel would sever his head from his shoulders.

Sidi Bombay nodded at Clive and said, "Yes, this is the one."

The ruler spoke to the vizier. The vizier spoke to Sidi Bombay. Sidi Bombay nodded and spoke to Clive Folliot. "The Grand Khalif Achmed Aziz al Karami commands you to rise to your knees, Englishman."

Without moving, Clive managed to whisper to Sidi Bombay, "Tell the fat pig that no officer of Her Majesty will respond to such impertinence." Clive thought he heard a moan from behind him. He dared not turn to see if it was Horace Hamilton Smythe.

"If I tell that to the khalif, he will order you killed at once. The choice is yours, Englishman, yes. Shall I tell him?"

Clive considered. He felt the Dayak's naked foot removed from his skull, but he sensed the continuing nearness of the steel blade. Carefully, he rose as far as his knees. He caught his lower lip between his teeth and looked the khalif in the eye.

Slowly and clearly Folliot said, "Your Magnificence, I am an officer in the service of Her Majesty Victoria. As a man I am at your mercy. You may kill me if you will. But as an officer of Her Majesty I have rendered you all the obeisance you are due. I will grovel no more."

Slowly and carefully he rose to his feet. "Sidi Bombay," he commanded, "tell that to the vizier, that he may tell it to his master." Clive looked directly at the khalif. He saw a new expression in the man's deeply hidden eyes.

Even as Sidi Bombay began his Hindi singsong, Clive heard the whistle of cold steel behind him. He neither turned nor dodged the stroke; to do so would lower him and would only prolong the inevitable.

The Khalif Achmed Aziz al Karami moved one jewel-encrusted hand. It was a tiny gesture, almost imperceptible.

But the polished blade changed its course even as it swung at the back of Clive's neck. It whistled past his head, actually clipping a tiny lock of his unruly hair and sending it floating through the air to slide slowly to the black marble floor.

The khalif made another gesture, this time to Clive. It was hardly larger than the move that had saved Folliot's life, a twist of one hand. Torchlight flickered and bounced from the gorgeous gems that covered Achmed Aziz al Karami's fat digits.

The gesture was suggestive of the spiral of the stars outside.

The kahlif spoke again, and Sidi Bombay, still on his knees, translated to Clive.

"His Magnificence says that you have the courage of your brother, Englishman. He says that your courage has saved you your life, and that he will spare English Smythe's and mine as well and place them in your hands."

"Tell His Magnificence that I thank him." Clive wondered how the khalif had known who he was, but he chose not to ask. His mind was racing furiously as he attempted to decide what next to do, what next to say.

The khalif gestured to his vizier, who gestured to a man standing beneath a torch at the edge of the chamber. The man advanced. He was a reddish-skinned individual with a peculiar look to his face—his forehead sloped and his eyes were crossed and he wore a feathered breechclout and cape.

From beneath the cape he drew something and advanced toward Clive. He spoke and held the object forward.

With a gasp Clive recognized his brother Neville's journal. He took it from the man and opened it to the last entry he had read—the one that had instructed him to sound the black gong in this very chamber. He had done so only a few hours ago, and all that had transpired since quite staggered the imagination.

There was a new entry in the book! Even before attempting to read it, Clive turned back to the beginning of the journal, to the entries that preceded the one he had read.

They were gone.

He turned back to the newly written page. There were only a few lines there. This time they offered no positive directions. The writing was cryptic, almost a riddle. *Beware your friends. Trust your enemies. Rise to the depths and sink to the heights.*

The writing was definitely that of Neville Folliot. And it was brand-new writing! What did it mean? Clive wondered. And even if he could fathom its import, was the journal to be trusted? He had obeyed a previous instruction, had sounded the black gong—and had promptly been attacked by an army of murderers! What result would come of obeying another directive from Neville Folliot's ectoplasmic hand?

From behind Clive, Quartermaster Sergeant Horace Hamilton Smythe moved forward.

Achmed Aziz al Karami gestured, and a squad of warriors seized Clive and Sidi Bombay and Horace Hamilton Smythe.

The warriors hustled Clive and his companions from the great chamber. They did not speak. They were a motley crew, the dregs of the armies of the world, not only of this year 1868 but of all time. A Roman centurion, a Grecian helot, an Egyptian in the garb of the Eleventh Dynasty, a blue-painted Celt, a feathered Maya, an Oriental in the rough and foul-smelling accounterment of the horde of Genghis Khan.

All were armed and powerful men.

As audacity had been the key to survival earlier, Clive decided, discretion was the course to follow now. He hoped that he could communicate this to Sidi Bombay and Horace Hamilton Smythe. Apparently he could—or else they had come independently to the same conclusion.

Single file, with Clive in the lead, an ill-matched pair of warriors as guards at the elbows of each, they marched through corridors and down ramps.

* * *

The Dungeon was huge, yet its very commodiousness was strained by the crowd of prisoners it contained.

What the khalif intended, Clive had no idea. The journal was still in Clive's possession, but other than that he and Sergeant Smythe and Sidi Bombay had no weapons, no tools, no supplies or equipment of any sort. They had only the clothes they wore and the resources of their own wit and experience.

The Dungeon was apparently carved from the living rock beneath the Black Tower of Q'oorna.

But carved by whom?

Or by what?

The answer to that soon became apparent. A narrow stream flowed through the Dungeon, perhaps a tributary of the broad body of water that Clive and his companions had seen from the mountain peak where they had found and left Neville's coffin. How many centuries the stream had flowed here, there was no way of telling.

But if the stream had carved out this cavern, then the water had to come from somewhere and exit elsewhere, and that meant that there were two possible paths of escape from the Dungeon, other than returning via the opening through which the guards had unceremoniously dumped Clive and Sidi Bombay and Sergeant Smythe.

The mouth of the cavern was closed by a wall of iron bars. The single gate in the wall was also made of iron bars. The guards had unlocked this, swung it open, and shoved their prisoners through. Then they had slammed the gateway shut once again, locked it securely, and marched back the way they had come.

The cavern was lighted by a row of torches that burned high on the walls. The torches were fed by oil. Where the oil came from, when or how or by whom it was replenished, the newcomers simply did not know.

Clive and his companions stood together, peering into the gloom.

How many prisoners did the huge cavern hold?

There seemed no end to them. Hundreds, possibly thousands of prisoners stood or lay or sat in huddled heaps on the cold, damp floor. The mix here was as polyglot as that in the chamber above, but here the men were not spruce as above, nor armed and equipped. Instead they appeared dispirited, their clothing in tatters, their faces gaunt, their eyes haunted by hopelessness.

They had clustered by nations and by races. There were gangs of dark-skinned men, probably African tribesmen. Others, equally black, might have been East Indians or Australian aborigines. There were yellow Asiatics and ruddy-skinned American Indians.

From each group there arose a buzz of talk, the whole so blurred and overlapping that Clive was unable to detect any meaning in any of the voices.

None of the men possessed anything other than his clothing.

Clive and his companions moved among the groups, studying them as they passed, gathering suspicious or assessing glances in return. They found the source of the black stream. It emerged from an opening in the wall of the cavern. Clive examined the opening. It was less than a foot in diameter. There was no way he could escape through that hole.

The three companions followed the course of the steam until it broadened into a basin. The basin was roughly circular, some twenty feet across. There was no telling its depth, but it was obvious that the water exited the Dungeon through the basin, for the stream flowed steadily into it and no visible watercourse emerged from the basin.

But that was not the most astonishing part of the circular body of water. Clive and his companions were not able to get close to it because it was completely surrounded . . .

By women!

Women of every conceivable racial type, white and black, yellow and brown. Most were of types recognizable to Clive, but others were so strange that they appeared hardly human. Heavyset, hulking, hairy women looking more apelike than human. Perhaps these were survivals of some ancient ancestor of humanity, some race that had arisen thousands or millions of years ago only to give way to a more advanced species when their time had run out.

Mr. Darwin would be beside himself, could he but see these persons!

And others! There were women with hairless skulls and slim, sleek bodies that might function better in a watery environment than on the face of the Earth. And still others with long torsos and extended, tapering limbs, women who might have grown to maturity in a world where the pull of gravity was slight—if not absent—and where the human frame could stretch to amazing heights.

The women clustered around the pond. Like the men, they were devoid of weapons or other implements, but they had found strength in union and were unmolested by the males.

One woman in particular caught Clive Folliot's attention. Despite her ragged garb and unkempt person, there was a dark-haired and dark-eyed beauty to her, and a grace to her carriage and her limbs that brought a tightness to Clive's throat and chest.

There was something of Annabella Leighton there! All women were sisters under the skin, or so ran a common army maxim. Surely there was a kind of sisterhood here, and Clive was deeply moved by the sight of this female.

He tried to move toward the woman.

To his astonishment, the other women stepped aside. They did not want contact with these strange males. Clive could sense Sergeant Smythe and Sidi Bombay beside and slightly behind him.

Even as the other women, black and white, tall and

short, hairy and primitive and smooth-skinned and sleek, moved aside, the dark beauty stood her ground.

Before her, Clive halted. He looked into her eyes. Her back was to the pool. She returned his glance, her face curious, courageous, perhaps even cunning. She did not step aside as the others had. She did not yield an inch. She did not flinch from Clive.

He raised his hand to touch her. He moved slowly, as one would toward a wild animal, seeking to reassure it, to tame it, above all not to drive it to panicked flight.

The woman tracked the movement of Clive's hand, following it with her eyes. The suggestion of a smile played at the corners of her mouth.

Clive placed his hand gently on her upper arm—or tried to.

When his fingers were the tiniest fraction of an inch from her flesh, a searing flame leaped from her to his skin. It spread across him, covering his entire body. His every nerve screeched, his eyes bulged, his hair stood on end. He could see blue flames crackling over his torso.

· CHAPTER 14 ·
"Too Many Creeps"

Clive Folliot sat on the floor of the cave, feeling its cold and damp through his khaki trousers and thick-soled boots. To his left sat Sidi Bombay, serene in lotus position, his face a blank, his hands resting palms upward on the inner sides of his knees. To his right was Sergeant Horace Hamilton Smythe, his face atwitch with eagerness to be on with things.

Opposite Clive sat the woman whose touch was so electrifying. She smiled now at Clive. "Clean run I dimp sizzle your circuits, user. Would have been a catastrophic error. Glad to download this message."

Clive shook his head and looked to Sidi Bombay and Horace Hamilton Smythe for help, but they failed to understand her any more than Folliot did. "Are you apologizing, young lady?"

She smiled and nodded. At least they were in accord on that score. She seemed to speak the English language, or some variation of it. Clive had known enough Americans to recognize some of the peculiarities that had accrued to the tongue in that country, but even Sergeant Smythe, who had lived in America for a time, got no more out of the woman's words than did Clive.

The woman nodded vigorously. "Firm tiff!" she said.

Firm tiff? Clive pondered. What could she mean? The phrase seemed meaningless—but, combined with her affirmative nod—*affirmative*! That was it! Some of her statements did make a kind of fantastic sense;

others were as baffling as if she were speaking in ancient Egyptian.

"This place is the Dungeon of Q'oorna," Clive said. "But my friends and I don't understand where Q'oorna actually is. We were exploring in Equatoria, trying to cross the Bahr-el-Zeraf, in the Sudd. We were headed for the Sudan, in search of the headwaters of the Nile. And in search of my brother Neville. Then—"

He found himself indicating his puzzlement with a shrug of the shoulders and a gesture of his hands.

"Linkage fault, sounds like. Nasty bug."

There she was again, speaking that baffling argot that sounded so much like English but conveyed no meaning.

"But you, young lady. We don't even know your name. Nor you ours." Clive introduced his companions and himself.

Now it was the young woman's turn to seem puzzled, but after a few seconds she nodded vigorously and said, "Tiff, tiff. Eyedee protocol, sure. User Annie, sure." She extended her hand to be shaken, but quickly drew it back, giggling. "Downs short your chips. Hah!"

Clive asked where the woman was from, and that, at least, drew a coherent answer. "San Francisco," she said. He'd heard of that place, a roaring seaport somewhere near the gold mines of America. "Default option San Francisco," she went on. "Absolute address was London before Dungeon."

Absolute address? Clive exchanged blank stares with Sergeant Smythe. But he was determined to press on. This woman, this User Annie or whatever her name was, was the only person in the polyglot conglomeration in the Dungeon who seemed willing and able to converse with him. If only he could fathom her meanings—and communicate to her his own!

"User Annie, do you mean you had moved from

San Francisco to London before you came to, ah, Q'oorna?"

"Tiff! Address London, Annie anna Crackbelles playing Piccadilly for two thousand openfile protocol when—*zap!*—bused to Dungeon, Stings, user, valid stings. Too many creeps here. Mostly tempoids." She burst into laughter, staring at Clive.

She reached inside her blouse and did something, then held her hand toward him again. Cautiously, Clive took the hand and shook it, then dropped it quickly. It had been warm and pleasant—the first touch of woman flesh in too long. User Annie reached inside her blouse again.

"You're a tempoid yourself, aren't you, Clive?"

He merely stared at her.

"Or maybe *I* am!" A curious look passed across her features. "Who can say? Where's the clock? How can anybody crunch that?" She appeared baffled.

"Tempoid?" Clive asked. But at least she was speaking comprehensibly. It was a struggle to understand User Annie, but to some degree at least he could do it.

"Io functional?" User Annie asked. That was a baffler. Io was the daughter of Inachus, was she not? He tried to remember his myths. Something about a magical transformation. Sometimes identified with the minor Egyptian deity Sis. Was User Annie trying to ask him something about Egypt?

"Closefile nineteen ninety-nine," User Annie said. "Big audio output function in Piccadilly. Openfile two thousand. *Zap!* Bus here." She spread her hands.

Nineteen ninety-nine?

Two thousand?

Was she talking about the *years* 1999 and 2000? But those were more than a century in the future? and tempoids . . .

"Tempoids?" he asked. "As in *tempus*—"

"*Fugit!*" she supplied, grinning. "Valid! What's your clock, anthro?"

Clive hesitated.

"Download!" User Annie commanded. She seemed agitated with him. Probably she was becoming as frustrated by their bizarre conversation as he was. "Activate your modem!"

She had asked something about his clock. That made no sense at all. But tempoids—*tempus fugit*—time flies—and she had spoken of 1999 and 2000. "This is the year of Our Lord one thousand eight hundred sixty-eight," he stated solemnly.

"Only relative," User Annie said. But she did seem pleased that they were getting some information to each other. Clive was pleased as well.

She waved her hand again, indicating the whole of the Dungeon. "Data insufficient for this address. Probably virtual anyhow. Absolute clock and address unavailable. Huh. Performance degrades, too bad, eh, user?"

Clive addressed his companions. "I think—strange as this seems—that, ah, User Annie is telling us that she was brought here from London. But not only that. She was brought here from the future. From the year 1999 or 2000. Closefile, openfile; 1999, 2000. I suspect she's talking about a New Year's celebration. Something happened to her on December thirty-first, 1999, and she was brought here. To the year 1868."

"Are you so certain, sah, that this is 1868?" Smythe inquired. "Maybe we were brought to the young lady's time, rather than she to ours. Or maybe something even stranger than that. Didn't the young lady make some remarks about relatives and clocks and virtues? Not that I took her meaning precisely, sah, but one thinks she's telling us that the Dungeon isn't quite in, ah, I don't quite know how to put it, sah. P'raps the major could 'elp me out with some o' his fine Cambridge words, sah."

Before Clive could respond, Sidi Bombay spoke. "Time and time, Englishmen, and space and space. Both have their shapes and their turnings. There are more times and more spaces than thou knowest."

Clive found himself staring at the gaunt face. What did he know of this man? That he came from India, that he was very old. But what was his philosophy? What were his thoughts? Clive did not even know whether Sidi Bombay adhered to the Hindu attitude or the Buddhist or the Muslim—although he had spoken of Allah and the coffin of the Prophet. That meant that surely there was something of the Mussulman in him. Nor had he unraveled to the slightest degree the connection between Sidi Bombay and Horace Hamilton Smythe and the strange symbol of the swirling, spiraled stars.

He looked at the roof of the Dungeon and saw only blackness—the blackness of rough, living basalt further blackened by uncounted numbers of torches that had burned and burned in the Dungeon. What would he give for a glimpse of the blue sky . . . or even of the black, crystalline sky of the swirling world of Q'oorna!

And yet, by persistence, he was able to gain some understanding of User Annie's story. And, he thought, to make the young woman understand something of his.

She was indeed an American. It was astonishing to ponder that she lived as she did, independently, with neither family nor chaperon. Traveling about her country—indeed, the entire globe—in company of a band of itinerant musicians known by the odd name of the Crackbelles.

He tried to grasp the music she described, but even the instruments that her companions played had strange names and were incomprehensibly described. But User Annie, at least, indicated that her own part in the enterprise was to sing and dance before audiences. She seemed hardly the music hall type of girl—independent and brash she was, but neither cheap nor crude.

The distressing effect of her touch was the result of something she called an electrofield, powered by a tiny device hidden beneath the bodice of her costume. The device was powered by her own body energies, and User Annie feared that if she became too weak or tired, it would fail. And then she would be at the mercy of those around her.

She cast a fearful glance at some of the more brutal types whose shadows seemed to dance and leer in the flickering light of torches.

Clive asked what the device was called, that powered User Annie's electrofield.

"A Baalbec A-nine," she answered. "Cono model. Couldn't bus bastante bux for a -ten. May be a catastrophic error, that!"

There had been no food since Clive and the others had arrived here, but there were more urgent concerns than meat and bread. Clive persisted, "Who are all these persons? What are tempoids? What are extroids? What are cybroids?"

"You're missing some chips, user!" Annie shook her head. "You joking me? You on downtime lately?"

Clive persisted.

User Annie heaved a sigh of exasperation. "Tempoids are clock busers. Future users, past users. Maybe even other kind of time users. Raghead understands that better than you do, User Clive. Raghead validates! Good data, crunch that, User Clive!"

Clock busers? As in omnibuses? Did she mean those who traveled on clocks? No—those who traveled in time! "And extroids?" he asked.

She shook her head. "Heepers, anthro! Open your file! CounterEarthers, Zimarzlans, Beta Tories! User never input planets?"

Clive jumped to his feet. "They're from other planets? From Mars and Venus and Jupiter?"

"All over the scan. Tiff, tiff, user. That's outside your protocol, dimp?"

Clive put his hands over his eyes. "Du Maurier was right after all," he whispered. "He should have been brought here, and I should have remained in England. Or at most, in Zanzibar." He lowered himself carefully so that his eyes were at the level of User Annie's. "And cybroids?" he asked. "Tell me please, what are cybroids?"

"Oh, anthro! You're really missing chips! System interface biomass with hardware, that's all. Proto- plasm seepeeoo, mekky perifs, mixed wetware and chips-resident routines. Get your program debugged, user! Upgrade your system specs!"

Sergeant Smythe interrupted the colloquy by plac- ing his hand on Clive Folliot's wrist. "Take a look this-a-way, sah." He jerked his head toward a group of savage-looking individuals dressed in maroon and yellow mottled gear. At least, the rags that covered their scabrous bodies showed the traces of those colors.

They were casting glances at Clive and the others, and a couple of the more energetic among them were indicating that they might have violence in mind.

"Miss, ah, Annie," Clive addressed the young woman. "Can your—what did you call it?"

"Electrofield."

"Yes. Can it include more persons than yourself?"

"Firm tiff. But high power drain, clock time, pos- sible system failure."

"Could you include all of us?" He indicated Sidi Bombay and Horace Hamilton Smythe as well as himself.

User Annie said she could include them.

Horace Hamilton Smythe strode to the pond into which the black stream disappeared. "What precisely does that thingumabob do, Miss Annie?"

She looked puzzled for a moment, then her face cleared. " 'Lectrolyzes impinging matter, bub."

"And water, miss? What would it do in water? Would it keep it away from yer, so's yer could still breathe—like a diving bell, so to speak?"

"Oh, firm tiff. Pozzi tiff! Pozzi tiff!" Her words conveyed their message, and her vigorous nods and gestures confirmed it.

"Well, miss, I propose that the four of us gets

ourselves out of here, because there i'n't much future with those blokes turning restless."

He jerked a thumb behind him, toward the parties in the maroon and yellow rags. Clive Folliot followed Smythe's gesture with his eyes. He couldn't determine the racial identity of the men, and their guttural language was completely foreign to him. By contrast, User Annie's odd argot was the Queen's English to perfection.

He looked more closely at the ragged group. There was a strange look to their eyes, as if they were pairs of tiny telescopes embedded in place of the natural organs.

One of the men opened his mouth and Clive caught the flash of metal and the glimmer of something else, the nature of which he preferred not to try to guess.

Were these cybroids? Something about protoplasm and *mekky perifs,* whatever those were. Mekky? Mechanical? A mixture of living matter and machine? He knew about crude artificial parts—peglegs and hook hands and carefully carved wooden teeth. But these creatures . . .

Clive Folliot shuddered.

Horace Hamilton Smythe led the way to the edge of the pond. The other women who surrounded it allowed the party of four to pass among them. When they reached the edge of the pond, Smythe said, "Now's the time, Miss Annie. If you can understand what I'm asking yer, miss, now's the time."

He pointed to the young woman's bodice, and User Annie nodded. She reached inside her clothing with one hand, and with the other took hold of Smythe's. Sidi Bombay and Clive Folliot linked their hands with the others'. User Annie made another adjustment and Clive Folliot felt a brief tingle. Then everything returned to normal.

"Don't decouple!" User Annie urged.

The four of them, by mutual consent, leaped into the pond.

Clive felt the water close over his head. It was pitch black and as cold as a North Country winter, but instead of rushing into his nostrils the liquid stayed a tiny distance away from him. He tried to recall the experiment in natural philosophy he had witnessed at Cambridge. Something about the application of a galvanic force to electrolyze water into oxygen and hydrogen.

The phenomenon had seemed merely a curiosity to him at the time, but now it meant that he and his companions could breathe even though they were wholly covered by water!

Their downward momentum had carried them to the bottom of the pond. Clive knelt on the rocky bottom, holding to one of the others' hands—he didn't know whose—and with his free hand feeling about the raw stone floor.

It tended toward a low point, and there Clive found what he had hoped against hope to find: an opening as large around as a man!

He tried to speak to the others, to explain what he had found, but the thin coating of air that permitted breath was insufficient to permit speech. The only sound that emerged from his mouth was an incoherent gurgling.

Counting on the others to follow his lead, he began to slide his foot into the opening. But he pulled back and reversed his posture. He felt the hand that he had clasped in his own slide down his flank and his leg, and grasp him at last by one heavy boot. He offered up a prayer to whatever deity might oversee this dark and terrifying world, that the precious contact of hand to ankle would not be broken.

He pulled himself slowly through the opening, feeling a slow, steady flow of water around him. What would he find on the other side? Another chamber? A lengthy channel? A passageway in which he would become lodged, there to die an agonizing death?

Or—freedom?

He could see nothing—at first.

He could hear nothing—save the pounding of his pulse, the rush of his bloodstream.

Then—perhaps his eyes were adjusting to their new surroundings, his ears to the watery medium—shapes and colors and sounds began to make themselves apparent.

Sleek-bodied denizens of the flowing water approached and stared at the humans. Luminous eyes peered into their own. Tentacles wove and thrust. Clive felt a rubbery, muscular appendage touch him. For whatever reason, the shocking effect of the electrofield did not deter these creatures; either that, or it had ceased to function in the watery medium.

The passage widened around them. They were swimming, now, borne along by the flow of the stream, no longer touching the walls of the passage through which they moved.

Clive felt the hand that had clutched his ankle work its way up the side of his body. He reached to find his companions. They could now link hands once again, and move forward through the water side by side. They were unarmed, defenseless against any attack that might occur.

With a jolt, Clive's toe collided with a solid mass.

He placed his foot carefully, found that there was a fairly smooth, rocky floor beneath him. He looked up and realized that above the water there was no longer a cavernous roof but the high black sky of Q'oorna. The familiar swirling spiral of stars glinted down, distorted and made to appear to waver by the moving stream.

In a while Clive and his companions were wading onto the bank of the black stream. They dropped one another's hands—perhaps a moment too soon, for the shield of force disappeared and they were suddenly drenched in the icy water—all except Annie, who remained protected by the electrofield. The others stood shaking like dogs to rid themselves of soaking water. Shaking and laughing all at once.

Clive trembled with cold. The stars were, if anything, brighter than ever. He peered into the blackness above and began to perceive distant nebulae
and constellations. Bands of light, unmeasurably distant, swept across the sky. The total illumination was
far greater than that of any ordinary night; the landscape and its occupants were bathed with the gloomy
illumination of a grim midwinter twilight.

"Has anyone an idea of where we are?" Clive asked
the others. "This is Q'oorna, of course—but where is
Q'oorna? *What* is Q'oorna?"

User Annie had reached inside her bodice to switch
off the Baalbec A-9. "Load some astronomy software, anthro." She swung a graceful arm above her
head. Clive could not help noticing the swell of her
bosom, the soft movement that accompanied her
gesture.

"Data inconclusive," she continued. "But high order probability Q'oorna is a rogue planet."

"A rogue planet? What can you mean?"

"Maybe people decided to take a jaunt, took their
world with them, left their sun behind." User Annie
looked at the stars. An unreadable expression flickered across her face. "Maybe somebody else aited
their sun. Left Q'oorna orphan, not rogue. Compu-
tation result equivalent, orphan or rogue. Nonsignif-
icant differentiation, User Clive Folliot."

Clive shook his head. "Ate their sun? *Ate* it? As in
mythology?"

User Annie snorted. "Not ate it, user. Read error,
data link fault. Aited. As in, propriated. Appropriated. Uh—uh—intermittent device jam. Correct and
proceed. Appropriated, equivalent term—uh—uh—
took, took away, lexicon software limitation, swiped,
crook'd—uh—uh—cross-ref bobbyvescoe, jamesboys,
robinhood, nickdixon. Linkage complete. user? Heepers!
file closing."

She started walking away.

Clive couldn't tell whether she really knew where
she was going or had decided arbitrarily to follow the

course of the stream, but in this baffling place that seemed as good as idea as any.

The party moved together.

They reached a level of fatigue and hunger just short of acute discomfort, and there they leveled off. Water was no problem—they paused to rest and drink from the stream every few hours. Horace Hamilton Smythe's turnip watch had miraculously survived both the battle and the soaking. How much longer it would function was subject to speculation, but for the moment at least it continued to tick away.

The landscape remained as black as ever but the sky continued to brighten. There was no sunrise as such. Instead the constellations and the vaguer bands of light in the sky became both brighter and more numerous.

It was as if Q'oorna were a world at the veritable edge of creation. As Q'oorna revolved in its daily course, a strange sort of dawn and dusk, daytime and night, would occur. When they faced the rest of the universe, the cumulative light of a billion suns would impinge on them. So distant was Q'oorna from these stars that their combined illumination was never greater than that of a grey and miserable late afternoon in England. And when Q'oorna's rotation brought the observers to face away from the rest of the universe, there was only the enigmatic spiral of stars, those few but almost painfully brilliant points of light, in the planet's sky.

Trying to imagine where such a place might be, where such conditions might obtain, Clive shivered.

Ahead of them a chasm yawned.

Even as they spotted it from afar, a distant roaring could be heard. Perhaps the stream they were following plunged over the edge of the chasm, and the sound was that of the waterfall.

No words were exchanged among the four. None were needed, and none could contribute. All of them knew that they would continue until they had reached the edge.

When they were a mile from the chasm a chance glint of light hinted to them that there was a way across. They could not see the far side of the chasm: its width was too great for that. But a great, graceful arch spanned the abyss, disappearing beyond in a faintly luminous mist that rose from below.

The roaring grew louder.

Clive halted and took Horace Hamilton Smythe's arm. "Do you hear it, Sergeant?"

"Hear what, sah?"

"That roaring—howling—whatever it is."

"Yes, sah. Of course, sah."

"It's no waterfall. It's—it's some kind of voice."

"Yes, sah, I detect as much, sah."

"And—and—Sergeant Smythe—it's—it's singing. It's a crude, a monstrously crude voice, like a lion's roar crossed with the howling of a gigantic wolf. But I swear by all that's holy, Sergeant, whatever that is that's making the sound is doing its level best to sing 'God Save the Queen'!"

▪ CHAPTER 15 ▪
Enter the Dwarf

Thus: *Finnbogg.*

He was like a man, but he was not a man.

Barely four feet tall, and so wide that from a distance Clive could have taken him for Tweedle-dee or Tweedle-dum, one of the rotund twins in Mr. Dodgson's fantasy. Here was a short, fat, jolly individual who would have been more at home on a music hall stage in Whitechapel than guarding a bridge across a forbidding chasm on this remote black hell called Q'oorna.

Closer to the bridge, he looked both more and less human than he did from afar.

He had two arms and two legs. His torso and hands and feet were shaped like those of a man, although Clive could not tell how many fingers or toes Finnbogg possessed.

His face had the look of a bulldog. His brow beetled, and his nose was puglike, broad and flat and with nostrils that flared against the flatness of his face. His jaw was underslung, and teeth like tusks protruded from his lower jaw, extending over his upper lip. He snapped them as he pranced about, and when he clashed his teeth, sparks literally flew in the black Q'oornan night.

And he howled and roared in a voice like a mighty beast, but as Clive and Sidi Bombay and Horace Hamilton Smythe and User Annie drew close, the tune and even the words of "God Save the Queen" grew clear.

When they were a hundred yards from the bridge and its amazing guardian, the creature gave them another surprise. He dropped to all fours, his almost apelike arms and his short legs working in perfect coordination. He sped across the black landscape at astonishing speed.

Before Clive and the others could react, before Annie could reach inside her bodice and activate her Baalbec A-9 electrofield, he was upon them. Almost more rapidly than the eye could follow he circled them, then threw himself on the black earth, rolling against their legs, rubbing his fangs terrifyingly against their legs.

Annie screamed.

Folliot winced and recoiled.

Horace Hamilton Smythe uttered an unprintable oath.

And Sidi Bombay knelt and embraced the monstrosity, running his scrawny black hands through its weird, bushy hair, rubbing its shoulders and back, finally pressing his cheek against its bristly face and its razor-sharp fangs.

"You see, Englishman? We have found a friend."

"You're right," Clive managed. He knelt beside the Indian, reached toward the massive being. It—he—was amazingly massive. Bones like iron stanchions, limbs like tree trunks, a face that, like a genial bulldog's, was strangely appealing in its very ugliness and its almost pathetic eagerness to please despite its ferocity.

At last the monster backed off a few paces. It raised itself to a standing posture and began a low humming, a humming of a song popular among the cadets at Sandhurst. Clive Folliot recognized the tune. It was one that his brother Neville had sung when deep in his cups, one with lyrics to make a Whitechapel trollop crimson.

"What are you?" Clive demanded of the creature. "Who are you? Where does this bridge lead?" He indicated the soaring span that disappeared into mist.

From here it could be seen that the bridge was cast of living basalt, black and polished and glittering beneath the Q'oornan constellations.

"Finnbogg," the creature answered. It howled and capered and gibbered like a mad thing—but it was not mad. "Happy," Finnbogg roared. "Happy, happy Finnbogg. Come to play, come to stay, come today. Good, good, nice, nice!"

He hopped forward and placed one heavily padded, pawlike hand against Clive's cheek, one against Annie's. "Nice tempoids play Finnbogg, happy Finnbogg, come and play. Tell Finnbogg a story."

Clive shook his head. "A story?"

The beast capered. "Story! Finnbogg love stories. Like 'Merry Thornbug and Merchant Lamprey.' Or 'Snowsnakes Three.' Know 'Snowsnakes Three,' being? Finnbogg's favorite story. 'One fine day Snowsnake One woke up. 'Yik, yak,' Snowsnake say, 'where to find redscratchers in blue ice? Try greenice witchfaery burrow.' But Sharp Treeclimber say, 'Witchfaery go hot lava, witchfaery swim in volcano, witchfaery out for birding soup.' So Snowsnake one—' "

Finnbogg stopped. He sat back on his massive haunches and peered from one face to another. "No being know story? Nobody know 'Snowsnakes Three' story? Know another story? Tell Finnbogg story. Finnbogg love story, save story, never forget good story."

Clive ignored the creature's pleas. "Are you a Q'oornan?" he demanded.

Finnbogg somersaulted, hopped straight into the air—at least twelve feet into the air!—landed on his hands, and did a spring back onto his feet. "Not Q'oornan!" he roared. "Finnbogg Finnbogg from Finnbogg!" he shouted. He peered deeply into Clive's face. "Finnbogg know you. Finnbogg friend, man friend, else Finnbogg *kill*!"

The last word seemed to give the creature an idea. He threw himself at an imaginary foe, fangs bared, clashing his great teeth fearsomely. He roared in mock rage—Clive hoped that it was merely mock rage—and tossed his great head to left and to right. If he had held an enemy in his jaws at that instant, its neck would have been snapped as easily as that of a rabbit in the grip of a terrier.

"Englishmen," Sidi Bombay said softly, "do you not know the totem of your own land? Even the Prophet, blessings be upon His name, was not perfect. This humble servant of God cannot comprehend the Prophet's dislike of the noble dog."

Clive stared at the strange creature. Sidi Bombay had merely confirmed Clive's impression of Finnbogg. The massive, muscular being was indeed a bulldog, or something that Charles Darwin might have predicted would emerge from a million generations of bulldogs striving to achieve humanity. He was as energetic, as enthusiastic, as affectionate and eager for approval as a bulldog. And he was a terrifying visage, and in combat would doubtless prove as deadly and as unyielding as a bulldog.

"You know me?" Clive asked the doggish being.

"Folliot," came the reply in a growl. "Folliot, Folliot, good major, yes, Finnbogg friend Folliot."

"P'raps the major's brother passed this way, sah," Sergeant Smythe offered.

"Perhaps he did," Clive replied softly. "If so, he seems to have made a favorable impression for once. Well, let us not look a gift horse—or dog!—in the mouth, eh, Smythe? It looks as if we've found a faithful friend and strong ally!"

The young woman took Finnbogg's pawlike hand from her face and held it between her own graceful hands. "Eyedee protocol Finnbogg," she said. "User Annie log-on, modem connect. Designate task assignment."

"Bad Q'oornans tell Finnbogg guard bridge. Tell Finnbogg not let tempoids cross bridge. Not let extroids cross bridge. Not let cybroids cross bridge. Only Q'oornans cross bridge. Where Finnbogg's littermates? Boypups, girlpups, Finnboggs, gone.

Down? All gone away down? Gone away? Where pups?"

The creature threw himself to the ground, whining and—Clive was certain of it—actually weeping.

Finnbogg dragged himself, belly to the ground, to the edge of the chasm. He leaned far over, almost tumbling from the black rocky ledge, but held himself back with fingers of immense strength. Mists rose from the depths. The stream that Clive's party had followed flowed over the edge of the chasm and crashed into the depths, spume rising to obscure the bottom of the abyss.

"Where does the bridge lead?" Clive asked. He was studying the span. It was narrow, barely adequate to permit their party to walk side by side. Certainly it could not carry a coach of passengers or a wagon of goods. It rose into the Q'oornan sky, silhouetted against the sparkling distant nebulae until it disappeared into the mist and the distance.

"Bad Q'oornans never tell Finnbogg. Beat Finnbogg, scold Finnbogg, never love Finnbogg, never never never. Take boypups, girlpups, where litter? Never tell story. Being know story of Farmer Fivefeet and Walking Wildhooper? No? Q'oornans never tell story! Bad bad bad." He made a sound that was a simple growl but that was the growl of a thousand creatures in one. He dropped to all fours once again.

The young woman knelt and put her arms around Finnbogg's neck. "Open data link, User Finnbogg. Sysop Annie buses love protocol." She pressed the bristly face to her bosom, the creature's great fangs held tight against the thin cloth that covered her soft, generous breasts.

"Wot's the young lady saying, sah?" Sergeant Smythe asked.

"I think she told Finnbogg that she loves him," Clive answered. "And somehow, Smythe, I believe she's telling the truth."

Finnbogg jumped to his feet, capered in a mad

circle around the others, and seized Annie's hand in his own.

"Come ahead, come ahead, tempoids. Come ahead. Finnbogg your Finnbogg now. Not Q'oornans' Finnbogg, no, no, no more Q'oornans'. Come, come, tempoids. Cross Finnbogg bridge. Cross, cross, come along."

Like an eager dog straining at its lead, he dragged Annie onto the bridge. The others followed.

They had gone hardly thirty yards when Clive realized with a shudder that the bridge was a bare span of cold, black basalt soaring above the chasm. There were no walls to it, no guardrails. The surface was smooth, and where it was wet with mist it was slick. A single misstep, a fall, would cast one into the black chasm and to certain doom.

Happy now to be with his new friends, Finnbogg was singing a song that Clive had heard on the streets of London, where it had arrived from Boston in America. "Champagne Charlie was his name," the creature roared, "Champagne Charlie was his name."

Clive was troubled by something that he could not identify and that would not leave him in peace until he had tracked it through his own mental labyrinth.

He had it! "Champagne Charlie" had arrived in England only the year before, he was sure of it. Sheet music had been imported from Boston, and overnight half of London was singing the same silly song. If Finnbogg knew the song, then it had arrived in Q'oorna within the past year. In all likelihood, it had to be Clive's brother Neville who had brought it.

Distractions and disasters notwithstanding, Clive was still on the trail! He had seen Neville's cadaver, or what had appeared to be Neville's cadaver. But there had been new entries in the journal, and now there was Finnbogg's evidence, however indirect, to suggest that Neville was alive.

They climbed slowly toward the peak of the bridge. It became increasingly difficult to keep steady footing and to move ahead. The upward slope was not steep—that alone made it possible to make the climb without equipment that the travelers no longer possessed—but as they ascended, the temperature plummeted. The droplets of mist that condensed on the bridge froze, and the already slick surface of polished obsidian bore a thin coating of ice.

Finnbogg alone had no difficulty in keeping his footing. His feet were bare, their bottoms divided into pads like those of a dog. The pads had been hardened by the long years of exposure to the hard ground and rough duty that Finnbogg had encountered at the bridge. His nails, like those of a dog, were strong and curved, and—perhaps as an amusing pastime—he had sharpened them to needle points, just as he had those on his fingers.

He strode happily along, singing "Champagne Charlie," "When You and I Were Young, Maggie," "Work for the Night Is Coming," and "Tenting on the Old Camp Ground." Occasionally he would burst into an especially gleeful chorus of his favorite, "God Save the Queen."

The climb settled into a routine. It wasn't especially difficult, save for the need to place each step carefully, avoiding the peril of a disastrous slip.

Even the jovial Finnbogg settled into a calmer mood, humming a medley of Negro spirituals. He loved each song and repeated each more times than Clive Folliot could count, before moving on to the next. And Finnbogg's humming had the general volume and tonal quality of the steam engines aboard the *Empress Philippa*.

Clive found himself reminiscing about Captain Wingate and Purser Fennely and the other persons he had encountered aboard that ship—the trio of cardsharpers, Lorena Ransome in particular. She had been a charmer, and she had seemed more than willing to share her charms with Clive.

A warm fantasy relieved him of the chill tedium of the basalt bridge. He was taken by a strangely pleasant melancholy. He could summon up the feeling, the very odor of—

A scream shattered his reverie.

User Annie leaped back, colliding with Folliot. He fell to one knee, clutching to keep from being swept off the bridge. A huge shadow rose before the party, blocking out a patch of sky where stars and fuzzy nebulae cast their ghostly illumination.

The shadow hovered briefly, then began to grow with alarming speed as it dropped back toward the travelers.

Features became visible on the thing, for it was a solid object, a living creature that blocked the stars and nebulae, not a mere shadow at all. It had huge wings that buzzed and sizzled in the mist-filled air. Its eyes glowed with a malevolent light of their own, and when they were cast upon Clive he felt a queerness pass through his flesh, as if the eyes had actually projected an invisible, harmful ray like those speculated upon in the papers of William Crookes.

It had rows of claws, and along the center of its body a pattern of openings through which a ruddy glow was visible.

Bringing itself parallel with the path of the bridge, it whirred and buzzed toward the travelers. Small black objects dropped from it, falling from the orifices in its torso. As each of them struck the bridge it exploded like a grenade.

The creature swept past, screaming its malice.

It swung in a broad curve, disappeared into the mist, then reappeared ahead of the travelers and far off to one side. Again it swept toward them, but this time as it completed its approach it did not pass overhead. Instead it reared in the air like an angry stallion. Clive could see the fires of hell burning inside the thing.

Finnbogg launched himself into the air.

The bulldog of a man and the monstrous flying thing collided with a single deafening crash, then fell back to the icy bridge with a second and louder impact that shook the very basalt.

Grappling like wrestlers, they struggled, sliding

forward and back, left and right, approaching within a fraction of an inch of their mutual doom, then struggling together, back toward the relative safety of the center of the pathway.

With a final grinding, wrenching, crunching paroxysm. Finnbogg tore the attacker in half. Finnbogg held the two pieces of the thing in the air. From within the halves ugly liquids poured, purple and lavender and magenta, that sizzled and then sublimed away into pungent gas when they hit the ice on the bridge.

Finnbogg plucked a segment of the thing and sampled it with his fangs. He growled and spit it out. "Bad meat, bad, bad, not taste nice, poor Finnbogg, bad thing, bad, bad, bad."

"Is it—was it alive, Finnbogg?" Folliot peered at the broken remnants, trying to understand what it was that he beheld. "Is it a natural beast or a mechanical contrivance? I thought it was a beast, but—"

He frowned, picked at some of the smaller fragments that had fallen to the icy roadway. They seemed of artificial composition, bits of metal or pottery or glass, certainly not the product of organic nature but of applied intelligence.

"Bad alive," Finnbogg growled. "Bad alive, make-uh—uh—more parts. More parts for bad alive. Not good to eat, not good to play, never tell Finnbogg story, not nice."

Quartermaster Sergeant Horace Hamilton Smythe joined Folliot in examining the fragments. "P'raps the major might wish to arsk, ah, Mr. Finnbogg if that was a servant of the Q'oornans. Seems to me they're a very odd lot, those Q'oornans. Hardly had time to talk wiv 'em back in their city, but I don't quite gavver as how they had the likes of this thing to send out to do their bidding. Doesn't the major agree, sah, if I might make so bold, sah!'

Clive half-expected the man to brace to attention and snap off a brisk salute, but he merely waited expectantly.

"Good point," Clive conceded. To Finnbogg he said, "Was that—bad thing—Q'oornan? Did the people who set you to watch the bridge send that thing after us, do you think?"

Finnbogg stood still, slowly shaking his shaggy head. Finally he said, "No, no Q'oornan. No, no. Q'oornans bad, sky thing bad. Bad, bad. Two bad, not one bad, not same bad, bad, bad. No, no." He swung his head mournfully.

Sergeant Smythe was meticulously picking through the remnants of the defeated attacker, confidentially exchanging low words with Sidi Bombay. The sergeant looked up at Clive. "Some very nice workmanship here, sah. If that's the right word for it. Har!" He grinned at his own joke.

"What do you mean, Smythe? What's the point?"

"Bit of salvage, sah. Look here, sah." He was carefully removing dozens of black pellets from the remnants of the attacker. "These little beauties seem to explode on impact. Could use 'em as bombs if we had to, doesn't the major agree? And look here, sah."

He had managed to separate one of the creature's claws. It was an odd contrivance of horny matter and metal, with a complex arrangement of hinges and gears in it.

"Don't even know what this might be good for, sah, but it looks as if it could be some sort of universal tool." He lunged with the thing, raked it across an imaginary opponent. The claw snapped viciously at the air. "Have to be mighty careful with this thing, sah; it looks as if it might turn on you, don't you know. But it might make a very nice weapon, don't you see."

He proceeded to remove and distribute undamaged claws to Clive, Sidi Bombay, and User Annie. Annie held the claw before her face, ran her hands over it, and nodded happily. "Eyedee protocol complete, cybroid device, Io linkage interrupted. *Hah!*" Her single burst of laughter was like a tinkling bell.

Horace Hamilton Smythe slipped one into a pocket of his tattered khaki garb. When he held one toward Finnbogg, the latter accepted it graciously, crunched it between his teeth, and threw it away. "Not taste nice," he growled. "Bad, bad." He snuffled and started forward again.

Soon they reached the peak of the bridge.

Clive stood at the apex, peering slowly in a full circle.

It was both the most magnificent and the most terrible sight he had ever experienced.

At last they had climbed above the level of the mist that rose from the gorge. Directly beneath the party, the mist floated like a thick London fog. It spread up and down the gorge, so that a seeming river of fog flowed to the travelers' left and right, winding and twisting away to the limit of sight in both directions.

But ahead and behind, the mist dissipated and the Q'oornan landscape stretched majestically as Roman Pluto's stygian realm. Black ground, smooth and rolling, stretched mile after miles. Here and there a stand of vegetation, recognizable by its brushy, irregular shape and mottled texture, but as black as the ground upon which it stood and the sky that towered above.

And at greater distances, scattered irregularly, clusters of gleaming diamond-white and diamond-brilliant lights. Lights that must mark cities.

And in those cities—what? There was no way of knowing, short of making their way to the far end of the bridge and then crossing the plain to investigate.

Clive felt a warm presence and looked down to find User Annie holding his arm. Her head was pressed against his shoulder. Obviously her Baalbec A-9 electrofield was shut off, for he felt no shock of galvanic fluid—only that of the press of female flesh.

"Little Annie," he murmured, "strange creature out of time. Do you understand this world? Do you understand Clive Folliot? Will I ever achieve the vaguest inkling of your world and of you?"

She looked up at him, and in her eyes he saw something both strange and comforting, both alien and familiar. What did he see? He shook his head in bafflement.

"Opsys malfunction?" Annie asked softly. "Error analysis program loaded? Debugging in process? Ah, User Clive, motherboard plug-in components, ah."

Clive thought he saw a tear on her cheek. In the strange half-illumination that was as close as Q'oorna ever came to daylight, a tiny spark glowed within the tear. But surely that was an oddity of their locale, a reflection of some immensely distant star.

"Aiee! Save me 'ere Vishnu strikes!" Perhaps it was the heat of Sidi Bombay's naked feet that had melted a thin layer of ice and caused him to lose his footing. Sidi Bombay fell to the black bridge and started to slide toward the brink. They had descended from the topmost peak of the span, and once within the milky mist the bridge was again slippery with ice.

Finnbogg growled and launched himself toward Sidi Bombay. At the same time that gaunt individual pulled the claw from within his tattered robe and punched its needlelike tip into the ice. It held, and he grasped it desperately with both hands, his body swinging in a circle around it until he dangled desperately over the edge of the chasm, flailing his limbs and crying for help.

Finnbogg extended a pawlike hand and grasped Sidi Bombay's wrist. The massive, doglike dwarf pulled the skeletal figure back over the edge of bridge. Sidi Bombay clung to Finnbogg, uttering soft moans and touching his forehead over and over against the muscular torso of his savior.

"Bad," Finnbogg intoned solemnly. "Sidi Bombay man fall, go away. Ah, ah, all break Sidi Bombay, no. Come Finnbogg, Sidi Bombay." Amazingly, Finnbogg lifted Sidi Bombay in one hand and cuddled him against his massive, bulldog chest.

"Others, come. Tempoids, come Finnbogg." He gestured over his shoulder.

Making a basket of his tree-trunk arms, Finnbogg lifted Clive and Annie and Horace Hamilton Smythe. There was hardly room for them, but the massive creature's thick bones and mighty muscles bore their weight as if they were dolls.

Finnbogg set a steady, rolling pace, the clawlike nails on his toes providing firm purchase on the ice-covered basalt. The powerful voice boomed out chorus after chorus of hymns, music hall tunes, and every so often a stirring reprise of "God Save the Queen."

Clive scanned the sky above them. The deeper they penetrated into the mist, the less visibility remained. That meant they could not see their potential attackers, but the handicap was mutual, and no more aerial creatures appeared.

But a slithering sound could be heard. Clive peered down at the bridge itself. Finnbogg's plodding limbs moved rhythmically, soothingly. It would be easy to yield to their soporific effect and doze, but the unexplained sound kept Folliot alert.

He thought he saw the flicker of a death-white *something* at the edge of the pathway. The motion of anything white in this black Hades was itself strangely shocking, but there it was. It appeared again, flickering over the edge of the basalt, waving about for a brief moment, then disappearing again.

Without other warning, the entire bridge shook.

Finnbogg emitted a startled grunt and halted, digging in the claws of his extremities to steady himself. He waited for a few seconds, then started forward again.

Again the bridge shuddered.

Clive peered at the edges of the roadway. Perhaps the white feelers were connected with the shaking. They had to belong to some creature that clung to the lower surface of the bridge just as Finnbogg was clinging to its upper.

Again Finnbogg started forward, but by now the vibration had grown into a steady, pulsing beat. *Thud-thud-thud,* and with each repetition of the sound the bridge shook.

"Put down little friends," Finnbogg grunted. He halted and shook himself as Clive and the others climbed from his arms and stood cautiously on the basalt, by now merely wet and slippery rather than coated with ice.

The massive dwarf Finnbogg planted himself in the center of the bridge.

Peering around him, Clive saw the source of the shaking. It was advancing, slow stride by stride. Silhouetted against the newest arrival, Finnbogg was converted, suddenly, into a pitiable midget.

· FOUR ·
MORE WORLDS
THAN THESE

▪ CHAPTER 16 ▪
"Damn You, Clive Folliot!"

The tentacles belonged to this thing, Clive Folliot realized. They were long, whiplike organs with which it felt its way along. It was a horror that consumed everything in its path.

In its totality it was like nothing Clive had ever laid eyes on. But in its separate parts it was familiar to him, and that made it all the more horrid.

It slithered forward on its tentacles. They were countless, some fat, some thin, the longest of them hardly less long than a polo field. Above the tentacles came its astonishing hulk of a torso. It was as thick as a great tree. It was totally covered with protruding organs. Suckers, feelers, mouths, mandibles, and claws. It was like a titanic war machine—but one that was the product of some mad, satanic deity. No human designer of munitions could ever have conceived this horror.

So huge was the thing that the upper end of its trunk faded into the layer of mist that engulfed and towered over the bridge. Clive peered at the monstrosity like a country bumpkin gawking at the Nelson Monument in Trafalgar Square. The upper end of the monster's trunk supported a second ring of tentacles that hung from it like the cape of an elegant matron arriving at a charity ball. Farther yet, hidden both by the upper ring of tentacles and by the thickening mist, must be the creature's head.

A slender tentacle slithered from beneath the basalt roadway and moved tentatively toward the travelers. Clive watched fascinated as it felt its way, rising and falling, feeling to the left and then to the right, like an independent being, a pitiable and yet deadly menacing blind creature trying to find its way.

It touched User Annie's ankle. She screamed and cowered away from it. Clive wondered whether she had switched on her Baalbec A-9. Had she forgotten her defensive electrofield, or was its jarring effect too tiny to bother the monster?

The tentacle rose and wove blindly to and fro. Another tentacle rose from the other side of the basalt and wavered toward the first. Sergeant Smythe stood between the two. With perfect coordination they moved to entrap him, wrapping themselves around his waist.

More quickly than the eye could follow, Smythe raised the half-mechanical claw he had taken from the aerial cybroid. As if his arm and the claw were a single organic whole, he attacked the tentacles that had wrapped themselves around him. The edge of the claw was miraculously sharp, and Smythe wielded it with astonishing skill.

Almost from the first moment the tentacles writhed and danced.

Smythe was spun around like a dervish.

A tentacle withdrew from his body and snapped like a whip a fraction of an inch from his face. Smythe grinned a grin that Clive Folliot had seen on Smythe's face more than once before, in the heat of battle. His expression was that of the berserker. His manner was that of the surgeon: cold and efficient and determined to perform his bloody but necessary task.

Smythe slashed the tentacles to ribbons, then with even more astonishing speed and skill he grasped the frazzled ends and wove them together in a sailor's knot.

From above them in the mist where its head was hidden from view the monster gave a howl like a thousand damned souls in one.

Sidi Bombay stood nearby, his own claw at the ready. With his empty hand he gestured to Horace Hamilton Smythe.

Sergeant Smythe nodded and tossed his claw to the Indian. "Go to it, old friend. Show this thing your special talent!"

User Annie had come to stand beside Clive Folliot. He placed his arm around her shoulders and held her. Fascinated, they watched Sidi Bombay.

The gaunt man held a cybroid claw in each hand. Using them like mountaineer's pitons, he scrambled up the thicket of tentacles that writhed and snapped in the cold mist.

Finnbogg, in the meantime, had reverted to his apparent ancestry. He seized a cluster of tentacles in his powerful underslung jaw and set his four limbs firmly against the surface of the bridge. He tugged furiously at the tentacles, all the while clamping down with his incomparable jaw muscles and grinding with his terrible fangs.

Above the roadway, Sidi Bombay was scrambling like a crazed mountaineer. The sight was truly incredible. He would swing a cybroid claw upward, plunging it into the writhing mass of tentacles, holding himself in place with his other hand and his bare feet, then swing the second claw upward, moving his feet as well until he had raised himself the length of his body. How he managed to keep his purchase in the jungle of slimy, squirming tentacles was a mystery to Clive.

In front of Clive and Annie, Finnbogg kept up his attack on the monster's lower tentacles. A writhing mass tore away from the creature, followed by a steaming gush of hot, stinking fluid. Wherever it struck on the basalt it formed into glittering puddles that steamed and sizzled and bubbled as they sublimed into a searing gas and drifted away into the blackness.

Sidi Bombay had disappeared into the mist overhead. The sounds of the creature were louder now.

A violent thrumming, something somewhere between the massed hoofbeats of a great, malevolent herd and the rumbling of a terrible landslide.

The monstrosity began to sway back and forth.

A nest of twisting tentacles seized Sergeant Smythe again, and this time he had no weapon to use against them. Frantically, with his bare hands alone, he attacked the imprisoning strands.

They coiled upward, lifting Smythe bodily into the air. Before Clive's and Annie's horrified eyes the sergeant was passed from tentacular cluster to cluster. His shouts echoed back to them but they were incomprehensible. The path that he followed was circuitous, moving him around the creature at the same time as it tended ever upward, toward the gigantic torso covered with its organs of terror and destruction.

Mighty Finnbogg had worked his way partially into the clustering tentacles. Only half of the canoid creature was visible. From within a curtain of tentacles could be heard his growls and the snapping of razorlike fangs against rubbery organs.

Until this moment Clive had been frozen in place by the horror and fascination of the sight. He shook himself and then he saw that Annie had joined the fray. Armed with a cyboid claw, cursing his failure to act more promptly, he ran to assist Finnbogg.

Clive grasped a rubbery tentacle and began hacking at it with the claw. He could see User Annie doing the same.

Without instruction in the use of the claw, still Clive felt a sudden surge of confidence. The weapon was so perfectly designed that it took no lessons but merely a will to make use of it. He cut away the first tentacle he had seized and reached for another.

He could see Finnbogg's hindquarters. The fearless but slow-witted Finnbogg had belatedly realized his peril. Struggling and fighting his way ever deeper into the nest of tentacles, he now ran the risk of becoming trapped, unable to withdraw.

Then, like a tree before the axman, the giant creature toppled toward the surface of the bridge. Slowly at first, it leaned away from the companions. Its thousands of chelae, tentacles, and feelers beat the air, setting up a clattering and whirring that sounded like a hurricane crossing the tropical jungle of an ocean isle. The atmosphere itself was whipped into a froth of mist and spume and human sweat and the stinking, sticky excretions of the wounded monstrosity.

The pounding and thrumming and grinding of the creature's internal organs grew louder.

Its voice rose, howling as if it would echo from the farthest nebulae.

It crashed against the roadway, rebounded once, and landed again, lying the long way and covering the entire width of the path. Its tentacles writhed and its chellae waved painfully in the blackness. It emitted noise like a moan of pain and despair.

A rumble sounded, and a creaking.

The bridge itself shifted.

Clive could see the base of the monstrosity. It was nearly round. Most of it was made up of a transparent membrane. The membrane was surrounded by a row of frantically writhing tentacles. Through the transparent membrane he could see partway into the thing's innards. He saw horrible things there, entire creatures, humans and aliens alike, swallowed whole and floating in a heavy, viscous liquid. Some of them were mere skeletons, others were still fleshy, and still others, most horrifying of all, were apparently still alive, waving their arms and legs, struggling feebly against their unavoidable fate.

Swimming lazily among the bodies were miniature replicas of the great monster. One or another would stop and extend a proboscis to pierce a human or an alien being. As Clive watched in helpless horror, the victim would shrivel while the feasting monstrosity swelled.

Now User Annie moved out of Clive's grasp. She reached inside her bodice at last and moved her hand. Folliot could see that she was switching on her electrofield.

She held a cybroid claw. She ran toward the transparent membrane, the claw extended in front of her.

Clive thought she was going to saw through the membrane in a heroic but futile attempt to save the captives floating inside the monstrosity. He shouted and ran after her. The creature's earlier victims were beyond saving. She would only free the creature's young, free them and then face their renewed attack.

Annie reached the membrane before Clive could overtake her. She attacked it, using the cybroid claw. But whatever her intention, the effect of the electrofield on the creature was far greater than that of the claw alone could possibly have been.

Every tentacle, pod, feeler, and cilium of the monster spasmed.

The howling voice rose to a pitch and volume beyond even that of any earlier moment in the battle.

The entire creature slithered and whirled as if it were a pair of spokes on a wagon wheel.

Annie and Clive were both swept backward, barely avoiding being swept from the surface of the bridge into the misty chasm below.

The monstrosity revolved through a full 180 degrees, so that its hitherto unseen upper end roared past Clive and Annie.

As the monster's end drew into sight, Clive had a horrifying premonition of what he was going to see. The upper collar of tentacles was still spasmed outward like an Elizabethan ruff, only they twitched and clutched at nothing as they approached.

They swept past Clive and Annie with an awful stench and spray of disgusting fluids.

Then the head appeared, a head fully twelve feet in height and four to five feet in width.

It had dark hair the color of Clive's and a military officer's sun-darkened skin the color of Clive's. The eyebrows and mustache resembled his also, but the mustache had been trimmed in a different style.

The lips were drawn back in a snarl to show teeth as large as rugby balls. The eyes were wide with terror and with rage. The mouth opened to speak, but before a sound emerged the face was gone.

It was a face that Clive recognized.

The great monstrosity tumbled over the basalt edge of the arching bridge. As it disappeared into the mist and the depths of the chasm it turned slowly, end over end. Its great voice roared with a timbre Clive found all too familiar.

"Clive Folliot," it boomed and echoed. "Damn you, Clive Folliot! Damn you to the nethermost pits of hell! Damn you to spend eternity in the Dungeon!"

Behind Clive and Annie the bridge creaked and shuddered. Ahead of them it did the same. Cracks appeared in its surface.

Annie's hand was inside her bodice. She turned off the Baalbec A-9. "Exit program," she shouted at Clive. "Log off! Crash system!" She grasped his hand and started to run.

It took him no time to realize that she was right. The bridge was crumbling, its delicate structure fatally damaged by the impact of the monstrosity's tons of mass. The only hope for the survivors of the encounter was to reach the other end of the bridge before it crumbled altogether into the crevasse.

Time and again they slipped in the greasy excretions that the monstrosity had left behind. In a while they gave up trying to rise and run, and simply slid along, like tobogganers on a slope, shifting their weight as best they could to keep to the center of the roadway and avoid its dangerous edges.

They came to Finnbogg, contentedly swallowing the last of a cluster of the creature's tentacles that he had chewed away. He saw them whiz toward him, decided that their form of locomotion was fun, and joined them.

Almost at the end of the bridge, they came across Horace Hamilton Smythe. He had been thrown there by the first great convulsion that had swept the creature when it was prodded by Annie's electrofield.

There was no sign of Sidi Bombay.

"I'll pray for his soul," Clive mumbled.

"Wun't advise that, sah," Smythe amended. He sat up, then let the others help him to his feet.

Clive snapped alert. "Just because the fellow had black skin, Sergeant Smythe, and worshipped in a funny kind of building not a proper church, doesn't mean he was not a child of God all the same."

"Don't doubt a word, sah, not a word. Still wun't pray for Sidi Bombay's soul yet, no sah. I've seen Sidi Bombay through more perils than this. I'd wager a pay packet we haven't seen the last of Sidi Bombay, sah, not by a long shot."

"I'll take your bet, then, Sergeant." Clive Folliot grinned. "And for once in my life I hope I lose my bet!"

"Sidi Bombay's a good chap, Major." Smythe bobbed his head up and down.

"But whom did he serve, Smythe?" Clive's momentary giddiness at their escape was fading now, replaced by more serious thoughts. "It was he who brought us into this terrible place. He appeared so conveniently with that barge as we entered the Sudd. And since then—well, I don't mean to lend credence to the legend of the inscrutable Oriental, Sergeant, but I'd give a pretty penny to know what Sidi Bombay was really up to.'

Smythe rubbed the back of his head. "I don't rightly know what to say, Major. But I'd trust old Sidi with my life, I would. I've done so often enough, over the years, and he's never let me down. I do expect we'll see him again, sah. And when we do, I 'spect old Sidi will acquit himself as nobly as ever he has."

To set up their camp they had found a relatively sheltered spot and settled in. There were no tents, there was no bedding, there were no real implements. The terrain on this side of the chasm was more varied than in the region around the city of Q'oorna. It was a region of rolling hills, grassy slopes, and wooded vales. Everything was black, as had been the case since their arrival on the planet. Clive found that his body was beginning to demand nourishment and sleep again. To this point it had run on its own resources, thanks to some mechanism developed, perhaps, in ancient times when primitive men had had to exert themselves for long periods without food or rest.

Finnbogg had proved invaluable to the party. With his immense strength and stamina he had carried the others when they were too weary to walk. It was a sight like that of an ant carrying a breadcrumb many times its own size.

They had settled on a location for their camp some miles from the end of the bridge. Despite their soreness and weariness, none of them wanted to remain anywhere near the site of the horror they had experienced. Finnbogg had left Annie and Smythe and Clive Folliot and tramped willingly away. He returned with brushwood for a fire and with berries and a few wild vegetables that he urged them, in his doggish, enthusiastic way, to sample.

While they tested the food reluctantly—coal-black berries and apples and potatoes, or rough analogues of those foods, were difficult to accept—the dwarfish Finnbogg built a fire of twigs and branches. He started the fire by using the ancient method of rubbing twigs together, an operation that would have tried the patience of any of the others, but which he pursued stolidly until he had succeeded.

The fire burned with a pure white flame. Thin smoke rose above the circle of branches. Clive knew that they should plot their strategy, combine their poor knowledge and limited intelligence and decide what to do now that they had lost Sidi Bombay—and now that they themselves were apparently lost in this strange world.

But he was too weary, and the food had settled

comfortingly in his belly, and User Annie was humming some melody from her own era a hundred and more years in Clive's future. Oddly, it was a familiar tune, a melody by one of the Italian composers of the eighteenth century.

Clive smiled. Perhaps something decent and worthwhile had persisted in the world, despite every effort by men to demean and destroy the good.

He lay back, and Annie lay beside him.

He had neither paper nor pen with him, so he composed a story for Maurice Carstairs in his mind. Perhaps if he thought it through vividly enough, the telepathic emanations would reach George du Maurier, and du Maurier would transcribe them for Carstairs's paper. Folliot laughed at the thought, and felt Annie stir at the sound. She had fallen asleep leaning against him, and he could feel her breath, soft and warm, on the side of his neck.

Special and exclusive to the readers of The Recorder and Dispatch. *Dateline Q'oorna. Your correspondent this day encountered a creature at least a hundred feet in height, equipped with tentacles and feelers, with a transparent window in its underside and a piteous sight within. The creature had the face of your correspondent's elder brother and it spoke with a human voice amplified ten thousandfold.*

He rehearsed the details of the battle in his mind, conjuring up an image of the great creature that might be reproduced on the front page of *The Recorder and Dispatch*. That would sell copies by the wagonload. And when Clive returned to England and wrote his book, he would outshine Burton and Darwin and the rest of them combined!

Somehow the pleasant prospect of best-sellerdom, with its attendant invitations to the lecture tour and the wealth that must inevitably accompany such success, became mixed with a repetition of the monstrosity's last words:

"Damn you, Clive Folliot! Damn you to the nethermost pits of hell! Damn you to spend eternity in the Dungeon!"

His brother. His own brother, Neville Folliot. They had never been close, had never even been friends. But what could Clive have done to evoke such hatred in his only sibling?

And—how had Neville become transformed into the hideous giant who had tumbled from the bridge? *Had* Neville been the giant? It had Neville's face, it spoke with Neville's voice, and it addressed him, Clive, by name.

But . . . was it Neville?

Sweet dreams turned into nightmares that ended only with the arrival of Q'oorna's pallid and depressing dawn.

Finnbogg managed to catch a string of fish in the stream. It was startling to see the dead-black creatures. Sergeant Smythe took charge of building up their campfire, and they roasted the fish on sticks. To take a first taste of the still-steaming black meat was a challenge, but the texture and flavor were excellent and they made a satisfying meal of Finnbogg's catch.

Then they had to decide on their plan of action. There was no turning back to the City of Q'oorna— the chasm they had crossed was bottomless, and the bridge was gone.

They could wander the countryside or they could make permanent camp where they had already made a temporary one. But there was no point to either of those courses of action.

They could set out for a goal—possibly one of the cities they had seen rising from the black landscape when they had stood atop the arching bridge. That course alone promised to bring them out of Q'oorna —or bring them an understanding of what they were doing in this black world.

In the midst of the debate Clive Folliot confronted Horace Hamilton Smythe. This questioning was long overdue, but until now there had been no opportunity to conduct it. They had been engaged in one absorbing activity or another, whether in the flat-bottomed boat crossing the Bahr-el-Zeraf, finding the casket of Neville Folliot, creeping down the Cliff of the Face, exploring the deserted City of Q'oorna, or crossing the bridge with Finnbogg. There had been a partial exchange on the subject of Sidi Bombay's disappearance, but Clive was by no means satisfied.

The time had come for deeper probing.

"You're part of this," Clive accused. "You and Sidi Bombay both, I suspect. But you *have* to be part of it, Smythe."

"Part of what, sah?" Smythe's expression was ingenuous.

"You're in with the Q'oornans. The priest in Bagomoyo probably was as well, now that I think of it. They are responsible for whatever it is that happened to Neville. They kidnapped me and they seem to have kidnapped Miss Annie here from the future itself."

He gestured toward Annie. She sat on the ground, listening intently to the dialogue. How much of it did she comprehend? Any at all? Clive wondered. Beyond her, Finnbogg lay stretched on the ground. Annie ran her fingernails through his hair. The dwarfish, doglike being sighed contentedly.

"They brought Finnbogg here, too, poor creature. And heaven knows how many others. The tempoids, the extroids, the cyboids that we saw imprisoned in the Dungeon. How many nations do they come from? How many worlds? How many eras?"

"You think I can answer all that, sah?" Sergeant Smythe grinned beneath his bushy mustache. "I'm a plain quartermaster, sah. A glorified supplies clerk, a military greengrocer. I don't know nothing about different worlds and cyber-whatevers and tempo-whodoyoucallems, sah. The major flatters me too much."

Clive half-expected Horace Hamilton Smythe to stand up and knock the dottle from a pipe and wrap a scarf around his face and head into the English night. It was the kind of performance he'd have given in a friendly pub after a long night over a series of pints of beer and a few tasty scones.

The black sky with its smears of milky nebulae and sparkling points of stars, the campfire that burned brightly, added to the illusion that they were in some setting far more prosaic than Q'oorna.

Smythe was so matter-of-fact, so perfect an example of the good, solid, steady Englishman, that Clive was nearly lulled into accepting his denials. But there was simply too much evidence to the contrary. There were simply too many unexplained aspects of Smythe's behavior.

"All right," Clive said. "You deny that you were the piano-playing mandarin aboard *Empress Philippa*? That you posed as an Arab guardsman at the palace of the sultan of Zanzibar?"

Smythe hesitated too long before he gave an answer.

"Your silence convicts you," Folliot accused. He pointed a finger angrily at Smythe.

"Well now, sah. It ain't exactly that I have to deny all that, sah," Smythe finally responded. "But I don't exactly admit it, neither."

"Oh, come along, man! We've known each other too long and too well for this sort of gaming. Own up, and let's lay our cards on the table. I've been totally open from the outset as to why I'm here. But you've never so much as given a reason."

Smythe was squirming now. In all the years Clive had known him, he'd never seen the sergeant so nonplussed. He decided that this was the moment to strike.

"We'll put that all aside for now," Clive stated. "I'll not forget it, and a time will come for accounting. Rest assured of that, Sergeant. But for now, I'll drop the subject if you will just answer me one question. Answer openly, honestly, fully. Will you do that, Sergeant, and then we'll be on our way? Will you do it?"

The Smythe whom Clive Folliot thought he knew

so well would have answered with a straightforward yes or no. But *this* Sergeant Smythe said, "Depends on the question, sah. It really does. Whyn't you try me, sah?"

Folliot almost spat the words. "What is the meaning of the spiral formation of stars that I saw on the grip of your revolver?"

▪ CHAPTER 17 ▪
A Ride on a Riverboat

Horace Hamilton Smythe laughed and rose to his feet. He took the few steps that brought him to the campfire and set himself to kicking it out. "Lord love you, Major Folliot! I never 'spected you were so wrought up over that. Bless me, let's get on our way, and I'll tell you the story as we march."

He shook his head in bemusement. " 'Pon my word, if that's the only thing botherin' the major, he's a lucky man indeed!"

"Local grid bearing due east," User Annie suddenly said.

Clive thought—not for the first time—that she lived on a different plane from the rest of them. Her thoughts were not their thoughts. And her perceptions of their surroundings must, in some utterly incomprehensible way, differ vastly from their own.

"Will that bring us to one of the cities we saw?" Clive asked her. "Preferably the nearest of them?"

Annie looked into his face, and for a fleeting instant it was as if Annabella Leighton were looking into his face. A wave of unbearable melancholia swept over Clive. He turned violently away from the woman.

Annie said, "Pozzi. Firm. Double tiff, User Clive."

"How do you know that?"

Annie reached inside her bodice and made the familiar motion that Clive knew involved her Baalbec A-9. She knelt on the black ground and pointed a long, slim finger at a smooth patch.

A map appeared on the ground, its lines glowing

brightly. Annie pointed to the brightest spot on the map and announced, "Absolute address user file." She laughed.

The sound wrenched at Folliot's heart. It was so much like the laughter of Miss Leighton. So much . . .

"Can your electrofield make maps anywhere, Miss Annie?"

Folliot was dropping into the mode of address he would have used in proper English society.

"Nega tiff. Baalbec A-nine alt function, topographic scan and visual readout, user."

Clive did not even pretend to comprehend that. His face must have conveyed his bafflement, for Annie offered a further explanation—a rarity for her.

"Will try nontech argot." She wrinkled her forehead in concentration. "Okay, I can make a map. Right on, bitchin' bad map. We ain't lost, we're right here, it's Mommy and Daddy got lost. You comprende usted, honcho?"

Clive did understand this much: User Annie's hidden machine could produce a map of the region of Q'oorna where they found themselves. What they would find when they reached the nearest city might be their doom as well as their salvation. It might be a new mystery as easily as the solution of the puzzles they already faced.

For better or for worse, they could choose their path. To an extent, at least, they could control their own destiny. " 'Men at some times,' " he quoted Cassius, " 'are masters of their fates.' " And Clive Folliot and Horace Hamilton Smythe and User Annie and squat, massive Finnbogg might make this such a time!

They set out together.

Clive studied the sky. "I wonder," he muttered, "is the North Star visible from Q'oorna? Since we shall never see true daylight here, we need some guide. Unless—Miss Annie—Baalbec A-nine can serve as a compass."

"Compass," Annie repeated. Her face clouded in

concentration. "Ah, grid orientation indicator. Tiff, tiff."

But did she mean *pozzi tiff* or *nega tiff?* Clive wondered.

She ran to the nearest stand of vegetation and returned with a broad, dead-black leaf in her hand. She held it carefully while she pointed her finger at it. The grid map she had shown them on the ground near the campfire appeared on the leaf. She held her finger above it for a while, then reached into her bodice to turn off Baalbec A-9.

The map remained on the leaf, white lines not so much imprinted on the black surface as glowing from within it. The glowing spot that represented the party of travelers—perhaps, Clive speculated, Baalbec A-9 itself—pulsed at them like a beating heart.

User Annie presented the map to Sergeant Smythe. Possibly she realized that he was a military man with long experience in maps and cross-country tracking. Certainly Clive Folliot was a rank amateur, and Annie herself with her urban background would be unaccustomed to traveling in the wild.

Finnbogg seemed cheerful today. He alternately plodded along beside the others or trotted off to investigate some intriguing scent or sound that they did not even detect. His canine nature was apparently becoming dominant over the human side of his being. Perhaps the two alternated, or perhaps it was the exposure to the countryside that was bringing about the change.

The dwarfish creature had taken a particular liking to User Annie. He would run to her side, nuzzle her with his heavy face and terrible fangs until she scratched his bristly skull. Then he would wriggle with pleasure and run off.

It was hard to tell the time, but after they had marched for an estimated two hours, Clive called a rest. They were in a clear area, the land relatively flat, a row of soft, wooded hills to their right, a level plain to their left.

Finnbogg sat on his heels, again as much doglike as manlike. He gazed at the sky, his bulldog face a melancholy mask. User Annie sat beside him, her arm around his heavily muscled shoulders.

The dwarf made a mournful snuffling sound.

Clive came and squatted before Finnbogg. "What's the matter, old fellow?" he asked. He could not decide whether to treat the creature as a man or as a beast—or as a child.

Finnbogg muttered in his throat.

Folliot shook his head. "What's that? Couldn't quite make it out, old boy. What say there, my good Finnbogg?"

The creature moved his head slightly, cocking it to one side. The gesture made him look more than ever like a giant mastiff. "Finnbogg pups, ooh, ooh, tempoid. Boypups, girlpups. Sire and dam. Ooh, Finnbogg want home. Ooh, home, home, home."

Clive patted him on the shoulder. "You want your home, eh? Can't blame you a bit, Finnbogg. Who wouldn't, eh?"

"'Tain't quite that simple, I don't think, Major, sah." Sergeant Horace Hamilton Smythe had joined the circle around Finnbogg.

"What do you mean, Sergeant?"

"I think the fellow's trying to tell us more than that he's homesick. Why, every raw recruit cries for his ma'am and his little trundle bed the first night. But brother Finnbogg here, why, he's been away from the family hearth a mighty long time, I warrant."

"Have you, Finnbogg? You weren't born on Q'oorna, were you? Who brought you here? How long ago, eh? How long have you been here? And—where *is* your home?"

Finnbogg raised a massive limb. It might have been a canine's paw, modified by some mad surgeon to simulate the hand of a man. "Finnbogg home," he wailed. He pointed his pad-and-claw-tipped finger at the sky, indicating a bright star. "Finnbogg home," he repeated. "Boypups and girlpups, sire and dam. Oh, oh, Finnbogg wants to go home."

"When did they bring you to Q'oorna, Finnbogg? How long have you been on this world?" Even as he asked the question, Folliot realized that Finnbogg would probably be unable to answer it.

Everywhere that Clive Folliot had traveled, whether in England or Europe or Africa, there had been a common experience of time. Even to people without calendars and clocks there was the daily turning of day and night, there was the slower turning of the seasons. Hours and weeks and months were human concepts, human inventions. But days and years were part of the natural order, and everyone understood them because everyone experienced them. Everyone on Earth.

But the mystical du Maurier, with his interest in interplanetary communication, had made a study of Mars and Venus, Jupiter and Saturn and Mercury. He had lectured Folliot to the point of boredom on the subject. Folliot's boredom, that was—not du Maurier's; the cartoonist could have gone on endlessly on the subject, or so it had seemed to Clive.

Du Maurier had said that the length of the day and of the year varied on all the worlds. Was the year of Mars not twice as long as that of Earth? And that of tiny Mercury far shorter? Finnbogg might answer, but what would his answer mean?

"Oh, many years," Finnbogg moaned. "Many, many years."

"How many years?" Clive persisted—but he wondered, now, if even the concept of numbers had meaning for the creature. He'd seen horses trained to count, although some skeptics insisted that the alleged mathematical skill was really just a conditioned response to a cleverly planned cue. Could dogs count? Was Finnbogg really a dog?

Clive Folliot's head whirled.

"Ten thousand years," Finnbogg moaned.

Clive stared and saw tears actually coursing down

Finnbogg's bristly cheeks. Ten thousand years? Surely the creature could not understand what he was saying. Perhaps this was simply his way of saying he'd been on Q'oorna for a long time—longer than he could express, or even recall.

Or maybe he had truly been on Q'oorna for ten thousand years.

"Annie home," Finnbogg was saying now. He kept his face pointed skyward, while with his paw-hand he indicated a star nowhere near the one he claimed as his own home.

"Annie home," Finnbogg repeated. Then he added, "Clive home, Horace home, Sidi Bombay home." All the while he pointed at the same glittering object. Perhaps he knew what he was talking about.

"Could that be?" Clive asked. "Does Q'oorna in truth circle a sun other than our own?"

User Annie looked surprised that he even asked. "Bubble failure, anthro? Not our sun. Not other sun. Dual negation. No sun. Q'oorna has no sun."

She was right, of course. Somehow the mental habit of a lifetime had persisted in Clive's outlook. He knew that Q'oorna had no sun of its own, else the planet's "day" would have revealed it. "And you believe that is truly our own sun? That tiny star to which Finnbogg is pointing?"

Annie nodded.

Clive was struck by an idea. "Can your, ah, Baalbec A-nine make a map of the sky, Miss Annie, as it does of the planet's surface?"

She nodded affirmatively.

"Please, then. As quickly as you can."

Annie obtained another, larger leaf. "Input Q'oorna," she muttered, her hand invisible as she manipulated the hidden controls of her wonderful mechanism. "Input Q'oorna, input Earth, input Finnbogg's world."

She looked at Clive. "Potential temporal displacement indicator available."

Clive said, "Pardon me, Miss Annie. I have no idea what you mean."

She smiled, and he would have given a kingdom to fathom the subtleties and complexities that underlay that simple expression. "My Baalbec can map time routes as well as space. If I want it to. But for now—run complete." She pointed at the black leaf. At first nothing happened, then gradually a chart of the heavens began to appear.

Folliot took Finnbogg by the elbow and directed his attention to the map. "Can you understand this, Finnbogg? Do you see?" He pointed at the heavens, then at the map. "This is a picture of the sky. You see?"

He pointed at the star that Finnbogg had claimed as home, then at the map. "You see, they are the same. The real star. The picture. Do you understand?"

Finnbogg looked between the map and the heavens. Slowly comprehension dawned in his eyes. "Finnbogg home." He pointed at the map, then at the sky. "Girlpups, boypups. Finnbogg want his home."

"Yes." Folliot nodded. "We all want our homes, don't we?" He cast a glance at Sergeant Smythe. "At least, I think we all do."

They had stopped their forward progress. Clive got them started again. As soon as they were under way, he asked Finnbogg if he could remember how he had come to Q'oorna.

The massive being shook his head lugubriously. "Finnbogg boypup. Ah, Folliot, long time ago. Ten thousand years ago, right, Folliot?" He grinned at Clive even though the paths of tears glistened on his bristly cheeks. He was desperate to please his new friends.

"Just boypup," Finnbogg repeated. "Remember home, ah, sire and dam. Smell so nice. Sire smell like wood, like dogsweat, like sky and grass. Dam smell so sweet, smell like milk, smell like love, sweet Finnbogg dam." He stopped speaking long enough to blow his nose, a great honking sound in proportion with the rest of this massive, simple, good-hearted fellow.

"Q'oornans come, I guess."

Finnbogg did not often use the personal pronoun, but he was catching some of the speech habits of the humans. That at least was a sign of progress. Even User Annie seemed to be breaking into coherence.

"Q'oornans steal whole litter. Ah, where Finnbogg's litter mates? Where boypups? Where girlpups? All sweet dogs and bitches."

"If you please, sir!" Clive interrupted. "In the presence of a lady—"

Simultaneously, User Annie burst into laughter and Finnbogg cringed as if he had been scourged.

"If the major permits, sah," Sergeant Smythe interjected, "the term, I believe, is quite proper, sah. If Finnbogg is truly of a canine derivation, which I believe the major will agree is likely the case, then the genders of his kind are properly referred to as dogs and bitches. Sah!"

Clive pursued his lips. "I suppose you're right, Sergeant. Still and all . . . well, very well. Do carry on, Finnbogg. The Q'oornans came to your planet, did they? It was a world, like earth?"

Finnbogg looked baffled.

"Hmm. You wouldn't know Earth, of course. Well, it was a world like, ah, Q'oorna, then. Was that it? Sky and seas and hills and lakes and such? Forests and cities and farmland?"

"Earth like that, then Earth like Finnbogg home, yes, Folliot," Finnbogg agreed.

"And how did these Q'oornans come to your world? Did they arrive through some sort of spirit mediumship? Do you know what I'm talking about, Finnbogg?"

The great shaggy head swept up and down, up and down. "Spirits, yes. Come by spirits."

"Then how did they bring you back to the Dungeon? To Q'oorna? Do they have a means of bringing you astrally?"

"Astrally, yes," Finnbogg agreed. "Bring astrally. Bring Finnbogg, bring littermates."

"Hah! And what of your sire and dam? Did the

Q'oornans bring them also? Are they in the Dungeon?"

Great tears rolled down Finnbogg's face. He ignored them, and they fell from his great jowl jaw and made a trail of tiny puddles on the ground as he plodded stolidly on. "Not in Dungeon, Folliot. Sire dead. Dam dead. Littermates—"

He paused and made a strangely human gesture, a shrug of helpless resignation, the palms of his pawlike hands tilted upward, his muscular shoulders elevated, his shaggy head tilted to the side.

For the time being, he had nothing more to say.

Not long after, they encountered a herd of grazing beasts. They were clustered at a waterhole. Magnificent, graceful things like ibexes, with long, curving necks and straight horns a yard long. They were jet black. The air was cold and moist, and when their lookout spotted the party he gave a piercing squeal of alarm. The herd bolted and disappeared across the plain in astonishing bounds fifteen or twenty feet in length.

They found a patch of vegetation that sported fruit trees and berry bushes. Finnbogg claimed to recognize the food and insisted that it was tasty and nourishing. Clive had deduced that Finnbogg's metabolism was enough like their own that his food would be at least harmless to them, and possibly nourishing.

They paused for another rest and meal. Clive—and Finnbogg—were right. The berries were tart but edible. They reminded Clive of wild blackberries that he'd found on his cousin's estate when visiting as a boy. The other fruit was also good. There was water, too, which Clive found more than welcome.

"All right," Folliot addressed Horace Hamilton Smythe. "Now that we've had our repast and a chance to rest our wearies, I think it's time for your story, Sergeant. Let's have it."

"My story, sah? You mean, like Finnbogg's? Good Lor', Major—I got here along with your majorship

and Sidi Bombay. We wandered in together, doesn't
the major remember? We 'ad our little tub in the
Sudd, pokin' around after the major's dear brother,
and we blundered into the Dungeon. That's all there
was to it, sah!"

Clive cleared his throat. "First of all, Sergeant
Smythe, by no means do I believe that was all there
was to it. Oh no! There's a lot more to it than that,
indeed."

He stood up and began to pace, his hands locked
behind his back. He halted and stared at the sky. A
great cloudy nebulae filled the center of his vision,
and off to the right of it, the star that User Annie
had said was Earth's own sun.

*Are you there, du Maurier? Have you been in touch with
Carstairs? Did my reports reach him? I'm sure the recent
ones have not done so. Would you forward this to him,
please? I am walking across the surface of a black world in
company of a woman from the future and a strange creature from a remote planet. We have encountered and defeated a beast to defy the lexicon of Mr. Alfred Russel
Wallace himself. . . .*

"Yes, sah?" Smythe interrupted his communion
with the distant du Maurier—if indeed there had
been communion. If there had in fact been any
communication between the two men, it had been
entirely one-sided. Clive had sent out his thoughts—or
had endeavored to do so. He had received no message of reply, nor evidence that his transmission had
been received.

"Yes, Smythe." *Back to the moment, Clive Folliot.* "I
don't for a moment believe that you and Sidi Bombay were the innocents that you claimed to be when
we entered the Bahr-el-Zeraf. But you still owe me
an explanation of your pistol."

"My Navy Colt, sah. Fine piece. Picked it up aboard
a paddle-wheel steamer on the Mississippi just before the Americans fought their War between the
States. Wish I had it on my hip again, sah. It's back

there, now." He gestured vaguely in the direction they had come from.

Of course. Smythe's pistol was lost in the great hall beneath the Tower of Q'oorna. If only Clive had been able to speak with the ruler of the city! If only Neville's journal had given more information about those people. Where had they come from? How had the black gong summoned them? Were they merely hiding, awaiting a signal to make themselves known to the strangers, or had they been summoned in some more mysterious, even mystical, manner?

Perhaps the Q'oornans were possessed of psychic powers. Surely Finnbogg's description of his trip from his home world to the Dungeon smacked of such forces, rather than of purely physical ones. Were the Q'oornans normally dwellers on some alien astral plane, who manifested themselves to ordinary mortals only when summoned by the gong?

But the battle that Clive and his companions had fought had been real enough, and quite physical. He still carried the bruises to prove that! And this world through which they moved seemed a very real and physical place, albeit a very peculiar one.

Clive whirled upon Horace Hamilton Smythe. "What about the swirl of stars? What does it mean?"

"Sah, it was there already, when I came into possession of the weapon. It don't mean nothing, sah! Leastwise, as far as I know. The, ah, the gentleman from whom I, ah, obtained the Colt said as much. It was a fine weapon. I wish I had it back, sah."

Clive advanced upon Smythe. He reached down and held his hands beside the sergeant's face, the palms of his hands parallel to the sergeant's stubble-tinted cheeks. "Stand up, Sergeant." Folliot raised his hands slowly, as if they were attached to the sergeant's jawbone.

And as if those hands were attached to his jawbone, Sergeant Horace Hamilton Smythe rose to his feet.

"You will tell me right now, Sergeant, and without

evasion, how you obtained that weapon, and from whom you obtained it."

Smythe looked at his toes. In the faint light that passed for high noon on Q'oorna, it was impossible to be certain, but Clive Folliot thought that he detected the enlisted man actually blushing.

"I met a young lady in America, sah. I was traveling on the *John C. Calhoun*, sah. From Memphis to New Orleans. I met a very fetching young lady, traveling with her brother on the riverboat. We, ah, became engaged in a very friendly game of poker. I'm afraid that I lost a great deal of money, sah. A very great deal."

"Don't tell me you lost more than you could pay, Sergeant! Not a responsible noncommissioned officer of Her Majesty's military service!"

"No, sah. I wouldn't do such a thing, Major Folliot! Never!"

"I'm relieved to hear that. Well, then?"

"Sah, I was, as they say in America, cleaned out, sah. Well, we reached New Orleans and I was without funds, and the gentleman and lady invited me to share their hotel suite, sah. They were most hospitable. They both said they were very sorry they had won all my money from me. They said they would like to return it, but they couldn't do that, sah. They needed the money to meet obligations of their own."

He was twisting his hands in anguish. "This is most distressing, Major. Is it really necessary?"

"Continue!"

"Yes, sah."

Clive could sense both User Annie and squat Finnbogg listening to Smythe's narrative. How much did either of them understand, she a woman with an incomprehensible mind, a tempoid, and he a creature from an alien planet?

"They were a brother and sister traveling together, did I tell the major that? He was a businessman, a very successful businessman. And the lady was a widow. Very young and beautiful she was, but a widow already. I felt dreadfully sorry for the lady, I did, sah. And since the gentleman had one room and the lady another, I assumed that I would put up in the gentleman's room. I hoped to leave the hotel the next morning, sah, and find an Englishman and explain my plight and perhaps borrow some funds."

He shook his head sadly.

"We assembled in the evening for a few drops of their American beverage, something that they call bourbon whiskey for a reason I could never learn, sah. We had a couple of little rounds of bourbon and then the gentleman said that he was very sleepy and retired to his bed in the other room, leaving me in the very pleasant company of his sister."

Smythe's eyes darted this way and that.

Folliot said, "Continue."

"Yes, sah. Well, sah, I don't rightly know what happened. The lady was quite lovely. The bourbon was very pleasant. I remember the lady was wearing a delightful perfume. The next thing I knew it was the following morning, sah. The gentleman came bursting into the lady's room and, ah, and, ah. . . ."

"All right, Smythe. Never mind the scene. I can imagine. If I had a sister—if you had one— Never mind that. What happened next?"

"I'm afraid that the gentleman challenged me to a duel, Major Folliot."

"Good God, no! This is getting worse and worse! What then?"

"We fought the duel with pistols. In a clearing beside the river. The Mississippi River, sah. I'm afraid that I killed the gentleman, sah. Everyone agreed that it was an affair of honor. No charges were brought by the local authorities. The gentleman provided the weapons. I didn't want to do it, sah. The gentleman fired first, sah, and his shot just grazed me. See the mark it left, sah, right here."

Smythe held out his hand to show Clive the scar. It was the same mark that Clive had previously taken to be a miniature representation of the spiraling

stars. He blinked, studied the scar. Perhaps the resemblance was happenstantial. Or, perhaps . . . He
simply could not tell.

"I wanted to call it off right then, sah. But the
gentleman insisted that I fire my weapon. He said
his honor would not be satisfied until I did."

Smythe managed to raise his eyes and look Clive
fully in the face. "I pointed my revolver at the ground
and pulled the trigger, sah. It was the worst bit of
luck I've ever had, sah. The ball struck a rock and
ricocheted straight at my opponent and struck him
in the heart. He was killed instantly, sah."

"The lady, sah, she said that I had acted nobly.
She insisted that I keep the dueling pistol. That's
what she called it, sah, but actually it was a Navy
Colt. The one you've seen, sah. With the swirl of
stars in the grip, sah. A fine piece. I wish I had it
back again, sah."

Clive put his hand on the other's shoulder. "All
right, Sergeant Smythe. That's past, and I think you
acted—well, perhaps unwisely, but not dishonorably,
with regard to the duel. As for the lady, what's past
cannot be recalled."

He signaled to User Annie and to Finnbogg. "Let
us get moving." Once they were again under way,
Clive said, "One more question, Sergeant. What were
their names—the gentleman and the lady in this
incident?"

"I'll never forget them, sah. They were a mining
millionaire, a Mr. Philo Goode. He'd made his fortune from a gem mine in Missouri. Remarkable, sah.
They turn up diamonds and emeralds and rubies, all
within a single site, Mr. Goode said. And the lady
was his sister. I mentioned that before, sah, didn't I?
She was a widow lady. Her name was Lorena Ransome.
Her husband was a preacher, a missionary, killed by
fierce Apaches in the Wild West. The Reverend Amos
Ransome, that was his name, sah."

Horace Hamilton Smythe heaved a heavy sigh.

"Ah, she was a beautiful one, Major. You can't imagine what a beautiful one."

"Yes, I can, Sergeant. Believe me, I can."

"Please, sah, don't rub it in so."

"I'm not rubbing it in, Sergeant! Don't tell me you have forgotten the trio of crooked gamblers who so nearly took me, aboard the *Empress Philippa.*"

"No, sah. Of course not."

"But think, man! They were the same trio! You never killed Philo Goode! His death was faked— heaven knows why! And Amos Ransome is not dead, nor is Lorena Ransome his widow. They traveled on board *Empress Philippa* as brother and sister, pretending not even to know Goode!"

"I—I—when you say it, sah, it all makes sense. Of course." Smythe's face had the expression of a poleaxed steer.

"But you didn't connect the incidents on the *John C. Calhoun* and the *Empress Philippa*? You recognized the trio as cardsharpers but you didn't connect them with the cardsharpers who had taken you in America? How can that be, Sergeant Smythe? They must have done something to your brain."

"I don't know, sah. I can't understand it. It doesn't make any sense at all, sah. No sense at all."

Smythe trudged ahead, his shoulders slumped. "I don't suppose, sah," he started to say after they'd gone the better part of a mile.

Folliot said, "Yes?"

"Well, I'm just trying to remember, sah. There we were, beside the river. The widow was there, Mrs. Ransome."

"Yes, Sergeant. If that's who she really was."

"And the seconds and witnesses. They take dueling very seriously in New Orleans, sah. There was quite an assemblage of ladies and gentlemen present. Seconds and witnesses and referees. Mr. Goode arranged all of that, since I didn't know anyone in New Orleans, you see, Major Folliot."

"Yes, Smythe. I quite understand. What is it that you are trying to tell me, man?"

"Well, sah, it was like this. I can remember the scene clearly. Very, very clearly. Up to a particular moment. The moment when Mrs. Ransome handed me the pistol. There was even a judge there, presiding over the event."

A wind had come up, a cold wind that bore moisture with it. Clive wondered if it ever rained on Q'oorna. It must, to maintain the vegetation and the wildlife they had observed. It must rain—or snow! He shuddered.

"The judge," Sergeant Smythe was saying, "took both the pistols. I handed him mine, and the other he took from Mr. Goode's dead hand, Major Folliot. After they were checked he returned them to Mrs. Ransome. She handed one of them to me. She said that she would keep one, and that I was to keep the other."

He shivered visibly. It might have been the cold wind that made him do so, or the memory of the events he was describing.

"She said—Major, I can remember it clear as my mother's face, sah—she said, 'You must look at this, Mr. Smythe.' I wasn't using my military rank in America, you see, Major. She said, 'You must look at this.' And she held the revolver so the grip was right before my eyes. I hadn't noticed the stars in the grip before that. Maybe they were there all along but I never saw them before."

A more violent shudder swept his frame.

"I don't know what happened, sah. I looked, as Mrs. Ransome asked me to. And—I don't know what happened, sah. Ever since then, I think I'm all right. I feel myself, I can do everything I could ever do, Major. But—sometimes I don't know *why* I do the things I do. Sometimes—I don't understand myself, Major."

He paused, then he said, "Maybe that's why I didn't connect the *John C. Calhoun* and the *Empress*

Philippa. Or the people. The people. I don't know, sah. What do you think, sah?"

"I don't know what to think, Sergeant. Either you were the victim of a plot and of powers that stagger the imagination—or you are a dissembler of monumental proportions!"

"A dissembler, sah? I beg the major's pardon!"

"Aboard *Empress Philippa*—and since, now that I think of it—you showed evidence of being a master of disguise, Smythe. Mandarin, Arab—you could put the West End's finest thespians to shame. And you did recognize the Goode-Ransome combine for what they were, when you penetrated their scheme in the *Empress*'s salon."

Smythe looked baffled.

"Now you tell me this wild tale," Folliot went on, "about Mississippi steamboat gamblers and seduction and dueling in New Orleans. You weave a yarn about the pistol, and you hint—at least you hint—that you must have been the subject of some sort of mesmeric spell cast by Miss Ransome. Or Mrs. Ransome. Whichever is her true identity. You tell this wild tale and you expect me to . . . to . . ."

He stopped because he had simply run out of words. Sergeant Smythe had been his mentor when he was a green lieutenant, had been his companion in war and peace. Clive knew that Smythe had more than once saved his very life!

And yet it appeared that Smythe was playing a secret and sinister game. A game in which the stakes were nothing less than life itself.

And Clive Folliot might yet be the loser of that game!

▪ CHAPTER 18 ▪
The Pool of Hades

They rounded the hill believing that they knew what would come next. They had Annie's map; they had followed it for days and it had proved accurate.

Then they learned better.

The map had indicated a low region. It appeared to be narrow, punctuated by swamps. To Clive it suggested a replay of the Sudd in Equatoria, but Horace Hamilton Smythe pointed out that the swampy area here was far smaller than the Bahr-el-Zeraf. By picking their way carefully, they could get through.

"I'm not convinced," Clive demurred. "Possibly we three can pick our way to the other side." There was no need for him to specify that he meant himself and Sergeant Smythe and User Annie. "But what about—"

He indicated Finnbogg with a movement of his head.

"Pity, sah. Hate to lose the beast, but if it must be. . . ."

"Beast?" Folliot was enraged. "He's no beast. He—"

"He's a doggy, sah. I'm as fond of the fellow as you are. Poor Sidi Bombay might not care so much for him, but I think he's a splendid old hound. Still, a man's a man and an animal is something different. You don't believe that Darwin chap, sah, I hope. We're all just a bunch of bloody beasts, that's what he's got to say. Can't accept that, I hope!"

"Oh, never mind Darwin! I'm talking about Finnbogg. I'll admit that he's rather like a dog. But we're rather like apes, Sergeant Smythe, in case you'd never noticed. We have the same number and arrangement of limbs, our other organs and features are pretty much alike. But that doesn't mean that a man's the same as a chimpanzee. And just because Finnbogg is rather like a dog doesn't mean that he is one."

Smythe backed down. Perhaps he still felt chagrined at his story of the *John C. Calhoun*. Or perhaps he was merely deferring to Folliot's rank. At any rate ... "No, sah. But we've still got to get through this little swamp."

They had Annie's map spread before them. Clive Folliot picked it up and folded it into a pocket of his khaki jacket. "Let's move on, then," he called.

That was when they rounded the hill. The swamp spread before them, as the map had indicated. It didn't look too bad. There were pools. There were marshy areas that might be quicksand and that would require great care. There were grassy tussocks and trees rising from the swamp with moss hanging from them and the Q'oornan equivalent of other earthly parasites—creepers, vines, and dead-black orchids.

"Does the major think we'll encounter any wildlife, sah?" Smythe peered ahead.

Before Folliot could answer, the water erupted in the center of the largest pool. The liquid spouted upward like a geyser, showering outward for hundreds of feet in all directions. The travelers were spattered. The water was startlingly warm, almost hot. It stank to high heaven. Wherever it touched the skin it left a scummy residue that itched and burned even after it was wiped away.

And with the spattering of black fluid came a shower of creatures ranging in scale from the size of a shilling coin to that of a giant swamp rat.

Folliot called to User Annie to switch on her protective field, but it was too late for that. The creatures were swarming over her and over all the rest of them.

Something that looked like a toad easily eight inches

long hopped onto Clive's shoulder and dug in with its toes. Each of its digits was tipped with a claw, and where the claws pierced his skin it felt like an array of red-hot dinner forks.

A formless blob looking like something Meinheer Leeuwenhoek might have observed through his microscope had fastened itself onto Horace Hamilton Smythe's face. At first it was a mere black splotch resembling an inkblot, but Smythe began to scream and wipe at it, trying desperately to clean it away, only to have it grow and spread until it threatened to cover his nostrils and mouth and smother him.

Finnbogg was swarmed by a brigade of insectlike creatures, scorpions and wasps and grubs and leeches and other beings of every type and description in uncounted hordes. The muscular Finnbogg rolled on the black earth, crushing his tormentors by the hundred—but they continued their attack by the thousand.

Folliot and his companions still had the cybroid claws they had taken from the flying beast. Clive used his claw to rip the toad off his shoulder and hurl it away from him, but a thing like a monstrous hellgrammite coursed up his body. He reached for it, opened his mouth to shout. The thing moved like lightning. Clive clamped his teeth shut, grasped the insect with one hand, and hacked at it with his claw. It loosened its grip on him and he flung it away.

He gagged, bent double, and retched. He had nipped off the head and forequarters of the hellgrammite, but the remaining part of the creature had continued to struggle, sending lances of fiery pain through Clive's tongue and lips. The contents of his stomach came up and splattered the ground, the partial insect still squirming feebly in the steaming mess.

A black snake reared and wove its hooded head a foot from Folliot's face. Its tongue flickered. It looked like the deadly Egyptian cobra, its black eyes reflecting the pale nebulae and stars that glittered above it.

"Crash system! Crash system! Catastrophic error!" It was User Annie's voice. Clive was frozen, facing the cobra. He knew enough of such creatures to realize that its mobility was limited, its movements not very rapid. But at this close range the cobra need merely permit itself to fall forward—that was the way the hooded vipers struck—and Clive would receive a lethal dose of venom.

Annie did not use her cybroid claw. Instead she raised her hand and pointed her finger at the cobra and it shrank away, slithering back toward the swamp. A thing like a giant leech had fastened itself to the back of her hand and Clive ripped it away and threw it as far as he could. Annie swept her finger over his body, dislodging half-a-dozen things that had got inside his garments without his even knowing it. Wherever her finger pointed, Clive felt a tracery of fire, but even this he could accept, knowing that the attacking beasts could not.

Annie gave the same treatment to Horace Hamilton Smythe.

The three of them ran to Finnbogg. The massive creature was still rolling on the ground, writhing and tearing at himself. Folliot and Smythe held him as Annie ran her finger over his body, dislodging one horror after another.

"What about you?" Folliot shouted at Annie. "Can you use that thing on yourself?"

She seemed to understand. "Electrofield power depleted. User exclusion mode. Manual intervention required!"

Even as she shouted the words she was stripping off her clothing. She did not hesitate at any point. Even before she was totally nude, Clive Folliot and Horace Hamilton Smythe were plucking hideous monstrosities from her flesh.

The whole thing was over in moments. Annie drew a ring in the earth, enclosing the four of them. Somehow her Baalbec A-9 left a charge on the ground. None of the horrors that had erupted—were still erupting—from the pool crossed the line.

In the battle to free themselves from the horrors that splattered them, the travelers had ignored the geyser that had produced them. Now they could see that it was still spouting its foul spew into the air, and that not only stinking black water but a steady stream of the hideous beings were scattering from the eruption.

When the geyser finally stopped its flow, the ground was covered with a living carpet of crawling, hopping, chirruping abominations. They crept upon one another, battled and killed and devoured one another, mated in a mad frenzy.

Only the ring created by Annie's Baalbec A-9 protected the four.

Clive estimated that the geyser spouted for only a quarter of an hour, and the orgy of feasting and mating and death went on for less than an hour. Then the creatures lapsed into lassitude. Sluggishly they began dragging themselves back into the swamp.

Like a living organism, the very earth seemed to move downward, downward. It was really the collective motion of tens of thousands of abominations, but they had the appearance of a single horror, and they entered the pool with a continuous, disgusting, surging sound, like that of a horrid beast sucking out the guts of a helpless victim.

Slowly, User Annie bent and picked up her garments. She trembled as she donned them, and Folliot gallantly held her arm to steady her. Sergeant Smythe suggested that she keep her electrofield turned on at all times, but Annie shook her head. For once she spoke comprehensibly. "Baalbec A-nine uses my power." She pressed a thumb against the soft flesh over her heart. "No battery pack on A-nine. No external power source." She smiled ruefully. "Baalbec uses only Annie's power. Not so strong. Not so strong."

She was clearly exhausted, and close to shedding

those tears that come to the emotionally and physically spent.

User Annie sank to her haunches and held her hand over her eyes. "Heepers!" she muttered. "Cuffin romchies, tubehead gig, unable crunch these cuffin numbers."

Clive knelt before her.

She looked into his face, tears falling at last from her eyes. "System overload, User Folliot. System cuffin overload. Circuits cuffin sizzled, user." She threw herself into his arms and butted his shoulder like a cat, weeping onto his jacket.

Once the ground was clear—which did not take long—they determined to press on. They had no idea how often the geyser erupted. It might be years between events, or mere minutes. They did not wish to remain there to find out. Nor did they wish to try to cross the swamp.

"Other ways off Q'oorna," Finnbogg volunteered. "Lots more of Dungeon than Q'oorna."

The others gazed at one another. If only they could understand one another fully, their chances of escape, or at least of survival, would be enhanced. But only Clive and Horace Hamilton Smythe could speak to each other with full comprehension. User Annie lapsed into and out of her strange futuristic jargon, and Finnbogg with his doggy eagerness to please had only the vocabulary one would expect of a bright canine.

They were marching southward, paralleling the edge of the swamp and tracing the foot of the row of hills they had penetrated.

"How else can we leave Q'oorna, Finnbogg?" Clive asked.

"Oh, big water mountain. Oh, yes, big water mountain, get off Q'oorna, Folliot. Oh, yes."

Clive turned to Horace Hamilton Smythe. "What do you think he means by that? Big water mountain. Think he means a glacier?"

Smythe asked Finnbogg, "You mean ice?"

Finnbogg only looked puzzled.

"Ice. Blimey! Look fella, ice is like water, only, ah, it's very cold, eh? When water gets cold enough it became hard. Hard like diamonds. Glass. Lord help me! Water rocks, eh, Finnbogg?"

Finnbogg nodded his massive head vigorously. "Hard, yes. Water like rocks. Yes. No. Not way out. Ice? Eh, Smythe, hard water ice, hey? Good! Good, good, good. No. Not hard. Not ice. Big mountain water like, ah"—he jerked a pawlike hand toward the now distant swamp—"water mountain up. Bad water mountain up. Good water mountain down."

He gestured vigorously, jumping up and down so that the very earth shook beneath his feet. "Water down! Water mountain down!"

"Jove!" Folliot exclaimed. "He's talking about a waterfall, Smythe! He's saying we can get out of here by passing through a waterfall!"

He imitated the motion of a waterfall with his hands.

Finnbogg said, "Yes, yes. Out of Q'oorna, water mountain down. Yes. More ways, too, Folliot. Many ways out of Q'oorna. Way of sky on ground. Oh, stars, clouds, black sky, white shining, get away from Q'oorna. Or heart of stone. Yes, like hard water rock and red heart shining. And house. House on"—he made parallel motions with his hands, upending them and sliding them through the air parallel to the ground—"on knives. Yes, Smythe. Yes, Folliot. Like house on knives. House move, knives stay, go out of Q'oorna. Out, yes, good, see boypups, girlpups, sire and dam. See Finnbogg home, good, yes, go."

Smythe said, "That sky-on-ground business doesn't ring any bells, but the rock with red heart shining—"

"Yes!" Clive interrupted. "That's a perfect description of the way we came through the Bahr-el-Zeraf! And the moving house on knives, did you get that, Smythe?"

"I'm not sure, sah, that I did."

"I'm not *sure* either," Folliot replied. "But I'd bet my monthly pay packet that good brother Finnbogg, in his own doggy way, was describing a railroad."

Smythe looked puzzled. Then he looked thoughtful. Then his face was split by a happy grin. "I think the major is absolutely right, I do! Yes, sah! A house that moves on knives. Two long blades, the rails. Can there be a railroad here on Q'oorna?"

"We don't know, do we, Sergeant? We don't know who the Q'oornans are, where they originate, why they are bringing people here. Not just people like ourselves, either. Extroids, tempoids, cybroids. We're just beginning to learn what this world is all about, Sergeant Smythe. And I think our goals may be changing, too."

"I don't quite take the major's drift, I'm afraid, sah."

They had put most of the swamp behind them, although the land to their left was still marshy. There were distant sounds—the call of wild beasts, the slither in the reeds that indicated the path of some water-dwelling serpent or amphibian, the occasional flapping of great wings, or the call of a bird.

Then a crackling and a whoosh like a Guy Fawkes Day rocket.

They halted and stared skyward.

Something gleaming and streamlined tore across the afternoon sky. It could have been a railroad train, but a railroad train snatched from some fantastic future and set down in the present. Only *set down* is hardly the term to use, for this apparition passed hundreds of feet above their heads. It was coming from the direction of the chasm and the ruined bridge, and as they stood watching, it passed over the swamp that had nearly taken their lives, and slid down the sky.

"It—it's going to crash!" Smythe gasped.

Even as the sergeant spoke, the great vehicle dropped toward the surface. In that frozen moment Clive could make out clearly the shape of the vehicle.

If he'd had pen and paper he could have made a perfect sketch of it for *The London Illustrated Recorder and Dispatch*. It was hundreds of feet in length, with a sleekly pointed tip. Rows of windows ran along the sides of the cars, which were jointed like those of a steam train.

There were no tracks, and no visible means of levitation. Enough attempts had been made to envision flying caravans of the future, and men had made efforts actually to build them, although only the most modest of gliders—in truth, little more than oversized children's kites—had achieved any degree of success.

Whatever had held this marvel in the air, the mechanism had failed. The aerial train did not plow nose-on into the ground, but instead dropped to the surface and ran along it like a true railroad vehicle, leaving behind it a long furrow of earth.

The four travelers began to run toward the vehicle. At first Clive Folliot was in the lead, but Finnbogg quickly outdistanced him and headed on.

They risked their lives by crossing the marshy borders of the swamp. Fortunately there was no quicksand there, and Finnbogg's broad, padded feet distributed his weight sufficiently that he was able to splash across the muddy areas undeterred.

It took several hours to reach the crashed vehicle. By the time they arrived, late afternoon was beginning to give way to Q'oorna's gloomy version of dusk.

The vehicle was very much like an earthly train. The travelers climbed onto an outside railing on the rearmost car. The cars did not appear severely damaged. Clive surmised that the vehicle had lost its power—rather as if the firebox in a steam locomotive had been permitted to go out, causing the boiler to lose pressure. The train would roll to a stop but it would remain undamaged.

Because this train had moved through the air rather than upon rails, it had come to earth with a heavy impact, and some damage would be expected. Still, should the power plant be repaired, the train might resume its journey.

Could the four travelers make their way on the train? Where would it take them? Possibly—probably!—to a major center of population, commerce, and authority among the Q'oornans. There, Clive thought, they would make a decision rapidly: whether to attempt to blend in to the local populace and seek information without contacting the authorities—or to head straight for the seat of power and confront the Q'oornan ruler.

Their experiences in the Black Tower did not encourage the latter course, but Clive was feeling increasingly confident and assertive. He had been half-hoodwinked, half-abducted into this mad world. He was not subject to its local tyrannies. He would not submit to the whims of any petty princeling.

He pulled back a door and led his party into the rearmost car.

He had stepped into a scene straight from the most scandalous work of Edward Gibbon. Marble columns rose in a stately arrangement surrounding a splendid bath. Statues painted in the most lifelike of colors captured the eye. All were nude, and some were engaged in astonishing activities.

The bath itself was filled with sinuous ladies and muscular youths. The ladies wore their hair bound up in colorful ribbons. These were the sole garments visible in the pool.

Beside the bath a group of musicians played softly on lyres and reeds, while servants brought baskets of fresh fruit.

Of all the sights and activities, perhaps the greatest shock to Clive was the variety of colors before him. Gone were the shades of blackness that had filled his every sight for days past. Reds and pinks, yellows and greens and browns and blues rioted until he felt that he could see no more. He was like a gourmand who had feasted to repletion and yet had to sample one more delicacy, one more flavor, one more and always one more.

User Annie dashed past him and ran to the bath. She plunged headlong into the blue-tinged water—and remained dry. The bathers around her continued their sport as if nothing had happened.

At Clive Folliot's side, Quartermaster Sergeant Horace Hamilton Smythe picked up a splendid yellow pear—or attempted to pick it up. Like a ghostly apparition passing through a wall, his hand passed through the fruit.

Clive recognized one of the statues, apparently a Roman sculptor's copy of a work by the great Greek artist Praxiteles. Clive touched the statue—or tried to, for he had no more success than Annie in swimming in the bath or Horace Hamilton Smythe in eating the yellow pear.

"It's unreal," he exclaimed. "All an illusion!"

"Or a mirage," Smythe amended. "It may all exist, but it's separated from us by distance. Ah, or by some more subtle thing than simple distance, Major. I think it *is* real. We can see it, but we just can't touch it."

As if to support Smythe's assertion, several of the Roman youths had given up their disporting in the bath and were staring at the newcomers.

One young man, startlingly physical, had approached User Annie. Annie had regained her feet and was staring at the Roman. He reached to place his hand on her shoulder, but the hand passed through her body. An expression of startlement appeared on his face.

Annie responded, placing her hand on the Roman—not on his shoulder—but with the same lack of contact. Annie giggled, made more advances, all without tangible effect.

"They are completely silent!" Folliot exclaimed.

"Holograms," User Annie said, between flights of giggles, "virtual images. Temporal displacement circuitry!"

Clive shook his head. "Wherever they are, whatever they are, we cannot do more than signal to them. Let us move on."

Finnbogg had remained quietly watching the activity. But he joined the others as they advanced to the next car of the train.

It was a scene from Dante, or perhaps from the preachments of some fundamentalist pastor who spouted fire and brimstone with his every breath. Flames danced about them, devils with pitchforks jabbed and twisted at tormented souls, rivers of glowing lava poured into pools of living sparks.

Finnbogg ignored the demons and the flames. Perhaps, to his distant mind, they were meaningless images. Perhaps, in his alien brain, they registered as sylvan glades and pleasant pastures—or did not register at all! In any case, he led the others through the inferno and on to the next car.

Each compartment of the train seemed a different world. Some were worlds of ineffable beauty, others of indescribable horror. Some offered temptation almost impossible to resist—until Clive and the others discovered that all was illusion, nothing was reality.

At length they stepped into what appeared—to Folliot and Smythe, at least—a most ordinary nineteenth-century railroad coach.

Ladies in long skirts and modest bonnets sat with baskets of knitting or hampers of food on their laps. Gentlemen in plug hats and side-whiskers attended them. Others sat quietly reading the latest newspapers or paperbound novels.

At the end of the car two seats had been arranged so as to face each other. A portable table had been set up between the knees of the four individuals who occupied the seats. A deck of cards and piles of colored wooden chips lay upon the table.

One of the four persons was a portly gentleman of advanced years, a brandy glass before him, his facial expression one of partial intoxication. Although he was richly dressed, there were no chips before him.

A gold pocket watch and chain lay on the table, as did a pile of large-denomination notes. The heavy-set man was perspiring freely and appeared to be distressed.

The person seated beside him was a comely woman. She sat very close to the man, and was whispering encouragement to him, her shapely lips held close to his ear.

The newcomers halted beside the group.

"Philo Goode!" Smythe exclaimed.

"Amos Ransome!" Folliot exclaimed.

"Lorena Ransome!" they both exclaimed.

The three sharpers sprang to their feet, leaving their latest victim startled and baffled as to what was transpiring. Without a backward glance they raced for the front of the car and leaped out.

Folliot and Smythe followed, trailing User Annie and massive Finnbogg in their wake.

Even as they leaped from the platform, hot on the trail of the sharpers, somewhere in a detached part of his mind Clive was considering that he had heard Lorena Ransome's whispers, heard the exclamations of the gamblers, heard the slap of their shoes on the floor of the railroad coach even as they fled. These persons were not mere images.

They were real!

But Clive had no opportunity to give thought to such metaphysical maunderings. The solid plain should have been a few feet below the level of the railroad coach.

Instead he found himself tumbling through a pitch-black void. As he revolved he could see Horace Hamilton Smythe and User Annie and the dwarf Finnbogg, all of them tumbling and falling like himself. And farther below, the three sharpers.

Somehow the sharpers were falling more rapidly than Clive and his companions. At first a few feet ahead of them, the sharpers moved faster and faster, shrinking to miniature versions of themselves, then to points of light and color. Then they disappeared altogether.

Wind whistled in Clive's ears and whipped past him, tearing at his clothes. He had the cybroid claw still—his only tool or weapon other than his bare hands and battered wits. He knew that Annie had her Baalbec A-9, a device of unknown and possibly crucial capabilities. Smythe was with him. Clive had regarded the man as his staunchest ally, but now he had become an enigma. And there was the eager, faithful Finnbogg.

The passage of air rose to a shriek. Then Clive realized that it was not merely the wind whipping past his ears that was responsible for the sound. Something else was shrieking, something huge and terrible, something that would make all the wonders and the horrors that he had encountered since leaving the flat of Miss Annabella Leighton pale to insignificance.

He revolved once more in the air, and beneath saw a face surrounded by tentacles, a face similar to the one he had destroyed in the fissure as he had descended the cliff. But this face was a hundred times more horrifying, and it was screaming at Clive, its mouth open wide, rows of terrible, razor-edged teeth chomping, and Clive was tumbling toward it, helpless to stop himself.

CHAPTER 19

Enter Shriek

Clive had time to wonder, *Is this what happened to the sharpers?* Then there was no more time to think, no more time for anything. The jaws clamped together. The glittering triangular teeth snapped shut, forming a solid surface of gleaming enamel, surrounded by horrid, fleshy lips that were drawn back in a hateful snarl.

With a jolt, Clive smashed into the granite-hard surface. With the impact of his boots on the teeth he bounded aside, tumbling over the snarling lips and falling onto a rock-strewn clearing. User Annie, Horace Hamilton Smythe, and Finnbogg all tumbled after him bouncing and tangling with one another. There were grunts and whooshes of rapidly expelled air but they all got quickly to their feet and checked themselves cursorily. There were no major injuries. That in itself was a relief.

But the quartet had no time to examine themselves for lesser cuts and bruises. The clearing was surrounded on three sides by shadowy woods. The fourth was a steep hillside where hardy shrubs and stunted trees struggled for purchase and for survival, nestling against boulders that might protect them from being swept away every time there was a rainfall.

At the foot of the slope an opening possibly four feet high and three feet across showed in stark contrast. It led into the hill, into a depth and a darkness that could not be judged from outside. For a split second, as Clive staggered to his feet and stood swaying uncertainly, staring into the opening, he thought that he saw a distant glimmer, a remote concatenation of lights that might—just might—have been the by-now familiar and menacing spiral of stars, glittering and revolving enigmatically.

Clive blinked. The outdoor illumination was dazzling. He swiveled his neck for a quick look at the sky.

The perpetual blackness that he had grown accustomed to on the plains of Q'oorna was no more. Here was a different sky, a sky of a different color, a sky the green of teal ducks' feathers. There were no brilliant, spiraling stars, nor the distant constellations and fuzzy-edged nebulae that had given Q'oorna its pallid daylight. Instead there were two suns in the sky!

One was a giant, lurking, red cinder that seemed prepared to plunge to earth, consuming the entire world in a final fiery orgy. The other was a point of brilliant blue that made its way across the orb of the red giant, unconcerned that it traversed the face of a neighbor a billion times its size.

"What now, sah?" Horace Hamilton Smythe asked Clive. "Shall we enter the cave?"

Clive shook his head, as if that could clear the cobwebs and give him an answer to Smythe's question. Before he could speak, the thunder of pounding feet sounded nearby. It was followed by the growling cacophony of a dozen voices.

A band of primitive huntsmen appeared, armed with spears and clubs, dressed in crudely fashioned garments of animal hide. Even these were a welcome sight to Clive. The hunters halted, facing Clive and his companions. This was as startling a moment for them as it was for the others.

Clive and his friends stood in a semicircle, its center the mouth of the cave.

Before anyone could speak, the primitives ranged themselves before the cave, blocking Clive and his band from the opening. Their leader disappeared within while his followers stood with their backs to the cave mouth, holding Clive and his friends at bay with their spears.

User Annie screamed.

Clive whirled and saw the newest arrival. It looked vaguely human, even as Finnbogg had at first glimpse looked vaguely human. But as Finnbogg's canine nature had become more noticeable upon closer examination, so also did this shrieker's nonhuman characteristics.

There were four arms instead of two, so the creature could perform several tasks at once, or could bring all four arms to bear upon a single task. And there were four legs instead of two, so that the creature could walk or run or climb or scramble with incredible agility and stamina.

Its torso was oddly made, with a thin chest and a massive abdomen, and its face featured not two eyes but eight that glowed redly beneath the double suns. There remained vestigial hair on the creature's body, hair of a stiff and spiky composition.

From its mouth extended toothlike projections, yet as Clive peered into the face he realized that these were not true teeth but mandibles like those of a spider. He thought of the giant spider that he had fought for his life, first on a jungle trail and then on a beach near the Wami River, and for an instant felt himself becoming light-headed.

He knew now what Mr. Darwin had referred to in his much discussed and much condemned work. If ever the race of spiders had advanced through thousands of millions of years of—he tried to remember Mr. Darwin's word—*evolution*—to attain a status comparable to that of humankind . . . then this amazing creature might be the result.

The primitives stood facing the strange newcomer. After a moment of stunned inaction, they fled, screaming in terror.

Now the strange creature settled itself into the

mouth of the cave. Clive had seen the leader of the primitive huntsmen disappear into that opening. He was trapped, cut off from the outer world and from his fellow tribesmen, by the newcomer's body.

The creature sat staring at Clive and the others. It made no sound, but Clive felt a message emanating from it. *Stay where you are,* it seemed to tell him. He looked at his companions. They nodded to him. All of them, even Finnbogg, had received the creature's message.

"What now, sah?" Horace Smythe asked.

"I wouldn't want to fight that thing," Clive said. "Even with the aid of our claws."

"No, sah. Do you think we might just quietly start to edge away? These woods look as if one could find a hiding place."

"I'm sure those huntsmen are all around us now, Sergeant. I think we might profit by standing our ground. This new creature doesn't appear hostile."

They settled themselves on the ground. As a spider will remain motionless, infinitely patient, at the center of her web, awaiting the arrival and self-entrapment of her prey—the great spiderlike being remained motionless in the mouth of the cave. The two suns made their way slowly toward the horizon.

Clive and his friends were alone, cut off from their ordinary reality, helpless there in the clearing.

Or were they?

"Annie," Clive said. "Have I mentioned my friend du Maurier to you?"

"No." Annie shook her head. "Eyedee reference Daphne?"

"Daphne? No. George du Maurier. The cartoonist."

Annie smiled. "Oh, pozzi tiff. I've input his books. *Trilby. The Martian.* Good entry level seffer."

"Seffer?" Clive asked.

"Uh, seffer. Uh, Wells, Verne, Heinlein, those. Seffer equivalent, uh, science fiction writer." She grinned. "I love seff. All Crackbelles love seff. Everybody loves seff."

"George du Maurier is my friend, Annie. He believes that mental communication is possible, between planets."

She grinned. "Clive believes, too?"

"I don't know. I really don't know. But I wonder—your electrofield device—"

"Baalbec A-nine."

"Could it—help me? If I attempted to send a message to George du Maurier . . . I've no real idea what kind of electrical or etheric or mesmeric waves might carry such a message. But perhaps your device could assist. Could serve as some sort of etheric telegraph."

Annie smiled. "Indeterminate, Clive. Make the attempt. Here." She took his hand with a gesture so rapid and unexpected that he had no chance to resist, and placed it so that the pad of his thumb rested on a spot directly above her sternum. He expected to feel warm, yielding flesh at that point, but he did not expect the peculiar texture and shape that he felt *beneath* her flesh. That must be the Baalbec A-9, implanted there within her bodice.

He closed his eyes and concentrated, conjuring the image of George du Maurier.

He thought, *Du Maurier, I have no idea whether you can hear me or not. If you can, I beseech you to act.*

I have fallen into another world, du Maurier. I have no idea where I am. Another planet . . . another plane of being . . . some altered state of existence that lies outside our usual notion of time and space.

I traveled from England to the Sudd, the region in Equatoria where my brother Neville was last seen. From there I passed through a strange gateway, one concealed in a great rock whose heart of ruby glowed and pulsed like a living organ. I was accompanied by Quartermaster Sergeant Horace Hamilton Smythe, of my own Guard unit, and by the East Indian, Sidi Bombay.

We found ourselves in a strange realm known as the Dungeon. Who rules this place, what their purpose may be, I have yet to fathom. I believe that Neville is here. At one point I thought that I had found his body, but I believe now

*that was a mere simulacrum, and that Neville is still alive
and somewhere in the Dungeon.*

*Within the Dungeon there are realms and realities, worlds
beyond fathoming, beyond even counting. Sergeant Smythe
is with me yet, Sidi Bombay has disappeared. With me also
are a being named Finnbogg, like a man yet not a man . . .
and a beautiful young woman who seems to come from the
year 1999, and is helping me to send this message to you.
Her name is Annie.*

*Du Maurier, I beseech you, in the name of our friend-
ship, in the name of your own psychic researches, in the
name of common humanity, do these things for me.*

Contact Maurice Carstairs at The Recorder and Dispatch. *Prepare a report for him based on what I have told
you. I will try to send you further details and later developments. If I ever do find my way back to England, I will be
rich and famous as a result of this adventure!*

*Contact my father at the family estate. Tell him that I am
still on Neville's trail, and that the title of Baron Tewkesbury shall never become extinct.*

*Contact the lady who accompanied me to the theater at
the opening of* "Cox and Box." *You will find her dwelling
on the top floor of the tallest house in Plantagenet Court. I
suspect that you know the street. If not, it is easy enough to
find. Tell her that I love her, and that I shall return to keep
my promise.*

*And then, du Maurier, the last and greatest favor of all.
You must get word back to me. Get material assistance to
me if you can, but if you cannot, then at least get word back
to me. Physically or mesmerically, however you can do it.
Let me know that I have reached you. Let me know that I
am not utterly and forever stranded here in the Dungeon.
Please, du Maurier—do this for me. When I get back to
London, you shall share in every bit of the wealth and glory
that I expect to reap.*

*God bless you, du Maurier! I can only hope that you
hear me, somehow. If you hear me in your sleep, know you
that this is not a dream! If you hear me while you wake, you
are not mad! I am real, I live, and I pray that this message
reaches you.*

Farewell, du Maurier! Farewell! Do not let me down, my friend! You are my only contact in the world I knew for thirty-three years!

He dropped his hand back into his lap. How long had he and Annie and Horace and great Finnbogg remained in their semicircular formation?

Annie looked pale, drained. She said, "I think—I think—but I'm so tired, Clive."

Clive had been in a fuguelike state himself. He blinked. The sun—or suns—of this world had sunk behind the woods that surrounded the mouth of the cave. A blazing dusk colored half the sky. In England, Folliot would have stopped to admire the picture painted from nature's magnificent palate, but here in the Dungeon he could only gaze at the eight-limbed being that yet blocked the entrance to the cave.

From somewhere deep within the cavern there came a single, agonized scream, followed by scraping and chomping sounds. The strange, eight-limbed creature that blocked the mouth of the cave nodded and slowly emerged from the opening.

Even as Clive watched the creature, fascinated, he first heard and then saw a few of the savages begin to creep back from the woods into which their tribe had disappeared.

The four-armed creature emitted another of its appalling shrieks, and with several of its hands tore patches of long, spiky hairs from itself, and hurled the hairs toward the woods. The hairs hurtled like miniature javelins, and where they struck the primitives those beings began almost instantaneously to swell and discolor. In seconds they fell to the earth and their bodies were tranformed into dreadful, distended travesties of the human form, writhing and puffing and discoloring and finally falling away into pools of horrid noisome fluids in which their bones lay like biscuits in bowls of cream.

Perhaps we would have been better off with the savages,

Clive thought. But the companions had no control over that choice. At least, they no longer had any.

Now something was happening to the face of the spider-being. Clive stared in fascination. He knew there was no point in attempting to flee, and as he watched, he realized that in some fantastically alien, arachnoidal way, the being was *smiling* at him. Smiling at him and his three friends.

The creature's four arms darted out, and with one hand for each it took Clive and Annie and Smythe and Finnbogg by their hands. Annie's electrofield had been changed from a weapon of defense to a tool of communication for Clive's benefit, and Annie had been too drained by the transmission of Clive's message to du Maurier to remember to switch it back!

With surprising gentleness but with a strength that overwhelmed even squat, massive Finnbogg's, the spider-being drew the others along as it scuttled on its four legs toward the mouth of the cave that the savages had previously surrounded.

And as the spider creature's hand grasped Clive Folliot's, Clive felt a strange sense of communion, both with the spider-being and, through it, with his three companions. Perhaps this was the mental telepathy that George du Maurier spoke of, or perhaps it was something else, some sort of electrical exchange of the brain waves of the three humans and the doglike being and the spider creature.

Clive could feel himself drawn into the mind of the great spider. He found that he could know the creature, not as if he were hearing it speak but as if, in some miraculous manner, he had *become* the spider creature.

The being had no name as Clive would have known the term, but it thought of itself as the source of the great blood curdling shriek that Clive had heard time and again, and to him that became the creature's name: *Shriek.* There was no other possible

name for the creature, no other name that Annie or
Finnbogg or Smythe could possibly apply.

And even as he was identifying the being by that
name he realized that the creature was not a neuter
it but a being of astonishingly powerful sexuality.
Unquestionably, a *she*.

He was plumbing the mind of a sexually aware,
perhaps even a sexually aroused, female spider—and
what had he learned of the mating habits of arach-
nids? He tried to recall a Cambridge lecture on natural history. Yes, he could see the side-whiskered,
pink-cheeked, bespectacled don, could hear the qua-
vering, aged voice. Yes. The female spider mated,
and having mated, she devoured her consort.

But—Shriek was not a spider, any more than
Finnbogg was a dog or Clive and Annie were orang-
utans. They were the evolved descendants of those
ancestral species. He prayed that Shriek was civilized, that in the course of her species' evolution they
had abandoned the grisly practice of their ancestors.
And in a surge of pure mentation he received his
answer from the being that held him by the hand in
a grip as powerful as the one in which a nanny holds
her toddling charge.

And through Shriek, Clive found himself in a
strange mental contact with Finnbogg and Horace
Hamilton Smythe.

In Finnbogg's mind he found odd memories. Memories of the doglike being's childhood. Finnbogg's
earliest recollections were of his mother and his sisters and brothers. These creatures were indeed doglike; and doglike, Finnbogg's earliest and most
powerful recollections were olfactory. The warm, comforting odor of his dam, of her familiar flesh, of the
milk of her dugs. The rasping feel of her tongue as
she cleaned him and his brothers and sisters. The
odors of his littermates, similar to one another and
quite different from that of their dam, and yet as
sharply distinguishable from one another as the faces
of Clive's own friends. First the males could be dis-

tinguished from the females, but beyond that no two of the pups could be taken for each other. And the odor of his sire, strong and dominating, tinctured with the tang of a thousand tantalizing creatures and substances that the great male encountered outside the cozy kennel where the dam kept and nursed her pups . . .

Clive knew that he was getting led across the clearing, that he was entering the cave. He knew that the whole act must take mere seconds of time, and yet in the mental exchange that took place with and within Shriek, years of memories and experiences were being exchanged.

He entered the mind of Horace Hamilton Smythe, and suddenly he had access to all of Smythe's memories and all of his feelings. He had a whole new set of recollections. A childhood that had its beginnings on an idyllic little farm in the south of England. Smythe and his bustling, cheerful mother. His father was more taciturn, more stern, far less pleasant than his mother, but still a good and loyal and reliable man who cared for his home and his family and his nation. And there were others. Little Horace had his littermates too, his brothers and sisters. And a dog, a great affectionate creature.

It became clearer in Clive's mind. It was a bulldog, exquisitely ugly and massively affectionate. It was like Finnbogg, greatly like Finnbogg. But somehow there came blight, and the failure of the farm, and the death of Smythe's father. His mother, driven from the land, had gathered her children about her and gone northward. The great bulldog had been put to death—the saddest event of Horace Hamilton Smythe's life: the boy had wept for days, inconsolable. No wonder, Clive realized, Smythe had taken so to Finnbogg.

Then the widow Smythe and her offspring had sunk from genteel deprivation in London's suburbs to abject poverty in the metropolis's slums. The mother had drifted to more and more menial forms of work, the daughters to lives of shame and the sons to lives of crime, until young Horace had found a new home for himself in Her Majesty's service. But for a recruiting sergeant who had seen a deep-hidden strength and potential virtue in the youth, Smythe would probably have wound up floating in the Thames with a knife gouge in his belly, or swinging from a gallows at Dartmoor, long before now.

Clive shared Smythe's memories of his campaigns. He saw himself as Smythe had seen him—a not altogether flattering view, but one colored by a certain affection. He recalled with Smythe the latter's earlier encounters with Sidi Bombay and he saw Smythe's American adventure, much as the sergeant had explained it not long before.

There were other interludes in Horace Hamilton Smythe's life, odysseys and events that startled Clive Folliot. He saw Smythe bundled in furs, buffeted by icy winds and stinging sleet, struggling to climb the peaks of the Himalayas, approaching the sacred precincts of the secretive lands of Tibet and Nepal. He saw Smythe in the jungles of Amazonia, probing the lost civilizations of the empire of Brazil.

What was a simple quartermaster sergeant of Her Majesty's army doing in these remote climes? With a jolt, Clive realized that there was far more to Horace Hamilton Smythe than ever he had realized.

If Clive had such sudden and deep access to the minds and memories of his companions, he realized, they must have the same sort of access to his own mind. There were events in his life of which he was not proud, but nothing could be done now to protect himself from mental scrutiny. Things he would never think of revealing in his articles for Maurice Carstairs, these others would learn, whether he willed it or not.

Until now he had not approached User Annie in this strange mental communion, and for the moment he wondered if he ought to do so. His brush with the mind of Horace Hamilton Smythe had been surprisingly easy to deal with. He and Smythe were natives of the same country, of course, and they were nearly of an age (Smythe being the older of the two). He might have expected greater difficulty in making mental contact with Finnbogg. The dwarf, after all, was a being of another species, the product of another world. But perhaps the very doggishness of the massive Finnbogg, and the natural affinity between human and canine, had made the contact possible.

But Annie . . . He approached her mentally, and it was like approaching a beautiful, subtle light. As weary as she had been after the attempt to communicate with du Maurier, she moved now—if that was the word—with ineffable and untired grace. She drew him to herself, and he found himself floating toward her, eager, excited. But before he could touch the light that was Annie, she slipped away, dancing before him, dodging his mental touch like a will-o'-the-wisp.

Later, she seemed to whisper in his ear. *The time will come, Clive, the time will come.* He thought he saw her dancing, dancing nude. He reached for her again, but instead he came up against the mind of Shriek.

What were Shriek's memories? What were her thoughts? Clive could sense them, share them somehow, even as Shriek probed and picked through his own mind. He felt an intelligence greater than his own, an older and wiser one. But whereas the alienness of Finnbogg was that of a warm-blooded, doglike mammal—or something very much like one—Shriek was far more alien to Clive. She was an arachnoid, a cold-blooded, egg-laying, eight-legged, eight-eyed creature.

The chemistry of her body was far different from his own. She secreted chemicals that permeated the stiff bristles on her body, and when she chose to do so she could vary that chemistry to bring about the results she desired, from terror and submission to willing cooperation, to uncontrollable lust, to death.

She had not used this chemistry on Clive and his friends because there had been no need for it.

She wanted Clive and Annie and Finnbogg and Smythe for something. Clive could see the purpose in Shriek's mind, but it was a purpose so remote from his experience and his comprehension that it came to him as a meaningless blur of impressions.

Shriek shoved Clive and the others through the low mouth of the cave. The strange spell of communion with the others snapped as Shriek released each of them, but in the final moment of that communion something else happened.

Clive received the distinct impression that he and the others could regain that communion, with or without Shriek's intervention. Under her spell their minds and their infinitely complex networks of nerves had been altered. Willingly or not, knowingly or not, Shriek had given Clive and Annie and Smythe and Finnbogg the power to share their minds simply by lacing their fingers together and permitting themselves to flow into one another.

Behind Clive the mouth of the cave was blocked by Finnbogg's massive torso—Annie and Horace Hamilton Smythe had already followed him inside. The light from outside returned as Finnbogg emerged inside the cave, then darkened again as Shriek's spiderish shape filled the opening for a moment.

Then Shriek, too, was inside, and Clive and the others beheld the world that they and the spider-being had entered.

▪ FIVE ▪
THE
NESTED
WORLDS

▪ CHAPTER 20 ▪
Into the Nest

It was an oval, cavernous enclosure, its shape like the inside of an egg. The very air seemed to scintillate with glowing particles, so that the chamber was as bright as day although it contained no single, identifiable source of light.

Because of the odd illumination, Clive realized, he and his companions cast no shadows: every atom of air glowed!

Clive turned to see Shriek apparently blocking the circular opening through which they had entered the chamber. There should be a disk of daylight and a glimpse of the outer world, but Clive could find none such. Instead, the walls of the chamber were dotted with openings. Some of them were above his head, even in the ceiling of the chamber. Others were in the walls, and still others in the floor of the chamber.

All of them were illuminated, and all were of different—and brilliant—colors. Reds and greens and shimmering yellows and gaudy purples and shades of blue and of every other color Clive could identify. And many he could not.

Clive examined the options optically. "What do you think?" he asked the others.

"I think we've no future inside this Easter egg," Sergeant Smythe said.

"Precious little anywhere else," Clive responded.

User Annie had edged beside him. He felt the warmth of her body, and a slight tremor that passed through it. He held her to him. He was relieved that her electrofield was turned off.

"Exit program," Annie suggested.

Clive was tempted to lace his fingers into hers, to attempt to gain communion with her, but this was not the moment.

Shriek made a clicking sound with her mandibles. It was the first sound she had made—at least the first that Clive knew of—other than her uncanny screaming. She gestured toward the holes in the ovoid chamber.

Her meaning was obvious. They were not to stay here. They had their choice of which exit to take— any that they could reach, at any rate—and they were to act quickly.

Clive said, "Well, which shall it be? Any suggestions?"

Finnbogg chose not to participate in a debate. He pounced on the nearest hole, a bright disk that glowed aquamarine.

Clive whirled, intending to restrain the dwarf, but the movement was unnecessary. Finnbogg stood baffled, held upright by what appeared to be a surface of pure, solid light.

Horace Smythe stepped gingerly on a crimson hole, first testing it with the tip of one foot, then standing squarely on it, grinning. "Give it a try, Major! It tingles! Really makes these weary dogs feel happy again!"

Behind Finnbogg, Annie was getting into the spirit of the game, jumping from opening to opening, bouncing off solid disks of yellow, green, orange.

Clive grinned, jumped onto a circle of brilliant magenta—and felt himself swept through it, the only sensation a not unpleasant prickling that danced across his skin as he passed through the opening.

User Annie followed him, then Finnbogg, looking happy and relieved not to have been left behind.

Clive heard a scuffling behind him and looked over his shoulder to see Shriek enter the opening as well. She was not abandoning them, then.

At least not yet.

In an instant Clive felt himself sliding, accelerating in a downward chute. The magenta illumination came from the walls of the tube, as the illumination had come from the atoms of air in the egg-shaped chamber.

There might have been pictures or inscriptions on the inside of the tube, but if so they flashed by so rapidly that only the vaguest of impressions of them could be gained. Even as he slid, Clive pondered the oddity of the different-colored openings. It had appeared, briefly, that the companions had their choice as to which exit to take from the egg-shaped chamber. But every exit was sealed to them—certainly every exit that they tried—until Clive had tried to stand on the magenta disk.

Someone, or something had forced this choice upon them!

The chute let them out high on a hillside. Clive expected to behold some exotic vista; in this he was to be surprised, although by no means disappointed. The hillside was covered with vegetation, and fell away before their feet, extending to a prosperous valley.

Beside him, Clive heard Horace Hamilton Smythe exclaim, "I say, it's like home!"

Finnbogg issued a sound that obviously conveyed the same happy meaning.

And the vista *was* much like parts of the English countryside. Rolling hills, green fields, yellow-brown paths of hard-packed earth. There were even buildings, thatch-roofed cottages and, in the distance where Clive could barely make it out, an impressively large manor house built in classic Tudor style.

He rubbed his eyes. "Is it England?" He raised his head, fully hoping and half-expecting to see the blue English sky with its puffy clouds and friendly sun somewhere above a distant horizon.

But the horizon did not drop away as it ought to.

In the distance the land *rose* so that tiny, remote objects hung suspended above closer ones. Still farther, the landscape was obscured by gathering mist.

And overhead, instead of blue sky and yellow sun, Clive beheld a constellation of tiny stars revolving in an eternal dance around some common center. He blinked and turned. Perhaps they should retreat through the tunnel they had used to enter this inside-out world.

The mouth of the tunnel was nowhere to be seen. Not for the first time since embarking on this adventure, he realized that there was no turning back.

Shriek's powerful hand grasped Clive's, and a cold clicking and rasping voice said in his mind, "No, Clive Folliot, it is not England."

Clive knew that he had heard the rasp of Shriek's mandibles. He knew that her language was something more remote from his own, more alien to him than the most exotic dialect of Tibet or of the Australian aborigine. And yet while the contact was maintained, he understood her.

"Why did you bring us here?" Folliot asked the spider-being.

"I have awaited you for a very long time, Clive Folliot. For you and your companions."

"But—why? What have you to do with us? There are persons and forces operating behind the scenes, manipulating all of us. Who are they? What is their goal?"

Shriek's face twitched into her bloodcurdling version of a smile. "What is your goal, Clive Folliot?"

"To find my brother." Shriek should have learned that much from their prior mental communion. But, forced to question his own motive, he found himself wondering if he really did wish to find Neville. He might be happier if Neville were dead—or lost forever in the Dungeon, a result nearly as desirable. Either way, could Clive somehow find his way back to England, he would in time gain control of the Tewkesbury estates and holdings, the family fortune. He would be made for life, with or without the fame and fortune that a book might gain for him.

How much of his thought Shriek had comprehended, Clive could not fathom. In any case, she released her grip on him and scuttled down the hillside on her four spidery legs. Clive considered briefly setting off in another direction, but he sensed from Shriek a goodness of will and a source of strength not lightly to be forfeited. He addressed his other companions. "Let's stay together, then. Whatever transpires, our best chance is to remain united, to pool our resources, to help one another."

Finnbogg alone seemed to have an inkling of their whereabouts. Doglike, the dwarf was pacing back and forth on the hillside, swinging his muzzle, nostrils distended. Little whines of distress came from his throat.

"What's the matter, old fellow?" Clive asked him.

"Bad place, bad." Finnbogg butted Clive, almost knocking him to the ground. The massive Finnbogg obviously wanted reassurance, and Clive rubbed his head.

"Why's it a bad place, Finnbogg?"

Annie and Horace stood watching the others. Shriek had scuttled away. She stood at the bottom of the hill, peering back up at them.

After a moment she went on her way.

For Clive it was a moment of difficult decision. He had just made up his mind—or thought that he had—to follow Shriek. But Finnbogg was unwilling to continue just yet. Clive had to decide whether to follow the spider-being while abandoning Finnbogg, or to stay with the massive dwarf.

He could not abandon Finnbogg. He turned his face away from Shriek, looked reassuringly into Finnbogg's great liquid eyes. When he turned back, Shriek was gone. But Annie and Horace, to Clive's gratification, had remained with him and the dwarf.

Clive repeated his question to Finnbogg.

"Bad Nihonjin here. Not like anybody else. Not

like Finnbogg people, not like major people, not like
Q'oornans. Not like any gaijin. Bad Nihonjin kill
everybody, everybody, everybody." He set up a snuffling that would have been funny had his sadness
not been so profound and so sincere.

"Nihonjin?" Annie exclaimed. "Gaijin?"

"Yes, yes," Finnbogg panted. "Annie knows Nihonjin?"

"High probability, User Finnbogg. Nihonjin an-
thros? Femmes?"

Finnbogg shook his head in puzzlement.

"Ah—boy Nihonjin or girl Nihonjin?"

"All boys, all boys, yes! Nihonjin here, ooh, bad,
bad."

Clive said, "What are you talking about?"

Before Finnbogg or Annie could respond, Horace
Hamilton Smythe said, "I think I know what he
means, sah."

"You do?"

Even as they spoke, the four companions had
drifted toward the base of the hill, toward the place
where Shriek had last been seen. Clive peered around,
looking for the arachnoid, but to no avail.

"I do, sah," Smythe nodded.

"Well?"

"Has the major ever been out East?"

"No farther than Zanzibar, Smythe."

"I've been farther, sah. Been to the Far East. As I
recall, sah, the Japanese call their country Nippon,
or Nihon. They call themselves Nihonjin."

"Those quaint little folk?"

"There's a lot more to them than that, sah."

"Why, I've seen their paintings and vases. Quite
lovely. Heard a lecture or two about their customs.
Think I met one of them once. Took him for a
Chinese. Chap seemed upset. Don't see why. They
look quite alike, come from the same corner of God's
Earth, don't they? What's the difference, eh? But the
chap was quite emphatic about it, wouldn't let it pass.

Finally had to excuse myself. Deuced odd fellow, I'd say."

"Yes, sah." Smythe's face was a study in neutrality.

Clive looked around. Annie and Finnbogg were engaged in quiet conversation. Annie had seated herself on the ground and was speaking earnestly to the dwarf. She asked him questions and he nodded his great head in agreement or dissent.

"Call themselves Nihonjin, do they?" Clive said to Smythe. "Well, I don't see why old Finnbogg's so exercised about them. Just a bunch of polite little chaps, interested in arranging flowers and drinking tea and wearing those funny robes, whatever they call the odd things."

"Kimonos, sah."

"Indeed." Clive addressed Finnbogg. "Well, old chap, if you think these Nihonjin are so bad, I wonder what you propose we do, eh? You're sure they live hereabouts? Don't think we've fallen through the earth like some characters of Mr. Dodgson's, do you? And landed in Japan? Eh?"

"Nihonjin here. Finnbogg know. Know about Nihonjin. Not many, but very bad people, very fierce people. Even Q'oornans afraid of Nihonjin, friend Clive."

"And what do we do?"

"Can go back?" The dwarf pointed up the hill behind them. The opening through which they had emerged remained an illusive prey. "Back home, maybe? Back to river?"

"Let's take a look." Clive gestured vaguely toward the place where they had emerged.

Finnbogg broke away from the others and raced up the hill. Clive, Annie, and Smythe followed him, struggling and panting. The hillside was dotted by scrubby trees and brush. It had been a lot easier to descend than it was to climb back up, and all except Finnbogg used the vegetation for handholds to pull themselves along.

The dwarf arrived well ahead of his companions.

He leaped for the place where they had emerged—
and rebounded. He thumped the earth with his massive fists, kicked at it with his great feet, to no avail.
He pulled at bushes with his heavy fingers, tearing
away clods of soil, turning this way and that, snuffling at the ground and howling miserably, but finding no sign of the glowing chute.

"Cannot go back," he moaned. "Lost. Finnbogg
lost. Finnbogg's friends lost. Everybody lost. Oh,
Nihonjin come. Will eat roast Finnbogg for dinner."

"They're cannibals?" Clive gasped.

Finnbogg moaned.

"I wouldn't take the doggy chap's fears too seriously," Smythe advised.

"Eh?"

"Finnbogg's a simple soul, Major. And we've seen
how much he loves fanciful tales. Where did he
learn about the Nihonjin, anyway? Don't think he's
been here before, I don't. He doesn't seem to know
this place in particular. May be giving us an old
wives' tale—or the doggy equivalent of one, if the
major takes my meaning, sah."

Clive looked over the landscape, shading his eyes
with one hand. It was so devilishly *normal*, he thought.
In a paradoxical way, that was the strangest part of
all. He tried to reconstruct his experiences since entering the Dungeon at the ruby-hearted rock in the
Sudd.

What was the nature of the Dungeon?

At first it had seemed like a world comparable to
Earth, however strange it was in its own way. A black
planet turning in solitude, the millions and millions
of stars that Clive knew, all to one side, and the
mysterious swirling spiral to the other. As the Dungeon revolved, any point would face first the millions of stars—what Clive was coming to think of as
the known universe—and then the spiral that he felt
contained the answer to the mystery of the Dungeon.

But as one passed through levels, all of that
changed.

There was the strange aerial train, with its cars seemingly snatched from different loci in time and space.

There was the strange tumble when Clive and his companions had pursued Philo Goode and his confederates from the train.

There was the egglike chamber with its glowing multicolored disks. Why had all of the disks save one been fixed and impenetrable, while the one that brought the travelers to this hillside had opened effortlessly for them?

The structure of the Dungeon was a mystery, as much so as its purpose.

"Major, sah?"

Clive blinked.

"Hadn't we best be moving on, sah?"

"Whither, Smythe?"

"I don't know, sah. The major is the commanding officer, sah. One had hoped that he would offer a plan, sah." Smythe's face was as bland and as expectant as that of an innocent child.

"Well, I suppose there is no constructive point in merely standing about. I wish I knew where Shriek had gone, but there appears nothing to be gained by waiting around this hillside. She may never return." He didn't really believe that, but he felt that Smythe was right. Passivity was not the means to survival in the Dungeon.

"Suppose we follow a generally downward path," Clive suggested. "What's your opinion, Smythe?"

"Lacking other information, sah, that's most often a good idea. Leads to water, most often leads to any settlement in the region. And it's easiest on the troops. Solid military doctrine, as I'm sure the major will recall from his training with the Guards."

"Very well—"

"Only, sah, if I might make so bold, sah. Perhaps Miss Annie could use that device of hers to give us a map once more."

"Splendid idea, yes." He looked at the young woman.

Without a word, she reached inside her bodice and did something to the Baalbec A-9. "How's this?" she asked.

In the air before her appeared a three-dimensional image of the landscape before them. It resembled one of the sand-table models that Brigadier Leicester's staff officers used in pointing out tactical problems when the Guards were preparing to go on maneuvers.

Clive could see the hillside where they stood. He searched in vain for a tiny representation of the glowing disk through which they had emerged. Hills and vales spread before them, and a few gentle streams that flowed together to make larger streams. Eventually, if the insubstantial model were large enough, Clive might learn where the streams led: to lakes, rivers, eventually to the sea. And of course to the distant villages that held such tantalizing hope of understanding, if not of ultimate escape from the Dungeon.

Was there a port? Were there ships and sailors who knew the full geography of this world?

To the right of the travelers, beyond a row of gentle hills, the model showed a flat plain, little more than a large meadow.

All of the landscape that the model showed was quiet, pastoral, still. All except the meadow.

There, something stirred.

• CHAPTER 21 •
Nihonjin!

"Let's find out," Clive commended.

Annie moved her hand and the ghostly miniature disappeared.

They started forward, Clive and Horace Smythe in the lead, Annie close behind them to encourage poor Finnbogg. The dwarf was trembling and whining, frightened to proceed but even more frightened at the prospect of being left behind.

They didn't keep track of how long it took them to reach the next range of hills, nor did they have to round the grass-covered slope to find out what it was that had stirred on the meadow. Something—something little bigger than a moving speck—rounded the base of the nearest hill.

Clive stared. "What's that?"

"Can't tell, sah. But it's coming this way. We'll know soon enough."

The four companions continued to move toward the hill and the object continued to move toward them.

"It—looks like a vehicle. A coach, perhaps."

"I don't like this, sah. I don't know quite what it is, or who's behind all this. I'm afraid Finnbogg may be right, though, about those Japanese."

Clive shook his head. "Whoever they are, Smythe, we can use all the friends we can get in this heaven-forsaken place."

"I'm not so sure they're friends, sah. That's my point."

Finnbogg, in the meantime, was whining and cowering behind Annie. Annie had halted and was peering beneath the shade of one hand at the approaching vehicle.

"It isn't quite a coach," Clive said. "Looks more like some sort of bicycle, rickshaw kind of thing. See those two chaps pedaling away there, side by side. And those roller things instead of wheels. And their grand muck-a-muck up on that seat in the back."

The contraption had approached within hailing distance, actually less than the length of a rugby field. Clive could see the two men who bent over handlebars, their legs revolving steadily on pedals that drove the rollers that propelled the vehicle. The man who sat in the center of the rear seat of the contraption held his arms crossed over his chest. Even as the machine bumped along, he reached to his side and brought up a peculiar device and held it to his face.

"What's that thing?" Clive asked.

Sergeant Smythe said, "Looks like a spyglass. Two of 'em, sah, lashed together. I think the chap's inspecting us."

The man lowered the device.

"Look at 'im now, sah. Really laying into those two blighters, ain't 'e? And they're putting their backs into it mightily. Making that cart go like the dickens!"

As the vehicle approached, its mechanism could be heard clattering and its parts creaking like a coach bouncing along a dirt road in rural Sussex, It skidded to a halt a few yards from Clive and the others. The two pedalers hopped off and stationed themselves between the cart and Clive's party. They were brown-skinned men with Oriental features, both apparently in their forties. They wore the much-patched but meticulously preserved remnants of tan military uniforms, cloth-wrapped leggings, and makeshift boots.

The man riding behind them stood without leaving the cart. He appeared to be ten years older than the others, and wore a uniform with more elaborate markings. He pointed at Annie and shouted a command in a language Clive did not understand.

Folliot drew himself up. Speaking in the local patois, he demanded to know his identity.

The man looked startled, but he recovered and switched from his own language to the patois. "I am Sergeant Chuichi Fushida of the Sixteenth Imperial Japanese Airborne Marine Detachment. And you are my prisoners. You will follow us to our base."

"Not a chance of that," Clive responded. "Sergeant, are you." He turned to Horace Hamilton Smythe. "Perhaps you'd better deal with this chap."

"Understand, sah," Smythe replied. "Smythe here, my brother. Regimental Chief Quartermaster Sergeant, Her Majesty's Fifth Imperial Horse Guards. Perhaps we can settle this thing, eh, Sergeant? What's that name again, Fushida?"

The Oriental appeared thunderstruck. "Horse Guards? Her Majesty? What majesty? What horse guards?"

Now it was Smythe's turn to show startlement. "What majesty? Why, Her Imperial Majesty Victoria."

The Japanese sergeant frowned. "Victoria? Of England?"

"The same."

"Victoria has been dead for years." He shouted a command to his two subordinates. They reached into the equipage of the cart and brought out carbines. Brilliantly polished bayonets protruded from the front of each weapon.

Annie had stood, staring at the entire exchange.

Finnbogg cowered behind her, whining and quivering.

The two armed Japanese ran forward, menacing the travelers with their weapons.

"This ain't working, Major Folliot. We'd best defend ourselves." Smythe brandished his cyberclaw.

Clive followed suit.

The first marine ran toward Folliot and Smythe;

the second, toward Annie and Finnbogg. "Doesn't look like they're going to shoot us, anyway," Smythe said. "Maybe they don't have any ammunition."

Finnbogg was backing away, shaking his head in fright, setting up a din of whines and whimpers.

Annie reached inside her bodice to turn on the electrofield but the marine nearest her swung his carbine butt-first against the side of her head. With a sickening thud the weapon connected with her skull and she collapsed to the ground and into an even more frightening silence.

Horace Hamilton Smythe was feinting and jabbing at the second marine, using his cyberclaw as a dirk. He was at a distinct disadvantage as the carbine and bayonet gave the Japanese marine a longer reach.

The cyberclaw clashed against the bayonet and slid along the barrel of the carbine. The marine reversed his weapon and swung its butt toward Smythe. Smythe danced away.

Clive started toward Annie, but came first to Finnbogg. The dwarf was curled up on the ground.

Folliot kicked him angrily, shouting, "Get up, you great coward. We're in a fight now! Get up and give an account of yourself." Finnbogg flattened himself on the ground, groveling.

"No," Finnbogg wailed. "No, n-o-o-o. Nihonjin kill everybody, cook everybody, eat everybody. Not eat Finnbogg! Go away, Nihonjin! Go away, Folliot man!"

Folliot bent over the supine Finnbogg. He seized him by the shoulders and tugged at him, enraged at the great dwarf's craven behavior.

Folliot snarled. He felt a glancing blow to the back of his head and tumbled, stunned, across the form of Finnbogg. He blinked. The bright sky whirled. For an instant he saw the face of one of the enemy marines bending over him, leering eagerly. He saw the marine raise his carbine. The weapon was held butt-downward over Clive's forehead. Apparently the Japanese intended to crush Clive's skull with the butt of the weapon rather than eviscerate him with the bayonet that gleamed in the sunlight.

It was a moment of strange clarity and calm. Clive felt as if he were separated from his body. He could see himself lying on his back, squinting against the sky. He could see the Japanese marine staring at him. He could see the carbine, a small rifle with a wooden stock and a heavily textured plate at its butt. He realized that this plate, weighted by the wood and steel of the weapon and powered by the wiry but muscular arms of the marine, would crush his skull and drive fragments of bone into his brain, obliterating him utterly, at any moment.

He even noted, with curiosity, a hinge on the carbine's stock just behind the receiver and trigger housing. He wondered at the purpose of that construction, and felt a pang of regret at the realization that he would never live to inquire.

Sunlight glinted again on the polished bayonet and the carbine began its descent.

The Japanese marine whirled across Clive, performing a perfect somersault. At the very edge of his vision Clive saw the man land on his feet, staggering.

The form of Horace Hamilton Smythe flashed above Clive.

Folliot was able to push himself to his hands and knees. He crouched on the grass, watching Smythe and the Japanese marine face each other. The odd moment of disembodied calm was past, and Clive heard a ringing in his ears, felt a pain in his skull and the nausea that he knew came with concussion.

The Japanese marine lunged at Smythe. He was using the bayonet now, performing a perfectly orthodox drill that Clive had seen a hundred times on the training fields and parade grounds of the Fifth Imperial Horse Guards.

Horace Hamilton Smythe was armed only with his cyberclaw, and to Clive Folliot's startlement, the sergeant had slipped the claw back into the waistband of his trousers. Instead of using his own weapon, he

sidestepped the lunging marine. The marine, his
weight committed to the bayonet stroke, fell easy
prey to Smythe. The Englishman caught the Japanese by shoulder and elbow, adding to his momentum
as he collided with Smythe's extended leg.

The Japanese tumbled through the air.

He landed on his back and stared up in astonishment at Horace Hamilton Smythe, who somehow
had plucked the carbine from his grasp as he spun
to the earth.

There was a clattering behind Clive. He turned
and saw the pedal-powered cart bouncing away. The
Japanese marine who had struck Annie to the ground
had loaded her inert form onto the cart. Now he was
pedaling furiously at one station while his commanding sergeant had unbent from his stiff posture on
the rear seat and assumed the other position as
pedaler.

"Stop them! They've got Annie!" Clive took a few
staggering steps after the cart. He realized that he
couldn't possibly catch it—even if he were not still
half-stunned.

"Down, sah!" came Sergeant Smythe's voice from
behind him. Clive dropped in his traces, turned to
see what Smythe was up to. The sergeant had raised
the Japanese carbine to his shoulder and was sight-
ing carefully at the cart.

Clive shouted, "No, Smythe—you'll hit Annie!"

But Smythe squeezed the trigger. Clive heard a
click from the weapon. Smythe lowered it, opened
the receiver. "No ammunition. An empty magazine
but no ammunition."

"We'd better get after that cart, Smythe!" Clive
took a few more unsteady steps, then halted, weak
and dizzy.

"No chance of that right now, sah. Let's see what
we can get out of this chap. We have to make a plan.
See what we can do with Finnbogg while we're at it.
Too bad Madame Shriek has decamped. Perhaps
we'll see her again, sah."

The marine, lying on the ground near Smythe, scrambled on his hands and feet. He launched himself at the Englishman. Without bothering to look around, Smythe stepped aside. The marine slammed past him and Smythe pricked him in the hindquarters with the bayonet.

"Chaps keep their pieces clean and their bayonets honed, anyway," Smythe murmured. "Pity they don't keep any bullets in their pieces."

The Japanese marine started to climb to his feet but Smythe stopped him with a sharp command. In the local patois he said, "You just sit where you are, fellow. Put your feet straight out in front of you and your hands behind your back. That's a good bloke. I don't want to kill you, but you've had too many chances already and you won't get another. Major Folliot—"

Clive looked at Smythe.

Smythe hesitated briefly. Then he said, "Sah, suppose I hand you this piece. Keep the bayonet pointed at this blighter, and if he tries anything, let's just spill his innards on the ground, eh?"

Clive took the weapon and stood over the prisoner.

Smythe knelt beside the man and unwrapped the cloth leggings from his ankles. "Always wondered what these things were any good for," he grumbled. He scuttled around the Japanese and with one unraveled legging tied the man's arms firmly together behind his back. He knotted one end of the second legging to the man's wrists so that it became, in effect, a leash.

"Don't want this chap to run away, now."

Keeping one eye on their prisoner, Folliot and Smythe examined the carbine. Smythe discovered the purpose of the hinged stock: the carbine could be folded, for compact packing.

"Why do you want to fold a carbine in half?" Smythe asked the prisoner.

The man stared blankly past Smythe.

"I asked you a question," Smythe snapped.

The Japanese continued to stare. His air was more
one of shock than of defiance.

"Maybe another little pricking with his own bayonet, Sergeant Smythe," Clive suggested.

Smythe considered briefly. Then he drew himself
up in his best parade ground manner. "Private, report!" he roared.

The Japanese squared his shoulders. His eyes grew
brighter, as if he were more on the alert even if
confused.

"Onishi, Shigeru, private, Sixteenth Airborne Marine Detachment, Sergeant, sir!"

"Good! And where are you stationed, Private
Onishi?"

"Onemak Island, Kwajalein Atoll, Sergeant, sir!"

"And your commanders?"

"Senior Lieutenant Takamura, sir! Junior Lieutenant Yamura, sir! Sergeant Fushida, sir!"

"You ever hear of those places, sah? What did he
say? Onemak, Kwajalein." Smythe looked at Folliot.

Clive said, "I think I recall Kwajalein. Some little
spit of coral out in the western Pacific. Don't think
the empire has reached that far, as yet. Don't know
why anybody would want it. Perhaps as a resupply
point for merchant ships."

There was a tugging at Clive's ankle and a whining
from his feet. He turned and saw Finnbogg cringing
and cowering. The dwarf's massive frame was still
quivering and his cheeks were wet with tears.

"Coward," Clive sneered. "Traitor. What do you
want, Finnbogg?"

"Finnbogg sorry, Folliot man," the dwarf sobbed.
"Finnbogg so afraid. Nihonjin, bad Nihonjin men—"

"Never mind. I know. Nihonjin roast people for
dinner. And they've got Annie now. We've got to get
her out of their clutches!"

"Japanese marines are not cannibals!" Private Onishi
snapped. The man was coming back to himself. These
were the first words he had volunteered. "We obey

the will of the emperor. You should know as much, you English. You have a king of your own."

"A queen, not a king. But yes."

"King."

Exasperated, Clive said, "Come now. Victoria reigns and all is well with the empire. She's been our sovereign for thirty-one glorious years. Since 1837."

The Japanese laughed. "What year is it now, do you think Englishman?"

"It's 1868, of course!"

"It's 2603 by the Japanese calendar. Meiji year '76. By your Western calendar, it is the year 1943."

Folliot stared into the man's face.

The Japanese lost some of his assuredness. "We have been in the Dungeon since 1943."

Sergeant Smythe stepped around the prisoner to stand beside Clive Folliot. He peered at the marine. "Since 1943, eh? Your chaps have been here since 1943? Your whole unit? Officers, sergeants, and all?"

"Yes!"

"And how long has that been? How old were you when this happened? How did it happen?"

The Japanese appeared even more confused. "I—do not know how long we have been here. We have suffered. We came at night. There were whirling stars. We thought they were some new weapon of the Americans. General MacArthur, Admiral Nimitz, President Roosevelt—the Americans have great leaders, more weapons than we have."

A shudder racked the man's frame. "But it was not the Americans. It was the Q'oornans. Since we have been here we have been attacked by monsters, raided by bandits. Men disappear. Our ammunition is all gone. Our fuel is all gone, so we converted our vehicles to pedal carts. Our Nakajima airplane no longer flies. The pilot, Sergeant Nomura, refused to let us salvage it for parts; he polishes and cares for the Nakajima as if it were a sacred shrine. We could get good parts from the Nakajima. Wheels, gears, good sheet metal."

"You've been here a long while, then. You didn't tell me your age."

"I was sixteen when we came to the Dungeon."

Smythe cocked an eye at the man. "Have you seen a mirror lately? Look at yourself, Private! Lines in your face. Gray in your hair. If you ask me, you're on the shady side of forty. If you're not there, you're close to it."

Onishi shrugged.

"They've been here twenty years," Smythe said to Folliot, "maybe a bit more. That would make it 1963 by their reckoning. Seems to me they just forgot about the passage of time, once they arrived here."

"But it's 1868," Clive insisted.

"It is for us, sah. We don't really understand the Dungeon even yet, do we, sah?"

"I wish du Maurier were here, Sergeant. You don't know the man, but this is the kind of puzzle that his mind loves to grapple with. Perhaps the Dungeon exists on some—I don't know what to call it—well, time track, I suppose. Some time track that is separate from our own. It isn't just a different place, it's a different *kind* of place, where geography and chronology don't work the same way they do on Earth. Oh, du Maruier would love it!"

Onishi said, "By 1963 the war will be over. General Tojo will dictate peace terms to President Roosevelt. Admiral Yamamoto will ride his white horse on the White House lawn!"

"I wouldn't know about that, Private. That's a problem for your century, not for mine!"

He threw a scornful look at Finnbogg, then a more respectful one at Horace Smythe. "Our problem is to find Private Onishi's detachment and rescue Annie."

"Oh yes," Finnbogg wailed. "Rescue Annie. Rescue Annie, find Shriek, go 'way from Nihonjin. Go 'way from Nihonjin!"

"Our council of war is convened," Clive announced.

▪ CHAPTER 22 ▪
New Kwajalein Atoll

It was Finnbogg who redeemed himself, who risked his life to save the life of another, whose great cowardice, in the end, was not as great as his loyalty and his courage. But before any of that could happen, Clive Folliot had to have his confrontation with the dwarf.

"They are ordinary men, Finnbogg. No different from Sergeant Smythe and myself. You're not terrified of us."

"No, not afraid of Folliot man, Smythe man."

"Then why are you so terrified of the Japanese—the Nihonjin?"

"Nihonjin eat people."

"How do you know that?"

"Know it."

"How, Finnbogg? Have you encountered Nihonjin before? Have you been in this part of the Dungeon?"

The massive being shook his head. "Not here before. Q'oornans tell Finnbogg. Show pictures. Tell stories."

Clive exchanged glances with Horace Smythe.

"Tell us the stories they told you, Finnbogg," Smythe urged.

Before the dwarf could answer, Clive said, "What about Annie? Why are we not pursuing the cart in which they took her away?"

"Cart moves too fast, sah. We couldn't catch up by direct pursuit. Have to do something better than that. Outsmart the Nihonjin if we can."

Clive rubbed his chin. "Suppose you're right, Smythe. But it's hard to remain calm and analytical with Annie in the clutches of those devils."

"Yes, sah." He gestured encouragingly to Finnbogg.

"Q'oornans say, Nihonjin have Crown of the Castle. Anyone who wears crown will become Lord of Castle. Nihonjin not let others get crown. Kill anyone who try. Cook 'em, eat 'em up."

"The Q'oornans told you this?"

Finnbogg nodded vigorously, completely human in the act.

"But—why would they tell you this? They used you only as a guard at the bridge, did they not?"

"Finnbogg was good guardian. Not ever let anyone pass. Only let Folliot men pass. Let Neville Folliot pass. Let Clive Folliot pass. Like Folliot men."

"Yes. But why would the Q'oornans tell you about the Nihonjin? They never intended you to reach this level of the Dungeon, did they?"

Finnbogg shook his head, bafflement written clearly upon his features.

"He doesn't know, sah." Smythe, keeping an eye on Private Onishi, lowered his voice to Clive. "The doggy bloke isn't too bright, sah, I don't think. There's a lot of questions old Finnbogg can't answer, sah. I suggest the major not waste too much time pursuin' so dim and flickerin' a lamp, if the major takes my meaning, sah."

Clive looked at Finnbogg, then back at Sergeant Smythe. "Point taken, Sergeant. What do you propose, then?"

Smythe turned to Finnbogg. "What else do you know about these Nihonjin, old fellow? What was that about a crown, eh?"

"Q'oornans tell Finnbogg since he was a puppy, Nihonjin kill everybody, cook 'em 'n' eat 'em. That's why Finnbogg scared. Finnbogg sorry, sorry friend Smythe, sorry friend Folliot. Finnbogg love sweet Annie. If Nihonjin cook Annie, Finnbogg kill Nihonjin. Kill 'em! Kill 'em! Kill 'em all!"

The dwarf's eyes blazed, his lips drew back to reveal rows of huge, pointed canine teeth.

Private Onishi cowered, trying to keep Horace Smythe between himself and the dwarf.

"You've got your courage back, Finnbogg?" Clive was not convinced.

"Finnbogg sorry he was scared, Folliot man. Next time will be brave. Next time kill Nihonjin if Nihonjin hurt Annie!"

Clive turned to Smythe. "D'you think we can trust him—after he funked on us?"

Smythe looked at Finnbogg and nodded. "I think so, sah."

"Cowardice to courage, just like that? Not easy to believe."

"I understand, sah. But I think the fellow was taught all his life to fear the Japanese. Never saw 'em, it seems. They were like boogeymen to him. Horrible fantasy figgers to scare naughty children, eh? Then—suddenly—there they are."

He jerked his head toward Private Onishi. "Now we've seen 'em. Finnbogg knows they're only human. *Pshaw*, we've got one of our own right here on a leash. He won't funk on us again, Major. I'd bet a year's pay vouchers on it!"

Clive rubbed his eyes with the heels of his hands. Images of Annie lying on the ground, of Annie being driven away in the Japanese pedal cart, rose to haunt him. For an errant moment he wondered how the marine had managed to hit her with the butt of his carbine if she had turned on the electrofield of her Baalbec A-9. Well, he wasn't certain that it had been turned on.

Annie had indicated that the Baalbec drew on her own strength for its power. For that reason, she used it only when the need arose. She did not keep it turned on when there was no immediate requirement. If the Japanese marine had caught her off guard . . . Or perhaps it *had* been turned on. A quick and heavy blow with the carbine might have succeeded anyway. And once Annie was unconscious, would the electrofield continue to function?

He didn't know, couldn't find out, and besides, the whole topic was a distraction from the business of the moment. He had to develop a battle plan, the objective of which was to free Annie from her captors.

"What was that about a crown, old fellow?" Sergeant Smythe was still trying to unravel Finnbogg's snarl of information, superstition, and fears.

Finnbogg, always volatile, had shifted from a sniveling coward to a raging warrior, eager to be away and at the enemy.

Private Onishi, formerly the aggressive marine, had traded roles with Finnbogg and become the coward.

"You've got to calm yourself," Smythe persisted. "We won't get anywhere by going off half-cocked. Now tell me, what was this about a crown? Was this something the Q'oornans told you? Something to do with the Nihonjin? Come along, Finnbogg, you've got to speak up."

Finnbogg slumped back on his haunches. The impact of his massive hindquarters literally shook the earth. "Q'oornans say, Lord of Castle had crown. Couldn't see crown. Crown like ice, like glass, like air. Crown there but cannot see it."

"All right, an invisible crown, eh? Invisible? You know what that is?"

"Yes, yes, invisible crown. But crown visible when True Lord wear it! Finnbogg know that! Q'oornans know that!"

"What Lord of Castle, then? What lord? What castle?"

"Don't know." Finnbogg was becoming downcast. "Don't know. Some castle, some lord. Only know what Q'oornans say."

"All right, then." Smythe cast glances at his prisoner from time to time; the man cowered from Finnbogg. Otherwise, the Japanese was docile enough.

As for Major Folliot, he was attending the dialogue closely. "Now," Smythe asked Finnbogg, "since we don't know anything about this mysterious Lord of the Castle, did the Q'oornans tell you why the lord doesn't have his crown anymore? What are the Japanese doing with it?"

Finnbogg nodded his massive head, delighted to be able to answer Smythe's questions. "Nihonjin raid castle. Long ago, Nihonjin had flying thing. Like cart, like train, like flying enemy on bridge. Nihonjin come to castle in flying thing, kill lord's soldiers, try to steal lady. Big battle. Many of lord's soldiers killed. Many Nihonjin killed, too. Many, many, many! Nihonjin get lord's invisible crown."

He rolled the word *invisible* gleefully. It was a new word for him. Even Clive Folliot, listening to the dialogue between Smythe and Finnbogg, watching them both as they conversed, could sense Finnbogg's pleasure in the word.

"And then, Finnbogg—what then?"

"Lord of Castle soldiers drive away Nihonjin. Nihonjin fly away."

"And they never attacked again?"

"Nihonjin flying thing no more fly."

"I see." Smythe nodded vigorously. He shot a glance at Clive Folliot.

"Out of fuel, eh, Sergeant? And no refueling station here in the Dungeon. Wonder what the thing worked with. Wood, coal, they should have been able to get something, don't you think?"

Smythe turned to Private Onishi. He tugged his leash to get his attention. "What about that, Private? You blokes have a flying machine? Broke down? Out of fuel? Why didn't you just stoke up with wood, eh?"

The Japanese frowned. "Nakajima requires petrol. No petrol in the Dungeon—or no way to get at it!"

"What's petrol?"

"Fuel! Engine fuel! You would not know about it

in your year. It is a liquid. You have alcohol, Englishman?"

"For drinking?"

Clive Folliot put in, "We used other forms of alcohol in the laboratory at Cambridge. The natural philosophers did, that is. It's inflammable stuff, all right. I 'magine it could be used to fuel an engine."

"And this machine—this Nakajima?"

"Model ninety-seven," the Japanese responded. "We were swept from Kwajalein to the Dungeon. We have encountered others here, other men from Earth and other creatures as well. We learned the patois. But we live together! Sixteenth Airborne Marines! Banzai!"

"Yes, that's all very well, Private Onishi."

Onishi looked away from Clive. "Sergeant—Sergeant Smythe." It was obvious that the other's rank had brought Onishi around. Trained in the authoritarian tradition of his empire, he would obey a military man of higher rank. "Sergeant, who is this man?" He indicated Clive.

"This is Major Folliot, Private. You mind your p's and q's around him!"

Onishi snapped to attention, every muscle aquiver.

Clive said, "And what of this crown that Finnbogg spoke of? Did you marines really raid some castle and capture an invisible crown? Sounds like a fairy tale to me."

"It is the truth, Major! I was not on the raid. The Nakajima ninety-seven normally carries only three men, four at most. Lieutenant Takamura has the crown now."

"And what's this invisibility business?"

"This is true, Major. The crown—when Lieutenant Takamura takes it off, you can see it, although just barely. It—it seems to flee to the edge of one's vision. Even holding it in the hand—I have never been permitted to touch it, of course, but I have been told—even holding it in the hand, one has to

look at the crown from the corner of the eye, and
then it can barely be seen."

He shook his head.

"And when one wears it—I have seen Lieutenant
Takamura—the crown cannot be seen at all."

"That sound right to you, Finnbogg?" Clive asked.

"Q'oornans say, when rightful Lord of Castle wear
crown, crown will glow like gold!"

"That true, Onishi? The crown ever glow that you
know of?"

"No, sir."

"Who was wearing it when your Nakajima attacked?
Did your officers see anyone wear it? Think this is all
a fairy tale, do you?"

"No, sir. But I never heard of the crown glowing,
sir, Major."

"All right. Now then, how are we going to get
Annie away from this chap's people? Don't suppose
they'd swap, do you, Smythe?"

"Don't think they would, sah. I don't know a great
deal of the Oriental character—"

"More than I, Sergeant!"

"As the major says, sah. But I don't think those
blokes would care to swap, no sah."

"Finnbogg go and take a look." The great dwarf
jumped up and down, shaking the earth.

"Look where, Finnbogg?"

"Look there." Finnbogg pointed. "Cart come from
around hill. Go back around hill. Finnbogg go take a
look."

"But they'll see you coming. There's just the one
of you."

A sly grin—the first Clive had seen there—creased
Finnbogg's massive face. "Finnbogg not go around
hill. Finnbogg go over hill. Peep down at Nihonjin."

"You're not afraid of them?"

"No more! Finnbogg ashamed! Finnbogg never be
afraid again." He walked around the prisoner, duck-
ing under the leash that Sergeant Smythe still held.
Private Onishi shrunk away from Finnbogg, but

Finnbogg grasped the leash and pulled the marine to him. The man, although shorter than either Clive Folliot or Horace Smythe, was still a full head taller than the massive dwarf.

Onishi shook visibly.

Finnbogg rubbed his jaw against the man's torso, circling him completely, dragging his great underslung teeth against Onishi. When he finished, Onishi trembled so hard that he had to crouch, pressing his hands against the earth to steady himself.

Finnbogg bounced up and down, laughing a blood-curdling laugh.

"I believe you, Finnbogg. But I'm afraid you'll become carried away by passion and try to charge the enemy camp. Can you carry me up the hill with you, Finnbogg? I could walk it, but it would take many hours. Too many hours," Clive said. "We can scout this out together. Promise me, Finnbogg, when we get there you'll stay down. Stay low. Just get to the top of that hill and peer down and when you've seen what there is to see, you'll just come back to me and report. No one-man raids. No heroics. Are you a member of this band? For better or for worse, I'm the commander of our little unit, and if you are a member of it you must obey me. Will you do that?"

Finnbogg shook his head up and down, his tongue lolling like that of a dog. "Oh, yes. Major Folliot, commanding officer, yes, yes, yes." Finnbogg snapped a crude version of a salute at Clive and stood clumsily at his version of attention.

"Wonder where Finnbogg learned to do that," Sergeant Smythe muttered.

"All I care about is Annie, now," Clive sighed.

Smythe said, "All right, Private Onishi. You can sit down now. Don't try anything or you're a dead man. How come you've no ammunition for that carbine of yours?"

Onishi, apparently relieved to engage in military shop talk with another soldier, opened up. Clive Folliot stood a few feet away, listening to the conversation without joining in. After all, he was a commissioned officer and these two were enlisted men.

Clive Folliot felt himself swept up and held under one of Finnbogg's mighty arms. Finnbogg started toward the hill behind which the Japanese cart had disappeared.

"Major Folliot all right?" the dwarf asked. He carried Clive as a child carries a doll, as if the man's weight meant nothing to him.

"I'm all right," Clive managed. "Just get us there, Finnbogg."

They jounced and pounded up the hillside. Clive knew that he would be more bruised at the end of this ride than ever he had been after the most strenuous of trips on horseback, but he cared nothing about that.

Annie. She was his only thought. *Annie.* Private Onishi had denied the report that the Nihonjin were cannibals. The man had seemed sincere enough, and yet, if his unit had been wandering twenty years in the Dungeon, any transformation, any accusation brought against them, might be true.

Twenty years!

What if they had indeed become cannibals!

Twenty years!

Another possibility, even more horrifying than that of Annie's death, dawned upon Clive. A band of men, marooned for twenty years in a world unimaginably alien and far from home—and suddenly, in possession of a beautiful young woman! Clive ground his teeth in anguish.

The hillside rolled by beneath Clive's eyes. He felt something chilly and wet on his face and turned his sight skyward. Beyond the shape of Finnbogg's broad shoulders and massive head, the sky over the Dungeon was darkening, darkening with the combination of dusk and rain clouds.

Another drop stung Clive's cheek, and another.

The wind began to whip past him, and the temperature dropped sharply.

Within minutes they sky was a somber gray. Huge, fat-bellied clouds roiled, and the air felt laden with moisture. A bolt of lightning shot from a black cloud to the earth and held its position, sizzling and wavering for a full second before it snapped back out of existence. A few seconds later thunder boomed across the valleys.

Clive looked ahead. They were approaching the crest of the hill. He hissed a warning to Finnbogg. The powerful dwarf halted and placed Clive carefully on his feet. Clive gestured with his hand—*down*. Finnbogg nodded his comprehension and dropped to the ground, crouching as low as his massive form permitted.

Clive slithered ahead. He peered over the crest of the hill. A cup-shaped valley opened beneath them, surrounded by hills except for an opening at each end. A stream flowed in one end of the depression and out the other. In the center of the little valley it broadened to form a lake. Clive wondered how deep it might be.

Tents and rude shelters were set up around the edges of the pond. Clive tried to remember his geography. The arrangement of the shelters was familiar to him. Yes! If the lake were a lagoon . . . if the hills and shelters had been low coral islands . . . the arrangement would have been almost identical to a Pacific Ocean atoll.

The Nihonjin had recreated their last base, Kwajalein.

· CHAPTER 23 ·
The Sacred

And now the storm struck in all its fury.

In the little valley, campfires had been built, and men in the meticulously preserved and repaired remnants of the uniforms of Imperial Japanese Marines cleaned their weapons, policed their areas, or prepared to cook their evening meal.

It was not clear to Clive what food they were preparing, nor could he fathom where they had obtained their supplies. There were a few patches of land with plants laid out in carefully tended rows. Perhaps the Japanese raised a few vegetables and obtained additional food by forage or hunting. Perhaps there were fish in the stream that passed through this otherworldly Kwajalein, or in the pond that stood in the middle of the encampment.

Marines ran to snatch up burning coals, shoveling them into stone boxes and carrying them beneath their simple shelters. Yes, if they had truly been stranded in the Dungeon for twenty years or more, they would preserve their fires as treasures.

But where was Annie?

Clive grasped Finnbogg by the shoulder, gestured down at the encampment. He had intended to make only a reconnaissance of the enemy position, but the storm offered an opportunity that would not soon return.

By now, the marines had retired to their shelters. Their guards—if they posted guards at all, after twenty years—were huddled in lean-tos, rain-drenched and wind-whipped, warming their hands over precious fires.

There was no path down the hillside, but the descent was fairly easy nonetheless. Clive made his way from one clump of vegetation to the next, stopping to lean against the trunk of a tree now and then and peer ahead. Massive Finnbogg had dropped to all fours; for him the going was easier yet.

Their only peril lay in the darkness and the teeming rain. Rain-soaked grass can become slippery, and uncovered patches of dirt turned to slippery clay and then to running mud as the downpour continued.

Some thirty yards from the bottom of the slope, and another ten from the nearest lean-to, Clive halted, crouched behind a clump of bushes as high as his waist. The rain was still falling but signs had appeared that the storm was beginning to dissipate. There were breaks in the black cloud cover, and a sliver of light from the enigmatic sky reflected off the wind-whipped surface of the lagoon.

The Japanese shelters were barely visible. Cracks of light glowed from most of them. On the opposite side of the lagoon he could make out a strip of land, cleared of vegetation and hard-packed. At one end of it stood a gleaming, streamlined machine unlike anything Clive had ever before laid eyes on. If he could identify it in any way, it was remotely like some of the incredible machines that visionary artists drew for inclusion in the most sensational of publications, machines that were intended to fly above the housetops, even to travel to distant worlds.

This must be the Nakajima that Private Onishi had spoken of.

Clive heard the slow breathing of Finnbogg. He reached to lay a restraining hand on the dwarf's arm. He pointed to the nearest lean-to. The storm was still creating a din, and Clive felt that he could safely speak to Finnbogg.

"There's no sign of Annie," Clive whispered. "We've got to locate her!"

Finnbogg grunted his understanding.

"We can separate, Finnbogg. We've got to keep low, keep quiet, get a look into each shelter until we find where she is being held. Then—"

"Then kill Nihonjin!" Finnbogg rumbled. "Kill bad Nihonjin, save good Annie, go back Smythe man."

"Don't be so quick to use violence," Clive whispered. "We don't know how many there are of them, but from the looks of their camp there must be dozens, at least. They have carbines with bayonets but apparently their ammunition was expended years ago. Our cyberclaws will be of some use, but we can hardly take on the whole camp."

"Then how save good Annie?"

"If we can overcome a guard or two and spirit her out—maybe she can do something to help herself with her Baalbec A-nine."

They started forward again.

A huge bolt of lightning flashed between earth and sky. As the bluish yellow bolt cracked and danced and the odor of ozone filled the air, Clive saw the bright metal of the Nakajima as if the machine were soaring through the heavens, the three-bladed screw on its nose whirling, the glass cage on its back covering a pilot and passenger.

It was the fantasy of a moment, he knew, but a thrill shot through him nonetheless. If this was the product of Earth's future, if this was the artifact of the world that had produced his dear Annie, it was a future he wished to see and to experience if ever the opportunity should present itself.

He started forward, moving stealthily toward the nearest of the marines' lean-tos. Finnbogg was to his right, and he gestured to the dwarf, pointing to the next shelter in that direction.

They separated.

Clive succeeded in reaching the shelter. It was

made of wood, painstakingly smoothed and fitted. If the Japanese had been here for twenty years, they had used the time to create homes for themselves with the precision and craftsmanship of true artists.

There was hardly a crack between two planks, but an opening had been left for ventilation, and perhaps to give the occupant of the shelter a view of the out-of-doors. Clive approached it, placed his eye to the opening.

A uniformed marine sat facing directly toward Clive! Only the fact that he was bent over his disassembled carbine, cleaning each piece with the care of a diamond cutter studying and polishing his tools, saved Clive from discovery. The shelter contained a single room, sparse furnishings, few decorations. The stone fire container that the marine had brought from outside cast a flickering light on his expressionless face. A handcrafted religious shrine stood against the wall.

The marine was gray-haired, his face lined by the passage of time.

There was no sign of Annie.

Clive drew away from the shelter, moved slowly to his left, toward the next. The architecture of this lean-to was similar, and he was able to peer within. Two marines sat on the floor, facing each other, the stone fire holder to one side. By its flickering light they were playing a game, moving dark and light pebbles on a wooden board. Occasionally one or the other would mutter a few syllables.

There was no sign of Annie.

The third shelter Clive approached was dark. He could see nothing within, but could hear the slow, steady breathing of a man asleep.

Were the shelters all one-man affairs? If so, then there must be at least one vacant shelter, belonging to one of the two men playing the pebble game. A vacant shelter might make a hiding place, a base of operations for himself and Finnbogg. Or—Annie might be held there!

Clive started once more across an open area.

The night was shattered by a shout in Japanese followed by a series of roars, thumps, grunts, and the sound of rending wood. The rain had almost ceased, the clouds had largely cleared, and there was enough light to see the Japanese encampment and the lagoon in its center.

With a crash the roof of a shelter literally flew into the air and clattered to the ground. The walls of the little building followed. Two uniformed Japanese ran from the lean-to, waving their arms and shouting. The massive form of Finnbogg bounced after them in close pursuit. Behind them they left a tableau illuminated by firelight from below and skylight from above.

Half-a-dozen more Japanese marines lay crumpled in a circle. Some of them moved, some of them moaned, some of them did neither. In the center of the circle, tied to a wooden chair, was a woman. Her chin was sunk on her chest but she looked up at Clive's approach and grinned at him.

"Annie!"

"Clive!"

He ran forward and tried to untie her bonds. The ropes were heavy, the knots too tightly drawn for him to open. He seized a carbine and managed to detach the bayonet from it. He attacked the knots with the razor-honed edge of the steel bayonet.

"They ran for help, Clive! They'll catch you," Annie sobbed.

"I'll face them!"

More voices rose in urgent cries, and through them the roar of the enraged Finnbogg could be heard.

"Poor Finnbogg," Annie exclaimed. "He saw me here and he went wild. Clive, what happened at our camp? Where is Horace?"

"Horace is all right. Never mind that. Here, turn your wrists a little. Good. Now, the other side." He bent and sliced the ropes that held her feet to the legs of the chair. "You're free now!"

Approaching voices drew nearer. Torchlight flickered.

An older Japanese in officer's garb, sword in hand, led the band of marines.

Clive leaped to his feet, bayonet at the ready. Without wasting a moment or a movement, Annie seized a carbine from a felled marine and stood by Clive's side. "Whatever happens, Annie," Clive murmured. "Whatever happens!"

The officer shouted a command and the marines following him skidded to a halt. He spoke to Annie and Clive, using the Japanese language. To Clive's astonishment, Annie replied, giving her brief answer in the same language.

"What did you say?" Clive asked her.

"I told him to speak in the patois. Where I come from, everybody has to know a little Japanese, but I don't know much and I don't think you know any, do you?"

"I don't, no." A flurry of thoughts whirled through Clive's brain, things he wanted to contemplate when he had the opportunity, things that he wanted to say to Annie. But now there was no time. "We've a standoff," Clive said to the marine officer. "I suppose your men could overpower us, but it will cost them dearly. And I know very well that we will die rather than be taken."

To his relief, Annie added an affirmative. It was a game of bluff that he was playing with the Japanese officer, and with Annie's backing, the game appeared to be working.

"Put up your sword, sir," Clive went on. "You are an officer and a gentleman, I take it."

Although Clive wore a civilian outfit, there was enough in his military bearing to carry weight with the other. "I am Major Clive Folliot, on detached service from Her Majesty's Fifth Imperial Horse Guards. And who are you, sir?"

"Yoshio Takamura, s-s-senior lieutenant, Sixteenth Imperial Airborne Marines."

"Very well, sir. May I have your word that neither you nor your men will betray my trust? If so, my companion and I shall lay down our weapons and ask you and your men to do the same. I give you my word as an officer and a gentleman that we bear you no ill will and will do you no harm."

The Japanese officer barked a short phrase at his followers. They lowered their carbines to the ground, then stacked them in a pair of neat cones. Lieutenant Takamura advanced toward Clive Folliot, his sword held across his chest. He stood barely a foot from Clive, his eyes a trifle below Clive's, gazing up into Folliot's face.

Slowly the Japanese raised his sword. For a moment he held it horizontal, its razor-sharp edge toward Clive Folliot at the level of Clive's throat.

Clive's cyberclaw was tucked into the top of his trousers. He still held the bayonet. He calculated the fraction of a second it would take him to plunge it upward into the other's unprotected belly as against the moment it would take Takamura to slash Clive's equally unprotected jugular with his glistening sword.

Their eyes met, and slowly, slowly, and simultaneously, Takamura and Folliot slipped the sword and bayonet into scabbard and belt loop. Out of the corner of his eye, Clive saw Annie give a sigh of relief.

"What is your demon doing to my men?" Takamura demanded.

"Demon? Oh—Finnbogg!"

The dwarf had reappeared. He staggered toward the grouping, a mixture of blood and mud covering his squat form. He was harried by marines. He would pick them up bodily and hurl them from himself but they kept coming, jabbing him with their bayonets, chivying him from every side. It was like a noble African lion harried by a pack of hunting Afghan hounds.

"Finnbogg, it's all right," Clive called, "Annie is safe."

Lieutenant Takamura shouted a series of commands at his men.

They abandoned their attacks on Finnbogg, and the mighty dwarf dropped to the ground at Annie's feet. She ran her hand into his hair, curling the muddy locks around her fingers.

"He is no demon," Annie told the lieutenant. "He is my friend and protector. You will not harm him."

"But you are an angel," the lieutenant said. "A sacred being."

Clive stared at the man. He seemed to be sane enough, but if he and his unit had been snatched from a war and dropped into the Dungeon to fend for themselves, left here for twenty years—what strange system of beliefs might they not have evolved? Annie an angel, a sacred and supernatural being? Finnbogg a demon?

And what would they have thought of Shriek? Apparently they had not encountered the arachnoid— but they might yet do so!

"I am a woman, Lieutenant Takamura. Not an angel. A human woman."

The Japanese officer drew a long, slow breath between his teeth.

"Your Private Onishi is at our camp in the next valley," Clive said. "You were brought here from Kwajalein Atoll, were you not?"

Takamura nodded. "And you? You are British?"

"Yes."

"You were at Singapore?"

Clive shook his head.

"Rangoon?"

"Zanzibar."

"Why are you here? What happened to you?"

"We were brought here, as you were, as many others have been. Finnbogg—my demon, you call him, but he is merely another kind of man, from a world different from ours, Lieutenant Takamura—Finnbogg was brought from his world, too. We come from different worlds and from different times. You are from 1943, Private Onishi said."

"Yes."

"I am from 1868. Annie is from 1999. So you see, Lieutenant, we are all the victims of Q'oorna, all prisoners of the Dungeon. What wars are fought on Earth are no longer our wars. We cannot be enemies here. Here we are fellows, brothers."

The Japanese reached into a pocket and brought out a cloth. He wiped his face. It was a commonplace enough gesture, but to Clive Folliot it was strangely comforting, a sign of the common humanity that exceeded their differences of race and of culture, of language and of era.

Takamura gestured to his men and they brought chairs for Clive and Annie and Takamura himself. Finnbogg had settled happily on the ground and sat with his eyes closed, his head pressed against Annie's knee.

"I must ask you," Clive went on, "why your men attacked us. We are strangers here, castaways. We had done them no harm."

"They took you for enemies. For agents of Q'oorna. How do we know that Britain and America are not allied with Q'oorna against the empire of Japan?"

"This war of the future—I pray it will never occur. There may be some way for us to prevent it. We face an opportunity unique in history, to meet, representatives of three distinct eras, and to see the events of the world through the eyes of those different eras. But for now, facing the plight we share in the Dungeon, it is folly of the most base degree for us to fight each other!"

"You are right. You are right and my men were wrong. As their commanding officer I bear the responsibility, the shame, for their misdeeds. Please accept my apologies, Major." The lieutenant lowered his head.

Good heavens, Clive thought to himself, *have I gone too far?* He'd heard somewhere of the curious Japanese practice of seppuku, ritual suicide in expiation of shame. Not of guilt, a concept familiar to a son of Brittania, but of shame. The difference was subtle but very real. He didn't want to. . . .

"Altogether understandable, Lieutenant. Think no more of it. There was no real harm done, anyway."

"And your—Annie?" Takamura said. "She forgives us also?"

"I do." Annie smiled. She raised her hand and rubbed her head, a puzzled frown replacing the smile on her face.

"Then let us toast. A small pleasure we have managed to reproduce here in the Dungeon." Takamura barked a command at his men. In the string of syllables Clive managed to decipher only the word *saki.*

"The little stream that flows through our valley," Takamura continued, "we have been able to dam its path and create a rice paddy. We were fortunate when we arrived here to cultivate new growth from the rice in our supplies. And we have learned to make saki."

They drank, they sang, they exchanged stories of military life in the British Empire in the nineteenth century and in the Japanese Empire in the twentieth. Clive felt the fumes of the saki rising from his belly to his head. He was warm and relaxed and he saw brown hands in tan uniform shirts reach and pour more saki. He drank, and the taste of the saki was pleasant and the feeling that it produced in him was pleasant. He felt his eyelids growing heavy, his head growing heavy, and even as he sank into warm, comfortable unconsciousness, he realized that if Takamura chose to betray him in the night, he was as good as dead.

CHAPTER 24

Nakajima Type 97

Clive awakened with the remnants of strange dreams whirling in his brain and the clubs of a thousand Equatorian bushbeaters pounding in his forehead. He blinked and flame seared his eyeballs. He shook his head and an African boa constrictor tightened its coils and crushed his skull to jelly.

He pushed himself upright, struggling against the worst morning-after of his life. He had never been much for heavy drinking, and the nausea and pain he felt reminded him of the wisdom of that policy— and the folly of his deviation from it.

He peered blearily around. There was mighty Finnbogg, the blood and the mud of last night dried on his body. Fleetingly Clive wondered how the multiplicity of miniature suns that illuminated this inverted world could yield to the darkness of night. That was a problem he would ponder another time.

The dwarf was sound asleep, and his snores were as remarkable as everything else about him. Clive reached toward Finnbogg and shook him by the shoulder.

Finnbogg opened a bloodshot eye and moaned.

Clive took a momentary satisfaction in the knowledge that Finnbogg's species was prone to both the human foible of drunkenness and the penalty that followed in its wake.

The dwarf shut his eye and gave the appearance of attempting to burrow into the earth itself, but

Clive persisted and finally Finnbogg sat up, rubbed his face, and stretched.

Senior Lieutenant Yoshio Takamura was nowhere to be seen.

More alarming, Annie had disappeared as well.

Had she partaken of saki along with her male companions? Clive tried to remember. Yes, he was certain that she had. But had she accepted a few token sips of the hot wine out of politeness, or had she imbibed as much as Folliot and Finnbogg, with similar or even more disastrous results?

Had the wine been drugged?

Had the entire party been staged by Takamura for some elusive, ulterior purpose?

From outside the wreckage of the shed came the distinctive creak and clatter of the Japanese pedal cart. Ignoring the lightning bolts that crashed inside his skull, Clive staggered to his feet and out of the wrecked shelter.

The day was bright, the sky blue. The circling suns glowed overhead. Life appeared to have returned to normal in New Kwajalein Atoll—as close to normal as life could be, in this unique setting. The pedal cart was at the far end of the village, a pair of uniformed Japanese propelling it at a good clip. Shading his eyes against the glaring sun, Clive could make out the form of Lieutenant Takamura seated in the rear of the cart, and beside him—Annie!

Clive ran toward the cart. It was moving faster than his wobbly legs could carry him. One of the pedalers seemed to control the direction of the cart. He swung it toward the stream that fed the lagoon in the center of the atoll, and the cart splashed across the shallow water, running onto the opposite bank with hardly a loss of speed.

Clive ran after it. Behind him he heard Finnbogg whining and moaning, his breath loud in the quiet morning air.

The cart turned again and headed toward the gleaming silvery machine, the Nakajima. The cart halted and the two pedalers handed Lieutenant Takamura and Annie down to the ground.

They walked together to the Nakajima, and Lieutenant Takamura courteously assisted Annie to climb onto one of the metallic projections that extended from the sides of the machine like the wings of a swooping bird.

Annie acted as if she had seen such contraptions before. Well, probably she had. To Clive the Nakajima was new and puzzling, but if it was a tool of war to the Japanese of 1943, then it would be a commonplace if not a virtual antique by the time Annie's world of 1999 came into being.

Annie slid the glass canopy of the Nakajima to the rear and climbed into the seat of the machine. Clive could see her moving to adjust the Baalbec A-9 beneath her blouse. The gesture made him wonder why she had not used the device the previous day. Even if the initial attack by the marines had caught her unprepared and the first blow she received had rendered her unconscious, she could have used the electrofield once she recovered herself.

But this was not the time for idle speculation. He shouted and waved after Annie, but she was too far from him to hear his shouts, and her position in the Nakajima prevented her from seeing his frantic gestures.

A whine arose from the machine, followed by a coughing sound, a snarl (all as if the Nakajima were a living thing), and finally a steady, throbbing hum. The silvery screw on the front of the Nakajima glinted in the sunlight as it began to whirl.

The machine was functioning—but how could that be? Onishi and Takamura both had said that the Japanese were long since devoid of ammunition for their weapons and fuel for their machine.

Somehow, Annie must be powering the Nakajima with her Baalbec A-9. Clive knew that the Baalbec drew its power from Annie's body—what a strain it must be, what a use of her physical reserves, to power that shining machine!

Life returned to Clive's legs—and apparently to Finnbogg's as well. They ran to the edge of the stream and forded it where the pedal cart had crossed. The water was cold and fresh. Clive and Finnbogg both fell more than once in their haste, but they struggled to their feet and continued.

They emerged on the far bank of the stream and began to run toward the Nakajima. Now Finnbogg's mighty muscles came into play and he outdistanced Clive in short order.

The Nakajima was rolling forward on three wheels like a child's wheeled plaything. Finnbogg raced past the stationary pedal cart, past the two marines, past Lieutenant Takamura. He very nearly caught up to the slowly moving Nakajima, but the machine accelerated just as Finnbogg dived for its nearest projection. His mighty hands, still dripping from the stream, slipped off its silvery polished skin and he crashed to the ground with a quivering jolt.

Clive caught sight of Annie, her hair whipped by the breeze created by the Nakajima's forward movement. The sun glinted on her flowing hair, on the glass of the open canopy, on the polished surfaces and silvery screw that pulled the Nakajima forward.

Then the machine lifted from the earth itself like a graceful sea bird rising from the surface of a pond. It rose into the air, shrank in perspective as it drew away from Clive, then curved away in a gentle swoop above the nearest hillside. Now the machine's aerial course drew it back toward the lagoon until it grew once more, the sun gleaming on its metal skin.

Was that truly Annie whom Clive perceived in the Nakajima's open canopy? Was she so close that he was able to see her wave, see her smile? Did she wave and smile at him—or at Finnbogg—or at her erstwhile captors?

The Nakajima shrank again, rising and glinting in the bright sun, climbing over the rows of hills that surrounded New Kwajalein Atoll. Soon it was a mere speck against the sky, glinting once and once again, and then it was gone.

Clive stood as one stunned. A groan from Finnbogg returned him to his surroundings.

He walked forthrightly to Lieutenant Takamura. The Japanese officer's uniform, though patched and thin, was spotless and was borne with precision and pride. A military scabbard depended from Takamura's belt, and from it protruded the pommel of his officer's sword.

"Major Folliot," Takamura snapped. He raised his hand in a brisk salute.

"Lieutenant." Clive felt a twinge as he returned the gesture; he had thought of himself in civilian terms, as an explorer and temporary journalist, since leaving the Horse Guards in England and beginning his journeys. Somehow he managed to summon a remnant of military punctilio.

"The Sacred is gone from us," Takamura said.

"Miss Annie. An ordinary girl, Lieutenant."

"Ordinary?" The Japanese sounded wistful.

Clive permitted himself a tight smile. "Extraordinary, then. But still, a mortal, a human."

"She is gone," Takamura said. "Lieutenant Yamura will succeed me." He drew his sword. It glinted in the light of the multiple suns. He raised it in a salute to Clive Folliot; then in another, to the disappeared aerial machine. He knelt, reversing the sword, holding its point to his sternum, and plunged it deep into his heart.

Where Takamura had moved and spoken with military correctness and had commanded the prompt and disciplined obedience of his subordinates, Yamura acted with the confident arrogance of the Oriental potentate that Clive Folliot had observed during his days in Madagascar and Zanzibar. The result was a fawning subservience that Clive found disquieting to observe.

Even during his brief stay in New Kwajalein, Clive had come to have high respect for Takamura—for the man's propriety, his sense of duty and honor. He was an officer with whom Clive would have been proud to serve, had circumstances been different. And the men of the Sixteenth Airborne Marine Detachment were men whom it would have been a privilege to lead.

But Yamura was another story. The assumption of superiority, the demand for obedience to person rather than to crown and empire, the abuse of the comforts and perquisites of command—Clive had seen these before and he knew to what they led: resentment, treachery, a shirking of duty, the placement of self above community. In a word, tyranny— and the ultimate, inevitable downfall of the tyrant.

The suns danced above New Kwajalein Atoll.

Junior Lieutenant Osamu Yamura sat behind a field desk, staring at the two strangers, the Occidental and the even stronger dwarf, who stood before him, staring back. Dislike was obvious, immediate, unspoken, and mutual.

"What am I to do with you two?" Yamura asked. His elbows planted on the table, he spread his fleshy hands before his shoulders, palms upward as if in exasperated supplication.

The question may have been a rhetorical one, but Clive Folliot answered nonetheless. "It is obvious, Lieutenant. We share a common plight. At best fellow castaways, at worst fellow victims of some plot so complex and remote that we can only guess at its nature, our only hope is to make common cause."

"Where is the Sacred?" Yamura jerked his head upward, indicating vaguely the sky into which Annie had disappeared in the Nakajima.

"I find it hard to accept your terminology. As I said to the late Lieutenant Takamura—"

"My predecessor is dead," Yamura cut him off. "I am commander now. I am in charge here. Do not forget that, Briton, and do not quote to me from

conversations between yourself and the dead man."
He stroked his salt-and-pepper mustache with a fleshy
hand. "A change in command of this unit was long
overdue, anyway. My predecessor did us all a favor
by removing himself from the picture."

"I do not share your obviously low opinion of
Lieutenant Takamura, Lieutenant Yamura—but be
that as it may, what has happened, regrettable though
it is, cannot be undone. I repeat, we are the common
victims of forces and operatives which we do not
comprehend, but which obviously wish us no well.
Our salvation, if salvation is possible, may well lie in
an alliance between us."

"You seem to regard yourself as my equal, Folliot."

"Major Folliot, if you please, Lieutenant. And while
my rank is clearly well above your own, I will not
insist upon excessive deferential displays on your
part. In fact, if the truth be known, I will confess to
certain impulses toward egalitarianism."

Yamura pounded the field desk with a heavy fist.
"You misunderstand me, Briton! You are my prisoner. You and your slave."

"Finnbogg is not my slave, sir."

"Your animal, then."

"Nor is he an animal. Finnbogg is a man."

"Enough!" Again the Japanese pounded his desk.
"I will brook no contradiction from you! You are my
inferiors! Both of you! As was the fool Takamura!
The fool! Takamura had no right to command! He
had no understanding of command! I should have
removed him long ago!"

The lieutenant's face was red, a spittle appeared at
the corner of his mouth.

A sergeant and two privates stood nearby. The
sergeant—Clive recognized him as Chuichi Fushida,
the commander of the raiding party that had captured Annie—signaled one of the privates and the
latter ran to Lieutenant Yamura with a cloth and
wiped the corner of his mouth. The lieutenant swung
a meaty arm and knocked the marine backward.

Yamura leaned forward, his forehead pressed against the palms of his hands. His breathing was loud and ragged.

"Are you all right, Lieutenant?" Clive turned and addressed Fushida. "Is your officer ill, Sergeant? He seemed almost—irrational. And now this display. He may be on the verge of apoplexy! Have you a medical officer with your unit?"

The sergeant said, "Prisoner, be quiet!" But as he said it, his eyes conveyed a different message. He was concerned, and his expression indicated that he was desperately seeking a way out of the dilemma that the death of Takamura and the accession of Yamura had created.

Yamura had returned to a more nearly normal condition. He lowered his hands, raised his face, glared at Clive Folliot and at Finnbogg. "The Sacred was an Occidental woman. She was in your company when my men took her, and it was you who freed her, last night."

"Yes," Clive acknowledged. "All of that is true."

"Where is she?"

Was the question an idée fixe? Was Lieutenant Yamura unshakably convinced that Clive and Annie were in communication, or at least that Clive had been aware of Annie's destination before ever she flew away in the glistening Nakajima?

"If you insist that Miss Annie is a sacred creature, I will no longer quarrel with you," Clive said. "Perhaps, in a way, she is—for she seems possessed of an angelic innocence despite having been raised in a world more perverse than either yours or mine, Lieutenant. But still I assure that I do not know where she has gone. The machine—you call it a Nakajima, do you?"

"Type ninety-seven, yes."

"A flying machine."

"An airplane."

"As you will. I must tell you that such things exist

only in the imaginations of visionaries and madmen, in my world. If in yours and Miss Annie's they are everyday objects, you are far ahead of 1868—as is quite proper. But I do not know how the airplane operates, nor have I the faintest idea of where Miss Annie may have traveled in it. As a guess, and nothing more, I might surmise that she has returned to the valley from which your marines kidnapped her. Does that not seem a reasonable supposition, Lieutenant Yamura?"

"Very well. You will lead us there!"

"You wish to go there? You and all your men?"

The fleshy officer sat in contemplation for an interval that seemed to drag on endlessly. Finally he said, "Sergeant Nomura will go. He is our pilot. The Nakajima is his responsibility. He will pay the penalty if it is lost. He will return it to New Kwajalein if it is recovered. He will bring the Sacred with him." Yamura nodded two, three, four times in agreement with himself. "Nomura and Fushida, Sergeant Fushida to command some men. Yes. That will be enough. And you, Major, and your animal as guides."

Clive had hoped to talk his way out of New Kwajalein. In a way, he had succeeded. But he and Finnbogg seemed to have reverted to the status of prisoners. Still, it might be easier to escape from a small party of Japanese marines than from the entire Sixteenth Detachment.

"Very well, Lieutenant. Finnbogg and I will accompany your men."

Yamura shouted at the sergeant who stood near him. He delivered a few sentences of instructions in Japanese. Clive Folliot and Finnbogg waited until the tirade subsided. When it did, Yamura stood up abruptly, knocking the field table tumbling.

Before it could crash to the ground, the two privates lunged forward and caught it, setting it back on its feet. The sergeant, meanwhile, had turned pale. He sucked air between his teeth, bowed to the lieutenant, then stood rigidly at attention.

Yamura disappeared into his lean-to.

The sergeant shouted a command to the two privates, who scurried off in opposite directions. As soon as the privates were gone, the sergeant turned back to Clive. He saluted smartly. "Sergeant Chuichi Fushida, Imperial Marines, at your service, sir."

Clive returned the salute. "I know you, Sergeant. My memory is not that poor."

"Yes, sir."

"I must apologize, Major Folliot, for my man's conduct."

"What conduct is that?"

"My man who struck the Sacred with his carbine."

"Poor decision. Not the right thing to do, I agree. Well, though, speaking for Miss Annie, she certainly seems unhurt. I would think the apology would be accepted."

"I am most grateful, sir."

"You're going back with us, eh?"

"I sent my men for Sergeant Nomura, our pilot."

"Quite understand. Here they come now." He turned to his side. "Come along, Finnbogg. You've been awfully quiet, old fellow. Not contemplating further acts of mayhem, are you?"

Finnbogg snuffled. "Want Annie."

"I'll bet you do. Suppose we all do, eh? Well, these Nihonjin don't seem quite as bad as they might be. Let's be off."

For whatever reasons, Lieutenant Yamura dispatched the party on foot. No pedal cart today, meaning that the expedition, which might have reached Clive's previous camp in an hour or less, spent all day trekking through the hills.

At first the two sergeants alternated as commander while the privates marched stolidly to their count. Clive and Finnbogg insisted on setting their own pace. When they set out, Finnbogg was grim and silent. The longer they paced, the more animated he became, scampering away and returning to the party. The Japanese carried their ammunitionless carbines with fixed bayonets. Whenever Finnbogg separated himself from the party, Sergeant Fushida or Sergeant Nomura would grow nervous. But Clive stayed nearby, and Finnbogg always returned.

The dwarf's spirits had recovered to the point where he began to sing, this time chorus after enthusiastic chorus of "The Old Rugged Cross."

Finally, they rounded the familiar hillside that would lead them to Clive's camp. Dusk had fallen. The multiple suns had not set—there was nowhere for them to do so in this strange, inside-out world— but they seemed to dim and brighten alternately, creating the equivalent of night and day. The storm of the previous night was not repeated; there were few clouds, and the evening was not unpleasant.

Finnbogg raced ahead, bounding joyously.

In a few minutes he was back, his head down, his shoulders drooping.

"What's the matter?" Clive asked.

Finnbogg took him by the hand and urged him forward.

This was the right place, no question about that. The features were exactly those they had left little more than twenty-four hours earlier. There were scuff marks on the ground where the pedal cart had turned.

But there was no sign of the Nakajima Model 97.

There was no sign of Annie.

There was no sign of Horace Hamilton Smythe, or of his prisoner, Private Shigeru Onishi.

There was only a roughened area in the dirt, where a struggle had apparently taken place not long ago, and a darkened patch in the middle of it.

Clive Folliot squatted beside the darkened patch,

rubbed his finger in it, and studied the result. The dark matter was red and sticky. There was little question that it was blood, and it had been shed so recently that it had neither dried completely nor been totally absorbed by the earth.

Behind Clive, Sergeant Fushida began to laugh.

CHAPTER 25

Like a Tale from the Brothers Grimm

"A fool! Lieutenant Yamura is a great fool!"

Clive turned his head. Still squatting beside the half-dried bloodstain, he peered up at the marine sergeant. Sergeant Fushida stood over Clive, a ceremonial sword in his hands. The two marine privates stood behind him at rigid attention, their carbines at the ready, bayonets fixed. In a moment of frozen awareness, Clive caught sight of Finnbogg behind the two privates, tensing the muscles of his mighty limbs to launch himself in attack.

Clive yelled, "Finnbogg, no!"

The dwarf drew back, a puzzled expression on his face.

Beyond him, Sergeant Nomura, the pilot, was scouring the area, possibly in search of tire tracks left by his Nakajima Model 97. There were tracks, all right, but Clive could see none that had not been made by the pedal cart. That was, if the tracks of the cart and those of the flying machine were distinguishable from each other.

"What do you mean?" Clive asked. He was taking a risk, he knew, by stopping Finnbogg at the very moment of the latter's attack on the Japanese. But they had proved amenable to talk prior to this moment. An attack by Finnbogg on the privates would probably have provoked an immediate—and fatal—stroke at Clive's neck by Sergeant Fushida's glittering sword. Talk was better.

"You say Lieutenant Yamura is a great fool. What do you mean by that?" Clive repeated.

"I mean that he is not a good leader. He has no respect for the men. No respect for the empire. He is concerned only with himself. Lieutenant Takamura was a good officer. Lieutenant Yamura is a bad one."

"I quite agree." Clive rose slowly to his feet. He didn't wish to alarm the sergeant. Not while he held a sword and Clive had only the cyberclaw tucked in his trousers—miraculously, after the events of the past two days, still tucked in his trousers.

Sergeant Fushida grunted—a peculiar verbal habit of the Japanese that Clive found both annoying and bewildering. The sound could mean almost anything, and a wrong guess on the hearer's part might prove disastrous.

"What do you propose to do?" Clive asked. "There is no apparent sign of your Nakajima machine. I suppose your colleague Sergeant Nomura will have something to say about that. But 'the Sacred,' as you call her, is certainly not here. And my colleague Sergeant Smythe and his prisoner have also disappeared, leaving *this* as a clue to puzzle us."

Fushida returned his sword to its scabbard, eliciting a sigh of relief from Clive Folliot, and squatted beside the Englishman. He peered at the thickening blood on the ground. "Huh! We may never know," he said aloud. Then, sotto voce, "I am supposed to have my men kill you."

Clive gaped at the man.

"Yes." Fushida nodded. "The only choice Yamura gave me was to do it myself. That is why I drew my sword."

Clive's mind raced. This was like a fairy tale, something from the Brothers Grimm, something that he had not heard in twenty-five years. "Hansel and Gretel," that was it. Finnbogg might have learned the story from Neville; the brothers had heard it together from their nanny. The cruel stepmother ordering the woodsman to take his children into the woods and kill them ... the woodsman too kind-hearted to perform the act. . . .

"Are you going to do it?" Clive asked.

"I cannot!" Fushida shook his head, fury and anguish mixed on his features. "I am a marine! I will kill for the emperor! I will kill in battle! But I will not commit cold-blooded murder!"

"Glad to hear that, Sergeant, believe you me!" Clive pushed himself upright.

Sergeant Fushida did the same.

They stood toe to toe.

"But what now?" Clive asked again.

Instead of answering the question, Fushida shouted at his fellow sergeant.

Nomura approached Fushida and Clive Folliot. "No," he grumbled, "the Sacred has not been here. My Nakajima has not been here. No, I would have seen its tracks in the earth."

"Then where?" Fushida asked. He spoke part of the time in the Q'oornan patois, part of the time in Japanese.

Nomura shrugged his shoulders and gestured toward the sky. "'You know as much as I, of this strange world.'

"I do not," Nomura disagreed. "I have never flown in the Nakajima Model ninety-seven, Hiroshi. In Kawanishis in the home islands, and to jump onto Kwajalein. But never in the Nakajima, and never in this world."

Nomura nodded. "You are right, Chuichi. Let me tell you, I saw very little of this world. Only the one flight, the flight to the castle when we obtained the crown. But this is a strange world. An inside-out world. Instead of living on the surface of a solid ball, we are on the inside of a hollow one."

"Everyone knows that!"

"Yes? Major Folliot?" Nomura turned toward Clive.

"We had surmised as much, Sergeant."

"Very well. They could be anywhere. I do not know how the Sacred was able to make the Nakajima fly. We have no fuel. I have even experimented with attempts to distill saki still further, to make pure alcohol and use it as aviation fuel, but without success."

Fushida permitted himself a small laugh.

From the direction opposite that of New Kwajalein Atoll there arose a hideous screaming sound. The Japanese marines, Finnbogg, and Clive all froze in their tracks, then turned slowly to see the source of the screaming, which grew louder by the moment.

In satisfaction of Clive's expectation, the screaming came from Shriek. The great arachnoid had rounded a hill and was scuttling forward on four legs, moving with astonishing speed, screaming at the top of her voice.

She halted as far from Clive and the others as a cricket bowler from the batsman. Clive could see two human forms held in two of her amazingly thin, amazingly strong arms. Her mandibles were gnashing, her eight eyes blazed.

The combination of the sight of the arachnoid and the sound of her bloodcurdling screams started the two marine privates to quaking. Their sergeants did better. Each of them drew his sword. They stood their ground, turning their eyes from Shriek to Clive and back. They seemed to guess that the eight-limbed creature was associated with Folliot, although they had no idea how this had come about.

Clive started toward Shriek.

With her two free hands she began plucking quill-like hairs from her swollen abdomen. She drew back her hands and then snapped them forward, each one once, then each one again.

Clive had covered perhaps a fourth of the distance toward her; from the corner of his eye he could see Finnbogg moving parallel to himself. Folliot halted and turned his head to follow the course of the quills as they whirred past his ears.

They struck the four Japanese—Fushida, Nomura, the two privates. The four marines set up a common howl, not of rage or pain but of sheer, distilled terror. Clive knew now what Shriek had done. She had caused her body to secrete a chemical that induced the reaction in the Japanese marines and had then used her flying quills to inject it into them, as if she had been a surgeon administering a hypodermic needle to a patient or a viper administering its venom to its victim.

Without speaking another word, without stopping for any purpose, the four marines turned tail and ran screaming back toward the row of hills that separated this valley from New Kwajalein Atoll.

Clive continued forward. When he reached Shriek she released her dual burden, placing Sergeant Smythe and his own erstwhile prisoner on the ground.

Smythe rose unsteadily, leaning on Clive with one hand.

The marine private lay on his back, staring sightlessly at the multicolored suns. He uttered an occasional moan, moved his hands and feet at random. His belly was swollen and his face was blank.

"Smythe," Clive said, "what's wrong with him?"

"Let's get away from here, sah. I don't want—I *cannot* watch the man. He attacked me, he very nearly killed me, sah. He had me at his mercy and he was prepared to dispatch me in a particularly nasty manner, sah, but I cannot stand near him."

"But—what happened?"

"It was Shriek, sah." Sergeant Smythe gestured at the arachnoid. "She arrived in the proverbial nick o' time, sah, and saved me. Yes, she did. But then, sah—I think she laid her eggs inside the man's body. I don't know how long it will take them to hatch, but I don't want to be here when they do, sah."

Clive's mouth dropped. He looked at the figure that lay on the ground, staring sightlessly at the multiple suns. He could not look, and turned his eyes away. But he couldn't *not* look, and had to turn his eyes back.

Wasps do that, Clive thought. *Lay their eggs inside their victims, and when the eggs hatch, the young use the hosts for food.* It was horrible. One of nature's adaptations—effective, efficient, and merciless. But he didn't know that spiders did it. And then he remembered that Shriek was a being from an alien world. She was *like* a spider, but she was not a spider.

What other horrors had he yet to learn of in the Dungeon? "I shall take a rock and bash his skull in, Smythe. Or take a cyberclaw and slash his jugular. Either would be more merciful than—than— He may have been an enemy, but he is still a man, Smythe! Kill him. In God's name, Smythe, as an act of mercy, let's kill him."

"If we do that, sah—I think she's got more eggs, sah. I'm as sorry for the man as you are, sah, I think. But I don't wish to take his place, sah, do you?"

"What then, Smythe? What can we do? What do you propose?"

"Miss Annie is gone, sah?"

Clive nodded.

"The Japanese are that way." Smythe pointed. "So I suggest we go *that* way." He jerked a thumb over his shoulder, pointing in the direction opposite New Kwajalein. "There are two passes out of this valley. Let's find out where the other one leads."

Clive looked at Shriek. She was preening her quills, gazing fondly at the distended belly of the helpless Japanese marine. With one hand she reached for the marine's distended belly. She pulled away his khaki shirt. The flesh beneath was swollen. A red circle marked the point at which the eggs had been inserted. Shriek laid her cheek against the man's belly, smiling serenely. She made the only sound other than her hideous screaming that Clive had ever heard her make: a warm, maternal crooning. It had the sound of a mother's loving lullaby.

Clive turned away, his stomach heaving. When he

finished being sick upon the ground he stood shaking, his hands cold and his face clammy.

Shriek seemed to pay no attention to Folliot or Smythe or Finnbogg. Clive looked at the dwarf. How much did Finnbogg understand of what had transpired? What was his desire, now?

Clive drew himself together. "Very well, Sergeant," he managed. "Let us see what lies in this direction."

▪ CHAPTER 26 ▪
Heaven in the Dungeon

There was no dissent.

They trekked along the base of a row of hills. When they had first emerged into this strange, inside-out world within the Dungeon, they had seen signs of habitation in the distance. Habitation, that is, far more substantial in appearance than the makeshift Japanese military encampment at new Kwajalein.

Now, after days of foot-wearying marches lightened by Finnbogg's spirited singing, they found a wheel-rutted roadway. It was a simple pair of parallel dirt tracks in the ground cover, but it filled their hearts with new hope and anticipation. They followed it and it brought them to an even more encouraging prospect: the sight of a distant cluster of buildings, a distant rise of chimneys, a distant curl of smoke.

At the edge of the village Horace Hamilton Smythe exclaimed, "Lor', Major, it could be my old home! Oh, Lord, how did this bit of heaven find its way into the Dungeon!" It was indeed like rural England. Clive wondered what it seemed like to Finnbogg—and to Shriek. What was comforting and homelike to himself and Smythe might be alien and threatening to the others. Or—the thought struck Clive like a blow to the solar plexus—their surroundings might appear different to the others.

Did Finnbogg see his home, a paradise of odors and tastes designed to make his canine heart rejoice?

Did Shriek see some terrifying world of webs and

nests, eggs and grubs and the fat juicy prey from which her kind sucked the very substance of life for their own sustenance?

He shuddered and bent to pick up a stone that lay beside the pathway. He felt it, pressed it to his cheek, dropped it again, and kicked it. Even through his trekking boots he felt the pain in his foot. "Thus I refute Bishop Berkeley," he muttered.

There was small comfort in the epistomological exercise.

And he found himself wondering melancholically, if only Annie were with the party, would she perceive some strange futuristic world of glittering glass and metallic machinery?

They reached the village as dusk fell. Clive gazed at the dimming stars and wondered, neither for the first time nor the last, how this strange world had come to be. Would God, even in His infinite power and creativity, have made such a place? Or was the Dungeon itself the handiwork of some great and wonderful—and possibly malign!—race?

They were greeted by a spokesman for the town. To Clive the leader and the villagers appeared fully human. Again he wondered how they looked to his companions, how the village itself looked to them. He could not even frame the question sensibly so as to ask it.

The leader was a chubby, jolly, gray-haired man. He wore a huge mustache and rough clothing, and when he spoke to Clive there was no difficulty in understanding him. The language he spoke wasn't exactly English. It was the patois that Clive had encountered before now, that had permitted him to speak with Finnbogg and with the Japanese marines of the Sixteenth Airborne Detachment. The accents and dialects were not identical. The villagers here spoke a form of the patois with enough English in it—mixed with generous portions of a dozen other languages that Clive at least recognized, plus others as baffling as Martian—to make good, clear sense.

The town leader introduced himself with a title, and Clive was unable to tell whether the word he used was *mayor* or *major*. Was he an elected official, or a retired military man who had simply assumed the village's leadership?

The mayor's—or major's—wife bustled around, serving platters of delicious food to the party of travelers. Clive was not surprised that Finnbogg happily dined on the same fare as the humans, nor that Shriek declined with a humanlike shake of her head and an enigmatic expression on her face.

They ate their meal and drank steins of foaming beer at the major's rough plank table. Even before they finished the meal there were horns and drums outside, and they retired to the town square.

Villagers in ranks performed evolutions to the sound of the musicians. It was a strange sight, a cross between a dance and something that a drill sergeant might have devised for the training of rough recruits.

Clive turned to the leader. "Your title is that of major, is it not?"

The man nodded.

A chilling suspicion was growing in Clive's belly. "Who taught you all this?" he demanded.

Silently, the major bowed his head.

A sense of urgency—and something close to rage—swept over Clive. He caught the other by the collar and jerked his head upright. "Tell me, man. Tell me! Who taught you this, or I'll shake the truth out of you!"

"I—I cannot tell you, sir."

"Cannot? You mean, will not!"

"Please!" The major's wife was dancing around them, fluttering her hands helplessly. "Please, sir, he cannot, he cannot."

Without releasing the major, Clive addressed the woman. "Why not? Woman, I've been through hell getting here. Through a series of hells. Where are we? What world is this? Why is the mayor called major? Who taught these people British drill? Tell me!"

Finnbogg was cringing at his leader's outburst. Horace Hamilton Smythe stared at the spectacle, thunderstruck. Shriek stood some yards away, gazing bemused.

Clive gave the major another shake.

"All right," the major gasped. "All right. I will tell you everything."

Clive released his grasp and the man started to squirm away, but Clive was younger and stronger, and his exertions had built up his muscles and his agility since leaving London on board *Empress Philippa*.

He caught the major by the scruff of the neck and hauled him back to his house, the man's wife still fluttering in circles around the tableau. Smythe, Finnbogg, and Shriek followed. The dancers in the village square continued their movements as if nothing untoward had transpired.

Inside the house, the major collapsed into a chair. Behind him a stone fireplace held a cozy blaze. The mantelpiece above the hearth displayed family treasures—two small paintings in ornate frames, a bouquet of dried flowers preserved beneath a glass dome, what appeared to be a Bible. A rectangular pier glass behind the treasures provided a doubled image of each. Against the wall a tall clock ticked monotonously, its long pendulum swinging back and forth with unvarying regularity.

It was a scene that could have been lifted from a thousand English villages, yet here it was, somewhere in the Dungeon. Were they still on Q'oorna at all? Was Q'oorna the whole of the Dungeon, or were there worlds beside worlds, worlds within worlds? Was this planet a hollow shell, like an egg with its contents blown clear? If so, then they had made their way from the outer surface to the inner.

Above their heads the miniature galaxy of stars

brightened and dimmed alternately to create the simulacrum of day and night. Beneath their feet—reachable through the glowing tunnel that had brought them to this place—was the terrifying world of blackness that they had crossed on foot, the world that they knew as Q'oorna.

How had they traveled to that black world from the Sudd?

Perhaps the Dungeon was not as simple a place as Clive Folliot had imagined. The tunnels might lead not merely into the ground, but might course through strange dimensions beyond his schooling and beyond even his imagining.

Which of his companions might help him to fathom the conundrum? Horace Hamilton Smythe was far too much the pragmatist; Finnbogg was too simple in his doglike devotion; Shriek was too remotely alien. If only he could be reunited with Annie—perhaps. A native of some future Earth, she seemed to possess a knowledge and understanding that would not have been found in a woman of Clive's own day and acquaintanceship. And the strange device that she wore beneath her very skin seemed to enhance her mental powers. She could create maps, Clive knew. Perhaps she could learn languages, analyze information of many sorts. . . .

Clive grinned wryly as he realized that the mystical Sidi Bombay would have been the best person with whom to discuss their situation. But where was Sidi Bombay?

Clive was trembling. "I—I apologize," he addressed the major. "I had no right to lay hands on you, sir."

The man stared blankly at him.

"You cannot imagine the experiences we have passed through," Clive continued. "Or the feelings that boil in our breasts. I allowed myself to become carried away, sir. I apologize. Will you help us, sir?"

The major's wife had disappeared into the kitchen, and now she returned bearing a tray with hot tea and scones. The mayor/major had regained at least part of his breath—and of his composure. "We seldom meet strangers. Ours is a simple village. We tend our farms. We trade on market days and we dance on holidays. We wish no trouble."

Clive was listening to the man's words, but even more so, as the official spoke, Clive was watching his face. The man's mustache twitched nervously. A tic appeared and disappeared at the corner of his mouth. And his eyes—

His eyes darted here and there. To Clive, to the bustling figure of his wife, to Smythe, to Finnbogg, and to Shriek. Well they might!

But they also darted in the direction of the mantelpiece above the cottage's cozy hearth. They darted there frequently, and each time they did so, the tic appeared at the corner of the mayor's mouth. And his eyes darted less frequently but more furtively in another direction.

If Clive read him properly, the major was not looking at any object within the cottage. He was looking toward something outside the cottage, perhaps beyond the village. And each time he looked toward that something it was with an air of foreboding and dread.

The major was nattering on, talking of some matter of crops and rainfall and harvests. Clive very nearly tuned out the droning voice. The major's wife handed Clive a cup of tea and held out a scone for him.

Clive watched the major's eyes. What was it on the mantel that kept drawing his attention, that kept filling him with concern?

Teacup in hand, Clive stood and walked to the fireplace. The logs inside burned with a steady, comforting flame. He turned his back to the others and studied the objects on display.

One painting was a scene of village life. Happy people going about their business, thatched cottages and green fields surrounding them. In the distance a darker structure soared skyward: one that rose with towers and turrets like those of a medieval castle. All else in the picture suggested contentment and joy, but the castle loomed grim and menacing.

The other was a wedding portrait. Clive recognized the major and his wife—younger and slimmer versions of themselves, but unmistakably the same two people. They were surrounded by well-wishers, villagers, and—apparently—family. And the priest beaming at the young couple was—a younger version of Timothy F. X. O'Hara! The face was thinner; the sparse, faded hair was thick and red. But this man was undoubtedly the white priest of Bagomoyo!

Clive seized the picture and shoved it in the major's face. "Who is this priest?" he demanded.

The old man stammered. "Why—why—that's the dominie."

"What dominie?"

"The preacher. Father O'Hara. That's our wedding portrait. Father O'Hara married the missus and myself. What's the matter, man?"

"Is he here? In this village? Is he here now?"

"Why, no. This is too small a town to support its own priest. Father O'Hara comes by every few years to shrive us of our sins. To solemnize weddings, say his blessings over the cradles of babies and the barrows of the dead. Why, the young courting couples can't wait for his next visit—sometimes they get dreadfully eager, living apart and waiting for the priest so they can be married."

Clive put his hand to his forehead. "Do you know where he comes from? How he gets here? Where does he go when he leaves?"

The major shook his head. "No, sir. He just walks up the road, same as you and your friends. He stays a few days or a week, then he walks on. That's all."

Clive put the wedding portrait back on the mantel and stood with his back to the others. He shifted his glance from the painting to the pier glass behind it. In it he could see the others gathered behind him. The major was watching Clive apprehensively.

Clive slid his feet to the left, toward the preserved bouquet. In the glass, the expression on the major's face showed relief. Clive slid back, to the paintings, then to the Bible.

The major stood up and took Clive's arm. "Please, sir, have something to eat. Can I get you more tea?" He took Clive's cup from him. "You are still upset, I can tell. Your apology is accepted, sir. You must consider yourself a guest here, an honored guest." He pulled at Clive's elbow, tugging him away from the hearth.

Clive let the major take his teacup but otherwise refused to budge. "What's this now?" he asked. He picked up the Bible from the mantel.

"Please!" the major and his wife exclaimed simultaneously.

"But it's just a Bible," Clive protested. He held the book, looked at it carefully. It was not a Bible. It was Neville Folliot's journal!

Clive strode furiously toward the major. "Where did you get this, sir? Where—"

The major's wife was pawing at him with her pink chubby hands. Her motions were half-placatory, half-directed at snatching the book away from him. But Clive was having none of this. The major, meanwhile, was stammering rapid bursts of words, alternately blustering and demanding the return of his property, and pleading with Clive to spare him disaster, averring that Clive did not understand, it was not his fault, it was the Lord of the Castle who was responsible, that the Lord of the Castle would punish him if he relinquished the book.

With a slicing gesture of one hand, Clive silenced the major and stopped his wife from her plucking at the book. "This book is the journal of my brother, Major Neville Folliot, Royal Somerset Grenadier Guards. My brother being deceased, it is my responsibility to take charge of the journal and return it to our father, Baron Tewkesbury. You have no valid claim upon the book, and I will not release it from my possession. That is the end of it!"

Quivering, the major collapsed into his chair. His wife knelt beside him, murmuring to him and wiping her tears with her apron.

"I assume," Clive said, "that the Lord of the Castle to whom you refer dwells in the castle pictured beyond the village." He indicated the painting above the mantel.

The major nodded silently. His face was drawn. He appeared hardly the same man he had been just minutes ago.

"And that is the same castle toward which you cast such worried glances as you spoke earlier," Clive continued.

The major nodded again.

Clive ordered his thoughts, turning the journal over and over in his hands, studying its binding as if to learn something from it. "You knew my brother, Neville Folliot?"

The major and his wife both nodded, conceding the fact.

But how could that be? Clive had regained his outward calm, but inwardly he was stunned, seething with shock and mystification. The major and his wife knew Neville? They had obtained the journal from him?

But Neville was dead. Clive had seen him, had opened his bier by his own efforts, had gazed upon Neville's cadaver, had pried the journal—this same journal!—from Neville's very hands!

No!

Neville's mind jumped from pole to pole like an iron filing in some experiment conducted by the late Mr. Faraday.

Neville must be alive, must be somewhere ahead of Clive and his companions, egging them on, drawing them on to some hidden purpose of his own! And the enigmatic journal with its messages, sometimes helpful, sometimes treacherous, had now reappeared!

Clive seated himself. He drew a small table toward himself and laid the book upon it. He opened it to the last entry he had read.

On the following page, there were new words. It was written in ink the color of freshly spilled blood, ink a color Clive had never seen before except in the heat of sanguinary battle. But the hand in which the new entry was written showed Neville's inimitable penmanship. The entry was brief and the words were clear even if their meaning was not:

Little brother, you astonish me. I never expected you to reach this place. I never expected you to live this long. You can still go back. You can still save yourself. Your companions are lost, but you can be saved. Turn back. TURN BACK NOW! Else the Lord of the Castle will have his glee. Turn back, brother, and tell Father that his will is being done, the Lord has seen the sign, the swirl approaches its vertex, and timing is correct, the formula spells true. Turn back, brother, or the Lord will toast your liver!

Clive was aghast. Turn back? How could he, even if he wished to comply? There was no returning through the colored tunnel, no flying back through the void to the strange trainlike vehicle, no recrossing the chasm, no. . . .

There was simply no turning back. Even if he were willing to give up his quest and return to England, he could not abandon Sidi Bombay and Annie. He could not abandon Annie!

Clive raised his eyes. He locked his gaze with that of the major. The look that he saw in the official's eyes he now realized was mirrored in his own.

The sign . . . the swirl . . . the vertex . . . the timing . . . the formula . . .

What did it mean? Was Baron Tewkesbury somehow involved in the strange plot? Clive's father and his brother, together?

Clive rocked in his seat. Instinctively, he reached his hand toward Horace Hamilton Smythe for aid or simply for the calming comfort that communion could provide. But before Smythe could respond, Clive leaped to his feet. He shut Neville's journal with a clap that made the others jump.

"We will go to the castle!" he ordered.

"No!" the major pleaded. "You do not know what you are saying!"

"We will go! How far is it? How long will it take to walk?"

"You cannot walk there, sir. It is impossible!"

"Then we will require horses, sir!"

"We have no horses in this village."

"What do you use?"

"We use—other beasts. We have carts and we have other beasts to draw them. Not horses."

"Very well," Clive snapped.

"Please," the major began again, but the look in Clive's face convinced him that the case was hopeless. "At least," the official amended, "not at night. We cannot take you in the night, and you would never get there without guides. At least wait for the morning, sir. Please."

Clive hesitated, exchanged silent glances with his companions, trying to read their thoughts. Then he made his decision. "No. Prepare the cart. Will it hold us all? Prepare the beasts. Then we will go!"

The major rose slowly to his feet, his face ashen, his hands trembling. Nearby, his wife collapsed to the floor, sobbing without shame.

▪ CHAPTER 27 ▪
The Hall of the Mountain Lords

A squad of villagers, working by torchlight, prepared the cart. While they went about their tasks,
Clive conferred with his colleagues.

Horace Hamilton Smythe was the most articulate,
and the most determined to push on. "We've come
this far, sah! I feel that I led the major into this
situation. I wish to tender my apologies for so doing,
sah."

Clive Folliot clasped Smythe by the hand. Everybody was apologizing tonight. "Not your fault, Sergeant. I was suspicious of your motives for a time,
that I will admit. But once I learned of your experiences in New Orleans—your encounter with the sharpers, your duel—I realized that you were not at fault.
You have not acted as a free agent at all times,
during this adventure."

Smythe bobbed his head. "Grateful that the major
understands."

"I do wish I could be sure that you are the old
Horace Hamilton Smythe right now."

"I am, sah!"

"And not going to lapse back into a mesmeric
trance, Sergeant? Are you fully free of Philo Goode's
influence—Philo Goode and whoever may be his part-
ners or his principals?"

"That I cannot say, sah." Smythe looked up as if
searching the heavens for some clue. "I feel entirely
myself, at this very moment. But if Mr. Goode has

his invisible net over me, I don't know but that he'll try to haul it in once more."

The man looked stricken. Clive's heart went out to him, but there was nothing he could do to help.

They stood in the square outside the major's house. The constellation of miniature suns above them glowed and pulsed dimly at the midnight hour. They had arranged themselves into the all-too-familiar spiral.

Like Smythe, Clive peered up at the heavens. Somewhere beyond those swirling stars lay the inner shell of this tiny world. Perhaps each of the tunnels they had tried to choose among led to a different world, each miniature, each self-contained, each unique.

"Besides, I can't just abandon old Sidi Bombay," Horace Hamilton Smythe resumed. "He's a good chap. I'm convinced he's alive, and if we keep on, we may find some sign to tell us where he's gone. Sidi's my oldest comrade, Major. We served together even before you and I met that very first day. If I was your mentor when you were a green lieutenant— you've said as much, and I feel honored that you did, sah—why, consider that Sidi was my own mentor. My initiator and my guide in a whole wide world, Major. I know it in my bones, Major, that old Sidi is alive. And I can't abandon the man."

"I understand." Clive nodded. "As you feel about Sidi Bombay, so feel I—about Miss Annie." The two soldiers stood silently, musing. Then, quite suddenly, Clive said, "Smythe, I am certain that my brother is alive. As sure as you that Sidi Bombay lives, so am I that Neville Folliot does."

"Are you, sah?"

"Well, I must admit that I am of two minds. When we found the casket containing his cadaver, I of course thought it was all up with Neville. But by some power he continues to add messages to his journal."

"The major read a new message tonight," Smythe commented.

Clive had not shared the latest entry with Smythe. Now he admitted as much. "Indeed. A disquieting one, at that. Still and all, it shows that Neville is able to communicate with us."

"Does the major believe in the spirits, sah? Not to be discouraging, but p'raps Major Neville Folliot has, how shall I put it, eh, passed over to the next plane of existence. Could it be that he's sending back ectoplasmic tendrils to write in his journal?"

Clive held the journal under his arm. He patted it. "Anything is possible, Sergeant. Anything at all. But—somehow I don't believe that Neville is dead. The body in the casket was a simulacrum. A mechanical thing, perhaps, or a dummy. Perhaps even a real cadaver—a corpse chosen for its superficial resemblance to Neville."

He squeezed his eyes shut for a moment, then opened them and said, "Dress the double in the right uniform, style its mustache and hair to resemble Neville's, apply a little makeup. See to it that the lighting is dim and the moment is brief and stressful. *Voilà!* The ruse could hardly fail!"

He kicked absently at a clod of dirt, then turned his gaze once more toward the enigmatically swirling stars. Who was behind all this? Whither did it lead? "I don't know," he answered his own question, "but I'm going to find out. And when I do, I know I shall find my brother again. Find him alive. And in all likelihood, I shall find my lost Annie and you too shall find your comrade, Sidi Bombay."

The cart rolled from its shed, a heavy wooden vehicle reminiscent of a London dray. The major/mayor of the village rode on a high wooden seat. He cracked a whip viciously against the rumps of the harnessed team that drew the cart.

A flickering oil lantern swayed at each corner of the cart, and a torch burned in a holder beside the driver's seat.

Finnbogg and Shriek followed Clive and Smythe to the cart.

Clive stared at the team. The major had said that the cart would not be drawn by horses. Clive therefore expected to find some other beasts used for the purpose—oxen, buffaloes, even giant canines.

But these draft animals were human beings. Giant, naked humans. One male, one female.

Clive emitted a scream of rage and lunged at the major, meaning to do no less than hurl him from his perch. But the official dodged his effort, and instead Clive ran to the front of the cart.

He peered into the pathetic faces. The man and woman must each have weighed half a ton at least, the male probably as much as twelve hundred pounds. "What have they done to you?" Clive gritted.

There was no response.

He took the head of the male in his hands and peered into the eyes. They were dull, with little sign of intelligence or awareness.

"You're a human being, man, not a dumb beast! Speak! What have they done?"

There was no response. He stepped to the female. Her features were only slightly less massive and crude than those of her consort. Long hair hung down on the sides of her face. A harness was fixed to her body, and a bit to her mouth exactly as if she were a horse. Her companion was similarly outfitted.

Clive's eyes shifted from the dull, spiritless faces to the bodies of the two. Their arms were long and heavily fleshed, their hands foreshortened into clublike appendages. They stood on all fours, rumps elevated, but only slightly so, for their legs were short and stumplike in shape. Their shoulders were massively muscled.

Tears of rage and of pathos came to Clive's eyes. "Speak!" he shouted at the human beasts. "Stand upright! Clothe yourselves! They have turned you into animals!"

The male and female stirred uneasily, as if somewhere, in a dim recess of their brutalized brains, some dim spark glowed in response to Clive's impas-

sioned speech. They shifted on their hands and made
a sound, a heartbreaking, sighing sound that contained the last, hopeless vestige of their lost humanity.

The major hopped down from his perch. He
reached into a pocket and extracted an apple and a
rude knife. He sliced the apple in half and jammed a
piece of it into the mouth of each of the human
beasts. Despite the bits in their mouths, they managed to chew on the apple. The dim light that had
appeared in their eyes disappeared.

"You shouldn't ought to do that, sir," the major
appealed to Clive. "You'll only get 'em upset. Let 'em
be, sir, please. For their own sake. There's nothing
you can do for 'em. Nothing anybody can do for
'em. So just let 'em be."

Clive looked into the major's face. The pain and
the grief and the hopelessness that he saw there
were too real to dispute. "All right," he said. "Let's
go, then."

"Thank you, sir." The major helped them all onto
the cart. Finnbogg insisted on sniffing at the team
first. He cocked his head to one side, then to the
other, then hurried away from them and climbed
laboriously onto the rearmost position. Shriek hopped
toward the human beasts but they reared and backed
away, until she, too, climbed onto the back of the
cart.

Clive and Sergeant Smythe sat nearer the major.

The ride to the castle was quiet and chilly and in
large part uneventful. There were occasional sounds
from the darkness, sounds that sent a shudder
through Clive Folliot. He had placed Neville's journal on the seat beside himself. Now, to keep it safe,
he shifted his weight and slid the black-bound book
beneath his leg.

The cart rolled and jounced along. No one spoke,
and even Finnbogg's musical impulses seemed to
have been dampened. How long the cart rolled, Clive
could not tell. The creaking of its wheels, the fresh
odors of the countryside, and his own tension and

fatigue combined to place him in a condition of semiconsciousness.

How perfect this moment would be, had he Annie beside him instead of the stolid Sergeant Smythe!

In his strange, half-waking dream, he held Annie in his arms. Beneath the swirling stars her face was singularly beautiful. The points of light from above were reflected in her eyes. Her hair swung gracefully. He wondered how women managed to tend to their hair in the midst of circumstances like these, but even in his semidream he conceded that there were mysteries utterly beyond male comprehension, of which this was one.

He lowered his face to hers, and their lips met.

They were unimaginably far from home, trapped in a world they had surely never made and would probably never understand. They traveled in the company of beings undreamed of in Clive's London. Each day—each moment— might be their last.

Some inchoate instinct drove Clive to press his lips harder against those of Annie, to hold her closer to him, straining the power of his hands to press her body against his own. And she responded, responded in ways that might be commonplace in her own strange world of the year 1999 but that were shocking—and delightful—to a man of Clive's staid era.

In that moment Clive felt a strange stirring. It was his brother Neville's journal, which he had placed beneath his leg. It shifted and squirmed like a living thing. He tried to ignore it, tried to hold his full attention upon Annie. This might be the last opportunity either of them would ever have to share a moment such as this one. He did not wish her to be deprived of it.

But the book demanded his attention. It grew hot, then cold. It sent the sensation of needles running into his leg. It stung like an injection of deadly acid.

With a moan, Clive released Annie and reached for the book. With a start he realized that Annie was not there at all. He was fully awake, seated on the hard seat of a jouncing, creaking conveyance. He drew the journal from its place on the seat beneath his leg.

Dawn had broken—or its equivalent in this hollow world. The galaxy of stars overhead had brightened. The castle loomed before them, little more than a mile ahead.

The book opened itself in Clive's hand, opened to the page after the last entry had read. There was a new entry, this time in ink the color of a cobra's eyes—a deadly, hypnotic green!

The gem of beauty is the diamond and the gem of sin is the emerald. Seek out the diamond. Seek out the emerald. You have traveled farther than was simple and farther than was wise. Your peril is only beginning and yet it is ending. Beware the sin that rests upon the peak of beauty. Beware the emerald set upon the peak of diamond. BEWARE, CLIVE FOLLIOT, BEWARE!

Unaided by volition on the part of Clive Folliot, the book shut itself with a snap. He tried to open it again, to reexamine this newest message, but the book refused to yield.

A squad of heavyset, gnomelike troopers barred the pathway. The major's cart had come close to the castle now, and he drew the human beasts to a halt.

The commander of the guards wore a heavy helmet, massive armor, and thick padding. He carried a huge double-headed battle-ax, and other weapons hung from the belt that circled his broad waist.

"You!" he snarled. He held his enormous ax in one hand as if it were an instructor's pointer in some sunlit classroom at Cambridge. He pointed the ax unmistakably at Clive. "Climb down! Come ahead!"

He pointed at the others in the wagon and made a contemptuous gesture. "You others, the rest of you—go home. Or wait here. Or be eaten by—" He made a sound, uttered a word, obviously the name of a beast to be found hereabouts.

"Die anyway," the commander growled. He pointed

again at Clive. "You come, quick!" He turned his
back without waiting for a response and trudged up
the dirt road toward the castle.

Still seated, Clive turned and looked at his companions and tried to read what he saw in their faces.
He held the journal toward Horace Smythe. He was
not sure why he did it, but he felt somehow that the
journal might more likely survive in Smythe's cus-
tody than in his own.

Clive climbed down from the wagon. He followed
the guard commander up the hard-packed path toward the castle. He would face whatever the castle
held, alone. *Alone*, the word echoed in his mind. He
repeated with each step he took. *Alone. Alone. Alone.*

The castle, upon closer approach, was a perfect
example of the medieval keep. It could have been an
illustration from some volume of folktales gathered
by the Brothers Grimm—perhaps the one containing
the story of Hansel and Gretel! High towers rose
gloomily above massive battlements. Notched walls
and narrow windows would facilitate the defense of
the castle against any besieging army. The only visible entrance to the pile was a great arched opening
sealed by an iron portcullis that could be reached
only by crossing a broad moat.

Through the portcullis Clive could see a broad,
open courtyard—the kind of courtyard that in centuries past would have been used as a marshaling
area for parties of traders—or of warriors.

It was something out-of-date by hundreds of years,
a nightmare from the Middle Ages. Yet here it stood.

Clive's guide had not spoken another word once
they had left the cart and Clive's companions behind. There was only the loping, gnomish stride of
the commander leading Clive up the path and the
heavy shuffling of the other guards behind him, to
accompany his melancholy march.

The drawbridge was raised when they reached the
moat. The guard commander found a heavy stone
and dragged it from the earth with filthy fingers. He

drew back and hurled it against the bridge; as the stone splashed into the moat, the sound of its impact on the bridge boomed through the air.

The morning was bright by now, and wisps of vapor rose and danced above the moat. A face appeared in a slit beside the bridge. The helmet-clad head nodded. Moments later, with much creaking and groaning, the bridge was lowered.

"Go, you!" Clive's guide commanded. Clive walked carefully across the drawbridge. When he was halfway across, the guard in the castle shouted, "Halt!"

Clive took the opportunity to peer over the edge of the bridge, into the murky moat. Something swimming by peered back up at him and seemed almost to grin, a hungry, anticipatory grin that revealed rows of gleaming, triangular teeth.

Taking a careful stride, Clive positioned himself closer to the center of the span. With the sound of protesting metal, the portcullis rose. Clive could see that its bottom edge was fitted with a series of terrible barbed spikes that fitted into the ground beneath—but that could as easily impale a man and shred his flesh.

More of the gnomish guards appeared and surrounded Clive. He cast a single glance behind him. The squad that had escorted him from the cart had turned and was marching away from the moat. The cart itself and its passengers were nowhere to be seen.

Were they safe? A lump rose in Clive's throat when he thought of his companions—those he had left in the cart and those from whom he had been separated earlier. Smythe and Finnbogg and Shriek would have accompanied him had he asked. He was certain of that. But the terms of the situation meant that he must advance alone. He must press on. He must see this through. Somehow, in the course of doing so, he would find his way back to the others, especially to Annie—or she to him—and they would discover their fates together.

But for now he must go on. Again he repeated to himself, as he moved step by step across the stone-paved courtyard and toward the main keep of the castle, he was *alone . . . alone . . . alone.*

This time the gnomelike guards refused to speak a word. Even their commander communicated by heavy gestures and harsh shoves. The thought flickered across Clive's mind that Neville's journal might have another message in it by now, but he had left the black-bound book with Smythe. There was no revising that decision: it was a fait accompli.

The guards marched Clive through corridors and passageways until they reached an audience room. The captain of the guards took Clive by the elbow and hustled him to the center of the room. Before a raised platform the captain shoved Clive forward, at the same time kicking him behind the knees. In a single moment Clive felt himself tumble to the floor. In a crazy flash of clarity he found himself examining the carpet that had been laid there—a rich oriental weave with a single pattern replicated hundreds upon hundreds of times in golden threads against a background the color of midnight.

The swirling spiral of stars.

There was a moment of silence. Then a smoothly masculine voice spoke. "Now, there's no need for that."

Clive raised his eyes. A man and a woman were seated on carved wooden thrones.

"Come," the man said. "There's no excuse for the way you've been treated. I'm really very sorry, old fellow. We try to instill some courtesy in these chaps, but they do have a long tradition behind them and it's hard to make them change." He gestured to Clive to rise, then indicated a third chair near the dais.

Clive made his way to the chair and sank into it. He was conscious of his raggedness and of the filth that covered him. He had not had a bath or a shave in days, nor a change of clothing in weeks.

By contrast, the man who spoke was immaculately

groomed. He was almost grotesquely tall and slim, yet his form and features were marked by an enviable grace. His costume was all of white, a pale silken material cut to accentuate the conformation of his body. When he moved, the impression was one of power and grace despite his extreme slimness.

His companion was his female counterpart, dressed also in a costume of white silk. Her clothing was tightly fitted to arms and body, although cut so low at the bosom as to draw Clive's unwilling attention. Below the waist, where the man's costume comprised tightly fitted trousers that disappeared into dark-tinted boots, the woman wore a long skirt that lay softly across her lap and against her legs.

Both wore jeweled rings, glittering emeralds mounted in silver bezels. A single dark emerald was suspended by a silver chain from the woman's throat—it lay against her generous bosom, rising and falling with her every breath.

But what most struck Clive about the two was their coloration. Their skins were white. Not the so-called white of the Anglo-Saxon, but a true white, as if they had been carved from living snow or ice. And the hair and the eyes of both were of a dark, glittering green, the color reflected in the emerald gems that both wore as decoration.

"You are Major Clive Folliot," the man said.

Clive acknowledged his identity.

The man smiled faintly. "Of the island of Angle Land on the planet Tellus, and of the Third Era of Technology of that world."

Clive could think of no response to make.

"And I," the man said, "am N'wrbb Crrd'f." He placed a hand deprecatingly against his chest, inclined his head courteously. "And my companion," he continued, "is the Lady 'Nrrc'kth." He extended his hand toward the woman. She took it in hers, smiling softly at Clive.

Her smile, despite her tall, slim conformation and startling coloration—or perhaps because of these characteristics—was breathtaking. Clive compared it to those of women he had known through his life and found none to which to compare it. She released N'wrbb Crrd'f's hand and he withdrew it. The magnificent woman touched the emerald that lay against her bosom, and Clive found himself wondering at the likely color of the areolae of her breasts. Would he ever see them for himself?

N'wrbb Crrd'f was speaking, Clive realized with a start. ". . . will wish to refresh yourself. In all honesty, it astonishes me that you have survived to this point. I will lose a wager." He laughed. "A friendly wager, but one that I regret losing nonetheless. I never expected you to survive to this point. I've thought you a weak link, Major Clive Folliot. Far stronger and more capable candidates than yourself have attempted this journey, and have not come anywhere near reaching the castle. But—"

He made a gesture with his hands, as if in self-deprecation. "For every winner there is a loser and vice versa, so I shall pay and my friend will collect and all will thus remain in equilibrium."

He took his lovely companion's hand and they rose and walked from the dais. Clive stood to face them. At this closer distance they were even more graceful, the man even more powerful, the woman even more breathtakingly lovely, than Clive had realized.

"My men will take you to your quarters. You will find a warm bath, soap, a razor, fresh clothing. I'm sure you will be happier and more comfortable when you have removed the evidence of your travels. Then you will join us for dinner, Major Clive Folliot."

Clive shook his head. "My friends. My companions." He pointed vaguely to the entrance of the room, indicating the whole path he had followed, the cart and Finnbogg and Shriek and Horace Hamilton Smythe.

"I'm sorry, Major. They cannot join us. I fear for

them—there is only a small chance that they are alive, although I certainly wish them well."

"No longer alive? Sergeant Smythe? Finnbogg and Shriek? No longer alive?" Clive began to tremble.

"But there is another guest," N'wrbb Crrd'f said softly. "I'm sure you will be pleased to share our board with the brigadier."

Numbly, Clive echoed the other's last word. "Brigadier?"

"Yes," N'wrbb Crrd'f smiled, "Brigadier Neville Folliot."

Clive luxuriated in the tub. It was made of wood, the pieces so perfectly fitted and finished that it was absolutely watertight. Servants had brought the hot water in buckets, had clipped his hair and shaved his beard, had washed and rubbed and pampered him.

The room contained little furniture—soft draperies upon the walls, a huge bed where fresh costumery was laid out, a heavy rug like that below, where the pattern of swirling stars repeated itself endlessly.

Left alone, he climbed from the water and dried himself in a huge, soft towel. The costume that had been set out for him was medieval in cut—jerkin and trousers and high-topped boots of soft leather. The colors were all shades of red and maroon. The clothing fitted perfectly. A dagger, golden-hilted and decorated with polished rubies, hung at his waist.

Clive stood before a tall mirror, admiring himself. The room was illuminated by torches mounted in brackets.

Behind Clive there appeared a tall, graceful figure in white. He whirled and saw the Lady 'Nrrc'kth. She pressed a finger to her lips, reached out a slim-fingered hand, and pressed it against Clive's mouth to silence him even before he had spoken.

He nodded and she dropped her hand.

His lips burned maddeningly where she had touched them. That fleeting contact was like a kiss of frozen flame, a sip of iced wine tinctured with a burning spice.

Operating by little more than reflex, he clasped the lady in his arms. She came to him, unresisting. He felt her lips at his ear, her warm breath close against his skin, her body strong against his own. For all her height, he could see the magnificent emerald that hung upon her bosom. As she shifted he learned the answer to one mystery that had puzzled him: the color of the areolae that decorated her breasts.

"Clive Folliot," 'Nrrc'kth whispered in his ear, "Clive Folliot, you must rescue me!"

These were the first words he had heard her speak, and he was flabbergasted by them. Was she not the consort of N'wrbb Crrd'f? He asked if the lord was not her husband.

'Nrrc'kth laughed, low and bitter. "He wishes to be my husband. I despise him!"

"But—I saw you together. Ruler and consort. Man and wife."

"We are nothing of the sort."

Clive shook his head. "Is this not your world? Your castle?"

"No, neither. I am not of this world, nor is the beast N'wrbb. Our world is far from here. Agents of the Dungeon came there and N'wrbb made league with them. If he would aid them in their plans, they would help him to capture me and force me here as his prisoner."

Clive was dizzy. Perhaps it was the hot bath that had drained the blood from his brain; perhaps it was the nearness of the Lady 'Nrrc'kth. He staggered and she helped him to the bed. He meant only to sit on its edge, but there was a ringing in his ears. Perhaps there had been some subtle infusion in the bathwater itself. He lay back, his eyes fixed on the ceiling where shadows cast by torches danced hypnotically.

He saw a face leaning over his own—a face that was somehow alien but yet was the most beautiful into which he had ever looked. The skin was pallid, the hair a glossy greenish black. He felt soft hands touching him, laid against the sides of his face. He heard words but could not understand them. His own hands felt smooth cloth and wonderful soft flesh.

Without warning the Lady 'Nrrc'kth was dragged from him. He felt a hand grasp him by the front of his costume, haul him unceremoniously to his feet. He stood looking up into the face of the Lord N'wrbb Crrd'f. "I should kill you," the lord snarled at Clive. His breath was hot and foul. "I should kill you both. But I'll do better than that. Much better. You think you know the meaning of the word *Dungeon*, Clive Folliot. You think you know that, but you know nothing. Nothing!"

N'wrbb drew back his hand and struck Clive with all his strength on one side of the face, then on the other. Still dizzy, still weak, Clive saw a blackness filled with N'wrbb's sneering face in the center of a spiral of swirling stars.

"You and the Lady 'Nrrc'kth together shall learn the meaning of the Dungeon—while Brigadier Folliot and I look on in amusement!"

He had come that close to finding Neville! That close! And now—what was to become of him?

Clive felt himself swung violently by the sinewy N'wrbb. He felt himself dragged toward the doorway. Even as he lost consciousness he wondered what was happening to the Lady 'Nrrc'kth.

▪ CHAPTER 28 ▪
The Army of Despair

Pain preceded full awareness, so that Clive seemed to swim up to consciousness through a sea of agony like a diver swimming from the ocean floor up to the surface. He blinked his eyes; the light that made him blink was a watery, wintry light that filtered faintly through tiny windows near the roof of the stone chamber.

He felt for the dagger that had been part of his costume. At the time he had thought it merely a ceremonial appurtenance of the red-and-maroon finery that had been provided for him. Now it would prove of supremely practical importance.

The dagger was gone!

He pushed himself to a sitting position. He was in a dungeon once again! Not only was the whole bizarre universe into which he had been unwillingly plunged called the Dungeon—it was well equipped with literal dungeons, and Clive was developing a most regrettable penchant for getting himself tossed into them.

The lovely, exotic 'Nrrc'kth was beside him, her magnificent white gown torn and stained, her breathtaking silver-and-emerald jewelry gone. They were surrounded by a motley crew of ill-assorted individuals. A stocky woman whose coloring resembled that of 'Nrrc'kth stood over them, Clive's ruby-hilted dagger in her hand. Her appearance was that of an oldster, but there was obvious strength in her limbs and agility in her movements. She was clearly in command of the situation.

The shambling creatures that surrounded them were obviously awed by the stocky woman, and the addition of Clive's dagger to her arsenal had helped to keep them at bay.

The woman flicked a sharp-eyed look at Clive. "Awake at last, are you, cookie?"

Clive staggered to his feet. There was no need to answer the woman's question, asked in the patois that served so much of the Dungeon.

"Call me Gram," the woman said. "And who are you, you queer-looking turnip?"

As well as he could in a few brief sentences, Clive told her who he was.

"Brigadier Folliot's brother, hey? Well, well, we're all related around here, ain't we!"

Clive averred that he didn't understand the comment.

"Well, I'm pretty-girl's great-aunt, as a matter of fact." She indicated 'Nrrc'kth's cool, green-and-white beauty.

"You were brought here from the same world?"

"Djajj—you'd know it as Baten Kaitos Omicron."

"No, I would not." Clive shook his head. "I don't know it at all."

"Where you from, boy? What's your planet? And what's your year?"

"Uh—Tellus. Terra. Earth. The year was 1868."

The old woman laughed. "I guess you'd call my year—our year"—she indicated 'Nrrc'kth—"801,702. Or close enough as makes no difference."

The old woman looked around the scores of ragged, filthy individuals who filled the dungeon. "Seems to me there was another fella here from Earth. Can't say as I remember the year." She paused to rub her chin.

Clive's mind raced. Another fellow from Earth—could it be Horace Hamilton Smythe? Or Sidi Bombay? The old woman knew who Brigadier Folliot was—Clive's brother must have awarded himself the promotion to a more exalted rank than that of a humble Guards major.

"Tomàs!" the old woman shouted.

The rows of shambling prisoners parted and a swarthy, unshaven man shuffled forward. He wore a sailor's knitted cap and vaguely nautical garb. He doffed his cap and bobbed his head to Gram.

"Yes'm."

"What year did you say you came from, Tomàs?"

The seafarer's eyes flicked from Gram to Clive and back, then from Gram to 'Nrrc'kth, then back once more to Gram. "It was 1492," Tomàs said. "Snatched right off the good ship *Niña* I was. Night watch, that was my duty. Settin' there doin' my duty, keepin' a sharp eye out for waterspouts and sea serpents. And sayin' my beads, too, so's we wouldn't fall off the edge of the world when we got there."

"Yes," Gram interrupted. "Get to the point, Tomàs."

"Yes'm. Well, there I sat, meditatin' on the agony of Our Lord and contemplatin' the stations of the cross, when all of a sudden there's a glare of lights in the sky, all colors, as bright as day. And then a bunch of stars breaks through a patch of clouds in the sou'west, I remember like today it was the sou'west. And they forms into a spiral and they swirls around and around. I felt so dizzy, I had to drop my beads and just hold on to the crow's nest to keep from fallin' to the deck. But it didn't do me no good, no. They got me anyhow. They just swept me up into the sky, and down to the Dungeon and all the things that happened to me then—"

"Never mind," Gram cut him off. "Is that enough?" She turned to face Clive. "This is Tomàs, then. Tomàs, this is Clive. You two being from the same planet, maybe you can do some good together. While I take care of my little baby, here." She put her arms around 'Nrrc'kth and tended to the younger woman's hurts.

Clive and Tomàs moved off together. Clive cast a

look around him, taking in the forms of the other prisoners. Why were they here? Why did the mysterious, shadowy figures who ran this world, be they Q'oornans or some even more alien race, capture beings of so many worlds and ages, and bring them to the Dungeon, only to abandon some and imprison others?

If he had just succeeded in locating Neville, Clive was convinced, he could have made a start at solving this even greater mystery. And he had been so close, so agonizingly close to finding his brother!

Nor was he prepared to abandon that goal! But he did not expect to locate Neville by remaining passive in this stone prison. He had traveled too far, endured too much, paid too great a price in pain and the loss of friends, to remain here.

"Tomàs," he addressed the sailor. "Portuguese, are you?"

"Yessir."

"Have you friends here, Tomàs? Are these prisoners a community whom we can mobilize against our captors?"

The Iberian looked solemn. "The Dungeon is Our Lord's way of testing us, sir. If we keep our faith, we will yet be saved. If we give way to rebellion or despair, we are doomed."

Clive Folliot was as pious as the next man, but there were times for salvation through faith and times for salvation through acts. This was clearly one of the latter.

"I've no doubt that your faith is strong, Tomàs. And of course no one would go against the will of heaven. But surely you don't think your captors are doing heaven's bidding! More likely the opposite! Won't you help us to win our freedom? Surely that is heaven's will—freedom, not misery, for the faithful."

Somehow, Tomàs took little convincing. Perhaps it was Clive's eloquence and obvious sincerity that swayed the Iberian. Or perhaps it was the thought of daylight and clear skies and running water as contrasted with the filth and misery of his present surroundings.

At any rate, Tomàs's saturnine features were split by an eager grin. "Aye, Major! Good old Gram is a mighty one, and I've other friends. Strange creatures here, Major! Wolfish ones and lionish ones and others that I can't even put words to—but they're all prisoners of the Dungeon and they're all ready for an escape. They only need someone to lead 'em. Are you it, Major? Are you it?"

Clive hesitated only a moment. He was a contemplative, passive man by nature. He would rather study, and think, and plan, than act. But this was no time for such conduct.

"I am your man, Tomàs! Yes, I will lead you! Come, let us gather with Gram. And with whatever others you believe have the will and the intelligence to join us at the center of our plot. We shall develop a scheme, and then we shall act. The Q'oornans brought us here against our will, every man and woman and inhuman creature of us. But they shall not keep us here. We shall become our own masters once again!"

'Nrrc'kth rested while Clive and Tomàs and Gram formulated their plan. Tomàs suggested two more prisoners to join the conspiracy. One was a strange creature with skin like a lizard's and claws like a tiger's. The other was far odder, a shadowy, whispery thing that Clive could never quite bring his eyes to focus on and that seemed to grow and shrink and shift restlessly.

There was the danger, always the danger, that some of the prisoners were traitors, double agents planted among the polyglot mass by their Q'oornan captors, for reasons of their own. There was no easy way to uncover such traitors, and the presence of turncoats seemed unlikely.

They would just have to trust Tomàs's judgment—and Gram's—Clive decided.

The plan that was evolved required the digging out of paving stones from the floor of the dungeon. The stones were not cemented into place, but were simply laid side by side, carefully fitted so that it was almost impossible to raise them from their places.

But Clive's ceremonial dagger had escaped the notice of his captors in the turmoil of his confrontation with the Lord of the Castle. Now, with its polished blade as a tool, Clive and his allies managed to raise a block near the window-wall a fraction of an inch.

And now the tigerish talons of Tomàs's friend came into play. No ordinary fingers could have held that stone in place—Clive estimated that it weighed nearly four hundred pounds, and its sides were smooth and slippery. But the claws dug in, and then the form shifter managed to penetrate the narrow opening with tendrils of its being and get part of its mass beneath the stone so that it pressed upward upon the block.

With a concerted effort they managed to raise the stone. With a common exclamation they shoved it sideways onto the adjacent block.

For a fleeting moment Clive hoped that the removal of the stone would give them access to some hidden escape route, some forgotten tunnel that would lead them from the dungeon to the outer world, whence they could make a full escape from the castle.

Such was not to be. They saw only black earth beneath the stones. In a way, Clive was relieved. He did not really wish to leave the castle and escape across country. Not after he'd got this close to Neville. Oh, no! Now Clive craved the confrontation that he knew awaited him.

They worked in shifts, digging at the dirt beneath the black stone. Their food was brought at regular intervals and it was an easy matter to shield the excavation project with the bodies of ever-moving prisoners. Nor did their warders pay attention to what they did. The prison had been secure for so long a time that they had been lulled into a treacherous overconfidence.

The wall itself shimmered and glowed and became gradually transparent. Clive found himself staring open-mouthed. 'Nrrc'kth was at his side. She had recovered her strength and become a vital part of the inner cabal that plotted the prisoners' escape. Tomàs was supervising the work of excavation, and he exclaimed aloud at the vision, calling upon his patron saint for protection.

He had been right all along, Tomàs exclaimed. The Dungeon was part of heaven's plan—perhaps it was purgatory! Perhaps it was a precinct of hell itself! And now—

Clive commanded calm. He had grown comfortable with the Dungeon's patois, and the problem of languages no longer impeded the exercise of his authority.

Now, standing where the wall of close-fitted stones had held the motley prisoners helpless, there was instead a shimmering, glowing field. And in the center of it, illuminated by an inner light, surrounded by Shriek and Finnbogg and Horace Hamilton Smythe, stood the dark-haired, willowy figure of User Annie!

Clive strode forward. He felt his brain execute a twist, his sense of time and space turning through some strange dimension so that he had access to the information he had carried in him since the strange communion he had experienced with Horace Hamilton Smythe and with Finnbogg and with Annie, through Shriek. He had thought, at the time, that he had refrained from merging his mind with that of User Annie. But he realized, now, that he had indeed shared his mind with her, and she had shared hers with him. He had repressed until now the shocking information that he had received from her, but in this moment of confrontation and reunion it came pouring forth from whatever chamber of the mind in which it had been sealed.

While the scene before him froze into a tableau, his mind traveled through the tale that he had received from Annie.

Yes, you call me User Annie but my name is Annabelle Leigh. My lovers call me Anne, or Belle. I like Belle. My grandmother knew Belle Starr.

You think I speak strangely, but that's the way we speak in my time, in my world. In my business. Computers are so much a part of our daily lives, our speech has taken on the jargon of the programmer and the systems designer. Your speech sounds as alien and incomprehensible to me, Clive Folliot, as does mine to you. Bless Shriek for helping us to understand each other. I do care for you, I am attracted to you, but there is something between us already that you do not understand—and yet you must.

I was born in San Francisco in 1980, so I'm nineteen years old. I was a virgin until I was fifteen—average for girls in my time. I have a good education and a good profession—or I did, at least, until the Q'oornans plucked me from Piccadilly Circus and brought me to the Dungeon.

My mother was a singer before me. She was born in Denver, in 1959, and made her way to San Francisco. She sang in the chorus of the San Francisco opera and she won a few small roles as a coloratura. She was twenty-one years of age when I was born. She was never married. That's a tradition in our family. I'm the fifth generation to maintain the tradition, and I won't change it if I can help myself.

We never marry. We take lovers of our choice, we bear daughters, we live our own lives, go where we will, and above all—we never marry!

My grandmother was born in Chicago in 1925. She was a saloon girl. She sang and danced and she was a part-time hooker on the side. She had few advantages. Her mother hadn't been able to give her much, but she taught her the family law: live as you choose—take the lovers that you wish—bear a daughter—never marry!

Grandmother had it hard, but she remained true to the family tradition. She bore my mother at the age of thirty-four. She raised her on her poor earnings, but she taught her what she had to learn, and she helped her to rise in the world.

My great-grandmother was a Boston scrubwoman. She was scorned there as a bastard. She had come to America in her mother's arms, a toothless infant. Her mother had tried to claim widowhood, but somehow word got out that she had never been married, that her child was illegitimate. She was the one who made the great resolve, who laid down our family law.

The family name was not always Leigh. It was shortened somewhere along the years, from Leighton.

Our line was founded by the Englishwoman Annabella Leighton. She had taken a lover, but this was before our great law had been created. She intended to marry. Her lover had promised to marry her. She trusted him, poor fool! Poor Annabella Leighton!

Her lover was the second son of a baron. His older brother was lost on an expedition to East Africa. Great-great-grandmother's lover went in search of his brother. Neither brother returned.

Great-great-grandmother waited to the bitter end. She gave birth to her child alone, alone and unattended in a freezing London flat. When she realized that her lover was not returning—when old Baron Tewkesbury died and the title and fortune passed to a distant cousin who turned Great-great-grandmother away from his door—she created the great law of our family.

She booked passage to America, and lived in Boston, and raised her child to live as she would, to take lovers as she chose, to bear a daughter and pass on to her the family law. And above all, never to marry.

That is the story of my family. That is who I am.

You played a part in that story, Clive Folliot. You know who you are. You know the part that you played.

My feelings about you are mixed, to say the least. If we get out of this alive ... if you find your way back to

England and to Annabella Leighton . . . if you marry her after all . . .

What will become of my family? What will become of our law? What will become of me? I don't know, Clive Folliot. That is the end and the answer to it all. I simply do not know.

Clive shook his head, as if that could change the universe and break the stasis that had held him, sound and movement resumed all around him.

User Annie—no, Annabelle Leigh—stood in the center of her glowing nimbus. Colors for which Clive had not the vaguest of names shimmered and wove around her as she moved her hands, melting away the stone wall of the dungeon.

He had no idea what the computers were that she had spoken of in that blinding moment of communication, save that they were machines of a wondrous sort, machines that seemed almost to have minds and consciousness of their own, and that could be used as either the servants or the masters of men. Baalbec A-9 was obviously one such.

The prisoners were pouring through the opening in the wall of the dungeon that Annabelle Leigh had made. Clearly this marvel was another wonder worked by her Baalbec A-9.

How much of her own strength this deed had consumed, how much remained, how much more the machine could do at Annabelle's command, Clive could not even guess. She had told Clive that the machine was powered by the energies of her body. When she was fatigued and her strength depleted, then the Baalbec must lose its power as well, until Annie had rested and taken nourishment and re-plenished her strength.

And, for that matter, how had she got here? He could only guess, and his guess was that she had flown in the Nakajima Model 97. Brought it to earth where? Perhaps in the courtyard of the castle. Or perhaps beyond the moat, and from there trans-

ported Shriek and Finnbogg and Horace Hamilton
Smythe.

Questions, always questions, and each answer
brought only a new freshet of puzzles in its train.
There was not time, certainly not time now, to pur-
sue the matter.

He looked back at 'Nrrc'kth. Her white gown, her
pale skin, her black-green hair, her unearthly beauty
still stirred him to the core. He looked away from
her, looked once more at Annabelle Leigh. Was this
young woman truly the great-great-granddaughter
of Annabella Leighton? She had to be; the story she
told fitted too well, for all its fantastic features, with
the realities of Clive's and Annabella's lives.

Annabelle Leigh—User Annie—was his own great-
great-grandchild. She was the flesh of his flesh,
the flower of his—and Annabella's—loins, of their
passion.

He thought of how he had held her on their ride
in the cart. He knew that if the situation had been
different, if the opportunity had presented itself, he
would have done more than hold her in his arms.
He would have . . . She was his own great-great-
grandchild, his direct descendant, his very daughter,
and he would have. . . .

But no, that had been only a dream, a curious
flight of fantasy, a thing half of the stuff of sleep
and half of wishful musings. And he had not known,
had not known at the time. . . .

But then he was swept by a more tangible force, by
the rush of the prisoners from the dungeon seeking
their freedom.

A few of them ran away, fleeing the dungeon, the
castle. He heard a series of splashes as they plunged
into the broad moat. Then a series of screams as the
denizens of that precinct began to feast.

Most of the prisoners remained, clustering around
Clive and Tomàs and Gram and 'Nrrc'kth. This group
merged with the newcomers, with Annabelle and
Horace Hamilton Smythe and Finnbogg and Shriek.

And all of them—all of them—were looking at Clive.

No, he realized in a stunning moment of comprehension. They were not looking *at* him. They were looking *to* him. Looking to him for decision and leadership.

He did not wish the role of commander, but it had been thrust upon him. There were guards in the castle above. It was a miracle that they had not yet responded to the mass escape of the prisoners, but at any moment, Clive knew, they would arrive.

He could lead his motley band in flight—or he could lead them as they stayed to fight.

The first course might save injuries, even deaths—for the time being. But someone had to face down the Q'oornans. Someone had to solve the mystery of the Dungeon. Someone had to conquer the overlords!

That someone would be Clive Folliot, along with his band of human and inhuman followers.

There was time for one brief exchange with Annie, and while the others took brief respite, Clive took this chance. "I understand now," he said to Annie.

She looked into his face and said, "I'm glad, Clive." In her look was the knowledge that Annie, too, knew what it was that Clive understood. She had learned as much of him, through that moment of psychic unity, as he had learned of her.

"Is there anything else—anything I must find out?"

Annie smiled. "Whole ROM libraries, Clive. Grandfather. The Q'oornans—they're just one group, one world in a universe you can hardly imagine. We're pawns, Grandfather. Pawns in a mad n-dimensional chess game where we don't even know whose hand it is that moves us."

"Is there no hope, then?" Clive almost pleaded.

"There is always hope, Grandfather! Always! Only when we surrender hope does it cease to exist for us. As long as we cling to our aspirations and as long as we do not give up the struggle, we may yet win. Someday. Somehow. We *will* win, Grandfather!"

Clive smiled at Annie. At this beautiful woman, this creature of courage and of mystification. He realized that he loved her, loved her in a way he had never loved before.

They would win! In his heart he knew that they would.

The first task that lay ahead was to confront Neville.

Clive Folliot set out to accomplish that task.

▪ CHAPTER 29 ▪
Chang Guafe

Of all the prisoners to join Clive's army outside the castle, the most striking in appearance was Chang Guafe. Not man, not beast, not machine, Chang Guafe was none of these and all of them.

His face was an ever-moving amorphous mass of eyes and teeth and other objects that must have been the product of a maddened experimenter rather than nature even at her worst. There were tentacles and gears, pincers and claws. Chang Guafe might have been the acromegalous parent of the monster of the great black bridge, outfitted with the product of a malevolent munitions maker.

In a rapid exchange of information with the monster, Clive learned that he—even that word is inaccurate and insufficient to designate Chang Guafe, but it will suffice—was the product of a world where life was simple and primitive. Chang Guafe himself had begun as little more than an amoeba.

But the great achievement of evolution among Chang Guafe's species was their ability to retain the features, and to a limited extent even the conscious personalities, of the creatures they encountered and absorbed.

Left alone, Chang Guafe's world had developed into the habitat of a formless mass of living, pulsating protoplasm. Undifferentiated, unspecialized, unintelligent, and even unconscious—until the first space explorers had arrived from a distant planet. Once the visitors' spacecraft had come to rest, it was inexorably absorbed, and both the mechanical devices of the craft and the physical and mental organs of its occupants were incorporated into the makeup of the native life form.

With the knowledge and the technique of its new members, the native life of Chang Guafe's planet had in turn become spacefaring—and had spread itself, enveloping and incorporating all life and all technology that it encountered.

Then Chang Guafe had reached a planet already dominated by the Q'oornans. It would be inaccurate to say that Chang Guafe traveled by spaceship, or alternately that he traveled without need of one. There was no distinction between occupant and vehicle. Chang Guafe and his supplies and equipment and spaceship were a single entity.

But something on this planet had frozen Chang Guafe's form. He could move, he could function, he could even change, within limits. But no longer could he absorb new organisms or new mechanisms. He was stuck. And he had been imprisoned in the Dungeon. And he sought vengeance against his captors.

Chang Guafe saw in the leadership of Clive Folliot an opportunity to gain that vengeance—and at least a hope of escape from this planet and the restoration of his power to grow and adapt.

And Clive Folliot saw in Chang Guafe an ally in his own fight against the Q'oornans and in his quest for his missing brother.

Clive and his band found themselves in an open area, the castle with its now breached dungeon wall behind them, the broad moat separating the castle from the mainland ahead. He wanted to talk with them, to tell them what he had experienced and ask what they had learned during the time of their separation. Above all he wanted to speak with Annie—Annabelle Leigh, his own descendant! But this was not the time to do that.

He threw back his head to scan the sky above. The ever-circling stars of the miniature constellation that lighted this world within the Dungeon were as bright as noonday.

What lay on the other side of this inside-out world? Clive knew that he *could* travel there, given the opportunity. Had Neville been at the castle of N'wrbb Crrd'f? Was he gone now—possibly to some point opposite the castle, some land in the sky of the Dungeon?

Clive had come this close—within an hour, possibly within a corridor, of Neville. He could not give up his quest!

A squad of gnomish guards poured from the gap in the castle wall that had been carved out by the Baalbec A-9 of Annabelle Leigh. His former carnal feeling for Annie had been transformed into a kind of grandpaternal pride and concern for her welfare. No longer was she merely an attractive, if exotic, young woman whom he had encountered in this nightmarish world.

She was the flesh of his flesh, the blood of his blood. She was his child, and he would watch over her.

The gnomes attacked with pikes and axes.

Clive's forces defended themselves with whatever makeshift weapons they could find. Sticks and rocks and, when need be, their own bare hands, their teeth, their claws. Some of them possessed organs for producing and administering venom.

Shriek bounded into the air, her four long legs propelling her in one direction and then another, her four thin but powerful arms twisting the limbs and necks of the gnomes. Her mandibles, which Clive had thought merely vestigial, proved to be anything but—she administered stings that sent her enemies into paroxysms of agony and their compatriots into tremors of fright. She pulled her own spikelike hairs and threw them into the faces of attackers, sending them spinning onto the ground to writhe and scream until they died.

One gnomish attacker managed to strike at Shriek

with a spike-headed mace. The impact shattered one
of the spider woman's four arms. She set up a howl
unlike any that Clive had heard before. With her
remaining arms she picked up her attacker and hurled
him bodily through the air. His own scream joined
hers, cutting off with the splash of his body into the
moat.

There was a thrashing, a sound of rending, a final
agonized howl, and the gnome disappeared beneath
the rippling water.

The gnome's mace had remained embedded in
Shriek's flesh, held there by barbed spikes. The spider woman's screaming dominated the entire field of
battle as she tore her own ruined limb from its socket,
pulled the spike-headed mace from the discarded
arm, and waded back into the battle, smashing gnomes
with the mace.

The attackers were almost decimated when a cry
of dismay went up among Clive's followers. Another
squad of guards—no, two squads!—were approaching. They had left the castle and circled, one mass of
troops moving clockwise, the other counterclockwise,
to converge, pincers-fashion, on Clive's band of
warriors.

Mighty Finnbogg broke away from a few remnants
of the original band of gnomes that he had been
harrying, and charged toward one of the new parties
of attackers. Clive heard his canine snarling, a basso
counterpoint to Shriek's piercing war cries. He saw
Finnbogg disappear beneath the mass of gnomes.

Clive could see the vague outline of Finnbogg's
figure, gnomes crawling over it like beetles over a
rodent. But Finnbogg was not a passive victim.
Gnomes and parts of gnomes flew from the hump
that was Finnbogg. Blood spattered, gore splatted on
the earth.

Annabelle and 'Nrrc'kth and Gram stood in a tri-
angle facing outward. 'Nrrc'kth and Gram had armed
themselves with weapons seized from falling gnomes.
Annabelle relied solely upon her Baalbec A-9. Clive

knew only a few of that device's potentialities. What it could do for Annabelle, what she could do with it, he could only guess.

Clive himself was armed with the ruby-handled ceremonial dagger he had received from N'wrbb Crrd'f. It seemed a pitiable tool to use against pikes and maces and battle-axes and broadswords, but Clive was a man inspired. He leaped and struck, dodged and twisted. He was covered with a sheen of sweat and dirt and blood, and he had no idea how much of the blood was his own, nor did he care.

This gentle, contemplative, perhaps unintentionally self-concerned man, had been turned into a machine for killing.

He sensed Sergeant Smythe at his back, heard the man's grunts of effort, shouts of triumph, cries of pain.

Clive heard Smythe shout, "Here, sah! Your hand!" The sergeant had managed to keep a few of the tiny explosive pellets that he had salvaged from the flying beast that had attacked them on the obsidian bridge. He slipped half of his supply into Clive's palm.

The pellets were hardly larger than orange pips.

Clive hurled one into the face of a howling attacker. It exploded with a roar that sent the attacker tumbling away, his face a bloody ruin. Clive hurled another of the pellets, and another. Each did its work. He heard Horace Smythe, behind him, cry out in triumph after each similar success.

But soon the supply of explosives was exhausted, and still the attackers kept coming.

Clive found himself face to face with a tall, slim figure in white and green. It was not the lovely 'Nrcc'kth, but her cruel would-be consort, N'wrbb Crrd'f.

The two men locked eyes. Clive wished for just one more of the minuscule, deadly pellets. *Just one!* But he had none. He had only the tiny, ruby-decorated dagger.

N'wrbb, armed with a longsword, swung his blade

downward. Its trajectory was such that the heavy blade and polished edge would chop Clive from shoulder to sternum, should the blow land as intended.

Folliot did not jump back or try to dodge the stroke. Instead he leaped forward, dagger held chesthigh, and plunged the blade at N'wrbb's heart. The blade dug into the pallid figure and blood the color of emerald sprayed out around it.

Clive pulled back the dagger, expecting N'wrbb to fall dead, but Folliot had assumed that the internal organs of these slim creatures were arranged as were his own. It was a mistake on Folliot's part—a mistake that saved N'wrbb's life and very nearly cost Folliot his own.

The taller man shouted with anger and pain. Reversing his weapon, he lifted his longsword point uppermost, and brought it down heavily on Clive Folliot's head. The massive hilt pounded against Clive's unprotected skull like a war club.

Clive heard the impact rather than felt it. He fell away from N'wrbb, collapsing helplessly onto his knees, then toppling onto his side. He saw N'wrbb clutch at his chest. Green ichor was spreading over the previously immaculate white garment.

N'wrbb spun and stumbled away from Clive.

Folliot dragged himself painfully back to his feet. Around him the battle still raged. Gnomish guards and escaped prisoners slashed and pounded at one another. Bodies of the dead and dying littered the ground, and at one point Clive saw a horrid tentacle emerge from the moat and drag a form, still bleeding and struggling, into the black water.

Somewhere in the fray were Annabelle and Gram, 'Nrcc'kth and Shriek, faithful Finnbogg and sturdy Horace Hamilton Smythe. Some of them might be wounded, some dead. Still the battle raged.

Staggering and stumbling with every step, yet regaining strength with every movement, Clive pounded across the bloodstained earth, pursuing N'wrbb Crrd'f.

The taller man had fled back into the dungeon,

and Clive pursued him there, unable to overtake the other's longer strides, yet grittily determined not to let him escape.

Down corridors, across echoing chambers, up flights of cold stone stairs they pounded. There seemed not a soul in the castle. Every soldier had been dispatched to the battle raging outside. The sounds of desperation, of triumph, and of death floated through the air, furnishing a cacophonous counterpoint to the thudding footsteps and panting breaths of the two men.

N'wrbb ran down a long corridor. Clive pursued him relentlessly. Behind him could be heard the sounds of other pursuers.

Clive permitted himself the momentary diversion of glancing over his shoulder. Behind him he could see a band of his companions and allies. Annie, 'Nrrc'kth, Gram, Tomàs, Smythe—and their inhuman or semihuman associates Finnbogg, Shriek, and Chang Guafe—followed in pursuit. They were like a polyglot army—but Clive did not stop to wait for them.

Suddenly N'wrbb disappeared. Clive reached the point at which he had last seen his enemy. An alcove had been cut into the smooth black rock. A rich tapestry depicting a scene of shocking lasciviousness covered the entryway.

Clive pushed cautiously at the tapestry, expecting to find N'wrbb hiding behind it, readying a treacherous sword stroke. But the pallid man was not there. He cowered instead at the end of a short corridor, his back against a massive wooden door. N'wrbb faced Clive, but with the hilt of his longsword he was pounding at the door, pleading to be admitted.

Clive started forward. Only the furtive flickering of N'wrbb's dark green eyes stopped him at the edge of a black flagstone that appeared no different from the others around it. Clive braced himself against the wall, extended one foot cautiously, and laid it lightly on the stone.

With a roar a huge cube of blackness fell from above. Clive had not looked up; he had concentrated too fully on the man who faced him. The cube was another stone, one that must have weighed easily five hundred pounds. It crashed onto the floor, shattering into a thousand pieces. Flying fragments stung Clive's face and body. He had managed to draw back his foot in time, or it would have been turned to jelly. If he had stepped fully onto the stone, he would have been killed outright by the falling cube.

N'wrbb cried again to whoever was on the other side of the door—or whoever he thought was there. There was no response.

Clive leaped over the shattered stone. He stood barely a yard from N'wrbb. Armed only with his ruby-hilted dagger, he would have been easy prey for N'wrbb, but his opponent had no fight left in him.

"Let me go," the pallid man pleaded. "Just let me by you." He pointed down the short corridor they had both traversed. "Let me by you and I'll go away, I'll leave you alone, you can do anything you want."

"Too late," Folliot answered. "Fight for your life, Q'oornan monster!"

"I'm no Q'oornan! Don't you see, they made me prisoner, too! I'm on your side, Clive Folliot!"

"It's no good," Clive started to say.

But N'wrbb threw his sword at Clive's feet and collapsed, weeping and pleading. Clive Folliot could kill in a flaming rage, but he could not kill in cold blood.

Behind N'wrbb there was a stir. Clive saw that his band of allies had reached the corridor. They stood on the other side of the fallen, shattered block of stone. None of them moved or spoke. They stood witnessing the confrontation between their leader and his enemy.

Clive reached a hand toward N'wrbb. The pale man lashed upward, a heavy chunk of black rock in his fist. The fragment connected with Clive, striking him on the cheek and sending him hurtling against the wall. In an instant N'wrbb had bounded over Clive's form and clambered up the pile of shattered fragments. He reached into the blackness that yawned where the rock had previously hung. With a grunt and a sneering chuckle he disappeared.

Clive pulled himself upright. He made a move, started once again in pursuit of N'wrbb, determined that this time he would not fall prey to any trick. But something stopped him. It was the feel of a hand on his shoulder.

He turned and found himself facing the tall, beautiful 'Nrrc'kth. Her emerald-green eyes were level with his own. Her warm mouth and tempting lips were inches from his.

"Spare him, Clive." She took his hands in hers.

"But he wanted to—"

"I know," 'Nrrc'kth said softly.

"You said—"

"Yes, Clive Folliot. But now I plead for him. A villain, a monster—but a man of Djajj nonetheless. Of our entire planet, only the three—N'wrbb, and old Gram, and I—survive in the Dungeon. If he should die . . ." She shook her head slowly. "Besides, Clive Folliot, you have mastered him. You do not know what it means to a man of Djajj to be beaten and humiliated as you have beaten and humiliated N'wrbb."

"Then—what would you have me do?"

She still held his hands. Now she dropped one, and by the other led him back through the castle. Followed by the others—by Annie and Horace Smythe, Finnbogg and Shriek and Chang Guafe—they made their way to the great hall where Clive had first seen the two figures of pale white and brilliant green— the diamond and emerald, he realized with a shock, of which his brother's journal had spoken.

'Nrrc'kth led him to the great carved chair that had belonged to N'wrbb. She stood before him. Annabelle Leigh—User Annie—stood beside her and slightly to her rear. The others, including even the bizarre Chang Guafe, stood behind the two women, all of them facing Clive.

"Clive Folliot," 'Nrrc'kth said, "by right of courage, by right of combat, and by right of conquest, you have won the title of Lord of the Castle. Now a final test remains. A final test which you must pass or . . ."

She did not complete the sentence. Instead she turned to Annabelle Leigh. The young woman of Earth's future looked pallid, drained of her energies by the incredible demands of using her Baalbec A-9 to power the Nakajima flying machine and then melting the wall of the dungeon. And yet she had never looked more beautiful.

Annabelle raised her hands. Her fingers disappeared into her flowing hair. She removed something, something that was almost invisible, but that Clive could see shimmering and glinting like polished glass when he looked at it from the corner of his eye.

He remembered, suddenly, another moment when Annie had raised her hands to her head. Another moment when her facial expression had seemed strange, when Clive had wondered, fleetingly, at the reasons, only to be distracted by more pressing considerations.

Somehow, during her stay in New Kwajalein, during the time when User Annie had become, for the Sixteenth Marine Detachment, a creature of myth— she had received from the Japanese castaways the crown of the Lord of the Castle. And when that crown was worn by the True Lord of the Castle, Clive remembered, it was to glow.

Annie stood at Clive's one side, 'Nrrc'kth at the other.

Each holding the nearly invisible crown with her fingertips, the two beautiful women lowered it carefully upon Clive's head.

The glow that the crown emitted filled the room, and in the moment that it did, a cheer rose from

Clive's assembled friends, and from the multitude of freed prisoners who had followed them.

Annabelle Leigh put her arms around Clive and kissed him warmly on the face. Her breath was sweet, and he felt a single, hot tear fall from her eye onto his cheek. Then she released him, and the Lady 'Nrrc'kth was miraculously in his arms, her mouth pressed to his, her hands pressing him to her. He hesitated for only an instant, then responded to her with ardor equal to her own.

From somewhere behind Clive there was the swish of heavy velvet curtains. He pushed the Lady 'Nrrc'kth away and spun on his heel, the crown of the Lord of the Castle forgotten, his friends forgotten, everything forgotten.

He dashed to the swinging tapestry, pulled it aside, and pursued the fleeing N'wrbb Crrd'f. Back through corridors thick with dust the two men fled. Back to the alcove where they had faced each other. Back to the place where a pile of shattered stone marked Clive's narrow escape from death.

Beyond the pile of stone Clive saw a glint of metal, a plaque of polished brass beside the heavy wooden door upon which N'wrbb had so fruitlessly pounded. Suddenly Clive realized that a secret was about to be unraveled, a secret far more important to him than the pursuit of the craven N'wrbb Crrd'f.

Eight words were engraved in neat, military script upon the gleaming brass. Clive read the words, mouthing each syllable softly to himself.

Brigadier Sir Neville Folliot
Royal Somerset Grenadier Guards

Clive rapped on the metal plate, using the hilt of his dagger as a knocker. There was no more response to his rapping than there had been to N'wrbb's pounding and pleading. "Neville," Clive shouted, "open up! Open up! It is I, your brother Clive!"

Still no response. Perhaps there was no one in the room beyond the heavy door. Or perhaps Neville was there, unable to respond—injured—even dead.

Clive's band of faithful followers were nowhere to be seen. For all he knew they still stood surrounding 'Nrrc'kth and Annie, shocked by Clive's abrupt exit. He knew that they would follow him, that they would appear at any moment. But he did not wait to ask their advice or their support.

This one thing he must do; this much he knew. If the others stayed with him, he would be strengthened and heartened. But if they did not, his course would remain unaltered.

He bent and picked up the heavy fragment of black stone with which N'wrbb had earlier struck him. He smashed it against the lock. The door shuddered. He pounded the rock against the mechanism again and again.

Finally the door swung slowly open.

The room inside was a perfect nineteenth-century gentleman's study. Heavy wooden furniture and a horsehair sofa stood neatly in their places. Rows of uniformly bound volumes filled tall cases, lining the walls. Where the bookcases did not cover the dark wooden paneling, portraits in gilt frames loomed portentously.

Soft gaslight illuminated the chamber.

In the center of the room, facing the doorway, stood a huge, ornately carved desk. A distinguished figure, garbed in beautifully tailored, proper gentleman's costume of the most modern civilian cut, sat industriously, engrossed in his task.

The work before him was a large journal bound in black leather. The man held a steel-tipped pen. From time to time he paused in his writing to dip his pen into an inkwell, then shake the surplus ink from the pen's nib and return to his task.

How long the tableau held, Clive could not guess. He knew only that his chest was tight, his breathing shallow. He could sense his band of allies waiting silently a half-dozen paces away. He could feel his heart pounding in his bosom, the blood rushing past his eardrums.

Neville!

Neville, at last!

The well-tailored man finished his page. He returned his pen carefully to its holder, lifted a square of blotting paper, and dried the sheet before him. He opened a drawer in the pedestal of his desk and drew something from it.

All of this—all of this—without raising his head from his work.

What was Neville's place in the Dungeon? What was his alliance with the Q'oornans? Which of the players in Annie's fabled n-dimensional chess game moved the piece called Neville Folliot—and for what purpose?

All of these thoughts raced through Clive Folliot's mind in the seconds during which the scene remained frozen.

"Neville!" Clive shouted.

The writing man raised his head and looked Clive Folliot directly in the eye.

Simultaneously he raised a gleaming American Navy Colt revolver and pointed it at Clive's chest.

"I fear you are mistaken, Major Clive Folliot," the man hissed.

Clive Folliot stared aghast into the countenance of a perfect stranger.

SELECTIONS
FROM THE SKETCHBOOK
OF MAJOR CLIVE FOLLIOT

The following drawings are from Major Clive Folliot's private sketchbook, which was mysteriously left on the doorstep of *The London Illustrated Recorder and Dispatch,* the newspaper that provided financing for his expedition. There was no explanation accompanying the parcel, save for an enigmatic inscription in the hand of Major Folliot himself.

At last, a brief moment of respite! This whirlwind of an adventure has reached a state of relative calm, and I intend to use this much appreciated time to document, as precisely as possible, the details of my extraordinary exploits in the confines of the dungeon.

My recollections of the many events that have transpired are so vivid that I feel compelled to put them down on paper. Who knows when I shall have the chance again?

CLIVE FOLLIOT —
MAJOR
FIFTH IMPERIAL
HORSE GUARDS.

— A RATHER
MOROSE SELF—
PORTRAIT.

ANNABELLE
LEIGHTON
— FROM MEMORY

Quarter Master
Sgt. Horace Hamilton
Smythe

Portrait from Life

In Disguise as a Mandarin.

A CREATURE WHICH
ATTACKED WHILE GUARDING
A RED GLOWING ROCK
FORMATION.

THE GONG
AT THE
BLACK TOWER

SGT. SMYTHE'S
REVOLVER

NOTE
PATTERN

THE DIARY OF
MY LOST BROTHER

A CUTLASS LIKE WEAPON
SALVAGED FROM
A HORRIBLE FLYING
CREATURE.

'User' ANNIE
STRIKING RESEMBLANCE
TO ANNABELLE. FROM LIFE.

FINNBOGG

BULLDOG
-LIKE,
CAN SPEAK
INTELLIGENT.

Sidi Bombay

An Aquaintance of Jet Smythes,
most inigmatic.

A strange star
formation, which spins
in the night sky.
... and also appears
on Sidi Bombay's hand!

SHRIEK

A SPIDER-LIKE CREATURE
A FEMALE, SURPRISINGLY GENTLE

NRRC'KTH

THE ROYAL LADY
OF A
MEDIEVAL
CASTLE,
WITHIN THE
DUNGEON.

Coming in January 1989

Volume two in the exciting
new fantasy series
Philip Jose Farmer's

by Bruce Coville

The adventure continues . . .